CH

England, between Hastings and the village of
St Leonard's, Sussex, May, 1826

THEY caught up with him when he was within sight of the harbour, dragged him from his exhausted horse, and threw him on to the rough gravel road that led to the sea. His hand twisted beneath him as he fell, and he heard the bones in two of his fingers snap. Thank God, it was his left hand.

Alexander's right hand closed around the small dagger tucked into the belt at his waist, shoving it deeper into its hidden sheath. Fortunately there was little chance that his attackers would shoot him. They wouldn't want him to pass too easily into the joys of Paradise, and so, with luck, he might manage to kill at least one of them before he died.

There were three of them surrounding him, all mounted, and all wearing the absurdly tight garments that passed for normal riding clothes here in England. But they weren't English, Alexander was sure of that. He had only heard them call out a couple of terse commands, but that was enough for him to recognise their language. They had spoken Turkish, the classical Osmanlica of the Sultan's court.

They did not deign to address him as they pulled him to his feet, slashing their riding crops across his face to give him a foretaste of the punishments they had in store. When the blood was coursing freely down his cheeks the leader of the trio held Alexander at sword-point, while the other two dismounted and stripped him of his jacket, waistcoat and boots. They ripped apart the seams of his clothing with methodical efficiency, then cut the supple leather of his boots with swift, shallow strokes of their knives. They exclaimed in unison when they discovered the two sets of much-folded paper, wedged one into the heel of each boot. Alexander could see their fingers shaking as they opened the wafer-thin sheets, and they laughed triumphantly as they scanned the documents before brandishing them high in the air.

Their leader grunted his satisfaction as he leaned back in his saddle, relaxing his vigilance for a single crucial instant. The blade at Alexander's throat wavered, and the punishing grip on his hair slackened. It was all the leeway he needed. He tore free, dodging between the flailing hoofs of the sweating horses, pulling his dagger from its sheath as he did so.

He heard the whistle of the leather whip only a split second before it landed across his shoulders, but somehow he forced himself to maintain his grip on the dagger. He didn't even hear the singing slash of the second and subsequent blows. Pain—raw, black and burning—filled his senses, but he blocked it out as he fell to his knees and crawled momentarily out of reach beneath the scraggy bushes of the hedgerow. He grovelled on his belly, feigning unconsciousness as he lay prostrate on the ground. He knew that death must be very near, and he fought back the waves of unconsciousness. Since the fates had decreed that he should leave this world Alexander very much wanted to take one of his murderers with him.

His thoughts were so rigorously focused to block out awareness of his own pain that he heard the rattle of iron wheels on the stony surface of the road without registering the significance of the sound. It was a shouted curse from one of his attackers that alerted him to the rapid approach of a carriage and horses.

The leader of the assassins tugged on the bridle of his gelding, speaking rapidly in Turkish. 'You two carry the papers to the boat, and I'll take care of this traitor.'

The command was instantly obeyed. His two subordinates leaped on to their horses and cut off across country without stopping to glance back. Alexander seized his chance. He uncoiled himself in a single swift movement, throwing his dagger even as the Turk's finger squeezed the trigger of his gun.

Biting, searing pain burned a path through Alexander's

shoulder. He heard the choked cry of his assailant, the scream of a frightened horse, and the pounding of hoofs, but the sounds seemed to come from far away, as if they echoed faintly on a winter wind blowing in from the mountains of the Caucasus. Except that he was thousands of miles away from the mountains, Alexander reminded himself. He was in. . . He couldn't remember where he was. He remembered only that he had to get the bank draft to Hank Barrett and deliver the naval charts to the ship that would soon sail into the cove near Hastings.

Mr Canning's bank draft. Alexander smiled. If only his attackers knew how they had been tricked, he thought drowsily. If only the sun had not disappeared so completely, he would have got up and ridden back to where he had hidden the secret papers. He didn't have time to be sleeping here on this comfortable road. Hank was waiting and so were the people of his homeland. . . Summer would be over all too soon and they were already starving. . .

How strange it was to die.

There was no sun. The darkness was becoming thicker, stroking him with freezing fingers that chilled his blood. Alexander shivered. He wondered why nobody had ever warned him that Paradise would be so cold. Surely, in Paradise, a man could at least expect the servants to light a brazier or two on chilly evenings. And why was he alone? Where were the *houris*, who were supposed to lead him out of life and into Paradise?

Then he remembered. There would be no beautiful maidens to welcome him into eternity. He had denied his father's faith, and so he would never enter the Garden of Eternal Delight. He was a renegade, a traitor, an infidel. He was a Christian. He sighed. No warm and friendly *houris* would come to greet him. He would have to content himself with a cool, Christian angel. He hoped very much that she wouldn't sing. His head was aching, and he had always hated harps.

He didn't know how long he waited before he felt the brush of the angel's wing against his cheek. He sighed with relief because she had finally arrived and opened his eyes to welcome her with a smile. He knew she was an angel because she had golden hair and eyes that sparkled with a blue as brilliant as the Aegean Sea on a sunny day. *Houris* had brown eyes, and black hair that gleamed like the wings of the raven. He wondered if God ever got confused and sent *houris* to meet Christians and angels to meet Muslims.

'Tom, for pity's sake get me a blanket!' the angel commanded.

How odd, Alexander thought. He would never have expected an angel to call out her orders in a barbaric language like English. He would have thought that any self-respecting angel would prefer to speak Greek.

'Dear God, Tom, he's been shot!'

The angelic system of communication didn't seem to be very efficient, Alexander decided. Surely the entire flock of heavenly assistants ought to know what incident brought him to the gates of heaven? He tried to sit up so that he could see his angel more clearly, and she cradled his head gently in her arms. She stroked him soothingly on the forehead, and he felt the power of her touch radiate throughout his aching body.

She held his hand when her assistants lifted him on to a bumpy storm cloud. 'Don't worry,' she murmured. 'Everything will be all right.'

Her voice was beautiful, Alexander thought, as he nestled deeper into the cloudy darkness. Almost as beautiful as her face.

He closed his eyes.

Lady Adeline screamed when she saw the blood on Charlotte's new green pelisse. Charlotte made soothing noises and hoped that her aunt wouldn't faint, but, judging from past experience, the odds were against her. Aunt Adeline had swooned three months ago, on Charlotte's twenty-fifth birthday, simply because she couldn't bear to think of her niece lodged so firmly on the shelf of spinsterhood, and, only a week ago, she had swooned when Charlotte refused the archdeacon's offer of marriage.

The groom and the footman were, like their mistress,

covered in blood and dust, and the man they held between them was a gruesome enough sight to make even Charlotte feel queasy. Miraculously Aunt Adeline's curiosity seemed to get the better of her susceptibilities, and, despite all the gore, she refrained from fainting. Taking advantage of this unexpected display of fortitude, Charlotte sprang nimbly into the carriage and sat down opposite her aunt.

'Tom,' she said to the coachman, 'if you and Harry will lift the poor man through the door, I will take his head on to my lap. I think that is how he will be most comfortable.'

'And what be us to do with his feet, Miss Charlotte?'

'He is too tall to fit on to the seat, so I'm afraid his feet will have to go on to the floor.'

Lady Adeline peered nervously out of the window. 'Are you sure the highwaymen are all gone?' she interjected.

'Yes, my lady,' Tom replied reassuringly. 'Rode off over the fields, they did. Two of 'em, flying over the hedges like they were a-running from the devil. Then another one heading in the same direction, riding a bay, he was. Looked like he was wounded, he did.' Tom looked gloomily at the man in his arms. 'Come to think on't, for all we know, this man is like as not to be another of 'em. Looks wicked enough to be an envoy sent straight from the devil, he do. How'm we to know if he be a highwayman?'

'It seems highly unlikely, since he has been attacked,' Charlotte pointed out calmly. 'And at the moment, whatever his past, he represents no threat to us or to anybody.' She leaned forward and held out her hands to the coachman. 'I am ready to take him now, Tom, if you and Harry are ready to lift him into the carriage.'

Lady Adeline emitted a series of alarmed squeaks as Tom and Harry heaved the prostrate, blanket-wrapped body through the door. Charlotte turned her attention to staunching the blood flowing from the bullet-wound in the man's shoulder while Tom leaned in and arranged the blanket as best he could over the man's half-naked body.

His efforts, alas, were less than successful. The blanket could either conceal the man's broad, bloody and hair-matted chest or it could conceal his long legs and tattered linen drawers. It simply was not large enough to conceal both highly improper areas at the same time. Charlotte finally settled the problem by deciding that the man needed to be warm rather than decent. She pulled the cover up to the man's chin, and indicated to the coachmen that they should drive home as quickly as possible. Lady Adeline blushed and averted her eyes.

The man groaned, then stirred as the carriage jolted into motion. He lashed out feebly, but only a few seconds passed before he relapsed again into unconsciousness. Unfortunately, as he sank into oblivion, one long, muscled and extremely masculine leg jostled against Lady Adeline's worsted skirt, and the sole of his foot slid down her calf, coming to rest neatly beside her ankle. Lady Adeline looked down and realised that only a layer of woollen stocking separated her ankle from naked male flesh. It was the final straw in a day already weighted by too much drama. She screamed, jerking her foot away as if she had been scalded. Her cheeks paled, and she clutched at her heart as she fell back, prostrate, against the squabs.

Charlotte sighed, wondering for the hundredth time why Aunt Adeline—and women in general—chose such odd things to faint about. Resignedly she pressed the pad of her torn petticoat against the man's wound with one hand while rummaging around with the other to locate her reticule. She managed to find the vial of smelling salts, and pulled it out, unscrewing the lid with her teeth and wafting the bottle as close to her aunt's nose as she could reach without disturbing the wounded man.

Lady Adeline took several gasping breaths, coughed, and opened her eyes. She blinked, fluttered her handkerchief in a vague sort of way, then stared dispiritedly towards her niece. 'Oh, dear,' she murmured. 'He is still here. I hoped it was only a bad dream.'

The man suddenly flung his hand upwards, and it landed squarely upon Charlotte's breast. Lady Adeline shuddered, and Charlotte reached hastily for the smelling salts, but her aunt waved them away, looking at her niece with genuine puzzlement. 'Dear heaven, Charlotte, he is so. . .so *muscled*. And so dark! For all we know he may be a gypsy, or a highwayman, or even a murderer! Why didn't you tell Harry to take care of him? You really ought to think more of your reputation, child.'

'I can't see how helping a wounded man will ruin my reputation.'

'But he is *naked*!' Lady Adeline exclaimed. 'Dear child, how can you possibly hold a naked man in your arms? And his head! Haven't you noticed that it's resting in a most indelicate position?'

'There is no other way for me to hold him, Aunt. I need to keep this pad pressed against the wound in his shoulder. Besides, he isn't naked. Surely you must have noticed that he is wearing drawers.'

Lady Adeline turned bright pink. 'For goodness' sake, Charlotte, I swear I shall never understand you. How can you mention such *unmentionable* garments without a quiver of embarrassment?'

'I don't know,' Charlotte replied seriously. 'Do you think it might be because I am the only girl in a family of five boys? I was sixteen when Mama sent me away to school, you know, and I think by then it was too late to turn me into a proper female.'

'But couldn't you at least pretend a little?' Lady Adeline wailed. 'What is the point of being so beautiful if you don't make the slightest push to get yourself a husband? What is the point of *anything* if you are determined to remain a spinster?'

Charlotte tried not to let her impatience show. 'I am not determined to remain a spinster,' she said.

'Then why did you refuse the archdeacon?' Lady Adeline asked plaintively, just as if she had not already asked the same question at least once a day in the week since the archdeacon's proposal. 'After all, Charlotte, you are several years past the age at which you should have married. And the archdeacon has a private income, and his brother is a baron. Just think, dear girl, you would have become the Honourable Mrs Quentin Jeffries. It is hard to imagine a more delightful match.'

Charlotte refrained from pointing out that the archdeacon was a pompous ass with a noticeable streak of cruelty hidden beneath his patronising smiles. 'I don't love him, Aunt,' she said mildly.

Her aunt so far forgot feminine delicacy as to snort vigorously. 'You are not seventeen any longer, Charlotte, so do not talk like a green girl. At seventeen a girl may indulge herself with dreams of love and romance. She will learn soon enough what such dreams are worth. At five-and-twenty you should have more sense than to imagine that love has anything to do with the practical business of marriage.'

'Sometimes I think I have far too much common sense,' Charlotte commented wryly. 'Unlike most women I cannot quite see how marriage to somebody one doesn't particularly like is a recipe for happiness.'

Lady Adeline clucked disapprovingly. 'Your dear mother was a wonderful woman and quite my favourite sister, but there is no denying the fact that she made a lamentable job of your education. You know, Charlotte, if you had only been taught how to play the pianoforte and embroider and do water-colours, like any other young lady of fashion, I'm sure you would have been happily married years ago. Instead you persist in clinging to this insane belief that a lady is capable of learning all the same things as a gentleman. Why, even I can see the absurdity of such an idea! God made women smaller than men, Charlotte. We have smaller heads, and therefore we also have smaller brains. Naturally we cannot think such profound thoughts as our menfolk, and the good Lord never intended us to. That is why every lady needs a gentleman to take care of her. That is why you should have married the archdeacon.'

'Because his head is bigger than mine? That is certainly a novel reason for contemplating matrimony.'

'You see, you are doing it again! Charlotte, can you not try to curb this unbecoming habit of treating serious matters with nothing but levity?'

The blood from the man's bullet-wound had seeped

through the pad and was beginning to drip on to Charlotte's fingers. She surreptitiously wiped her hand on a corner of the blanket, then tried to squeeze the jagged ends of torn flesh closer together. She wondered if her aunt, who was kind-hearted by nature, saw anything at all incongruous in discussing the archdeacon's proposal while the man in Charlotte's arms slowly spilled his lifeblood on to the carriage floor.

She sighed with relief as the chaise turned in through the wrought-iron gates of Rippon Manor. It was only the second week of May, but the weather had been unusually mild so that the oak trees were laden with rich green foliage and irises bloomed in huge yellow clusters along the edge of the drive, creating an illusion of midsummer brightness.

Harry jumped down from the box and ran up the steps to the front door, grasping the bell-pull and sending a tumultuous peal ringing through the quiet household.

The servants responded with quick efficiency to the emergency on their doorstep. Within minutes the housekeeper had organised a makeshift stretcher, and the wounded man was lifted out of Charlotte's arms and carried into the room near the kitchen that was kept expressly for sick or injured servants. The butler tactfully removed Lady Adeline from the sick-room with the promise of tea in her bedroom, and Tom drove the carriage back to the stables, saying that he would send one of the lads out for the doctor.

The man lay still upon the bed, his breathing rapid and shallow, his eyes sunken deep in their sockets. Charlotte didn't like to contemplate how close to death the man had already travelled, so she stripped off her pelisse and rolled up the lace-trimmed sleeves of her gown. Activity would help her to feel less useless as they waited for the doctor, and surely it could not hurt to remove some of the dirt caking his face and body?

'Mrs Stubbs, I shall need water, soap and linen washcloths,' she said with a great deal more briskness than she felt.

The housekeeper pursed her lips. 'Better if you don't

revive him, miss, not until the surgeon's finished with him.'

'I think it will take more than a damp cloth to revive this patient,' Charlotte said. 'Would you bring me the water, Mrs Stubbs?'

The housekeeper saw that her mistress was adamant, so the kitchen maid was set to heating pans of water while Charlotte washed away the grime from the man's face. He was probably quite young, she thought, not more than thirty. He might even be handsome when his cheeks were not hollowed and his facial bones starkly protruding.

With Mrs Stubbs's help, she rolled the man on to his unwounded shoulder, and his back was visible to them both for the first time. The housekeeper gasped when she saw the mangled strips of bloodied flesh, and Charlotte turned away hastily, taking several minutes to wring out the linen cloth she was holding.

'What in the world has happened to him, Miss Charlotte?' The housekeeper's voice shook noticeably. 'I've never seen anything so horrible, not in all my born days.'

'I think he has been whipped,' Charlotte replied. She turned back to their patient and carefully wiped away the grit and dirt that clung to the open welts. 'I saw similar cuts once on a horse that had been mistreated by its owner.'

'He's nobody from around these parts,' the housekeeper commented. 'He looks like a heathen, his skin is so dark. And his hair! It's like jet underneath all that dust. You never see a man from these parts with hair that colour.'

The housekeeper managed to make black hair sound immoral, Charlotte thought with secret amusement. 'His face certainly doesn't seem familiar,' she agreed.

'That's because he's a foreigner.' The housekeeper grimaced as she took the blood-soaked washcloth from her mistress. 'The highwaymen were probably foreigners, too. Take my word for it, Miss Charlotte, that beating was the work of heathens. Or maybe gypsies. Englishmen wouldn't have nothing to do with a carry-on like that.'

Charlotte did not bother to dispute the housekeeper's logic. As far as Mrs Stubbs was concerned civilisation began and ended at the Sussex border. The housekeeper, like Lady Adeline, did not find it surprising that a foreigner should be found half dead on the highway. The only surprise would be if he turned out, by some shocking mischance, to be an Englishman.

Charlotte's attempts to cleanse the man's back obviously caused him pain. He moaned, then muttered several rapid incomprehensible syllables as he thrashed about on the bed, causing blood to gush freely out of the bullet-wound in his shoulder. She quickly stopped her ministrations, wringing out a fresh cloth and placing it soothingly across the man's forehead. His feverish muttering ended just as a knock at the sick-room door heralded the arrival of Dr Macfarlane.

The doctor did not believe in wasting time on frivolities, or even on normal courtesies. After the briefest of greetings he told Charlotte and the housekeeper to hold the patient quiet. He then sat down on the bed and extracted a slender steel surgeon's knife from his leather bag, looking closely at the wound before probing deep into the patient's shoulder. Charlotte felt her knees begin to buckle, and she had to grasp the bedpost for support.

'Don't you dare faint, woman,' the doctor barked, not even glancing up. 'Hold him down and keep him still, or I'll splinter his bone.'

Charlotte closed her eyes and swallowed hard, forcing herself to picture the flowers blooming in the garden rather than the work being performed under her nose. She eventually managed to open her eyes again, but she was careful to keep her gaze firmly averted from the gently twisting steel blade.

The man's complexion was grey from loss of blood when the doctor finally gave a quick grunt of satisfaction, and held up the bullet. He washed the wound swiftly with hot, clean water, a move that had Mrs Stubbs clucking doubtfully under her breath. He then dusted the hole left by the bullet with basilicum powder before binding the shoulder tightly to prevent movement. He made a splint for the fingers of the man's left hand, commenting brusquely that at least the man's right side was uninjured, so that he would have one comfortable position to lie in. He then paid Charlotte a curt compliment on the skilful job she had done in cleansing the cuts from the whip and announced that if the man survived the inevitable fever he would have a fair chance of living, with no more than a few scars to show for his dreadful experience.

'Here's ointment for his back. It doesn't smell very good, but I've found it works well to keep down the inflammation.' The doctor tied a final knot in the intricate web of bandages. 'Remember, he'll need nursing night and day. If those wounds are ever to heal, he must be kept still.'

'There are several of us to share the burden,' Charlotte said quietly. 'And we have Harry and two stable lads to cope with the heavier tasks.'

'Don't wear yourself out, now. I know you of old, Charlotte Rippon, and ye've no sense of moderation.' Dr Macfarlane clapped his hat on his head and snapped the lock of his leather bag. 'Ye're a fine woman, Miss Rippon, and you ought to be married.'

'Are you offering for me, Dr Macfarlane?' she asked, with a quick, teasing smile.

The doctor turned brick-red. 'Your tongue's so sharp, young lady, that one of these days it's going to cut you.' He reached for his hat, discovered it was already on his head, and stomped off down the corridor without bothering to say goodbye.

It was so hot that it was agony to remain closed inside his skin. Alexander clawed at his body, trying to rip off the red-hot coals that the devils had stuck all over him, but the monsters came again and grabbed his arm, holding him pinned to the rack so that they could continue their torture. The fire was consuming him, and he cried out, begging for water.

The angel heard him. His own angel, who had met him at the Gates of Paradise. She walked towards him, her white gown and golden hair shining with a cool luminescence in the hot red darkness. She touched him, and for a blissful moment his forehead became cool, and he smelled the sweetness of lemon blossom. She lifted a crystal goblet to his lips, and the cold water trickled into his mouth, soothing the aching roughness of his throat.

She stood up and turned away. 'Don't go,' he rasped and reached out his hand to call her back, but one of the monsters seized his arm, preventing him from moving. He forgot about the pain, forgot about everything except the need to bring the angel back so that he could be cool again. He dragged himself up, using every ounce of his strength to tear away from the restraining hold of the devils. He launched himself at the angel, clinging to the softness of her body as he begged her to stay with him, begged her to take away the pain.

She held him quite gently, but she didn't answer him, didn't even seem to understand his frantic pleas for mercy.

One of the monsters spoke laconically. 'This be the wust I've seen him, miss, and he's been bad the whole two days he's been here. I reckon this'll be the end, like as not.'

'Then we had better make sure that the end is favourable,' the angel said with unexpected sharpness. 'He still has amazing strength, so if this is the crisis of his fever there is no reason why we should not bring him through safely.'

'If you say so, miss.'

The heavenly cold touched Alexander's forehead again, and he felt the caress of the angel's fingers against his face. With a surge of joy he realised that she had heeded his pleas after all. She had defied the power of the monsters and stayed with him. He turned his lips and pressed them against the delicate palm of her hand.

'Thank you,' he whispered. 'You are brave to defy the emissaries of Satan.'

He thought that the angel smiled, but she did not answer him, and, too late, he realised that he had spoken to her in Greek. His angel, he remembered, was a very odd angel who only seemed to understand English. He tried to translate his words into her language, but his tongue was too thick to curl itself around the awkward, clipped English sounds.

'Don't try to talk,' the angel said. 'You should rest now.' He closed his eyes obediently, grateful for the unexpected respite from pain.

The sun shone into the room, casting an intricate pattern of light and shade on to the rumpled white linen cover. Alexander opened his eyes and glanced towards the window. The angel was sitting in a chair, reading. Except that she wasn't an angel, of course. She was a slender young woman with curly golden hair, and a perfect pink and white complexion. She wore a blue woollen dress in the stiff European style, but, despite the ugly clothes, Alexander thought that he had never seen such a beautiful woman.

She would probably glance up from her book at any minute, and then she would notice that he was awake. What ought he to say to her? For her sake, as much as for his own, it was imperative that she should discover as little as possible about him. His French was almost faultless. Should he pretend to be French? A merchant from Paris, perhaps? What should he call himself? Which region should he claim to be from? Normally he would have been able to invent a tissue of convincing lies in a matter of seconds, but at this precise moment his thought-processes were so fuzzy that he couldn't even come up with a realistic-sounding French name.

The woman finally looked up and saw that he was watching her. She smiled—an enchanting, dazzling smile that drove the last of Alexander's wits into a state of drowsy befuddlement.

'Oh, you are awake! How wonderful!' Her voice was low and musical, and it lilted with a genuine note of pleasure. She tossed her book carelessly to one side and hurried across the room, tugging the bell-pull as she passed the door.

'How good it is to have you with us at last! We began to think that you would sleep forever. I am Charlotte Rippon, by the way, and my aunt and I found you last Wednesday, about three miles from St Leonard's. What is your name, and is there some way we can notify your family to let them know you are safe?'

Charlotte. He repeated her name slowly inside his head and decided that it suited her. Its soft sounds fitted well with her generous smiles. He was on the brink of telling her his name when he suddenly remembered how many reasons he had for being discreet. He cut off his reply with a tiny harsh exclamation, turning his head on the pillow to avoid her friendly gaze. It was tempting to respond to her frankness, but trust and honesty were two qualities he couldn't afford. The grim reality was that as soon as he identified himself as Prince Karim Alexander the inevitable questions would begin. And he had not yet decided how he should answer them.

She did not seem unduly troubled by his silence. 'It will probably take you a few minutes to find your voice,' she said, adjusting the pillows behind his back. She took a glass from the table beside his bed and discarded its cover of white muslin. 'You must be thirsty,' she said, holding the glass out to him. 'We made the lemonade fresh this morning. Dr Macfarlane says it is probably the lemon juice that has helped to keep you alive. Fortunately, even at the height of your fever, we could always manage to make you swallow water and fruit juice.'

Fresh lemonade sounded like heaven and paradise rolled into one, Alexander reflected, and hard on the heels of that thought came the realisation that he was not only thirsty but also ravenously, voraciously hungry. He was also so weak that his hand shook as he reached out to take the glass. He found that it required more co-ordination than he possessed simply to prop the glass against his lips and swallow the cool, honey-sweetened drink. Trickles of juice ran down his chin and on to his chest, and Charlotte eventually had to hold the glass for him so that he could drain the last delicious drops. When he had finished he fell back against the pillows, swearing softly in Greek.

She took his empty glass and returned it to the bedside table. 'Oh, dear,' she said, observing him with a distinctly wry expression. 'You're no easier to understand now than you were when you were delirious. What's more, I have the most horrid feeling that you haven't understood a word I've said. Why did it never occur to me that you don't speak English?'

In a sudden flash of inspiration Alexander suddenly saw exactly how he could protect both Charlotte and himself. He would simply pretend he didn't understand English. If he didn't speak English he couldn't be expected to explain who he was and what he had been doing on a lonely road leading to a deserted strip of the Kentish coastline.

Even as this fortunate idea occurred to him Mrs Stubbs hurried into the room, her black skirts rustling. She immediately noticed that Alexander was awake, and her somewhat fierce features relaxed into a slight smile. 'Why, and so our patient is on the road to recovery at last,' she said cheerfully. 'Well, young man, you look as weak as a kitten, from what I can see of you underneath that stubble of beard, but you'll be looking forward to some food, I'll be bound. I'll fetch you some broth and some barley water. The doctor said you were to have nothing solid for a week, but I dare say we could coddle you an egg later on this afternoon, and I've already put by some calves'-foot jelly. It's invalid food, of course, but the taste is hearty.'

Smiling, but keeping his eyes carefully blank, Alexander looked straight at the housekeeper. 'I'm sorry,' he said in Greek, 'but I'm afraid I don't speak a word of English.'

Mrs Stubbs wheeled around and looked at Charlotte, her expression distinctly suspicious. 'What did he say?' she demanded. 'Is he speaking French?'

'No, nor German either,' Charlotte said. 'I'm very much afraid that our patient speaks no English, and I'm not quite sure what language he *is* speaking. A dialect of Italian, perhaps?'

'Ha!' the housekeeper exclaimed, her suspicious expression changing into a look of deep satisfaction. She folded her hands across her ample stomach and exhaled triumphantly. 'Well, Miss Charlotte, it's exactly as I warned you. It's no surprise to me that he's turned out to be a foreigner. And a real *heathen* foreigner, not even one of those fancy Frenchmen. All that black hair, and whip marks, too. I knew what he was from the moment I first saw him. You heed my words, miss, we'd better be careful to lock all the doors at night, or we'll have his murderers coming back here and attacking us in our beds. Those foreigners don't care who they kill once they start swinging their knives.'

'The people who attacked him don't even know he's here, Mrs Stubbs. How could they? Harry saw them running away before our carriage turned the bend in the road.'

The housekeeper pursed her lips and peered down at Alexander, her eyes darkened by foreboding. 'Foreigners have their own ways of finding things out,' she said ominously.

Charlotte swallowed a smile. 'Maybe so, but in the meantime our patient needs food,' she pointed out.

The housekeeper's expression softened once again. 'Yes, poor lamb, he looks proper poorly.' She fixed her gaze on Alexander as if willing him to understand. 'I'll bring you something to eat,' she said, drawing out every syllable to twice its normal length. 'I'll bring you food. Broth. Soup.'

'That's very good of you,' Alexander replied politely in Greek.

The housekeeper stared at him in mingled irritation and pity. 'He doesn't understand a word a body says,' she remarked sadly. Alexander glanced at Charlotte and saw that she was trying not to laugh. He repressed an unexpected urge to share her laughter and stared at Mrs Stubbs with a convincing portrayal of blank incomprehension.

'Well, there's no use in trying to talk to him, Miss Charlotte, and that's obvious for all to see. I'll bring him his food, and I'll send for Tom or one of the stable lads. We don't want you sitting in here unprotected with somebody who doesn't even speak the King's English. There's no knowing what he might get up to.'

'I don't think we need to take anybody away from the stables,' Charlotte said calmly. 'I assure you, Mrs Stubbs, that this poor man is too weak to lift his head from the pillow. I suspect he will fall asleep again as soon as he has eaten.'

'If you say so, miss.' Mrs Stubbs paused in the doorway, unable to resist savouring her moment of triumph. 'But I told you all along he was a foreigner.'

Charlotte waited until the last rustle of the housekeeper's skirt had faded into the silence, and then she drew up a chair alongside the bed. 'Mrs Stubbs is really a very good woman,' she said to Alexander. 'For all that she rants and raves so much about foreigners she would never turn away from somebody truly in need.' She paused for breath, then looked at him with a hint of exasperation in her blue eyes. 'You know, it is exceedingly inconvenient of you not to speak English. I suppose you don't speak French? *Parlez-vous français*?' she asked hopefully. '*Sprechen Sie Deutsch*?'

Alexander looked vague.

She sighed. 'Well, that takes care of that. I suppose I am going to have to teach you English, or I shall expire from curiosity. I have spent the past four days wondering what you were doing riding along a country road in the direction of a deserted harbour, and it is extremely frustrating to know that I am not likely to find out, at least within the next day or two.'

Alexander obligingly smiled. 'It is much better that you should never know,' he said in Greek.

Charlotte's alabaster-smooth brow wrinkled in frustration, then she pointed towards her chest. 'I am Charlotte Rippon,' she said. 'Charlotte Rippon. Charlotte.'

'You are very beautiful, Charlotte,' he murmured.

'I wish I knew what you were saying,' Charlotte said. She pointed to herself again, then lifted her hand and laid it gently against his chest. 'I am Charlotte,' she repeated. 'What is your name?'

It was obvious what she was asking, even to somebody who was not supposed to understand the language, and he knew that he would have to give her some sort of a reply. If he were wise, he would invent some plausible fiction, but he discovered with surprise that he didn't want to lie to this woman who had worked so hard to save his life. Cursing himself for a soft-hearted fool, he put his hand around her fingers and held them for a minute against his heart.

'Alexander,' he said quietly. He turned her hand around and pressed it lightly against her breast. 'Charlotte,' he murmured huskily. 'Charlotte Rippon.'

He watched, fascinated, as a delicate flush of colour ran into her cheeks. Neither of them moved for several seconds, then she sprang to her feet and walked jerkily towards the doorway. 'Well, Mr Alexander, here comes the housekeeper with your chicken broth,' she said.

Mrs Stubbs appeared in the doorway. 'Tell him not to eat it too fast,' she warned.

'I shall feed him myself,' Charlotte told her. 'He is scarcely strong enough to lift the spoon.'

With the housekeeper's help she raised him higher against the pillows, then sat down beside him and began to spoon small quantities of soup into his mouth. For the first half-dozen mouthfuls Alexander thought he would die of hunger between sips. By the end of the next half-dozen he scarcely had energy left to swallow. His eyelids were so heavy that it was rapidly becoming impossible to keep them open.

'He is already three parts asleep,' he heard Charlotte say. 'I won't try to make him eat any more broth. If you will ask Harry to sit with him while I have lunch with my aunt, I shall come back in an hour and give him some barley water. Dr Macfarlane recommended that he should be fed small amounts about every two hours.'

'What you need, Miss Charlotte, is an afternoon nap, or you'll find yourself just as much of an invalid as the foreigner. You've scarce slept five hours in the past two days.'

'It's true, I am a little tired. If you would please help me to adjust his pillows again, Mrs Stubbs, so that he can lie down, then perhaps I shall have time to rest for five minutes before lunch.'

Alexander was too tired to open his eyes, but he recognised the touch of Charlotte's fingers on his forehead as she brushed a lock of hair away from his face. He smiled contentedly and burrowed back into the pleasures of sleep. 'Goodnight, sweet Charlotte,' he murmured. 'Enjoy your afternoon nap.'

Just before sleep claimed him he remembered to thank God that he had spoken in Greek.

CHAPTER TWO

RAIN set in before dawn on Monday and continued, without let-up, throughout the afternoon. Charlotte, feeling unaccountably restless, sat across the fire from her aunt, knitting a cap for her youngest nephew and listening to Lady Adeline sing the praises of yesterday's sermon by the archdeacon. She heaved a small sigh of relief when the butler announced the arrival of a visitor.

''Tis a Mr Henry Barrett,' he said in his usual funereal tones. 'And he says he comes from Americy.'

'America!' Lady Adeline exclaimed. 'Good heavens! Why in the world are all these foreigners suddenly descending upon our quiet little home?'

Charlotte welcomed the interruption, whatever its cause. 'Please show Mr Barrett in,' she said to the butler. 'And ask Mrs Stubbs if she would make us tea.'

Their visitor was ushered into the drawing-room. To Lady Adeline's disappointment he looked very much like any ordinary middle-aged English country gentleman, with nothing particularly exotic about either his clothes or his appearance. He was fair-skinned, hazel-eyed, of medium height, and wore neat grey pantaloons topped by a sober, well-tailored jacket. His accent, however, betrayed his transatlantic origins.

'Lady Adeline, Miss Rippon, I apologise for the intrusion,' he said, laying his hat, stick and gloves neatly on the floor beside his chair, just as etiquette demanded. 'I wouldn't have called on you so unexpectedly, but the matter I must discuss with you is somewhat urgent.'

Lady Adeline smiled graciously. 'You are not intruding, sir. My niece and I welcome visitors, especially on such a rainy spring afternoon. I trust you are enjoying your stay in England, Mr Barrett?'

'Very much so, my lady, and I appreciate your kindness in receiving me.' He waited politely while the butler brought in a tea-tray and set it in front of Lady Adeline.

'Do you take sugar and milk, Mr Barrett?' she asked.

'Yes, please, my lady,' he replied, inclining his head in thanks as he accepted a cup of tea and refused an almond macaroon. He chatted with perfect correctness about the inclement weather while Aunt Adeline poured tea for herself and her niece, but Charlotte could see that he was clearly impatient to be done with social inanities.

She was as anxious as Mr Barrett to conclude their discussion of the afternoon's rain. 'You mentioned that you had some special reason for asking to see us,' she said as soon as the subject of puddles, chill winds and muddy roads had been dutifully examined.

Mr Barrett smiled at her gratefully. 'Yes, I did, Miss Rippon. To get straight to the point, ladies, I am from Boston, in Massachusetts, and I have been in England for some three months in connection with the settlement of my grandfather's estate. Last week I was supposed to meet a young friend in Hastings. Unfortunately he didn't turn up at the time and place we agreed upon, nor did he send any message cancelling our appointment. As you can imagine I have been greatly worried, and I have delayed my return to London in the hopes of hearing something from him. I have been staying at the White Swan, and this morning I heard that you have been caring for a young man who was attacked by highway robbers. Naturally I wondered if the gentleman you are caring for might be my young friend.'

'Oh, I do hope so!' Charlotte exclaimed. 'We asked Dr Macfarlane to tell as many people as possible about our patient because we hoped that somebody might be able to identify him for us.'

Mr Barrett glanced up quickly. 'Does that mean your patient is too severely wounded to speak?' he asked.

'He can speak,' Lady Adeline remarked gloomily. 'But the trouble is, he can't speak English.'

Mr Barrett paused in the act of bringing his teacup to his lips. 'Your patient can't speak English?' he repeated.

'Not a word,' Lady Adeline declared. 'And not a word of French nor even of German. So, of course, we cannot understand a single thing that he says to us.'

'I see,' Mr Barrett said slowly. 'Then, if your patient cannot speak to you, I imagine you have no idea what he was doing here?'

'Not the least idea in the world,' Lady Adeline confirmed. 'He was in a delirium for four days, you know, and even the doctor wasn't sure he would live. But Charlotte nursed him night and day, and the fever finally broke on Saturday morning. He spent most of yesterday sleeping, so we haven't had much opportunity to question him, even if we could understand anything that he says. Would you care for some more tea, Mr Barrett?'

'No, thank you, my lady, although it was delicious.' He returned his cup to the tray. 'Am I to understand, ladies, that you don't even know your patient's name?'

'That, at least, we were able to discover,' Charlotte said. 'His name is Mr Alexander.' She looked thoughtfully at their visitor. 'Is that the name of your young friend, sir?'

'Alexander?' the American repeated slowly. 'Miss Rippon, are you sure that this gentleman identified himself as Mr Alexander?'

'Well, in point of fact, we're not entirely sure of anything. As my aunt explained to you, Mr Barrett, our patient has been extremely sick, and he speaks not a word of our language. Naturally communication between us has been something of a hit-and-miss affair.'

Even as she spoke Charlotte found herself thinking back over the brief time she had spent with their patient yesterday. True, she and Mr Alexander shared no common language and yet, on occasion, she had experienced the oddest feeling that they were communicating very well. It had sometimes seemed as if they were laughing together at jokes which only the two of them shared. Which was absurd, of course. How could she imagine she had communicated with a man whose English vocabulary was limited to heavily accented versions of the words soup, lemonade, nightshirt, and shave?

'Believe me, Miss Rippon, I understand your difficulties,' Mr Barrett said. 'But I wonder if I might visit with your patient for a minute or two? If he is sleeping, I shall not disturb him. I merely wish to ascertain whether or not he is indeed my young friend.'

'But of course you must see him,' Charlotte agreed, rising to her feet. 'He is not well enough to be moved as yet, but my aunt and I would be delighted to know that he has a friend in the neighbourhood.'

They trooped down the hallway towards the sick-room, where the kitchen-maid was watching over the sleeping patient. Mr Barrett strode silently across to the bed and stared down at the sleeping patient, his face betraying nothing of his reaction to Mr Alexander's pale, hawklike features and the swath of ebony-black hair spread out against the white linen pillow-case.

It occurred to Charlotte that Mr Barrett was a man of exceptionally well-controlled emotions. Now that she thought about it she realised that his face had conveyed nothing save conventional courtesy since the moment he first walked into the drawing-room. It also occurred to her that Mr Barrett had mentioned neither the name nor the nationality of his missing 'young friend', and Charlotte was not convinced that the omissions were accidental.

She looked across the bed at their American visitor, resolving not to be fobbed off with any more half-answers. 'Is this the young man you are looking for, sir?'

She spoke softly, but the sound of her voice seemed to penetrate Mr Alexander's slumber. He stirred against the pillows, wincing as he rolled on to his back. He opened his eyes and his gaze fell directly upon Mr Barrett. He stared at the American for no more than a couple of seconds before his eyelids swept down, shuttering his expression. When he opened his eyes again he looked at Charlotte rather than at his visitor, murmuring something that was, as usual, frustratingly incomprehensible.

When he had finished muttering Charlotte turned

towards Mr Barrett. 'You can see for yourself, sir, the sort of difficulty my aunt and I have encountered. I suppose you did not understand what he was saying?'

'What? Oh, no, no. Not a word. I've no idea what lingo the poor chap was spouting. I only speak English, you know. There's no call for foreign languages in Boston, none at all. You may be sure that the King's English is quite good enough for me and my friends.'

This sentiment was so much in line with Lady Adeline's own thinking that she unbent sufficiently to smile warmly at their American visitor, but Charlotte cut in before her aunt could speak. 'Nevertheless, you have not answered me, sir. Is this wounded man your missing friend?'

Mr Barrett opened his mouth to respond but, before he could speak, a deep, heart-wrenching groan from her patient distracted Charlotte's attention. She feared that he must somehow have re-opened the wound in his shoulder, and she quickly unbuttoned his nightshirt so that she could check the bandages. There seemed to be no sign of fresh blood, but Mr Alexander had never before given voice to any overt sign of discomfort since the moment he first regained consciousness, and she suspected that his groans could only have been caused by some acute form of pain.

She touched the back of her hand to his forehead. Sure enough his skin felt hot and his cheeks seemed unexpectedly flushed. He groaned again, cutting off the harsh, choking sound in an obvious endeavour to disguise the extent of his discomfort.

'I do hope the fever isn't returning.' Charlotte turned to the maid. 'Peggy, please run out to the stable and ask Tom to send one of the lads to fetch the doctor.'

Mr Alexander tossed his head weakly against his pillows, occasionally calling out brief disjointed phrases. After a few minutes his restless movements ceased and he lay silent, his eyes closed and his body limp.

'I can see that my visit has occurred at a most inconvenient moment,' Mr Barrett said. 'You good ladies will want to devote your full attention to your patient, so I will take my leave of you, with many thanks for your kind hospitality. Perhaps the housekeeper could be summoned to direct me towards the front door?'

Charlotte straightened and looked steadily at the American. 'There is no need to rush away, Mr Barrett. Our patient is uncomfortable, perhaps, but I cannot believe he is in any immediate danger. And you still have not told us whether or not this man is your missing friend.'

Mr Barrett sighed. 'No,' he said sadly. 'I'm afraid I have never seen this young man before. I had so much wished. . .so much hoped. . .' He pulled a handkerchief from his pocket and blew his nose firmly. 'Well, well, there is no use in lamenting over spilled milk, I suppose. I am sorry that I can't be of more help to you and your Mr—er—Alexander, Miss Rippon, but there it is. This young man is a total stranger to me.'

'I am very sorry to hear that,' Charlotte said. 'But you must tell us the name of your missing friend, Mr Barrett, and give us some sort of a description, in case we hear of any other wounded men in the neighbourhood.'

'Yes, yes, you are quite right. I should tell you my friend's name. He is called—er—Mr John O'Malley. Yes, that's it. Mr O'Malley. He is a fine-looking young man, but not at all like this fellow who is your patient. My friend has—er—brown hair and blue eyes. He is from Ireland, and he speaks their language, which is Gaelic, you know. Yes, he speaks Gaelic just like a native, which of course he is, and that's why I thought your wounded foreigner might be the man I was looking for. Of course, my friend Mr O'Malley speaks English in addition to Gaelic, otherwise I'd never be able to talk to him.' Mr Barrett glanced towards Lady Adeline and gave a self-deprecating little laugh. 'You know how it is, my lady, with these foreign lingos. Anyway, I thought my young friend might have sustained a blow to the head during the attack upon him, in which case he might remember only his Gaelic.'

'I don't think this patient of ours is suffering from any loss of memory,' Charlotte said. 'Indeed, his wits always seem to be well about him as far as I can judge.'

Mr Alexander turned feebly on his pillow and suddenly addressed two or three swift, sharp sentences to Mr Barrett. As was to be expected, the American merely looked blank, and eventually Mr Alexander shrugged dispiritedly and turned away.

'That is how he carries on all the time,' Lady Adeline told Mr Barrett. 'He seems to think that if he gabbles on long enough somebody will eventually understand him.'

'Perhaps he hoped that I might recognise his language,' Mr Barrett suggested.

'But of course you did not,' Charlotte said.

'I'm afraid not,' Mr Barrett replied without a moment's hesitation. 'I've often thought the world would be a better place if only all these foreigners would learn to speak English.'

A faint choking sound issued from the direction of the bed, but when Charlotte looked down she saw that Mr Alexander's eyes were tightly shut, and his mouth drawn into a rigid line. She frowned slightly and picked up his wounded hand to examine the broken fingers. They did not look swollen or discoloured—two danger signs that Dr Macfarlane had warned her to look out for. She replaced his hand gently against the covers, and sighed.

'I hope the doctor arrives soon,' she said. 'I can't imagine what is causing Mr Alexander so much pain. He has groaned more in the past half-hour than he has in the previous five days.'

Mr Barrett spoke soothingly. 'I should not trouble yourself unduly, Miss Rippon. Your patient looks well on the road to recovery as far as I can see. I am confident that any pain he feels is temporary.'

Having delivered himself of this opinion, the American inclined his head courteously, first towards Aunt Adeline and then towards Charlotte. 'Ladies, I must not detain you any longer. I wonder if I have been foolish to wait around in Hastings, expecting to hear from my young friend? I believe I shall return to London first thing tomorrow morning. I may find some simple message there that will explain why my friend Mr O'Malley did not manage to keep our appointment.'

'Well, we must certainly hope so,' Lady Adeline said. 'But with all these foreign highwaymen around there's no telling what might have happened to your friend. Shall we wait for your carriage in the drawing-room, Mr Barrett? I'll send word round to the stables to let them know that you're ready to leave, and you shall tell me all about Boston while we are waiting.'

'It will be my pleasure, my lady,' Mr Barrett agreed, then bowed in Charlotte's direction. 'Miss Rippon, your patient is fortunate to be blessed with a nurse of such outstanding dedication. I only wish that I had been able to tell you something of his past history.'

'Yes, it would have been very helpful,' Charlotte said. 'But the philosophers tell us that we must not waste time in useless regrets. I shall look forward to hearing any news you may glean about your own missing friend, Mr Barrett.'

'You are overwhelmingly kind, Miss Rippon, and you may count upon a letter from me as soon as I arrive in London.' Mr Barrett paused by the bedside, and patted Mr Alexander lightly on his uninjured shoulder. 'Good-bye, young man, whoever you may be. I hope you will be better soon and that you appreciate the devoted attention you are receiving.'

Mr Alexander looked straight into Mr Barrett's hazel eyes and uttered two or three short quick sentences. Mr Barrett clamped his lips together, then shook his head sadly. 'Poor fellow! It touches my heart to hear him rattling away like that, knowing that nobody understands a word he says.' He patted the patient's shoulder for a second time. 'Take care, my good man. I hope you will feel better soon.'

'Goot-by,' said Mr Alexander.

Mr Barrett looked more astonished than anybody else. 'Well, well, he certainly learns fast, does he not? Perhaps he may communicate quite satisfactorily in English when he becomes a little stronger.'

'Goot-by,' said Mr Alexander again.

Mr Barrett lost none of his good humour. 'If I didn't know better, I would think the poor chap was anxious to see me gone,' he commented, smiling at the ridiculousness of his own suggestion. 'However, I do have business awaiting me in Hastings, so I will take my leave.' He bowed gallantly to Charlotte, then swept his arm to one side to indicate that Lady Adeline should precede him through the door.

Charlotte watched his departure with a slight speculative frown. Mr Barrett, she decided, might or might not have a missing friend named Mr O'Malley, and he might or might not be in England to settle his grandfather's estate. One thing, however, was absolutely certain. Mr Barrett knew more than he was telling. Charlotte had been watching him closely during that final exchange with Mr Alexander, and she had seen the flicker of wry laughter that had darkened Mr Barrett's gaze for a mere split second before his mask once again dropped into place. And if Mr Barrett had been hiding something that meant that Mr Alexander was hiding something as well. Charlotte was surprised at how much such a realisation hurt.

She looked down at her patient with an unusually severe frown. 'You seem remarkably recovered from your earlier attack of agony,' she remarked tartly. 'Dr Macfarlane is going to wonder why I bothered to call him.'

Mr Alexander smiled sweetly and plucked at his nightshirt. 'Nitshut,' he said.

'Nightshirt,' Charlotte corrected, thinking abstractedly that he had the most beautiful mouth and the straightest, most even teeth she had ever seen.

'Nit-shurt,' said Mr Alexander. He lifted his right hand and wriggled his fingers. 'Vingers,' he said.

'Fingers, not vingers,' she responded automatically. 'Fingers.'

'V—fingers,' he mimicked obligingly.

'You are doing very well, Mr Alexander. Very good.'

He lay back against the pillows and watched her with dark, laughing eyes. 'Charlotte,' he said softly. 'Charlotte—very good.'

Alexander made no complaint when Dr Macfarlane arrived later that evening and poked him about for a solid half-hour. The discomfort was no more than he deserved, since he had caused the good doctor to be called out for no better reason than an urgent need to distract Charlotte's far too acute attention from Hank Barrett.

He was not at all sure how successful he and his partner had been in their efforts to deceive Charlotte, but, on the whole, he could only conclude that their meeting had gone well. Whatever Charlotte suspected, it was unlikely to be anything that came close to the truth. Moreover, between moans, he had been able to instruct Hank to wait for him in London. They would then sail together to the Adriatic port of Brindisi, which was on a direct sea route to the Peloponnese—and the headquarters of the Greek freedom-fighters in Nauplia.

There was nobody in the world whom Alexander totally trusted, but Hank was one of the few men whom he would almost trust with his life. Having made a fortune as a shipping merchant, Henry Barrett was now eager to spend that fortune to help the Greek people win independence from the feudal tyranny of their Turkish Ottoman overlords.

During his years as a merchant captain Hank had spent many months in the various Greek ports, and—contrary to his claims—he had learned to speak fluent Greek. He was now one of the leading figures in the powerful American committee that was dedicated to aiding the cause of Greek independence. But, despite Hank's familiarity with the Greek language, Alexander knew that his American friend didn't fully understand the complex strands that had woven Greeks and Turks together in a love-hate relationship that spanned more than four centuries. Hank Barrett had never really understood how Alexander could have a Greek mother who was both a Christian princess of Wallachia and a slave of the Ottoman Empire. He had never understood Alexander's deep respect for his Muslim father, and he certainly didn't understand Alexander's willingness to obey the laws of Islam whenever he was forced to spend time in the imperial capital of Istanbul. Hank's straight-thinking mind couldn't begin to grasp the tortuous philosophical processes by which Alexander had come to support both the reforming efforts of Sultan Mahmud II and the cause of freedom for the Greek people.

However, Henry Barrett understood one part of the Greek problem very well. He understood that men had no energy to worry about abstract concepts like freedom and democracy when their bellies were empty and their children dying of hunger. Hank understood that the Greek countryside, already reduced to abject poverty by three hundred years of Ottoman misrule, could not endure the additional devastation caused by six years of unremitting pillage, civil war and siege. With Yankee practicality he was now using his vast personal fortune to save hundreds, perhaps thousands, of starving people.

The peasants in the Peloponnese had been hungry for so long that the word hunger had almost lost its meaning. A slice of bread soaked in olive oil had long since become an unimaginable luxury. Figs and grapes were no more than beautiful memories from a distant, unreal past. The revolutionary government was holed up in the fortress of Bourdzi, besieged by the Egyptian armies of Ibrahim Pasha, and their treasury could not conjure up the price of a week's supply of bread, let alone an entire winter's supply of grain. And without food Alexander knew that the Greek struggle for freedom was very soon going to die a muddy death on the rain-swept hillsides of the Peloponnese.

Alexander clenched his fist in frustration, swept by a need for action so intense that his body literally ached with it. God, how much longer would he be condemned to lie helplessly in bed while Canning's bank-draft rotted in a hole in a stone wall, and the wheat-sacks rotted in an inadequate warehouse in Brindisi? Not to mention the large-bore English rifles that waited in the deepest hold of Barrett's ship and might mean the difference between life and death to the besieged garrison of freedom-fighters in the Acropolis. Hell's fire, he simply couldn't afford to lie here, sipping barley water and taking days to recuperate from a simple bullet-wound!

He struggled frustratedly against the doctor's restraining hand, then smelled the faint perfume of lemon blossom and realised that Charlotte had come into the room. Reason returned, and he allowed the doctor to push him gently down on to the pillows.

'Hello, young lady,' Dr Macfarlane said, and Alexander saw a definite twinkle in the doctor's eyes. 'I hear ye had a visitor this afternoon. A gentleman from America.'

Charlotte laughed. 'I shall never understand how news travels so fast in this part of the world! You have doubtless already been given a full account.'

'Aye, I dare say I have.'

Charlotte glanced towards the bed, and Alexander felt a sudden unexpected tightening in the pit of his stomach. He quickly suppressed the sensation and forced himself to stare vacantly into Charlotte's eyes.

The doctor slowly replaced his instruments in his bag. 'I also heard that Lady Adeline was impressed by Mr Barrett's gentlemanly behaviour. She has formed a whole new opinion of the standard of civilisation in America.'

Charlotte laughed. 'Well, at least of civilisation in the city of Boston. My aunt was captivated by the charm of our visitor's stories.'

'And you?' the doctor asked quietly. 'Were you captivated, Charlotte?'

Alexander was watching her closely, and he had no difficulty in seeing her hesitation. 'Mr Barrett was very courteous,' she said finally. 'But there was something about him. . .'

The doctor looked up sharply. 'What do you mean, Charlotte?'

'I dare say I was imagining things, but the fact is, Doctor, I'm not sure Mr Barrett told us the truth. He repeated several times that he spoke only English, and yet I had the oddest feeling that he knew what language our patient was speaking—that he understood what Mr Alexander was saying.'

The doctor glanced immediately towards Alexander, who covered a nervous leap of his stomach with a blank, cheerful smile. Dr Macfarlane frowned. 'Do you think Mr Barrett was lying when he denied knowing our patient?'

'Why should he pretend not to know Mr Alexander if in fact he does?'

'You are too intelligent a woman, Charlotte Rippon,

to be asking such a foolish question. There are a dozen reasons why a man might deny his friend, and none of them good ones. Our patient has a winsome smile, but remember that a villainous heart can disguise itself as easily with smiles as it can with curses.'

Alexander did not like the direction the conversation was taking. He contemplated creating a diversion by falling out of bed, and was relieved when the housekeeper came in and saved him the discomfort of rolling out on to the thinly carpeted wooden floor—a ruse which would undoubtedly have damaged his right shoulder, the only part of his body that had so far escaped injury.

'I've brought the foreigner his dinner,' Mrs Stubbs announced, indicating a bowl of thin gruel and a cup of steaming hot milk. 'Should I give it to him now, Dr Macfarlane?'

'I can find no reason why not. His wounds all seem to be healing well, and I cannot see why he should have been in pain this afternoon. Perhaps we should take his moans and groans as a good sign. I have learned over the years that patients sometimes feel more pain when they are recovering than when they are at the height of their illness.'

'Do you think he is strong enough to eat some solid food?' Charlotte asked as she balanced the tray on Alexander's knees and handed him a spoon. 'He seems to be very tired of his invalid diet.'

'If he can keep down the gruel and the milk, you may try him next with a slice of bread and a poached breast of chicken.'

Alexander's stomach rumbled in pleasurable anticipation of a crusty mouthful of bread, well spread with butter. Fortunately he managed to control his hunger before he betrayed his understanding of their conversation.

The doctor and Charlotte waited until he had finished his gruel, then left the sick-room together. The housekeeper brought him a second cup of hot milk, but it did not seem to taste quite as good now that Charlotte was no longer sitting in the chair beside his bed.

She was extraordinarily beautiful, Alexander reflected,

even though she was thinner and taller—and several years older—than the women he was accustomed to taking into his bed. Her skin had the delicate bloom of a peach when the sunlight first fell upon it in the morning, and her clear blue eyes seemed so unawakened, so unaware of the possibilities of passion. He could imagine all too clearly how she would look when some man finally broke through the barrier of her innocence and first roused her to desire. Her cheeks would darken to the dusky pink of a wild rose, and her lips would soften as they parted to receive her lover's kiss. . .

Alexander pushed the cup of milk away, deliberately shutting out the tantalising images of a woman who was beginning to occupy far too much of his thoughts. He could not afford to let Charlotte Rippon into his dreams, much less into his life. If anything about his precarious future was absolutely certain, it was that there was no place in it for a woman like Charlotte.

Perhaps in divine retribution for his earlier pretence of pain Alexander found it impossible to sleep that night. The cuts in his back felt raw, his broken fingers ached, and the bullet-hole in his shoulder felt like a tunnel of fire. Harry, the footman, was sleeping on a truckle bed at one side of the room, and Alexander made every effort not to disturb him, but three or four times he dozed off just sufficiently to turn over on to his back, and he cried out as the sheets rubbed against the wounds left by the whips.

By the time morning came he was exhausted, too weary to pay much attention to the whispered conference of Harry and the housekeeper in a corner of his room. He was too tired even to be hungry, and turned aside from his bowl of gruel before it was half eaten. Mrs Stubbs pursed her lips, took the bowl back to the kitchen and returned with a cup of steaming barley water.

'Now you drink that all up,' she said. 'It will do you good, and no need for Miss Charlotte to be worrying herself silly about you. If you drink this, you'll get a few hours of peaceful sleep, and you'll be right as ninepence when you wake up. And, what's more, Miss Charlotte won't spend all afternoon troubling herself about you.'

If he had not been so tired, he might have analysed the housekeeper's words a little more carefully. He might even have paused to wonder why the drink had a familiar and faintly cloying scent. As it was, he gulped the drink down to please Mrs Stubbs, and it was only as the waves of unconsciousness swept over him that he realised he had been drugged. He fought to keep hold of his senses, but he knew that it was a losing battle. Whatever happened for the rest of this day he would know nothing about it, for the housekeeper had laced his drink with that curse of the Ottoman Empire, tincture of opium—the drug that the English called laudanum.

By Tuesday afternoon the rain had finally stopped, but a damp north-easterly wind continued to sweep across the downs so that the ground remained sodden, and a walk was out of the question.

The housekeeper brought in tea to break up the long afternoon. She had scarcely placed the tray in front of Aunt Adeline, however, when the butler appeared at the drawing-room door. 'Sorry to disturb you, my lady, but there be another gentleman to see you and Miss Charlotte.'

'Another gentleman!' Lady Adeline exclaimed. 'How amazing! Is he an American?'

'No, my lady. He is from London, and his name is Sir Clive Collins.' The butler coughed discreetly. 'He is a very *distinguished*-looking gentleman, my lady, and quite young.'

Lady Adeline read the proffered visiting-card and perked up considerably when she saw that Sir Clive was a baronet, not a mere knight.

'Please show him in, Arthur,' she said happily. 'And let Mrs Stubbs know that we'll be needing an extra teacup.'

Sir Clive Collins followed the butler into the drawing-room and swept both ladies a deep, flourishing bow. He was tall and pink-complexioned with thick blond hair and a superb refinement of manner. His grey jacket stretched taut and smooth across a pair of slender shoulders and his cravat would have been the envy of Beau Brummell at the height of his fame. His linen gleamed white and his boots shone with unspeckled lustre despite the muddiness of the highways. His mere presence seemed to bring the perfumed elegance of a London salon into the cosy comfort of Rippon Manor's country drawing-room.

'My dear ladies, I beg that you will forgive this intrusion,' he said, drawing off his kid gloves. 'But I have heard that you two kind souls have been playing angel of mercy to an unfortunate gentleman found prostrate by the roadside.'

'Oh, la, indeed we have!' exclaimed Aunt Adeline. 'Please do sit down, Sir Clive. Do you know, you are the second gentleman in twenty-four hours to enquire about Mr Alexander?'

'Mr Alexander?' Sir Clive paused in the act of bestowing his ebony cane alongside his chair. 'Oh, but of course—Mr Alexander.' He smiled agreeably at Aunt Adeline. 'How. . .ah. . .fortunate, my lady, that I found my way to your door, for it seems that you and your niece have discovered my missing companion. How *very* relieved his friends will be.'

'And what a relief for us to find somebody who will at last be able to tell us what he is saying!'

The faintest of frowns crossed Sir Clive's noble forehead. 'I'm not sure that I quite understand your meaning, my lady?'

Charlotte spoke for the first time. 'Surely you knew, Sir Clive, that Mr Alexander speaks no English?'

'Not only *our* language,' Lady Adeline interjected. 'The poor man doesn't even speak French or German. He rattles away at us all the time, and he might as well be talking Greek for all the sense we can make out of it.'

The baronet laughed easily. 'Well, my lady, you haven't quite hit the nail upon the head, but you are approaching the right area of the world. Mr Alexander is probably speaking Osmanlica.'

'Osmanlica!' exclaimed Lady Adeline. 'I have never even heard of such a language.'

'It is a form of Turkish spoken by the Sultan and the governing classes of the Ottoman Empire,' Sir Clive explained. 'Mr Alexander's family is from Wallachia, you see, which is one of the provinces of the Ottoman Empire, to the east of Hungary. He and I were due to meet in Hastings last week, prior to sailing for France. You may imagine my concern when the appointed time for our departure came and went without any word from my good friend.'

'Why would somebody from Wallachia speak Osmanlica?' Charlotte asked with genuine curiosity.

Sir Clive's smile became a shade more patronising. 'It is confusing, is it not? But the Sultan of the Ottoman Empire appoints the governors of each of his provinces, and for generations the ruler of Wallachia has been a Turkish-speaking Greek, even though the people he governs are Slavs. The ruler of the province is known as the Hospedar of Wallachia. Mr Alexander's mother is the youngest daughter of a former Hospedar of Wallachia.'

'Oh,' said Charlotte. 'Do you speak Turkish, Sir Clive? That is a rare accomplishment for an Englishman.'

'Just a little, Miss Rippon. Enough to communicate with my good friend, Mr Alexander.'

Lady Adeline had no clear idea where the Ottoman Empire was located, and she had never even heard of Wallachia. But she was sincerely pleased to think that Mr Alexander had friends and family waiting to claim him once he was well. She smiled warmly at their visitor.

'My dear Sir Clive, you cannot guess what a relief it is to learn something about our poor Mr Alexander! We were so disappointed yesterday when it turned out that Mr Barrett had never met him.'

Sir Clive's smile never wavered. 'Mr Barrett must be the other gentleman who enquired about my friend Alexander. I confess that I do not recognise the name.'

'That isn't surprising,' Charlotte said before her aunt could speak. 'Mr Barrett made a mistake. He discovered when he came here that he had never met Mr Alexander. Mr Barrett's missing friend is, unfortunately, still unaccounted for.'

'What a pity,' said Sir Clive.

His words couldn't have been more innocuous, and yet Charlotte found herself searching the baronet's handsome features with unusual intensity. She wondered why she had suddenly become so suspicious of everybody, and with so little real cause. Yesterday she had suspected that Mr Barrett knew her patient even though he claimed that he didn't. Today she suspected that Sir Clive didn't really know Mr Alexander well, even though he claimed to be an intimate friend. Logically speaking, her reluctance to trust Sir Clive seemed ridiculous.

She was so preoccupied with her thoughts that she lost the thread of the conversation and only found it again when Sir Clive and Aunt Adeline rose to their feet and walked off towards the sick-room. She hurried after them, wondering if Mr Alexander would be awake. When she had visited him immediately after lunch he had been sleeping deeply.

He was still sleeping. Sir Clive stared intently at the motionless form, his gaze sweeping from the ebony hair to the splinted fingers, visible above the bedclothes.

'He does not look as sick as I had feared,' he commented softly.

'The doctor assures us that he gains strength every day,' Charlotte replied.

'That is good news, but let us not disturb him before it is essential,' Sir Clive said. 'Perhaps we should return to the drawing-room before we make the final arrangements for his removal?'

'His removal?' Charlotte repeated blankly.

'Shh,' her aunt said, tiptoeing into the corridor. 'You heard what Sir Clive said, Charlotte. We should discuss this in the drawing-room.'

Sir Clive was at his most charming while Mrs Stubbs brought fresh tea, entertaining them with witty stories about the London *ton*. Lady Adeline was in seventh heaven as she listened to a delightful piece of gossip about the new Duchess of Blanchford, but Charlotte could barely restrain herself until there was a suitable pause in the conversation.

'About your plans to take Mr Alexander back to London,' she began finally.

Sir Clive smiled, and Charlotte realised that his smiles only made her feel more uncomfortable. 'I can see that you are worried about your patient, my dear Miss Rippon, but I can assure you that your worries are needless.'

'Mr Alexander is not yet anywhere near recovered, Sir Clive. He really isn't ready to be moved.'

'He is blessed with a remarkably strong constitution, Miss Rippon, and you need not think that I came unprepared to care for him. My travelling-chaise is well sprung, and it is crammed with pillows and blankets. Moreover, my personal physician will be waiting to tend to Alexander as soon as we arrive in London. I have no wife, but my housekeeper is an excellent creature with considerable experience of nursing the sick.'

Charlotte found herself trembling with the force of her resistance to Sir Clive's plans. 'I realise that Mr Alexander is a friend of yours, and that my aunt and I are merely chance intruders——'

'Never intruders,' Sir Clive murmured. 'Surely handmaidens of Providence would be a more apt description.'

Lady Adeline blushed at the charming compliment, and Charlotte smothered an impatient sigh. 'Whether my aunt and I are handmaidens or chance intruders, Sir Clive, Mr Alexander is our patient. The doctor has assured us repeatedly that he is still too weak to be moved, so I'm afraid I couldn't possibly allow you to take him all the way back to London this afternoon.'

Sir Clive's smile thinned. 'London may seem far away to you, my dear Miss Rippon, but I can assure you that it is little more than sixty miles. No very great distance to those of us who are accustomed to travel.'

Charlotte took a firm grip on her temper, which was in imminent danger of running out of control. 'As a seasoned traveller, Sir Clive, you must know that at this time of year it will require somewhere between ten and fifteen hours to travel even that short distance. The roads out of Sussex are little more than mud paths at the moment. Believe me, your friend is simply not strong enough to endure so many hours of constant motion. Our doctor expressly warned us that his wounds would never heal unless he rested. The flesh on his shoulder is only now beginning to knit together. One unexpected jolt of the carriage and a week's worth of nursing care would be thrown completely away.'

'You are very persuasive,' Sir Clive said. He smiled again, a charmingly boyish smile that almost concealed the slight angry flare of his nostrils. He turned towards Lady Adeline. 'How about you, dear lady? Do you share your niece's determination to keep Mr Alexander here?'

'Charlotte is the nurse in our family,' Lady Adeline replied placidly. 'An angel of mercy if ever there was one, Sir Clive. If she thinks Mr Alexander ought not to be moved, you may certainly trust her judgement.'

Lady Adeline was feeling less placid than she sounded. She was, in fact, delighted at the turn that events were taking. She had spent the past several minutes contemplating the happy news that Sir Clive Collins had no wife. A baronet who lived in London was clearly a matrimonial catch to bring a light to any woman's eye, and even Charlotte must surely be bowled over by his handsome features and elegant manners.

'With regret,' she said dolefully, 'I fear I must agree with my dear niece and our good doctor. Mr Alexander is not yet ready to be moved, but we would be honoured, Sir Clive, if you would stay with us for a few days until your wounded friend is strong enough to accompany you to London.'

There was only the tiniest pause before the baronet answered. 'You are goodness itself, Lady Adeline, but, alas, my commitments in London don't permit me to remain out of town even for a single night. I must set out upon my return journey without further delay.'

Lady Adeline had not really expected Sir Clive to accept her invitation, and she was too seasoned a campaigner on Charlotte's behalf to be put off by such a trivial set-back. Her second line of attack was already prepared. 'I am confident that it will not be too long before Mr Alexander is ready to be moved. Charlotte and I plan to travel to London within the next ten days in order to spend some time with my eldest nephew Giles. It would be the easiest thing in the world for us to bring your friend with us to London.'

Sir Clive was picking up his hat, cane and gloves, so he did not notice that Charlotte's mouth had fallen open, or that Lady Adeline shot her niece a quick glance, ordering silence.

Sir Clive rose to his feet. 'Your kindness appears to know no bounds, Lady Adeline. You have my card with my direction. Permit me to say that I look forward with great eagerness to your arrival in town with my dear friend.' He hesitated momentarily before adding, 'Mr Alexander and I have business in France that remains somewhat pressing. I know I can rely upon you to see that he is brought directly to London as soon as he is capable of undertaking the journey?'

'If all goes well, sir, my niece and I will be leaving for London next week, and Mr Alexander will be with us.'

Sir Clive pulled on his gloves. 'If I may be permitted to drop a word of warning, dear ladies. My friend comes from a troubled part of the world, and not everybody from Wallachia wishes him well. Do not, I beg of you, release Mr Alexander into anybody's care save my own.'

Charlotte looked searchingly at the baronet. 'I gather that Mr Alexander holds a position of some importance in Wallachia?'

'Not at all,' Sir Clive responded briskly. 'My friend is still a young man and his time is devoted almost exclusively to entertaining himself. Nevertheless he attracts attention from some undesirable elements among the lower orders of society because his family, you understand, is of considerable importance in Wallachia.'

'My aunt and I will certainly see that your friend is not placed in any danger,' Charlotte said.

'Thank you, Miss Rippon. And will you send me word the day before you leave here, so that I may have everything in readiness for my friend's arrival?'

'Certainly, Sir Clive, and in the meantime may I give Mr Alexander a message from you?'

'My most profound good wishes for his speedy recovery. If you are able to make him understand your meaning, of course.'

'You could write him a note, perhaps,' Charlotte suggested.

Sir Clive took the time to smooth out a wrinkle in the elegant grey kid of his gloves. 'Unfortunately, my dear Miss Rippon, I do not write Turkish. The characters are Arabic, you know, and quite different from our own. I can only speak it a little.'

'Never mind,' Lady Adeline interjected cheerfully. 'I dare say he will recognise your name, if nothing else.'

'Of course, and that should certainly reassure him.' Sir Clive gave them a final charming smile as the butler appeared at the drawing-room door. 'It seems my carriage is here, so I must take my leave, but I shall look forward to seeing you both in London. Good afternoon, Lady Adeline, Miss Rippon, and many thanks.'

When Alexander woke up he realised that, however much he normally loathed the destructive powers of opium, in this instance his drug-induced sleep had carried him a long way towards recovery. His head ached and his mouth burned with dryness, but the cuts in his back no longer pained him and even the wound in his shoulder had ceased its pounding. The bullet-hole now signalled its presence by nothing more than a persistent, dull throb.

He pushed himself up on his right elbow, revelling in his new-found energy, and looked around the sick-room. Charlotte was seated in her usual chair by the window, sewing, and her hair gleamed in the pale light of the morning sun. She was in profile to him, and he couldn't help noticing how her breasts thrust against the form-fitting grey challis of her morning-gown. Her waist and hips might be smaller than was fashionable in his part of the world, but her breasts were unexpectedly full and seemed to invite a man to take them into his hands.

His stomach gave the tiny involuntary leap that her presence always seemed to provoke, and for a moment he allowed his gaze to rest on the delicate curve of her cheek and the smooth perfection of her complexion. He felt the swift, unmistakable response of his body and deliberately turned his gaze away. He must be recovering his strength more quickly than he'd realised, he thought with a wry smile. In normal circumstances he would surely find Charlotte Rippon eminently resistible. After all, once he had taken a woman into his bed he invariably found her exactly like every other woman, and his growing attraction to this Englishwoman could only be a reflection of his weakened state of health. Or perhaps it was simply that he had been too busy recently to pay attention to the demands of his body. It was many weeks since he had last found time to enjoy the pleasures of a night spent in a woman's arms. No wonder this thin English spinster caused such an unexpected reaction every time he saw her.

He hauled himself upright against the pillows, noting with satisfaction that the movement no longer hurt his back. Charlotte heard the rustle of the bedclothes and she stood up quickly, putting down her sewing and walking across to the small table by his bed. She poured him a glass of barley water and handed it to him with a friendly smile at the same time as she pulled on the bell-rope to summon a servant. 'I'm sure you're hungry,' she said. 'It's Wednesday morning already, and you've slept for more than twenty-four hours. You missed seeing Sir Clive Collins when he called yesterday.'

Alexander drank the barley water in a single long swallow. Sir Clive Collins. Was he supposed to know somebody called Sir Clive Collins? He handed the glass back to Charlotte just as the housekeeper came into the room.

'I've brought the foreigner his breakfast,' she said, setting a large wooden tray on Alexander's lap. 'Just you wait and see what we have for you this morning,' she added, whipping off the covering napkin to reveal a boiled egg, two slices of bread and butter and a cup of steaming tea. After so many days of gruel and milk Alexander thought that his breakfast looked almost as beautiful as Charlotte.

'Zank-you,' he said to Mrs Stubbs with heartfelt gratitude.

'My word, he's getting quite good with his speaking,

isn't he?' she remarked, watching him with a proprietorial air as he cut off the top of his egg.

'Yes, his vocabulary increases every day,' Charlotte agreed.

'Well, I'll be getting along if you don't need me for anything else, Miss Charlotte. Peggy will come for the tray in a few minutes. Lady Adeline wants to count the contents of the still-room before you both leave for London.'

Alexander took a large bite of bread and butter as Charlotte sat down on the small stool beside his bed. He had only half registered the housekeeper's comment about London, and Sir Clive was completely forgotten as he chewed blissfully on the fresh, crusty bread, trying to remember any mouthful of food that had ever tasted more exquisite.

'Did you understand what I told you?' Charlotte asked. 'Your friend, Sir Clive Collins, came to see you yesterday. He drove down from London. You slept right through his visit, but my aunt and I agreed to take you to his house in London as soon as you are strong enough to travel.'

Alexander stared at Charlotte with a blankness that was totally unfeigned. Who the devil was Sir Clive Collins? he wondered. Alexander racked his brains, trying to recall anybody in the Foreign Secretary's office with a name similar to Sir Clive Collins. Only a minor functionary, Sir Clive Bottomley, came to mind. Could Sir Clive be an emissary sent by Mr Canning? Alexander's mission was vital to British interests as well as to Greek ones, so Sir Clive might well be an official messenger. On the other hand he could equally easily be a spy working to oppose the Foreign Secretary's plans for an independent Greek nation. There were innumerable factions within the Ottoman Empire, all determined to go to war rather than to surrender a single inch of imperial territory, and they had wealth enough to buy the loyalty of all the spies they needed.

Alexander smothered an impatient sigh. It was infuriating not to be able to ask any questions because of his self-imposed pretence of speaking no English. But if he wanted to protect Charlotte and her household he had no choice other than to continue with the masquerade until he was strong enough to make his escape from Rippon Manor. Please God, that would not take more than another couple of days.

'Zir Clive?' he said slowly, hoping that Charlotte would tell him something more. 'Zir Clive Collinz from London?'

'Yes, Sir Clive wishes you a speedy recovery, and he looks forward to your return to perfect health. He told us about your family in Wallachia and explained that you speak Turkish. He would have left you a note, but he said that he couldn't write Turkish because the Arabic script is too difficult to learn.'

That seemed to settle the question of Sir Clive's loyalties, Alexander decided. The baronet almost certainly hadn't come from Canning's office, or he would have done a much more efficient job of passing on a message. Which left wide open the interesting question of who and what Sir Clive actually was. Alexander silently cursed the well-meaning Mrs Stubbs and the opium-laced milk that had kept him sleeping during the baronet's visit. If only he had seen the man he might well have recognised him.

It was suddenly intolerable to be confined to bed when so much was happening in the world outside his sick-room. He set his breakfast tray on the bedside table and threw off his covers before Charlotte realised what he planned to do. He swung his legs over the edge of the bed and forced himself to stand. He stayed upright for all of twenty seconds before his knees buckled beneath him. He was compelled to grab hold of the wooden bedframe to prevent himself collapsing ignominiously on to the floor. He was too weak even to climb back into bed, and he leaned against the mattress, cursing long and fluently in Greek.

Charlotte was beside him in less than a minute, taking his weight on to her own shoulders and scolding him angrily as she tried to return him to the bed. She was obviously conscious of nothing save the need to return a feeble patient to the safety of his sick-bed, but Alexander was burningly aware of the supple curves of her body and the fragrant silkiness of her hair as it brushed against his jaw. Her total lack of awareness of him as a man merely added fuel to the flame of his anger. By heaven, he could not tolerate his role as an idiot invalid very much longer!

'No!' he said sharply, resisting her efforts to make him lie down. With a distinct effort of will he made himself speak in heavily accented English. 'No more bed, Charlotte. I walk!'

She looked at him in astonishment, and, at that precise moment, he neither knew nor cared whether her surprise was caused by his unexpected display of temper or by the sudden increase in his command of the English language. Pushing himself away from her, he drew in a deep breath and stepped away from the bed. His muscles wobbled a bit but, thank heaven, this time they held him upright as he walked four or five paces across to the window. He leaned against the wall for a moment, panting, then turned around and walked back to his bed. He would not admit, even to himself, how glad he was to let his knees fold under him and collapse on to the mattress. He made no protest when Charlotte plumped up the pillows and gently pushed him back under the covers.

'That was very well done,' she said, smiling softly. 'But you must not over-exert yourself, Mr Alexander. Rest now, and perhaps this afternoon you will be able to repeat your success.'

Alexander vowed silently that, by the end of the day, he would be capable of walking the length of the corridor and that, within two days, he would be strong enough to leave Rippon Manor. He knew that his speedy return to health was largely due to Charlotte's devoted nursing, and he was aware of the unpleasant irony of his situation. The best way of showing his gratitude was to leave everybody in total ignorance of who he was and what he had been doing in Kent, but he suddenly found it intolerable to contemplate leaving Rippon Manor without ever offering Charlotte his thanks. He reached out his hand and clasped her delicate fingers tightly within his grasp.

'Thank you, Charlotte,' he said huskily. 'For everything.'

Her gaze widened, and he thought irrelevantly that he had never in his life before seen such incredible blue eyes. 'Mr Alexander,' she whispered, 'precisely how much English do you speak?'

He looked at her for a long time before he replied. 'Goodbye, Charlotte,' he said quietly. He lifted her hand to his mouth, defying all the rules of etiquette and common sense as he pressed his lips first against the tips of her fingers and then against the pulse throbbing in her slender wrist.

She sat very still until he released her hand, and when she finally spoke her voice was little more than a whisper. 'You should not have done that, Mr Alexander.'

Sanity returned just in time to prevent him replying. He closed his eyes and turned his face into the pillow, feigning sleep without any real hope of deceiving her. Perhaps, he thought bleakly, if he resisted the temptation of saying anything further, he might still rescue the tattered remnants of his masquerade and protect Charlotte from the dangers of knowing too much.

CHAPTER THREE

THE day after Sir Clive's visit Mr Alexander walked the length of the downstairs hallway completely unaided. In celebration of his achievement he borrowed some clothes and took tea with the ladies in the drawing-room, delighting even Lady Adeline with his droll attempts to master such useful English phrases as, 'Would you care for cream and sugar in your tea?' or, 'The weather is much improved today, is it not?'

After an hour's practice Mr Alexander still stumbled over the sentences that Lady Adeline had so carefully selected, but she was not greatly put out by her pupil's lack of success. As she explained to Charlotte during dinner that evening, for a man raised in a country that nobody civilised had ever heard of Mr Alexander was doing far better than could be expected. Lady Adeline was helping herself to steamed purée of parsnips at the time and consequently didn't notice that her niece mumbled something rather non-committal in reply.

The tea-party marked the beginning of Mr Alexander's return to normal health and the end of Charlotte's duties in the sick-room. Lady Adeline pointed out, with perfect truth, that her niece's reputation would be ruined if it became known that she had entered the bedchamber of a man strong enough to walk by himself around the room. Fortunately the weather reverted to mild breezes and warm sun, so Charlotte was able to work off an inexplicable surge of restlessness by long rides across the countryside and visits to the outlying tenant farms on the Rippon Manor estate.

On Saturday, eleven days after Mr Alexander's arrival at Rippon Manor, Dr Macfarlane announced that his patient would be fit enough to travel to London by Tuesday morning, providing that the journey was taken in easy stages. Lady Adeline was immediately a-flutter with excitement and turned the entire household upside-down with preparations for their departure.

For her part, Charlotte tried hard to share her aunt's enthusiasm for the forthcoming trip. In truth she couldn't quite understand why the prospect of two or three weeks spent with her favourite brother in London left her feeling so strangely flat. She also wondered why she didn't feel more gratified by the knowledge that Mr Alexander was now healthy enough to leave Rippon Manor. There was no logical reason for her stomach to twist into a painful knot every time she thought of the fact that she would never see him again once he was safely returned to the bachelor comforts of Sir Clive Collins's household.

Harry was sent off to London with two letters in his saddle-bag, the first a brief note informing Sir Clive Collins of the imminent arrival of Mr Alexander, and the second a long letter to Charlotte's brother Giles, explaining the reason for their unexpected visit to town. Lady Adeline was able to sit down to dinner on Sunday night secure in the satisfying knowledge that their preparations for departure could not possibly have been in better train. She retired to bed within an hour of finishing her meal, admonishing her niece to follow her good example so that they would both be well rested for the journey on Tuesday morning.

By one o'clock in the morning Charlotte finally acknowledged that she was not going to fall asleep any time in the near future. She tiptoed down the stairs without lighting a candle, feeling her way down the steps by means of the carved oak panelling. Her brother Giles had recently sent a parcel of novels down from London, including Sir Walter Scott's latest publication, *The Talisman*. She hoped that reading his new tale of high adventure might help to induce sleepiness.

She had reached the downstairs hallway and was about to cross into the library when she heard the faint echo of something banging. The sound seemed to come from near the sick-room and her first thought was that Mr Alexander must have taken a sudden turn for the worse and be seeking assistance. No thought of propriety or maidenly modesty entered her head as she ran silently down the corridor towards the kitchen quarters.

The door to the sick-room was indeed open, but she realised at once that their former patient had not been seeking help. Far from suffering a relapse, Mr Alexander was obviously in fine fettle. He was out of bed and fully dressed in a white shirt and dark pantaloons borrowed from one of her brothers. He was, moreover, busily occupied in an attempt to prise open the rear door of the house. He was trying to lift up the massive iron bar that protected the entrance, but he was hampered by his inability to use both hands. The noise she had heard, Charlotte guessed, must have been the sound of the iron bar slipping out of Mr Alexander's grasp and falling back into its socket.

She did not stop to wonder whether it was altogether wise to reveal her presence. She was aware only of an intense feeling of betrayal. 'What are you doing?' she asked harshly. 'Just where were you planning to sneak off to, Mr Alexander?'

He whirled around, his features stark and unnaturally pale in the silvery moonlight. 'Charlotte, for God's sake, you startled me! What are you doing out of bed at this hour of night?'

She looked at him long and hard, and when she spoke her voice was colder than the wind in February. 'You have suddenly become an amazingly proficient pupil, Mr Alexander. I'm sure my aunt would be astounded to see how much success her English lessons have had. Would you be so kind as to inform me *precisely* how much of our language you speak?'

The faintest trace of colour darkened his high cheekbones. 'Enough to justify your anger,' he said quietly.

'I see. And would it be expecting too much if I asked for an explanation as to why you chose to deceive my aunt and me about your ability to understand us? I would have thought that we deserved better than to be made the butt of your perverted sense of humour.'

'You and Lady Adeline deserve only my gratitude,' he insisted. 'Believe me, Charlotte, you have received it in full measure.'

'That, of course, is why you allowed us to think that you understood nothing that we were saying to you.'

'I understand your anger, Charlotte——'

'Since you speak such excellent English, Mr Alexander, I am sure that you realise my name is Miss Rippon.'

His glance swept her face. 'Miss Rippon, I ask you to forgive me for the deception. My only excuse is hat I thought it absolutely necessary. I know all too well that I owe both you and your aunt more than I an ever repay.' He hesitated for a moment, then reached inside his shirt and withdrew a folded sheet of paper. 'You should know that I didn't intend to leave without at least expressing my thanks. I wrote this note, which I planned to set here on the kitchen table.'

Charlotte took the sheet of paper from him. She noticed, with an odd sense of detachment, that her hand was quite steady although beneath her calm exterior she trembled with a potent mixture of hurt and bitter anger. She started to open the note, then was swept by an unexpected surge of revulsion. She crumpled the paper into a tight ball and stuffed it into the pocket of her robe without even glancing at it.

'We'll leave your expressions of thanks for some other time,' she said coldly. 'For the moment I am more interested in hearing exactly how you intended to leave Rippon Manor. Were you planning to add the theft of one of our horses to your list of ingratitudes, Mr Alexander?'

He drew in a deep breath. 'I was not planning to steal a horse.' He stopped, and after a moment continued with some constraint. 'I intended only to borrow one. I would have sent the animal back to you as soon as I reached a posting-house. And later, when I returned to my home, I intended to send you one of my. . .to send you an Arabian breeding mare as a token of my esteem.'

'Of course,' she said, turning away so that he would not see the tears that gathered so annoyingly in the corner of her eyes. 'It sounds a most likely tale, Mr Alexander.'

He closed the gap between them in three quick strides and halted only inches away from her. 'Please look at me, Miss Rippon,' he asked. She kept her gaze averted obstinately as he continued in a low, earnest voice, 'Is it too late to ask you to trust me? Will you accept my word that I lied about my ability to speak your language only because it was safer for you and for your aunt if you thought I couldn't understand you?'

'Safer!' she retorted bitingly. 'Indeed, I can well believe that it was safer for you.' She saw that she had twisted the ribbons of her robe into a tight knot around her fingers and she carefully untwisted them. 'Are you a smuggler, Mr Alexander?'

'No,' he replied at once. He sighed, thrusting his uninjured hand impatiently through his dark hair. 'The truth is that I am undertaking a mission on behalf of my government—a mission, incidentally, which meets with the strong approval of Mr Canning, your Foreign

Secretary. Unfortunately it is also a mission which threatens the interests of several powerful nations, and there are many people who would be delighted to see me dead. I assure you, Miss Rippon, that I am thinking of you and your aunt as well as my own skin when I tell you that the less you know of me and my activities the safer you will be.'

She lifted her head, not bothering to disguise the contempt blazing in her eyes. 'You are despicable, Mr Alexander! What a marvellously convenient story, to be sure! In an instant you are converted from a dishonourable sneak-thief into a national hero, risking his life for the good of his country. And I, of course, am supposed to flutter my eyelashes, sigh over your gallantry, and then return quietly to my room. Unfortunately, sir, you have mistaken the degree of my gullibility. You do not look like a noble patriot, Mr Alexander. You look like a villain.'

His saturnine features broke into a smile—a warm, tender smile that had the most extraordinary effect on Charlotte's breathing-system. Before she had time to gather her wits he crooked his finger under her chin and tilted her face up, staring laughingly into her eyes.

'Ah, my dear Miss Rippon,' he murmured teasingly. 'I never expected Mrs Stubbs to convert you to her point of view so swiftly. Am I to be condemned simply because I am a foreigner with dark hair and eyes that are too black to belong to an Englishman?'

She avoided looking into the eyes he had mentioned and forced herself to ignore a treacherous desire to smile back at him. 'No, sir,' she said crisply. 'You are to be condemned because of your behaviour, and because of your many lies.'

'Tonight, trust me, I have told you nothing but the truth. I am leaving the protection of your home because I am on a mission that can no longer be delayed, and I deceived you about my knowledge of English only for your own safety.'

Her heart stopped beating for a moment, then raced forward at a quick, uneven pace. She wanted so much to believe him, to believe that those strange moments of intimacy they had shared had not been mere figments of her imagination. Somewhat belatedly she realised that his hand still held her chin captive and that less than six inches of space separated her inadequately clad body from his. It was clearly imperative that she move. She reminded herself that she was notorious throughout the entire neighbourhood for the unfeminine, no-nonsense practicality of her character. She wondered ruefully where her much-vaunted practicality had disappeared to now that she needed it most. With a final stern admonition she pulled herself out of Mr Alexander's embrace, then swung around so that her back was towards him. The few tattered remnants of her common sense seemed to function better when she wasn't looking at him.

'Who is Mr Barrett?' she asked abruptly.

'He is what he told you, a merchant from Boston. A very wealthy merchant.'

'You know him.'

'Yes,' he acknowledged. 'Mr Barrett is my. . . partner. . .in a humanitarian venture.'

'Why did you each pretend not to know the other?'

'My answer is the same as it has been before. It seemed safer that way for all of us.'

'Is he part of this mission you are undertaking for your government? For Wallachia?'

She heard the almost infinitesimal hesitation before he replied. 'Yes, Mr Barrett is working on behalf of my government, and also on behalf of Mr Canning and a committee of friends in the United States of America.'

'I didn't realise that people in America troubled themselves with the distant affairs of eastern Europe,' she said, turning around so that she was once again facing him. 'Tell me, Mr Alexander, are you really from Wallachia?'

'In a manner of speaking,' he replied. 'My mother is the youngest daughter of a former governor of Wallachia, but I, personally, have not spent much time in that province. My father is a loyal servant of Sultan Muhmad II, and most of my youth was spent in the city of Istanbul.'

'Are you a follower of the Prophet Mohammed, Mr Alexander?'

'No,' he said slowly. 'When I became a man I chose to follow the religion and customs of my mother's people.'

'What about Sir Clive?' she asked. 'Was he telling the truth when he claimed to know you?'

Mr Alexander bent down to pick up his cloak from the housekeeper's chair by the fireplace. 'Remember that I was asleep during Sir Clive's visit and have not seen him,' he said, swinging the cloak awkwardly around his shoulders. He fumbled with the metal frogs, not quite managing to conceal a grimace of pain when he inadvertently jolted his shoulder.

Even though he was obviously making preparations to leave Charlotte couldn't quite credit the evidence of her own eyes. Surely he didn't expect to walk out of the house and steal one of her horses while she stood by silently and watched? He must know that one loud scream on her part would bring half a dozen servants rushing to her rescue.

'Where do you think you're going?' she queried sharply.

His hand stilled on the buckle and his mouth tightened into a grim line. 'To the stables,' he said, his voice surprisingly gentle. 'I must leave Rippon Manor tonight.'

She ran to the door and positioned herself squarely in front of it. 'You may be a dishonourable man, Mr Alexander, but I am a conscientious nurse, and I will not allow you to kill yourself. You cannot control a strange horse on unknown roads, in the dark, with a half-healed bullet-wound in the middle of your shoulder.'

'I regret, Miss Rippon, that I have no choice in the matter.'

She pressed her palms flat against the wooden panels of the door. Her eyes met his across the width of the kitchen, and, for a moment, she had the oddest sensation that time stood still. She suddenly saw Mr Alexander not as a patient but as a man, and the vision was distinctly unsettling. Why had she never noticed the dark, sardonic sweep of his eyebrows across his high forehead? Why had she never noticed the hard line of his jaw and the arrogant thrust of his chin? But his mouth wasn't hard or arrogant. His mouth was—— She cut off the thought, angered by the strange byways that her mind kept pursuing tonight, and clasped her hands primly in front of her.

'If you try to open this door, Mr Alexander, I shall scream with all the force of my lungs.'

'My knees are quite knocking together,' he murmured, smiling as he walked purposefully towards her. 'I dare say there is no hope for me unless I make sure that your lungs have no breath left to carry out such a terrible threat.'

His words sank like stones into her heart, and, too late, she realised just how foolish she had been to place herself in the power of a man about whom she knew virtually nothing. His body loomed over her, tall and menacing in the pale moonlight. Fear closed her throat and widened her eyes as she looked up at him, but, illogically, she did not scream while she still had the chance.

He raised his hand and all trace of laughter vanished from his expression. His fingers were trembling, she saw with a kind of detached horror. She wanted to close her eyes, but even her eyelids seemed temporarily paralysed. His hand moved slowly towards her face and suddenly she felt the delicate touch of his fingers caressing her cheek.

'Ah, dear God,' he whispered. 'Charlotte, do not look at me so! You misunderstood my foolish words. How could you think that I would harm you? Has nobody ever told you that there are a thousand ways for a man to silence a woman without ever resorting to violence? Sweet Charlotte, I threatened to drown your cries in pleasure, not in pain.'

Sweet Charlotte. The words echoed strangely inside her, and she was shocked to discover that one small sinful part of her actually longed to find out how a man could cause a woman to drown in pleasure. She wondered how it would feel if his hand tore off her silly nightcap and curled itself in the long strands of her hair. She wondered how it would feel if he bent his head and pressed his lips against her forehead. . . She gulped, amazed at the extraordinary direction her thoughts were taking yet again. Thank heaven that Aunt Adeline couldn't read her mind at this precise moment, Charlotte thought wryly. The poor lady would fall into a swoon and take a week to come out of it.

'Mr Alexander,' she said with a firmness that she was far from feeling, 'this is not at all a proper conversation for us to be having. I think it would be better if you returned immediately to your bed——'

The tension fled from his features and laughter warmed his voice. 'In certain circumstances that might be a most enticing prospect, but tonight I regret that I really cannot avail myself of your offer. Sweet Charlotte, I have already told you that I must go.'

'If you try to leave tonight, I swear I shall rouse every servant in the place within two seconds of your walking outside that door. Mr Alexander, be reasonable. On Tuesday, scarcely thirty-six hours from now, we shall all be on our way to London. What can be so urgent that you must risk your health, and perhaps your life, in order to leave Rippon Manor tonight?'

He was silent for so long that she thought he might refuse to answer her. 'I have something to retrieve from this neighbourhood before I go to London,' he replied at long last. 'Something which is vital to my mission.'

'But if you tell me what you must retrieve, and where it is hidden, we can easily send one of the grooms tomorrow morning. If it is not too far distant I can even go myself.'

'No,' he said sharply. 'That would be much too dangerous.'

'Dangerous?' she repeated in astonishment. 'Mr Alexander, I ride five or six miles almost every morning. No harm is going to come to me in this neighbourhood. Everybody knows me!'

'I think I envy you,' he said. 'You are so incredibly foolish, so splendidly naïve. Your life has always been so safe that you cannot imagine the possibility of treachery, or betrayal. You cannot understand what it means to consider every stranger your enemy, and every acquaintance a potential traitor. How do you know that Rippon Manor is not being watched?'

She laughed. 'What would they be watching? Peggy slipping out of the house to tryst with one of the stable lads? Or my good aunt consulting with the dairymaids? Mr Alexander, you are allowing your suspicions to run riot. True, you were attacked by highwaymen, but that doesn't mean the countryside is crawling with potential thieves and robbers. Except for the attack upon you this neighbourhood has been free of highway robberies for almost a dozen years.'

He looked at her in a manner she found hard to interpret. 'I was not set upon by highwaymen,' he said firmly. 'I was attacked by assassins, hired and paid for by my country's enemies.'

She gasped. 'How can you be so sure?'

'I heard them speak,' he replied laconically.

'What is it that you have to retrieve before we go to London?' she asked in a somewhat subdued tone of voice.

'A package of documents,' he said. 'As soon as I saw that I was being followed I knew that I had little hope of escape. My horse was already on the edge of exhaustion, and my pursuers were freshly mounted. My first priority was to save the papers I was carrying from falling into the wrong hands, so I cut off the highway and rode across country for half a mile or so, searching for a place to hide the documents.'

'You found somewhere, obviously.'

He nodded. 'About a mile and a half northwest of the place where you and your aunt discovered me. But I'm not at all sure of finding the hiding-place again. I rode at frantic speed, and I may not recognise the terrain. It will probably require several hours of searching before I find the spot I'm looking for.'

'I will strike a bargain with you, Mr Alexander. If you will return to your room now, tomorrow I will harness up the pony-trap and drive you anywhere that you choose to direct me. Remember, I know the countryside around

Rippon Manor intimately. If you will allow me to help you your search may be much quicker.'

'Why are you so willing to help me?' he asked abruptly. 'You have no way of knowing that I am telling you any part of the truth.'

She didn't know the answer to his question. For all his claim that she was naïve she certainly wasn't naïve enough to believe that he was telling her anything like the whole story. Her gaze flew to his, seeking reassurance. His fathomless ebony eyes met hers steadily, and she was suddenly aware of the heavy, pounding beat of her heart. She drew in a long, shaky breath.

'I believe you have told me as much of the truth as you can,' she said. 'Am I a fool, Mr Alexander?'

For a long moment they stared wordlessly at each other, then he turned abruptly on his heel and strode across the kitchen to the sick-room. He paused on the threshold. 'No,' he replied quietly. 'You are anything but a fool. Goodnight, Charlotte.'

Long before dawn Charlotte had managed to convince herself that it would be positively unkind to worry Aunt Adeline with details of what had transpired in the kitchen with Mr Alexander. Accustomed to examining her actions with scrupulous honesty, on this particular occasion Charlotte allowed her thoughts to slide neatly around the truth. Last night's conversation was really too trivial to discuss with anybody, she decided. Why burden her aunt with the knowledge that their patient spoke English almost as well as everybody else in Rippon Manor? After all, they would be leaving for London first thing on Tuesday morning. By Wednesday, less than forty-eight hours from now, Mr Alexander would be out of their lives forever. There was no reason to throw the household into turmoil by revealing worrisome facts about him that were of no real interest to anybody, and certainly not to dear Aunt Adeline.

Having reached this very convenient conclusion, Charlotte's only remaining problem was how to help Mr Alexander search for his missing documents without explaining to her aunt what she was doing. She had already spent a couple of fruitless hours debating this knotty problem when, by great good fortune, the squire's wife happened to come calling.

Mrs Hubertson was a plump, amiable lady who enjoyed a position of considerable prestige in the neighbourhood. This was due in part to her comfortable financial circumstances, but even more to the fact that she had married off all three of her daughters within months of their leaving the schoolroom.

Satisfaction in her achievements as a wife and mother had not made Mrs Hubertson proud or stand-offish. She bustled into the drawing-room, barely concealing her excitement as she held aloft a book of fashion-plates that were hot off the Parisian printing-press.

'Only see what my daughter Jane has sent me!' she exclaimed, hastening to dispose her ample curves against the sofa cushions. 'My dears, we must take her word for it. Muslin is *finished*. Jane swears she hasn't seen a single gown that isn't made of silk.'

Charlotte, who could rarely work up the enthusiasm over clothes that her aunt deemed appropriate, nevertheless blessed Mrs Hubertson's arrival. Looking fascinated by her aunt's pronouncement that the waistline on evening dresses would continue to drop, she mentally calculated how long she would need to stay and chat before she and Mr Alexander could set off in pursuit of his documents. A quarter of an hour should do it, she decided.

At that moment Mrs Hubertson emitted a gusty sigh. 'Oh, my! Will you look at those magnificent satin sleeves? They must surely reach almost to one's ears! Charlotte, dearest, do you not find them positively adorable?'

Charlotte glanced at the enormous down-filled sleeves and forgot to be tactful. 'Just think how hot they would be in summer, and how inconvenient. You'd have to keep puffing up the feathers, or they would settle in a clump around your elbow.'

'What has that to do with anything?' Aunt Adeline asked, wrinkling her brow in genuine puzzlement. 'What has comfort or convenience to do with the question? We were discussing fashion.'

Mrs Hubertson adjusted her kindly features into the sternest gaze she could manage. 'Charlotte, dear, I have known you since you were a baby, and I speak with the frankness of an old friend. You are simply never going to marry unless you control this deplorable tendency towards the eccentric. Your aunt is quite right, my dear. Convenience has nothing to do with fashion. We ladies must suffer to be beautiful otherwise how can we ever hope to please the gentlemen?'

Charlotte had enough sense not to reply that if her chances of marriage depended on wearing pillows stuffed under her sleeves then she would rather remain single. 'You are quite right,' she said with a resigned smile. 'When we arrive in London, Mrs Hubertson, I shall pay particular attention to the exact size of everybody's sleeves and report back to you the moment we return.'

This mention of their forthcoming trip to the capital city served its intended purpose by giving rise to a delightful new train of conversation. Aunt Adeline and Mrs Hubertson were soon so deeply engrossed in their discussion of which warehouse carried the best selection of lace neck-ruffs that Charlotte was able to make good her escape with no more attention from her aunt than the instruction to take care when driving the gig.

Summoned by one of the footmen, Mr Alexander arrived promptly in the courtyard, followed by Mrs Stubbs, who was almost invisible beneath a pile of knitted shawls and soft cushions.

'I brought these for the foreigner,' she said, helping Alexander into the gig with a care that belied the brusqueness of her words. 'We don't want him ripping open those wounds after all the nights you spent nursing him, Miss Charlotte. Hold him steady, if you please, and I'll tuck this pillow behind his back.'

The housekeeper finally had the pillow arranged to her satisfaction, and she gave it a quick pat. 'There now, young man, you relax, and you'll feel all the better for a nice ride in the sunshine with Miss Charlottte.'

'Thank you, Mrs Stubbs.' Alexander smiled, and

Charlotte's stomach gave another of the odd little somersaults that it had begun to perform recently.

'Is there any special direction you think we should take, Mr Alexander?'

'The fever has blurred my memory somewhat, but I believe I had travelled less than two miles south and east from the spot where I hid the documents before my pursuers caught up with me.'

'Last night you mentioned that you had ridden cross-country.'

'Yes, directly towards the coast where Mr Barrett was expecting to meet me. I left the documents hidden behind a broken stone in a wall that marks the boundary of a small estate.'

Charlotte drove Daffodil around a treacherous hole in the gravel road, then urged the mare back into a brisk trot. She frowned, trying to visualise the neighbouring countryside. 'You were riding down the main road from London?'

'Yes. I passed through the little town of Battle about fifteen minutes before I hid the papers. You realise that I was working at frantic speed, with no time to take much stock of my surroundings, but I remember looking up and seeing a fine old Norman church as I dismounted.'

'I think I know where those papers must be,' Charlotte said, smiling with a touch of secret amusement. 'I do believe they are hidden in the wall that marks the boundary of Archdeacon Jeffries's estate.'

'Pray God they are still there.'

She glanced up as Alexander spoke and saw the unmistakable tension tightening his mouth. For the first time she realised the true significance of what she was doing. She was not taking a recovering invalid on a pleasant afternoon ramble through the countryside. If Mr Alexander could be believed the papers he had hidden were vital enough to have precipitated an attempt upon his life. If he was not telling the truth, then she might be putting herself in the path of real danger.

Somewhat belatedly Charlotte considered the possibility that once they found the all-important papers Mr

Alexander might simply knock her over the head and make off with Daffodil and the gig. By coming out with him alone, she realised, she had presented him with a better opportunity to steal the horse that he'd been trying to steal the night before.

Alexander reached out his hand and touched her gently on the cheek. 'Miss Rippon,' he murmured softly. 'You have an uncommonly expressive face, and I see that a whole series of dreadful suspicions has just occurred to you. I beg you not to trouble yourself unnecessarily. Believe me, I do not intend to murder you, nor do I intend to leave your wounded body by the wayside as I steal Daffodil and gallop to freedom. Apart from anything else, I doubt if Daffodil understands the meaning of the word gallop.'

Charlotte stiffened. 'Daffodil is a very good horse.'

'I'm sure she is, but not exactly the steed on which I would choose to race for freedom. Trust me, Miss Rippon, my intentions are wholly honourable. My aim is simply to retrieve the papers I have hidden and to accompany you to London, where I hope to make contact with my friend Hank Barrett. I don't intend to repay your generosity by harming you in any way.'

'You mistake the matter, Mr Alexander. I did not think——'

He pressed his finger to her lips, preventing her from speaking, but his eyes were warm with unexpected laughter as he turned to look at her. 'I regret to inform you, my dear Miss Rippon, that you are a hopeless liar. You thought me capable of all kinds of wicked deeds. Your blushes betray you.'

'I do not blush, Mr Alexander. For your information I am notorious throughout the neighbourhood for my inability to blush, faint, or otherwise comport myself in the manner expected of any young lady of sensibility.'

He leaned back against the pillow, his expression distinctly amused. 'Despite your fearsome reputation, Miss Rippon, I promise you that you blushed. In fact you are doing it again.'

Charlotte cleared her throat, which felt unaccountably constricted, and used her whip to point ahead of them.

'The rear entrance to the archdeacon's house is less than half a mile away, and over there is the tower of the village church. As you can see, it's in the Norman style, although it dates from the thirteenth century. Does anything hereabouts look familiar?'

Mr Alexander stared at the surrounding countryside with a concentration that wiped away all trace of laughter. 'Yes, it does indeed seem familiar. I think I crossed those fields over there, between the southern boundary of the archdeacon's estate and the churchyard. Do you know if there is a road for you and the gig to follow, Miss Rippon, or should I get out and walk?'

'There is a bridle path that Daffodil could take without too much trouble. Besides, you shouldn't walk unnecessarily. Mrs Stubbs will be cross with me if I return you to her in an exhausted state.'

They drove for a few more minutes, but they had scarcely reached the point where the dry stone wall turned sharply to the right when Mr Alexander asked Charlotte to stop the gig. As soon as Daffodil came to a halt he jumped out of the small carriage and strode around to offer Charlotte his assistance.

She looped the reins around the brass ring that acted as a carriage brake, then leaned forward, careful to rest almost none of her weight on Mr Alexander's arm. When he realised what she was doing he gave an impatient exclamation, grasped her waist with both hands and lifted her down on to the path.

'Mr Alexander, you must remember your injuries!' she insisted.

'Why in the world should I remember such a boring subject?'

His hands were still around her waist, and she suddenly experienced the oddest wish to lean closer to him, to discover how it would feel if she rested her cheek against the lapels of his jacket. She shook her head to dispel the strange fuzziness, feeling quite relieved when her voice emerged with all its usual briskness. 'Because I do not wish you to bleed all over the carriage when we drive up to London tomorrow. And, if you open up your shoulder-wound, that is assuredly what will happen.'

'I promise not to bleed over you or your carriage,' he said softly. '*Now* may we forget the subject of my injuries?'

'If you wish.' As she spoke she felt the heat rush up into her cheeks and realised, to her astonishment, that she was blushing—again. What in the world was the matter with her today? she wondered. If she wasn't careful she would soon be out-blushing Aunt Adeline. And then, presumably, she'd be fainting and needing smelling-salts.

Mr Alexander released his hold on her waist, and her breathing slowly returned to its normal rate. 'I'll tether the horse,' he said, stroking Daffodil on the muzzle. 'There's some grass for her to eat over there in the shade.'

He secured the reins to a nearby oak tree, then glanced up at the sun to get his bearings before walking swiftly along the length of the wall in a westerly direction. He ran his fingers over the rough, flat stones about ten inches from the top, and Charlotte followed behind him, checking at a lower level. After fifteen minutes of fruitless pacing and searching Alexander brushed a layer of grey dust from his hands and gave voice to a torrent of incomprehensible curses.

Charlotte waited until he had finished, then looked up at him with the hint of a smile. 'I think it's probably fortunate that I don't speak Turkish,' she said drily.

Alexander shrugged ruefully. 'I happened to be speaking Greek, but I apologise anyway. Most sincerely.'

'Why don't we pull away some of this ivy?' Charlotte suggested, tugging at a luxuriant crop of dark green leaves. 'It looks like quite recent growth.'

He pulled at a particularly thick clump. 'You are right,' he said. 'The leaves are abundant, but the roots are barely formed, and I remember there was ivy growing near the place I hid the documents.'

Charlotte laid bare another small stretch of wall. 'Do you usually think in Greek?' she asked, testing the stones.

'Not necessarily. The advantage of speaking several

languages is that you can select the one most suited to your mood.'

'And Greek is the language in which you lose your temper?'

He grinned. 'Well, it does have a very satisfying collection of curses. Turkish, on the other hand, is perfect for exchanging elaborate compliments and evading a precise answer to a difficult question.'

'And what about English?'

'English is the ideal language for honest, straightforward conversation. Commerce should always be conducted in English, whereas French might have been invented for——'

He broke off with such abruptness that Charlotte's curiosity was aroused. 'Please don't stop your explanations now, Mr Alexander. What might the French language have been invented for?'

His eyes met hers, their dark, unfathomable depths warmed by a definite hint of laughter. 'Since you insist, Miss Rippon, I will tell you that French is the perfect language for a man to use when he takes a woman into his bed. It is the language I always choose when I make love to a beautiful and desirable woman.'

He had made her blush *again*! If it weren't for the fact that she was never ill Charlotte would have sworn she was coming down with some virulent new disease. She turned away to hide her burning cheeks, and at that moment her fingers encountered a pair of broken stones so loose that they wobbled as she touched them. She pulled hard, ripping impatiently at the strands of overhanging ivy, and the stones toppled to the ground. She bent down and peered into the long, narrow hole.

'Mr Alexander,' she breathed, staring at the shadow-shrouded outline of an oilskin pouch. 'I do believe we have found your missing papers.'

He was at her side in a trice, pulling the pouch from the musty hole and rifling through the contents. When he was satisfied that everything was safe he seized her gloved hands and pressed them to his lips, indifferent to the dirt and stains soiling the leather. 'Charlotte, thank you, from the bottom of my heart. There are no words——'

They heard the sound of horse's hoofs just in time to spring apart as the rider trotted around the corner. 'Miss Rippon!' exclaimed a high, reedy voice. 'What an unexpected pleasure this is, to be sure! Such a coincidence, too! I was about to call at the manor in order to wish you and your good aunt a safe journey to London.'

Charlotte clasped her dirty hands behind her back and did her best to look delighted. 'Why, Archdeacon J-Jeffries! How are you? We—um—we didn't expect to see you here.'

His smile tightened. 'You did not? But why else, Miss Rippon, would you and your. . .companion. . .be walking in this particular spot if you did not plan to call upon me?'

Why indeed? Charlotte looked desperately in Mr Alexander's direction, hoping for inspiration. He slid smoothly in front of the hole in the wall and then stood there, alternately gazing up at the sky and smiling with half-witted good nature towards the archdeacon. Charlotte found herself suppressing an entirely inappropriate desire to giggle.

'Well, of course we intended to call upon you later,' she improvised hastily. 'But I wanted Mr Alexander to attempt a little exercise before we disturbed you. You know all about our invalid, of course. We are fortunate that he recovered his strength so swiftly.'

'Ah, yes, the wounded foreigner, picked up from the side of the road.' The archdeacon turned his gaze towards Alexander, and his nose wrinkled as if in the presence of an unpleasant smell.

'My dear Miss Rippon, far be it from me to question the wisdom of your decisions, but do you think it is safe for a young, unprotected lady like yourself to be roaming the countryside in the company of such a person? He doesn't even speak English, which we all know any decent foreigner learns in the nursery.' The archdeacon's full, damp lips tightened into a condescending line. 'Your heart is so generous, Miss Rippon, that I fear your good nature often overwhelms your common sense.'

'Taking an invalid for a walk—even a foreign invalid—does not strike me as a very hazardous undertaking, Mr Jeffries.'

The archdeacon was not accustomed to having his wisdom questioned, and he frowned irritably. 'Dear Miss Rippon! So blissfully unaware of the evils of this world, which is as it should be, of course. My dear young lady, trust the word of one who has seen more of the world's vices than it would be seemly for me to mention in your presence. I am sure your good aunt must have warned you that unless a man has been raised as a gentleman he is no more to be trusted than a ravening beast on the prowl.'

'However ravenous his intentions, I think Mr Alexander is still too weak to harm anybody.'

'Miss Rippon, you speak with all the charm of your sublime innocence. But what do we actually know about this man except that he comes from some country in the wilds of the East? That is hardly a background to inspire confidence.'

Charlotte clenched her teeth, then stretched her lips into a grimace that she hoped might pass for a smile. 'Mr Alexander doesn't come from an unknown country. He comes from Wallachia, which is a province of the Ottoman Empire. He is, I assure you, quite harmless.'

A muffled gurgle that sounded suspiciously like laughter drew the archdeacon's attention back to Mr Alexander. 'What in the world is the fellow laughing about?'

Alexander bobbed his head up and down as if delighted that the archdeacon had once again deigned to look at him. Then, in front of the minister's disbelieving gaze, he unbuttoned his loose, ill-fitting jacket and began scratching his ribcage. His gesture, while shocking the archdeacon, afforded Charlotte an excellent view of the oilskin pouch, tucked safely into the inner pocket of his jacket.

The archdeacon visibly recoiled in the face of Alexander's continued scratching. 'Good heavens, do you think the fellow has fleas?'

Charlotte bit her lip and stared at her toes. Usually Mr Jeffries reduced her to a state of barely concealed fury.

Today, for some reason, she kept wanting to laugh. 'Nobody who has been nursed by Mrs Stubbs would ever have fleas,' she said mildly.

'What's the matter with him now? What's he bobbing his head like that for?'

Charlotte carefully avoided meeting Mr Alexander's eyes. 'I expect he wishes to communicate his friendly feelings towards us. He speaks only Osmanlica, you know, and naturally we don't understand him when he tries to speak to us.'

Mr Alexander obligingly mumbled something totally incomprehensible, meanwhile bobbing his head up and down at an even faster rate than before.

The archdeacon's mouth compressed into a scornful sneer. 'Good heavens, Miss Rippon, I don't know why you and Lady Adeline lavished so much devotion on the wretched fellow. He looks positively half-witted to me.'

Charlotte was seized with a sudden inspiration. 'Oh, you are so observant, Mr Jeffries! Our patient suffered several blows to the head, and I'm afraid his wits are still a little feeble. But he is very content rambling around out here in the sunshine.'

Alexander, after exchanging one swift, laughing glance with Charlotte, allowed his mouth to hang open vacuously and leaned back, surreptitiously kicking the two fallen stones closer to the wall.

'Poor fellow, he is a pathetic object,' the archdeacon remarked.

Charlotte glanced hurriedly towards the wall and saw that the hole had been covered over expertly with strands of ivy. She heaved a quick sigh of relief. The archdeacon, meanwhile, had replaced his condescending smiles with pinched nostrils and a general expression of disdain. He glared at Mr Alexander, who was running around and flapping his arms in a fashion that forcibly reminded Charlotte of a duck about to lay a very large egg.

'What *is* the wretched fellow carrying on about now?' the archdeacon demanded. 'Good heavens, these foreigners have absolutely no manners.'

Charlotte was finding it more and more difficult not to

laugh. 'I think he wants to get back to Rippon Manor before it starts to rain.'

The archdeacon stared up at the solitary white cloud scudding across an otherwise cloudless blue sky. Not without justification, he wanted to know why in the world anybody, even a demented foreigner, would imagine it was likely to start raining any time soon.

'Mr Alexander seems terrified of rainstorms,' Charlotte replied glibly, somewhat horrified by the ease with which she was beginning to lie.

The archdeacon was not mollified and began to express himself at length on the subject of foreigners who had the bad taste to get themselves attacked in front of respectable people's carriages. Mr Alexander cut the conversation short by the simple process of untethering the reins and climbing noisily into the gig.

'Everything you say is very true, Mr Jeffries,' Charlotte said, backing up towards the gig. 'But I really must go now, I'm afraid. My aunt will be wondering what has kept me out so long, and I don't want her to be worried.'

At this mention of Lady Adeline the archdeacon had no choice other than to say goodbye. He manoeuvred his mount alongside the carriage and gave Charlotte an elaborate set of polite messages for transmission to her aunt.

In desperation Charlotte finally flicked the whip on to Daffodil's well-fed rump, and the mare lurched forward in outraged protest. 'I will see you in Church when we return from London,' Charlotte called out, encouraging Daffodil to reach her maximum speed of a slow canter. 'Good day to you, Archdeacon Jeffries.'

'Thank God he didn't volunteer to escort us home,' Mr Alexander remarked as soon as the carriage was out of earshot.

Under Tom's expert guidance the Rippon carriage rolled into the village of Hurst Green shortly after noon on Tuesday. The innkeeper at the Three Crowns, alerted by Harry several days previously, had already prepared a delicious meal of fresh bread, boiled potatoes and cold roasted chicken. The minute the coach stopped he was ready to usher the travellers into a private parlour, where his daughters had set out laden platters of food and jugs of creamy milk, still warm from the cow.

Lady Adeline, who was delighted to be twenty miles closer to her favourite nephew *and* the London warehouses, ate heartily, then leaned back in her chair and smiled cheerfully at Mr Alexander. 'You are looking in excellent health, dear sir. I trust that means your wounds are not paining you?'

'Wounds. . .good, zank you. No more pain.'

Lady Adeline dabbed her mouth with a napkin and smiled at her niece. 'He really has learned to understand us quite well, don't you think, Charlotte? Sir Clive will be pleased to see the rapid progress his friend has made in speaking English.'

'Yes, I expect he will.' Charlotte glanced out of the window, anxious to change the subject. Although Mr Alexander outwardly appeared all smiles she sensed his discomfort. He disliked deceiving her aunt about his ability to understand English, and yet they both knew that there was no point in destroying Lady Adeline's peace of mind by revealing the truth. A dark cloud momentarily blocked out the sun and provided Charlotte with the fresh conversational topic that she needed.

'Thank heaven the roads have all been dry so far. I hope those clouds get blown back out to sea before they can do any damage.'

'Tom says there will be no rain before nightfall,' Lady Adeline remarked comfortably. 'And you know his rheumatics never fail him. We have made such good time, I'm sure we shall reach Tunbridge Wells before dark.'

Lady Adeline's predictions proved correct. It was early evening, with dusk scarcely beginning to fall, as the carriage approached the small, fashionable watering-place of Tunbridge Wells.

Charlotte glanced out of the window and squinted to read the lettering on the white milestone. 'Three miles and we shall be there. And not a speck of rain in sight. Tom's rheumatics were infallible as always.'

'Thank goodness we've had no delays,' Lady Adeline said. 'I am more than ready for my dinner.'

Charlotte gave another idle glance out of the window, but the trees overhanging this stretch of highway made it too dark to see anything of interest. She yawned. 'I'm not hungry, but I'm very bored, and it would be nice to wash off some of this dirt. The grit from the road seems to penetrate everything.'

'I think I shall order a veal and ham pie,' Lady Adeline mused happily. 'Have I mentioned before that the cook at the inn here is famous for his pastry?'

Charlotte's eyes twinkled. 'Indeed you have. Several times. And if you want my opinion, Aunt Adeline, you're asking for nightma——'

Mr Alexander suddenly leaned across the carriage and grabbed Lady Adeline around the waist, dragging her forcibly to the floor of the carriage. Then he pulled Charlotte into his arms and thrust her head unceremoniously against his chest, holding her clasped tight against him. Seconds later they heard a shout from Tom, and the coach seemed to take a lurching leap forwards.

Lady Adeline struggled to get up from the rocking floor, her lips quivering in outrage. 'Mr Alexander, have you gone mad? Unhand my niece this instant!'

'Not safe,' he said tersely. 'Bandits. Brace yourself against the seat, my lady. Tom may lose control of the coach at any moment.'

Lady Adeline stared up at him out of wide, panic-stricken eyes. 'B-bandits?' she stuttered, too frightened to remark on his sudden amazing ability to speak English.

'Three of them. They rode out of the trees, and they're almost upon us.'

'Th-three of them? Oh, dear God!' Lady Adeline gave a ladylike little moan and immediately collapsed across the floor in a dead faint.

'Stay still!' Alexander commanded as Charlotte instinctively moved to help her aunt. He tightened his grasp around her waist until it was impossible for her to move. 'At this moment Tom is still in control of his team, but if the horses bolt you will be thrown and give yourself a concussion.'

'How can you be so sure they are band——?'

The sound of a gun-shot rang out into the gathering darkness, and the carriage teetered dangerously before careening at breakneck speed along the highway. Above the terrified neighing of the horses Charlotte heard Tom's voice barking out commands as he struggled to bring his team back under control. At least he is not dead, she thought, and the highwaymen probably won't be able to reload their weapons as they ride.

As if to extinguish even this feeble flicker of optimism two more gun-shots exploded, the sounds much closer this time, and Charlotte could not repress a shiver. Mr Alexander clasped her tightly around the upper arms, holding her so that she could not avoid looking into his eyes.

'Charlotte, I'm sorry. It is purely my presence that has led you into danger, and I beg your forgiveness.'

'It isn't your fault there are highwaymen——'

He placed a finger against her lips, cutting off the words. 'We have no time left for explanations. I ask of you one more favour—not for my sake, but for the sake of all the people whose lives depend upon me.'

Supporting her between the side of the coach and his body, he pulled the oilskin pouch of documents from inside his jacket pocket and thrust them into her hands.

'Hide these papers,' he said urgently. 'Our attackers will expect me to have them, not you. Give them to Henry Barrett when you reach London. He's lodging in Portman Square, number nine. Promise me, Charlotte, that you will take the papers to him!'

She could hear the pounding hoofs of their pursuers only yards away from the carriage. After the briefest of hesitations she stuffed the pouch into the side pocket of her travelling-gown. 'I promise, Mr Alexander, but I don't understand why you won't be able to make the delivery yourself.'

'Perhaps I will,' he said, but Charlotte could tell that he didn't believe his own statement. She looked up at him again and, for the briefest instant, his mouth softened into a smile—the warm, crooked smile that always played havoc with her nervous system. Even his eyes, which were usually so guarded, seemed suddenly tender, filled with apologies and regret.

'Goodbye, sweet Charlotte,' he murmured, his voice husky. 'I wish very much that we could have met in another place and time.'

Before she had even the slightest suspicion of what he intended to do he captured her face between his hands and bent his head until his lips covered hers, kissing her with swift, devastating thoroughness.

No young lady brought up by Lady Adeline could ever be in doubt as to what she ought to do when exposed to such an intolerable assault upon her virtue. Charlotte knew very well that she was supposed to gasp with horror and slap Mr Alexander's face. The trouble was, his kiss sent the oddest and most pleasurable quivers of sensation racing through her veins. A delicious languor invaded her limbs, and instead of reaching up to slap his face her hands developed a deplorable urge to tangle themselves in the thickness of his hair. The pressure of his mouth against hers deepened inexorably and, for a moment, her stomach knotted with strange anticipation. Then he parted her lips with his tongue, probing the inner softness of her mouth. Pleasure immediately turned to panic. Dear God, she thought wildly, feeling her body freeze into icy stiffness. This must be some extraordinary Turkish perversion! I cannot possibly be enjoying it.

The carriage came to a rattling, bone-jarring halt, which probably explained the strange plunging sensation in the region of Charlotte's heart. She tore herself out of Mr Alexander's arms, retreating to a far corner of the coach. 'What were you *doing*?' she demanded breathlessly. 'I think my aunt must be right. You have gone mad.'

He smiled ruefully. 'On the contrary, sweet Charlotte, I am all too sane. Although I fear I'm going to die a frustrated man.'

She had no idea what he was talking about, but there was no time to express her outrage at his behaviour because at that moment both doors to the carriage were torn open, and she found herself staring into a pair of very black, very threatening gun-muzzles.

The gust of cool, fresh air from the open doors blew over Lady Adeline's face, and she stirred groggily. 'Wh-what has happened?' she moaned, struggling to sit up. 'Where am I?'

Her gaze fell upon the glint of gun metal, then travelled inexorably upwards to encompass two pairs of eyes glinting eerily behind two crumpled white face masks. A strangled gasp wrenched its way out of her throat before she fell back to the floor in another dead faint.

One of the masked men dismounted from his horse and leaned into the carriage, pointing his gun straight at Alexander's stomach. 'Kip out the way,' he warned Charlotte. 'I jest wants the gent. You ladies won't be harmed if you does what I sez.' He jabbed the gun against Alexander's ribs. 'Out of the carriage, my fine cove. And take care 'ow you comes out or my finger might slip and do some mortal damage to one of the fine ladies here.'

Alexander moved slowly but unresistingly toward the edge of his seat. 'I'm willing to surrender myself provided you move away from the door so that I can make sure you honour your promise.'

The man sniffed. 'You 'ave me word on it, don't yer? And Gentleman Jem always keeps his word.'

Charlotte interposed herself between Jem and Mr Alexander, ripping at the buttons of her gloves and tearing them off. 'Why take this man when he has no money or valuables of any sort?' she said, tugging frantically at her rings—a heavy gold signet and a delicate pearl set in diamonds and white gold. 'Here, you can see these jewels are worth a lot of money. Take them, and let us be on our way.'

Gentleman Jem looked longingly at the jewels, but he merely scowled when Charlotte thrust the rings towards him.

'If you will just let us pass unharmed,' she pleaded, 'I

will give you more, much more. My aunt and I have other pieces of jewellery inside the carriage.'

Avarice flared hot and naked in the rheumy eyes behind the mask, and Jem stretched out his hand to grab the rings. The highwayman on the opposite side of the carriage spoke sharply. His voice was muffled by the thick woollen scarf wound over his nose and mouth, but his tone of voice left no doubt that he was the leader.

'Don't be a fool, Jem. Don't get so excited that you forget what we're here for. We want the man, not a few paltry jewels.'

'These 'ere jewels ain't eggsacly what I'd call paltry, Cap'n.'

'Nevertheless, we don't want them,' the captain replied. 'Remember, you are being paid to deliver the man to the place I will direct you. And paid well, I might add.'

'I can pay you, too,' Charlotte interjected quickly.

''Ow much?'

'Do not waste your money or your time, Miss Rippon,' Alexander advised softly. 'If you are not careful you will find yourself several hundred guineas lighter of purse, and I will still be a prisoner.'

'We can at least try to bargain,' Charlotte said, impatient with Mr Alexander's unnatural resignation. Foreigners, she thought crossly, could never be relied upon to grit their teeth and fight with a decent British sense of determination. 'Be reasonable, Mr Alexander. You cannot be more valuable to them than money. Well, Jem, are you interested in receiving a hundred guineas in exchange for allowing us all to ride safely into Tunbridge Wells?'

Gentleman Jem scratched his head. 'Well, I dare say for two 'undred I might——'

'You dare to say nothing at all,' the captain interrupted with deadly menace. His masked gaze flicked towards Charlotte. 'Forget your attempts to purchase Mr Alexander's safety. Believe me, you do not have sufficient funds for such an undertaking. Please allow him to get out of the carriage and then you can be on your way, a little delayed, but otherwise unharmed. Mr

Alexander, if you wish to avoid any unpleasant accidents to your erstwhile benefactors you would be wise to step out of the carriage immediately. Clasp your hands together behind your back, if you please.'

Long years in attendance at the Sultan's court had taught Alexander how to keep his expression neutral and his temper under absolute control. He had seen—all too often—what happened to men who indulged themselves in brave gestures. A meek, humble demeanour sometimes bought the time necessary to work out an escape plan. He had little hope of coming out of this abduction alive, but he knew that a cool head was essential if he hoped to take advantage of any slight, momentary weakness in his opponents. He rose to his feet and clasped his hands behind his back, obeying the captain's instructions implicitly. Apart from any other considerations, honour required that he should first get Lady Adeline and Charlotte on their way to safety. After that, perhaps, he could flirt with attempts to escape if he saw an opportunity.

He stepped down from the carriage, exaggerating the clumsiness of his movements. His attackers undoubtedly knew that he'd been wounded. No harm in allowing them to think him weaker and more awkward than he actually was.

'That's the way.' Gentleman Jem aimed his pistol straight at Alexander's heart, jerking his head to indicate that he should stand next to the two coachmen, who were lying, hands bound, under the supervision of a third highwayman.

Jem surveyed the scene, then rubbed his nose worriedly. Spur-of-the-moment planning didn't seem to be his strong point. 'Now we've got the gent, Cap'n, wot are we goin' to do wiv the ladies and the grooms?'

'Leave them. The coachmen are both wounded and the horses winded. They will never catch us.'

'If you sez so, Cap'n.' Jem sounded depressed. 'Shall I jest give the young lady a little tap on the 'ead to keep 'er quiet while we rides off?'

Lady Adeline's nervous system chose this most inauspicious moment to return to active duty. The captain was directly in her line of vision, and she recoiled from the gruesome masked figure with a violent start.

'Take care, Aunt!' Charlotte cried, but it was too late. Lady Adeline's floundering attempts to raise herself from the floor of the carriage caused her hand to flail out in the direction of Gentleman Jem's midriff. Jem, proving that his nickname was not to be taken as a serious indicator of his normal behaviour, swung around swiftly, lashing out with his fist and hitting Lady Adeline hard in the stomach. She collapsed into a tight ball, gagging as she tried to catch her breath, and Jem dragged her out of the carriage, indifferently tossing her on to the grass by the roadside.

'If you want to throw up you can use the grass,' he said crudely. 'No point in stinking up the carriage.'

Alexander forced himself not to react. He was all too aware of the pistol which the captain still held, aimed squarely at Charlotte's head. Not by a tremor of an eyelash did he allow the rage churning inside him to be revealed. With any luck, he thought, if nobody over-reacted, the two women would be allowed to proceed unharmed.

Charlotte, unfortunately, had no experience of thinking coolly in dangerous situations and at the sight of Lady Adeline lying crumpled on the damp, moonlit grass her temper snapped. 'How *could* you treat a lady in such a fashion?' she demanded, springing to her feet and lunging at Jem. She jumped down the carriage steps and tried to elbow her way past the highwayman. 'Move out of the way, you oaf, and let me tend to her!'

Alexander had rarely experienced such difficulty in standing stock-still. He gave a silent sigh of relief when he saw that Jem seemed to be amused rather than offended by Charlotte's efforts to attack him.

'Enough of this nonsense,' the captain said, his voice cold with anger. 'Get the prisoner on to the horse we brought for him. I'll take care of the girl. Quickly! We have been here far too long.' He didn't wait for Jem's response but simply leaned down from his horse and grasped Charlotte by the scruff of her neck, dragging her back towards the carriage.

Not since her childhood fights with her brothers had Charlotte been treated with such lack of respect, and she twisted around to confront the man, clawing at his face in her fury. The strings on his white velvet mask tore away from their moorings, and the mask dropped around the captain's neck.

The sounds of scuffling instantly died away to be replaced by an intense, tension-filled silence. Charlotte held her breath as she looked up at the man on the horse, aware—too late—of where her temper had led them.

'You should not have interfered, Miss Rippon,' Sir Clive Collins said softly. 'Knowledge can often be very dangerous to its possessor. Now I shall have to kill you, which I really never wanted to do.'

'Don't be a fool, Bottomley,' Alexander said. 'You'll get no co-operation from me if these ladies are harmed in any way.'

Sir Clive looked speculatively at Alexander. 'You recognise me, of course,' he said.

'You were present during several of my discussions with the Foreign Secretary, so naturally I remember you. Besides, when Charlotte told me that my friend Sir Clive *Collins* had come calling, I suspected that Sir Clive Bottomley might be your real name. The only question in my mind was whether or not you remained loyal to your government, or whether you had sold out to your country's enemies. Your presence here answers that question. I hope you demanded payment in advance for your treachery. In my part of the world it is never wise to work on credit.'

'And you, perhaps, are not very wise to call me a traitor, *Prince Karim*. A subject of the Sultan who foments rebellion among the people of the Ottoman Empire is hardly in a position to question another man's loyalties.'

Prince Karim. Mr Alexander was really a prince! Charlotte turned and stared at the man whom she and her aunt had picked up from the roadside. His hands were still clasped behind his back as the captain had ordered, his borrowed clothes scarcely fitted across the breadth of his shoulders, but when she saw the arrogant tilt of his jaw and the thin, aristocratic flare of his nostrils she had little difficulty in accepting the fact that this man was indeed a prince of the Ottoman Empire.

Alexander did not even glance in Sir Clive's direction. 'I do not have to account for my actions to you, only to His Highness the Sultan.'

'That is so. Fortunately, once I have taken you to Istanbul, you will be able to do precisely that. I am confident that the Sultan will take care of you as you deserve.' Without pause in the flow of his words Sir Clive raised his pistol and brought the butt crashing down upon Alexander's head. He watched impassively as Alexander toppled over on to the grass, then nodded curtly towards Charlotte.

'I hope you will find this a useful lesson,' he said. 'You have just seen what happens to people who don't please me. Be prudent, Miss Rippon, and learn to obey me.'

Jem stirred Alexander's inert body with his toe. 'We ain't goin' to kill the ladies, Cap'n?'

'No. I have decided it might be more useful to take them with me to Istanbul. Get all three of them back into the carriage. The Prince first. And please hurry, or we'll miss the tide.'

Jem muttered something inaudible under his breath, and Sir Clive directed his horse towards the bank of grass where the third highwayman kept vigil over the coachmen.

'Are they unconscious?' Sir Clive asked.

'Yessir. The young 'un don't look very grand. He took a bullet in the leg, but the old feller ain't hardly wounded. He oughtta come round soon. Do you want me to shoot 'em?'

'I don't share your lust for exterminating my fellow men, even such insignificant creatures as these two. Neither of them has seen us unmasked, so they can cause no trouble. Leave them, and get the prisoners into the carriage.'

'Yessir.'

Charlotte waited until all three abductors were busily engaged in stowing a hysterical Lady Adeline inside the carriage, then she hurried over to Tom's side. Under the guise of tending to the bullet-wound in his upper arm, she shoved the pouch of documents under his body. To her intense relief he murmured into her ear that he was only feigning unconsciousness.

'I'm sorry, Tom, there's no time to explain,' she whispered, tearing off a strip of her petticoat and binding it around the surface wound in his arm. A series of ear-splitting shrieks from Lady Adeline usefully drowned out all sound of her talking. 'Take these papers to Mr Henry Barrett at number nine Portman Square. Tell him the man we knew as Sir Clive Collins is really Sir Clive Bottomley and that he's taking us forcibly to Istanbul. Can you remember that, Tom?'

He looked at her with a pathetic attempt at fierceness. 'I bain't losing me wits yet, Miss Charlotte.'

She smiled, blinking back tears. 'Thank you, Tom. Can you walk to Tunbridge Wells to get help for Willy? I estimate there's still two miles to go.'

'I can make it.'

She squeezed his uninjured hand and moved over to begin tending to Willy. She had scarcely done more than look at his wound when she heard Jem's footsteps swishing through the damp grass.

'Into the carriage, pretty lady,' Jem ordered. His eyes fell on the torn strips of petticoat and narrowed ominously. 'What you bin doin' over here, anyway?'

For the first time in her life Charlotte was grateful for the convention that required ladies to faint at the smallest provocation. 'I wanted to care for my wounded servant,' she murmured brokenly. 'But there's so much blood, and dirt, and. . . Oh, it's simply all too terrible.'

She clutched a blood-stained hand to her bosom, doing her very best imitation of Aunt Adeline having palpitations. Then she drew in a dramatic, shuddering breath and collapsed on to the cold earth alongside Willy.

'Oh, lawks, git over 'ere, Bart,' Jem called. 'Let's git this last haybag into the carriage. At least she ain't screaming like 'tother 'un.'

Charlotte felt herself carried the short distance to the coach. She was dumped without ceremony next to her aunt, and the doors were slammed shut. With the blinds down and no lamps lit the interior of the carriage was pitch-black. She strained her ears to detect what the abductors were doing, but the men worked in virtual silence and all she could hear was the clop of horses' hoofs and the jingle of harness. Maybe the abductors had decided to change carriage horses, she reflected.

Within minutes Charlotte heard Sir Clive issue the command to give the horses their heads, and the coach trundled off along the highway.

She lifted the blind a crack, but all she could see was the shadowy outline of trees fading into the black horizon. She contemplated jumping from the coach, but even if she survived the fall and wasn't immediately recaptured she wouldn't achieve much. Aunt Adeline and Mr Alexander would still be inside the coach, unconscious, and she had no idea where the coach was headed. Sir Clive had mentioned a port, but England was a nation of ports stretched out along hundreds of miles of coastline.

The ride seemed endless, although Charlotte suspected that her sense of time had become distorted. Finally, when she had begun to wonder if the journey would last forever, the carriage drew to a halt. The doors were flung open and the salty tang of sea air filled the coach. She opened her mouth to scream, but Jem clapped his foul-smelling hand over it.

'No noise from you, pretty lady, or the cap'n jest might decide to drop you into the harbour.'

He stuffed a gag into her mouth and dropped a thick linen sack over her head, rendering her totally, frighteningly blind. Rough hands dragged her toward the carriage door, and she was carried off into impenetrable blackness.

CHAPTER FOUR

IGNORING the pounding ache in his head, Alexander gritted his teeth and levered himself up on to his right elbow. When the pain subsided to manageable proportions he opened his eyes.

He was in a small cabin, aboard a ship. The tiny porthole provided a view of heaving grey water and leaden skies. It was a relief to realise that the swaying motion of his stomach was not an illusion brought on by weakness but the reality of a vessel under sail.

A carafe and a pewter cup rested on a narrow shelf by his bunk, and Alexander drank the tepid water gratefully. Swinging his legs to the floor, he ignored the throbbing agony of his left shoulder until blood fell on to his hand and warned him that his wound had opened again. Using his teeth, he tore off a strip of shirt, trying to find some cloth that was reasonably clean. He pressed the linen pad against his scar, willing the flow of blood to diminish. Time to stop playing the invalid, he told himself grimly. Time to confront Sir Clive and demand some answers—not least the fate of Charlotte and her aunt. Until he knew what had happened to Charlotte he wouldn't know what had become of the precious bank-draft and the secret navigation charts for Hank Barrett.

If Sir Clive had carried out his threat to kill the two women—— Once again Alexander cut off the thought with ruthless efficiency. He had learned long ago not to torment himself with useless worries and even more useless regrets. If Charlotte and Lady Adeline still lived he would do his best to protect them. If they were already dead, then he would have no choice but to forget them. He wouldn't have time for mourning personal friends until he and Hank brought their cargo of food and ammunition safely into Greek harbour.

And yet, infuriatingly, he found that he couldn't quite erase Charlotte from his mind. The cool touch of her fingers against his forehead seemed as vivid now as during those nights when he burned with fever. And he longed to hear the soft, silvery sound of her laughter. Despite all his years of stern self-discipline Alexander found himself hoping that Charlotte and Lady Adeline had not been added to the long list of martyrs to the cause of Greek freedom.

He rose to his feet, forcing himself not to sway, not to give in to the longing to lie down again on the comfort of his bunk. He had become weak during those convalescent days at Rippon Manor, and not just because of his wounds. Charlotte had made him aware, for the first time, of what it could be like to live in a household where trust and security and mutual affection formed a constant background to the mundane tasks of daily living. Charlotte, lucky lady, had no idea what it was like to scrutinise every visitor, every chance acquaintance, wondering if this was the messenger who'd been sent to kill you. Sometimes, when he had been alone with Charlotte, he had felt a fleeting understanding of what ordinary, everyday happiness must be like. And therein, he realised, lay acute danger. Physical weakness could be overcome, but mental weakness—an attachment to people and places—left men vulnerable to manipulation and treachery. He had seen it happen all too often, and he would never permit his irrational interest in Charlotte's well-being to influence his actions.

Alexander finished the last of the water and straightened his shoulders, refusing to acknowledge the fresh stab of pain from his wound. The aftermath of his fever seemed to be having a strange effect on him. He couldn't remember another occasion when he had wasted so much time thinking about a mere woman. While he didn't accept his father's orthodox Muslim view that women lacked souls, he certainly didn't think that a man's happiness could ever be bound up in his relationship with a woman. If Sir Clive had allowed Charlotte to live Alexander hoped very much that she and her aunt had both been left behind in England.

Impatient with the obsessively circular train of his thoughts, Alexander crossed to the cabin door and discovered, without surprise, that it was locked. He pounded on the heavy oak panels. As he had expected a sailor was stationed somewhere close by in the corridor, and the noise attracted an instant response.

A wizened middle-aged seaman entered the cabin, leaving another sailor on armed guard outside the door. 'I'm Sam, and this 'ere is your dinner,' he said, setting down a wooden platter on the narrow shelf by the bunk.

Alexander viewed the loaf of barley bread and lump of hard cheese impassively. He had eaten far worse. 'Thank you, Sam. Could you tell me what time it is?'

'Jest passed two bells. You've bin sleeping for fifteen hours, mebbe more.'

'Do you know what happened to the ladies who were travelling with me? Are they on board?'

'Couldn't say, I'm sure. You'd have ter ask the cap'n.'

'Who is the captain?'

Sam looked surprised. 'Why, Sir Clive Bottomley is the cap'n. Didn't yer know that?'

'No, I didn't know Sir Clive was a sailing man. Is this his own ship?'

'I dunno nuffink about that. We're all new crew, hired on for the trip to Istanbul. Half our wages paid in advance. That ain't easy to come by.'

'I'm sure it isn't. Well, Sam, do you think you could find me some water to wash myself with, and a fresh shirt? This one is ripped and dirty, as you can see.'

'I reckon I could boil up some sea-water. We ain't got no fresh water to spare for what ain't necessary.'

'Hot sea-water would be very welcome.'

The bread and cheese were filling, if not appetising, and Alexander had scarcely finished eating when Sam returned with hot water, a hairbrush and a clean shirt. He seemed so pleased with the success of his efforts that Alexander didn't have the heart to comment on the glaring absence of soap and a towel.

''Urry up, if yer don't mind. The cap'n wants ter see you in his cabin. 'E said I'm ter take you there, pronto.'

Alexander took his time, mentally steeling himself for the interview ahead. 'I'm ready whenever you are,' he said finally.

Sam, who evidently recognised that escape from a ship in the middle of the ocean was impossible, took his duties as a guard lightly. 'Follow me, matey,' he said and strolled off down the corridor, finally halting outside an imposing brass-decorated door.

'This 'ere is the cap'n's quarters,' he declared, tapping on one of the polished mahogany panels. 'Stand 'ere alongside of me, matey.' He raised his voice importantly. 'It's me, Sam, Cap'n. I brung the Turkoman to see you, jest like you said.'

'Enter.'

Sam flung open the door and jerked his head to indicate that Alexander should precede him into the captain's cabin.

Sir Clive was seated at a large desk, reading. 'You may leave us, Sam,' he said without looking up from his papers. 'Wait outside until I call you.'

'Yessir.'

The door closed, but Sir Clive continued to read, totally ignoring Alexander's presence. Alexander, who had twice faced the terrors of the Chief Eunuch's interrogation office, was almost amused by the obvious attempt at intimidation. He parted his feet, bracing himself comfortably against the slight rolling motion of the ship, then narrowed his lids and glanced around the cabin, taking advantage of Sir Clive's silence. His brain clicked off impressions. Large room, ostentatious decoration, furnished in the European style with a carpet of Persian design on the floor. No charts in evidence, no sextant, nothing to suggest that Sir Clive was anything more than a titular captain. No paintings on the walls, no obvious clue as to the origin of the ship.

The rustling of papers ceased, and Alexander immediately schooled his features into blankness. After a quick survey of his prisoner Sir Clive cleared his throat, aware that he had somehow lost the advantage and not at all sure how to retrieve it. He picked up a pen and began to sharpen it, furious to realise that he actually felt nervous.

'I hope you've found your quarters comfortable,' he said at last.

'Adequate, thank you. My head would no doubt ache less had it not encountered the butt of your pistol.'

'Certain actions couldn't be avoided, but I've now given my men instructions to fulfil any reasonable request from you. Provided you co-operate, Prince Karim, I see no reason why I should need to harm you.'

Alexander allowed himself the luxury of a small, tight smile. 'That is generous of you, Sir Clive. I trust that the sailors on board follow your instructions more accurately than your hirelings who attacked me on the road to Hastings.'

'Those men had instructions to capture you alive and unharmed,' Sir Clive said coldly. 'They were foolish enough to exceed their orders, and they have paid the appropriate price for their foolishness.'

Alexander didn't reply, and Sir Clive asked irritably, 'Don't you want to know what my plans are for you?'

'If you care to explain them to me.'

'You have been causing considerable amounts of trouble to various important people in Istanbul, Prince Karim.'

'I am sorry to hear that. It was not my wish.'

Sir Clive got up and walked over to the porthole behind his desk. He looked out at the white-capped waters of the North Sea, contemplating the attractive idea of having the Prince clapped in irons and locked up in the hold without food or water. With a regretful sigh Sir Clive acknowledged that the idea of torture, pleasurable as it might be, wasn't practical. At the moment he found himself in the delightful position of having been paid twice to perform the same task: both the Emir Ibrahim and the Grand Vizier had advanced large sums of money for bringing Prince Karim back to Istanbul. It was unfortunate that the two of them were sworn enemies, who presumably wanted Karim back for quite different reasons.

Sir Clive swung around. 'You will find that the Grand Vizier has other ideas. The concept of an independent Greece is ridiculous. The people living in the Morea are either peasants or bandits without a decent administrator among the lot of them. The Greek peninsula has been under Ottoman rule for nearly four hundred years, and there is no reason why it should not continue in the same relationship for the next four hundred years.'

'None, perhaps, except that the people of Greece will not allow such a situation to continue. Not to mention the growing ambitions of the Russian Emperor.'

Sir Clive expelled his breath in a small hiss. 'You and Mr Canning are both romantics, like Lord Byron. You confuse the illiterate Greek peasant of today with the noble Greek philosopher of the past. But many Englishmen, including the Duke of Wellington, take a more realistic view of the situation.'

Alexander laughed. 'Believe me, Mr Canning has a very clear understanding of the limits of Greek power. He does not share one shred of the quixotic impulse that caused Lord Byron to die defending the besieged town of Missalonghi. Canning merely wishes to avoid a bloodbath that could compromise the safety of half of Europe. You should know that the Russians can hardly wait for the Ottoman Empire to explode so that they may gobble up the debris from the explosion.'

Sir Clive's mouth twisted into a sneer. 'I am aware of Mr Canning's alarmist views about Russia.'

'Ah, yes, I had forgotten.' Alexander smiled mockingly. 'You are the Foreign Office's resident expert on the Ottoman Empire. Attached to the personal staff of Mr Canning, if my memory serves me. No wonder you are so familiar with his views.'

The quill that Sir Clive was holding snapped in two. 'It is *your* position and *your* loyalties we are discussing, Prince Karim, not mine, and you would be wise not to annoy me. You are intelligent enough to realise that I can make your life on board comfortable—or very much otherwise.'

'Then by all means let us discuss my position, since I am greatly in favour of comfort. Why are you taking me to Istanbul, Sir Clive?'

'Because I've been paid to do so. Does it shock you that I'm so honest about my motives? You feel, perhaps, that an English gentleman should be above mere considerations of money?'

'I have not said so.'

Sir Clive smiled bitterly. 'That's because you are an Oriental. In England, however, a gentleman is supposed to support himself on the land left to him by his father. And if his father happens to gamble away the family inheritance then society has no answer to the dilemma. Except to be quite, quite clear about the fact that a gentleman may not engage in commerce and still remain a gentleman.'

'I see. How odd that trading in human lives is not considered commerce. No wonder we poor Orientals have such a hard time understanding the finer points of British etiquette.'

Sir Clive's plump cheeks paled with anger. 'You jump to false conclusions, Prince Karim. It's your father, the Emir Ibrahim Hussein, who wishes your return to Istanbul. I'm not leading you into any danger, and I'm certainly not trading your life for money.'

'Is that so? And yet I was attacked by four members of the Grand Vizier's staff on the road to Hastings—and only you and Mr Canning knew my destination. Are you sure it is not the Grand Vizier who requires my return?'

'How can you be so certain that the men who attacked you were from the Grand Vizier's office?'

'I recognised Ahmed Mustafa, the leader.'

Sir Clive was not pleased by this piece of news, but he was capable of some very quick thinking when his financial well-being was at stake. 'You haven't been in Istanbul for three years,' he said, leaning back in his chair. 'You have no idea how political alliances have shifted at court. Believe me, your father is anxious for you to come home. He told me that he had written to you twice without success, asking for you to return to Istanbul.'

His father had asked him to come home? Alexander inwardly acknowledged how much pleasure that news gave him. No letters had ever reached him, but he moved around so much that it was easy to believe he had missed some correspondence. On the other hand Alexander was well aware that Sir Clive was more than capable of lying.

'My father might have wanted me back in Istanbul,' he said finally, 'but there is no reason for him to have any interest in the papers that your minions were so anxious to steal. The Emir is in charge of financial matters. The Grand Vizier, on the other hand, is in charge of the Sultan's foreign policy and would have every interest in intercepting papers outlining Mr Canning's plans for Greece.'

'Ah, yes, the documents from Mr Canning's office.' Sir Clive stared contemplatively at the tips of his fingers. 'That was an interesting package of papers you were carrying stuffed into the heel of your boot, Prince Karim. Very enlightening to many people other than the Grand Vizier of the Ottoman Empire. However, I will admit that I resent Mr Canning's willingness to give you so much information that he withheld from me.'

Alexander controlled his body movements so that they revealed not the slightest reaction, but deep inside he felt a quick spurt of relief. Thank God he had persuaded Mr Canning to provide a set of fake papers—and thank God Sir Clive had accepted those fake papers as genuine! Now, if he could only find out what had happened to Charlotte and the *real* package of documents, he could get a message to Hank Barrett and make arrangements to meet the ship in Brindisi and then. . .

He looked up, deliberately allowing his expression to reveal a hint of scorn. 'I'm sure it's useless to remind you that those documents were highly secret and certainly not intended to be seen by anybody in the Ottoman Government.'

Sir Clive didn't respond directly. 'At first, you know, I found it odd that Mr Canning should encourage you to liaise with the Russian Government. But then, upon reflection, I decided that such a move would be typical of our wily Foreign Secretary. He plans to work secretly with the new Russian Emperor and thus undercut the French influence in Istanbul. I should have realised Canning would never ally himself with the French, whatever declarations of support he may make in public.'

Alexander resisted the impulse to crow with triumph.

'You've read the papers, Sir Clive, I have not. I was riding too fast to take time to study the letters I carried.'

'Well, Prince Karim, enough of this dry discussion of politics; it must be time for us to pass on to pleasanter matters. We have a long journey ahead, three weeks at least, even if the wind is in our favour. Enjoy your voyage home, Prince Karim. You are permitted to walk on the upper deck whenever one of the hands can be spared to accompany you.'

Sir Clive reached out for the bell in order to summon Sam. Alexander realised that he was about to be dismissed, and before he fully grasped the significance of his action he reached out and grabbed Sir Clive's hand. 'No, wait. Before you summon Sam there's something I must ask you.'

Sir Clive's eyebrows rose into his fringe of smooth blond hair. 'Yes?'

Alexander stepped back from the desk, already regretting his impulsive gesture. He understood Sir Clive well enough to know that it was risky to show concern for another person's welfare. On the other hand he desperately needed to know what had happened to Charlotte. For the sake of the documents, of course. This anxiety gnawing hard at his gut had nothing to do with any personal involvement.

'The two women who travelled with me,' he said finally, doing his best to keep his voice flat and uninterested. 'What happened to them?'

Just as Alexander had dreaded Sir Clive's gaze immediately became speculative. 'Why should you care?'

Alexander shrugged. 'They were kind to me. Naturally I feel some sense of obligation.'

Sir Clive leaned back in his captain's chair and rested his hands over the slight mound of his belly. 'I haven't seen them recently, but the women are well, I trust.'

'In this world or the next?'

'They are both alive, if that is what you want to know.'

'Alive and prisoners?'

'Prisoners is such a crude word, don't you think? Let us say rather that they are enjoying my generous hospitality for the journey to Istanbul.'

'In that case,' Alexander said mildly, 'I would like to meet with my fellow guests.'

Sir Clive's eyes narrowed, and for a long moment he stared consideringly at Alexander's face. Whatever he read there seemed to satisfy him, for he leaned forward with sudden energy and shook the brass bell.

'Yessir?' Sam was inside the door in a trice, waiting for instructions.

'There are two women in the aft cabin on the poop deck. Bring them here right away.'

'Yessir.'

Sam returned only five minutes later. 'I only brung one of them, Cap'n,' he said anxiously. 'The older one was too sick to move. Groaning something 'orrible, she was, but the young 'un is 'ere with me. I could send two men back to get the old 'un if you want her carried in.'

'That probably won't be necessary.'

'Aw right, sir.' Sam stepped to one side and pushed Charlotte into the cabin. 'Look lively. The cap'n wants to speak to yer.'

Charlotte entered the cabin at a dignified walk. Her face was stark white with fatigue, her blue eyes bruised with shadows. Alexander felt a curious ache somewhere in the region of his heart when he looked at her filthy, mud-spattered travelling-gown and tangled, dust-streaked hair. She had obviously been less fortunate than he in getting help from the crew, and he experienced an odd little flare of anger when he imagined her humiliation.

Charlotte appeared briefly startled when she saw Alexander, but she glanced at him only once, half-questioningly, before turning away as if something about his appearance disturbed her.

Sir Clive rose to his feet and executed a tiny mocking bow. 'I'm delighted to see that you've recovered from your accident, Miss Rippon. Welcome aboard my ship.'

She looked at him as if he were a particularly repulsive slug that had just crawled out from beneath her foot, but her voice, when she spoke, was scrupulously polite.

'My aunt is suffering greatly from seasickness, Sir Clive. She needs gruel to eat and hot water so that I may bathe her. Will you please tell one of the sailors to bring it to us? They won't listen to my requests.'

Sir Clive flicked one plump, pale finger in the direction of the door. 'You may leave us, Sam. Oh, and send the cook in to me so that we may discuss the dinner menu, if you please.'

'Yessir.'

'Sir Clive, about my aunt——'

'All in good time, my dear Miss Rippon.' Sir Clive's smile was spiced with cruelty. 'You are heading towards the Orient, and you must learn not to be impatient. In the Orient even simple tasks can take a long time to accomplish, isn't that so, Prince Karim?'

'It depends.'

Sir Clive gave an exaggerated sigh. 'You will find, Miss Rippon, that Prince Karim is sometimes a man of annoyingly few words.'

'My aunt is not well enough to be left on her own for very long——'

'Patience, my dear Miss Rippon. What did I just tell you about the Orient? Once you arrive in Istanbul you will find that even the simplest progress waits upon the pleasure of the Sultan and his eunuchs.'

'Do you see yourself as some sort of substitute sultan, Sir Clive?'

'Perhaps.' A faint smile played around Sir Clive's lips as he watched Charlotte sway visibly on her feet. She was obviously close to fainting from fatigue. He saw the Prince look at the girl and then quickly turn away again, his lips compressing.

'Dear me, Miss Rippon, your impatience almost made me forget my manners,' Sir Clive said, rising to his feet. 'The Prince already knows you, of course, but perhaps you might be interested in learning Mr Alexander's true name and title. He is the Prince Karim Alexander, only son of the Emir Ibrahim Hussein, Defterdar of Rumeli. You probably aren't familiar with the titles of the Ottoman Empire, so I will explain them to you. Emir is roughly the equivalent of our Prince, and Defterdar of Rumeli is the honorary title given to the Chief Treasury Officer in the Sultan's Imperial Government.'

Charlotte looked quickly at Alexander, bewilderment momentarily replacing the fatigue and the wariness in her eyes. 'Why didn't you tell me who you really are?' she asked quietly.

He couldn't look at her, couldn't risk the infuriating weakness that came from sensing her hurt. When he spoke Alexander recognised that his voice was cold with the effort of choking back the urge to go to her and offer comfort. 'It seemed the right decision at the time,' he said, shrugging offhandedly.

Hurt by the impenetrable remoteness of his expression, Charlotte turned back towards Sir Clive. 'Why does Prince Karim have a European title when his father's title is Turkish?'

'Titles are not inherited in the Ottoman Empire,' Sir Clive explained, well pleased with the tension that seemed to be building between his two captives, 'although the Sultan often chooses to bestow the same title on successive generations. As it happens, Prince Karim's title is inherited from his mother's family, the Ypsilantis of Wallachia.'

'So your name is really Prince Karim Alexander Ypsilanti?'

'In the Ottoman Empire we don't use family names,' Alexander replied curtly. He spoke into the space a few inches beyond Charlotte's left shoulder. 'I trust your cabin is reasonably comfortable, Miss Rippon?'

It was a major mistake to have allowed himself to meet her eyes, and he felt his heart contract with an ache of fellow feeling when he saw the stormy hint of challenge in her delicate features. 'The cabin is reasonably comfortable, thank you, Your Excellency. As I already explained to Sir Clive, we lack food and water to wash in. You are more fortunate than we, Prince Karim, since you don't seem to have been similarly deprived.'

'The sailor guarding my door proved helpful.'

Helpful indeed, Charlotte thought, looking at the Prince's crisp white shirt and generally spruce appearance. The boat heaved in response to a patch of rough water, and she clasped her hands around her waist, refusing to give in to the nausea clawing at her stomach.

She was all too aware of Prince Karim's presence only a few feet to her left, and yet she didn't want to look at him. It was difficult to believe that this remote, self-contained aristocrat was the same man who only a few days ago had shared tea and buttered muffins in front of the drawing-room fire at Rippon Manor. 'Mr Alexander', Charlotte reflected sadly, didn't seem to have much in common with His Excellency Prince Karim of Istanbul and Wallachia.

She pushed the memory of her time with 'Mr Alexander' to one side, annoyed by its power to captivate her. Prince Karim had probably lied to her about everything, she reflected angrily, refusing to consider why the knowledge of his dishonesty should leave her feeling so desolate.

Perhaps he wasn't even a prisoner. Surrounded as she was by this morass of double-dealing, it didn't seem beyond the bounds of possibility that the Prince and Sir Clive were actually working together. In which case there was no knowing what danger she might have sent her servant into by telling him to deliver the Prince's papers to Hank Barrett. Charlotte resolved that, whatever pressure was brought to bear upon her, she would never reveal what had happened to the package of documents. It had been one thing to help friendly 'Mr Alexander', but, as far as she was concerned, His Excellency Prince Karim could go hang.

A tap at the cabin door interrupted her thoughts. 'Enter,' Sir Clive commanded.

Sam came in at a brisk trot. 'Send one of the men to escort Miss Rippon back to her cabin. She is to be given gruel for her aunt, hot water so they may bathe, and something for her own supper. You may take Prince Karim back to his quarters.'

'Yessir. The lady was askin' if she could go up on deck. Is that allowed, Cap'n?'

'Certainly, provided she and the Prince don't speak.' Sir Clive waved dismissively.

A one-eyed sailor arrived to escort Charlotte back to her cabin, and as she and the Prince passed through the door they were no more than a few inches apart. Prince

Karim bent his head and spoke urgently into her ear. 'Where are the documents? Do you have them on board?'

Charlotte stared straight ahead, fury and a strange regret warring inside her. How typical of him, she thought angrily. Not a word about her sorry plight, not a word about her poor aunt, not a word about their forcible abduction halfway around the globe. Nothing except an obsessive concern about his silly package of papers.

She paused and looked back over her shoulder. 'Your touching concern for our welfare is deeply appreciated,' she said. 'Unfortunately my memory of all the events leading up to that disastrous journey to London seems to have vanished. Goodnight, Your Excellency. I trust you will sleep well.'

She stormed along the remainder of the narrow corridor without looking back again. Alexander watched her departure and quietly cursed himself for a fool.

The gruesome battlefronts of the Greek peninsula had taught Alexander both patience and practicality, and he needed a full measure of each as the ship sailed through the stormy seas off the coast of Spain and finally entered the Mediterranean through the narrow Strait of Gibraltar.

He had long since resigned himself to the fact that he couldn't escape from a ship sailing in the middle of the ocean, unless he planned to commit suicide, and since there was no point in wasting time planning an escape that couldn't succeed Alexander disciplined himself to concentrate on the one task within his grasp—that of recovering his usual good health. He spent hours on deck, stripped to the waist, allowing the hot spring sun and the salty sea-winds to heal his wounds at the same time as he regained his strength by working alongside the sailors.

He had always known that his constitution was basically strong, but he was surprised at the speed with which his previous energy returned to him. After a couple of strenuous days working on the rigging he realised that the muscles in his shoulder had survived the bullet-wound almost unscathed. As for the broken bones in the fingers of his left hand, they were already no more than a distant memory. Even his back no longer pained him. The scars from Ahmed Mustafa's whip stood out, starkly white against his tanned skin, but at least the wounds were all healed without any residual infection.

Sir Clive would undoubtedly have been furious if he'd known just how much his prisoner was enjoying the journey home to Istanbul. In fact only one cloud marred Alexander's bright blue horizon—his inability to talk to Charlotte and find out what had happened to the precious documents.

Charlotte was frequently to be seen on deck looking, if possible, even more beautiful than she had done in England. One of the sailors had lent her a wide-brimmed cotton hat, so that her eyes were always hidden from Alexander's view, but beneath the floppy brim of her makeshift bonnet he could see that the sea air had bestowed a golden-pink glow to her complexion and her blonde hair was streaked with silver where tendrils had escaped from confinement and been bleached by the sun.

Although Charlotte was often on deck she was invariably surrounded by a stalwart group of sailors who refused to allow Alexander anywhere near her. He would have found their separation less frustrating if he hadn't nursed the suspicion that Charlotte herself encouraged the seamen to maintain the impenetrable barricades.

It was not, he assured himself, that he had any personal interest in talking to Charlotte. Lord knew, it wasn't as if women were in short supply in his life. If the Grand Vizier didn't seize him the minute he landed in Istanbul he would soon have more women available to him than he could possibly want.

Alexander heaved a few more feet of water-sodden rope on to the deck. Among the exotic beauties of his harem, he told himself, Charlotte would be unremarkable. His pleasure in her company, the odd sense of closeness he experienced when they were together, was simply a consequence of his weeks of celibacy. It was only the need to reclaim possession of Mr Canning's vital papers that produced this gnawing ache in his gut every time he saw her. Without the sea charts showing the whereabouts of hostile Turkish ships Hank Barrett would never be able to bring his supplies safely into Greek harbour. And without Mr Canning's bank-draft there would be no money to pay for the grain and oil and ammunition waiting for them at the Italian port of Brindisi.

An unexpected shift in the direction of the breeze allowed the ripple of Charlotte's laughter to drift down the deck towards him. Alexander let the rope fall from his hands, watching intently as she leaned against the brass deck-railing and continued her conversation with the first lieutenant. What in the world did she find so amusing about the fellow? Alexander wondered irritably. Didn't she have enough sense to realise that he must be hand-in-glove with Sir Clive?

For all practical purposes Lieutenant Haye served as the ship's captain, since Sir Clive limited his command to issuing orders about the dinner menu and pacing the length of the bridge when the weather was particularly clement. The lieutenant wasn't a young man, but even from a distance of fifty feet Alexander could see that he hung on to Charlotte's words like a lovesick puppy. Alexander gritted his teeth and grimly returned to his self-imposed task of winding rope around the sail-winch. It was a back-breaking chore, hated by all the sailors, but he had recently felt the need to work off an alarming build-up of inner tension. God, he would be relieved when the ship finally reached Istanbul and all this waiting was over!

Lieutenant Haye followed the direction of his companion's gaze and found it fixed on the figure of Prince Karim. 'We should arrive in Istanbul early tomorrow morning,' he said. 'Are you looking forward to being on dry land again, Miss Rippon?'

With some difficulty Charlotte tore her gaze away from the fascinating picture presented by the half-naked body of Prince Karim Alexander. She had no idea why he chose to spend the voyage labouring at all the most arduous tasks—Sir Clive had made it quite plain that the Prince was at liberty to behave exactly as he chose—but she certainly wished she hadn't been compelled to see him so often.

The long idle hours of the voyage had provided ample time for introspection, and Charlotte had soon acknowledged precisely what sort of romantic fantasy she had been weaving about her relationship with 'Mr Alexander'. Now, however, reality had set in with a vengeance, and she recognised that it was past time for her to put such naïve fantasies behind her. Charlotte blushed when she remembered the cosy little daydreams she had spun during those afternoons at Rippon Manor. At least pride had stiffened her will-power sufficiently that she had refused to speak to him during the voyage. If he had smiled at her, if he had spoken to her in his husky, coaxing 'Mr Alexander' voice, she didn't know if she would have stuck to her resolution not to tell him what had happened to his wretched documents.

With an impatient toss of her head she turned her back on Prince Karim and looked up into the kindly but weak face of Lieutenant Haye. Not for the first time she dismissed all possibility of appealing to him for help. She had realised weeks ago that the men on board Sir Clive's ship were all carefully chosen. They were competent sailors, but each of them had some reason for obeying Sir Clive's instructions which was far more important to them than obeying the dictates of either their honour or their conscience. Recognising Lieutenant Haye's weakness, Charlotte accepted him for what he could offer.

Pushing a stray curl back under her hat, she looked up at him with a polite smile that she hoped masked her true feelings. It was amazing, she thought with a flash of amusement, how many of the skills learned in the drawing-room at Rippon Manor were proving useful on board a ship of criminals in the middle of the ocean. Dissembling, she was learning, had other uses than masking boredom with the archdeacon's conversation.

'For my aunt's sake I'm delighted that our journey will soon be over,' she said, responding to the lieutenant's earlier question. 'As you know, the poor lady has suffered a great deal. The motion of the waves seems to overset her completely, even though she is a good traveller on land.'

'I'm sorry to hear that. But am I correct in thinking you yourself have enjoyed being at sea, Miss Rippon?'

'My pleasure would be greater if I had undertaken the journey voluntarily, just as I should be looking forward to our arrival in Istanbul more if I had any idea of what might happen to me when we land.'

'The Ottoman Empire is structured in a way that seems very odd to us,' he said. 'From the very beginning they have built their administration and their households upon the use of slaves, and yet they pride themselves upon the fact that these same slaves can aspire to the highest positions in the land. Moreover it is illegal to keep any one person enslaved for more than a few years.'

'Slavery is still slavery, however benign the terms and however kindly the master.'

'True, and yet if you consider that the mother of every Sultan who has ever ruled was herself a slave, and usually a Christian, you will see that the Turks do not view slavery quite as we do.'

Charlotte's brow wrinkled in amazement. 'The Sultan's mother has always been a *slave*? And a *Christian*? How in the world does the ruler of a Muslim empire come to have a Christian mother?'

'Odd as it seems to us, it's really a typical example of Oriental logic. The Sultan is considered too noble and too exalted to enter into any binding legal contracts with his subjects. Marriage, however, is a legal contract. Therefore the Sultan can't marry. He can only take concubines, not wives.'

'But are all concubines necessarily slaves?'

'Yes, they are, at least in the Sultan's household.' Lieutenant Haye chuckled. 'And now we get to the most amazing part of the story. You see, it's against the religious law of the Ottoman Empire to enslave anybody who is Muslim, even a woman. So you have the intriguing situation whereby the Sultan needs to perpetuate his dynasty but cannot do so with any of his Muslim subjects. He cannot marry them but neither can he make them slaves.'

'So what does he do?'

'In the past the solution has been simple. He simply waited for his armies to provide him with a selection of good-looking female captives, usually Christians, but any religion was acceptable so long as it wasn't Muslim. Then these captives were carefully trained by the palace eunuchs to become the Sultan's concubines. Nowadays, however, the women in the Imperial harem are often gifts from important subjects, or from foreigners seeking favours.'

Charlotte shuddered. 'It sounds a dreadful life to me. How could those poor women tolerate slavery when presumably they have all grown up in freedom?'

Lieutenant Haye looked at her pityingly. The poor girl had no inkling of the fate that Sir Clive almost certainly had in store for her. 'The Sultan's concubines are usually treated with considerable kindness, Miss Rippon, and the first four to produce a son are elevated into positions of great honour.'

'I treat my favourite dogs with great kindness, Lieutenant Haye, and we are always delighted when one of them produces a healthy litter of puppies. Women, however, have more to offer than life as a household pet, even an honoured household pet.'

The lieutenant stirred uncomfortably. 'Theory and practice don't always march hand in hand, Miss Rippon. In theory the ladies of the Sultan's harem are slaves. In practice these ladies are much envied and admired. Their lot, you know, is no worse than that of many other members of the Sultan's Government. The Chief White Eunuch at the Sultan's court holds a position almost equivalent to the role of our Prime Minister and yet he, too, started life as a slave.'

The wind picked up a little force, tugging at Charlotte's skirt and sending a sudden chill racing down her spine. 'Lieutenant Haye, what are you trying to tell me? Why are you explaining the intricacies of the Ottoman slave system?'

As usual when the prospect of telling the truth became too painful the lieutenant lost his courage. 'Why, I'm not trying to tell you anything, Miss Rippon. I simply thought you might be interested in a little background information before we land. You must be ready bright and early tomorrow morning, you know. The Bosporus at dawn is a sight to treasure for a lifetime.'

On this fact, at least, Charlotte soon discovered that the lieutenant hadn't lied. Standing at the ship's rail with Sam for an escort, she watched the sun rise over the hills of the city. Despite the early hour the harbour was crowded with caiques, plying from one bank of the city to the other and occasionally rowing close to the ocean-going sailing ships to offer their wares for sale.

As they watched, a small boat was lowered into the water, together with one of the sailors to act as oarsman. 'What is happening?' Charlotte asked.

'The cap'n's sending a message to shore. Now we're close to land that little boat can travel faster than a barkentine like us. Must be somefink urgent on the cap'n's mind.'

Charlotte watched the swift passage of the rowboat through the calm waters of the harbour with an increasing sense of foreboding. Even the magnificence of the seven hills of the city, silhouetted against the bright morning sky, couldn't quite restore her earlier mood of optimism. The domes and the minarets, which moments ago had looked so fascinating, now looked both sinister and threatening, alien to every value and principle she held dear. It was borne in upon her that Sir Clive, who lacked any trace of honesty or kindness, held her destiny clasped firmly within his corrupt control.

At this inauspicious point in her thoughts Lieutenant Haye appeared on the bridge and smiled apologetically.

'The captain wants to speak to you in his cabin right away, Miss Rippon. Lady Adeline is already there. Would you see that Miss Rippon gets there safely, Sam?'

'Better 'urry, miss,' Sam said. 'Don't do ter keep the cap'n waiting.'

Prince Karim Alexander was the first person she saw on entering the overblown opulence of Sir Clive's cabin. The Prince was bent low, listening to Lady Adeline speak. He had obviously been making some polite enquiry as to the older woman's health, but when

Charlotte entered the cabin he moved away immediately, acknowledging her presence by no more than a cursory nod. Charlotte was naïve enough to accept this indifference at face value.

Sir Clive rose to his feet. 'Welcome to Istanbul,' he said. 'I'm sure you must all be delighted to have reached our journey's end.'

Lady Adeline scowled. 'On the contrary, my good man. I have no interest in reaching any destination other than my nephew's house in London.'

'That, alas, is impossible. You have interfered in matters that ought not to have concerned you, and I cannot allow you to return to England.'

Charlotte swallowed hard. 'N-never?' she asked, cursing the tremor that she couldn't quite eliminate from her voice.

'Never,' he agreed softly. 'But don't worry, I have other, quite pleasant plans for you and your aunt. I have made arrangements for you to stay in Istanbul.'

Charlotte was aware of the same chill running down her spine that she had felt when Lieutenant Haye spoke to her yesterday. 'Where have you arranged for us to stay?' she asked curtly.

'In very comfortable accommodations, my dear. You need not worry.' Sir Clive's plump lips formed a smug, self-satisfied smile. 'In fact the Prince will no doubt vouch for their comfort. I am sending you to the household of the Emir Ibrahim Hussein, the Prince's father.'

Alexander managed to control his reaction so that only a slight hiss betrayed his sudden furious exhalation of air. He knew at once exactly what Sir Clive had planned, and from the bewildered glances which Lady Adeline and Charlotte were exchanging he knew that they still didn't understand their fate.

Lady Adeline spoke tentatively. 'It is good of the Emir to extend his hospitality to us——'

Sir Clive's laughter interrupted her. 'You have misunderstood my meaning, Lady Adeline. I have already sent a message to the Emir announcing that I have brought back his son. I also gave him the glad news that

I have brought him an extra gift for his entertainment—a charming, golden-haired English girl to grace his harem and an older relative to act as her maid.'

White-faced, Lady Adeline turned toward her niece. 'For his harem?' she murmured, her voice quivering. 'Do you know. . .? Is a harem what I think it is, Charlotte?'

'Pray allow me to explain.' Sir Clive folded his hands across his waistcoat, scarcely able to contain his satisfaction. 'You ladies must realise that marriage in the Ottoman Empire is not quite the same institution as it is in our own dear England. No, indeed. Muslims expect a woman to know her place, and they take care to see that she stays there. In Istanbul a man is master of his household, and his wives must obey him every bit as much as his lowliest servant. They are not allowed to forget that their only purpose in life is to serve his pleasure—whatever that may be.'

Lady Adeline turned even paler. 'Wh-what has such a system to do with us?'

'Why, quite a lot, dear lady. Powerful officials of the Ottoman Empire—men such as Prince Karim's father—are entitled not only to four wives, but also to as many slaves and concubines as they can afford to keep in comfort. The Emir Ibrahim is a very wealthy man and so his household contains many slaves, both male and female. The women, of course, are all segregated, according to Muslim custom, into a separate part of the palace known as the harem.'

'And we would be housed in the harem along with all the Emir's *concubines*? Sir Clive, you cannot be serious! My niece's reputation would be ruined forever!'

'Oh, no, Lady Adeline, you won't be housed *with* the Emir's concubines. You will *be* one of his concubines. Or at least your niece Miss Rippon will be his concubine. You personally will simply be one of the household slaves. At your age you couldn't expect to be lucky enough to attract the attention of the Emir and be invited into his bed. Even Miss Rippon will have to struggle first to catch his attention and then to please him once he has noticed her.' Sir Clive smiled. 'Fortunately her blonde colouring is unusual in this part of the world, so her task shouldn't be too difficult. Her life—and yours—will be a great deal pleasanter once she has been bedded, particularly if she can manage to get herself with child. I have noticed that Turks seem positively to dote upon their children, and I don't suppose the Emir is any exception. If she bears him a son I can almost guarantee you both lives of considerable luxury.'

'If she bears him a son!' Lady Adeline sat bolt upright in the chair, for once in her life too shocked even to faint. Charlotte, struggling to grasp the full implications of what she had just been told, found herself literally speechless. Her gaze turned instinctively towards the Prince, who so far had been no more than a silent, unmoving presence in the corner of the cabin. He met her gaze with an infinitesimal nod of reassurance, as if to tell her that he would take care of things, then his eyes became dark and cold once again, before he turned his back on her and stared out of the porthole at the sun-dappled waters of the harbour.

As soon as he had seen his fill of the stark horror etched into the faces of the two women Sir Clive glanced at Prince Karim. Unfortunately the Prince's profile, far from displaying shock or anger, revealed nothing more than faint boredom.

Charlotte finally recovered her voice. 'There is no possible reason for you to condemn my aunt and me to a lifetime of slavery, Sir Clive. Why are you doing something so cruel?'

'So cruel? Miss Rippon, surely you jest. I must return to England on one final secret mission for the Grand Vizier. You and Lady Adeline are the only two people who can identify me, other than Prince Karim, and yet I have allowed you to live. A cruel man would have killed you by the roadside with your servants. I, out of the generosity of my heart, have made provision for a comfortable future. Don't worry, my dear Miss Rippon. The Emir is an elderly man and his carnal demands upon you probably will not be excessive.'

Charlotte, who had no idea what carnal demands actually were, didn't feel in the least reassured or grateful. If she had thought it would do any good she would have prostrated herself at Sir Clive's feet and begged him to reconsider. She was, however, wise enough to recognise that if Sir Clive didn't give her and Lady Adeline to the Emir Ibrahim then he would undoubtedly arrange to have them killed. My honour or my life, she thought with a bitter, inward smile. Funny how she had always assumed that in such a situation choosing life would be easy.

The Prince's cool, unemotional voice put a stop to her rising sense of panic. 'My father's official barge is approaching, and so is the Grand Vizier's. If you want to be sure of getting your money, Sir Clive, I recommend that you hand me over to my father.'

Charlotte's attempts to convince her aunt that the Emir Ibrahim would never risk offending the British authorities by keeping two English ladies as prisoners in his harem were interrupted by the return of their guards, each carrying an ominous-looking length of thin cord. Now that the ship had finally stopped moving Lady Adeline was ready to take charge of their situation once again. She crossed her arms and planted her feet squarely in front of the two sailors. 'And just what do you think you're going to do with that rope?' she asked tartly. 'I demand to see the British Ambassador this instant!'

Neither sailor wasted his breath replying. With silent efficiency they grabbed the two women and bound their arms close against their bodies. Like chickens trussed ready for roasting, Charlotte reflected with a gasp of faintly hysterical laughter.

When the knots were all secured to the sailors' satisfaction they took two large squares of white muslin and threw one each over Lady Adeline and Charlotte. The plain, semi-transparent cloth hung down over their bound arms and swirled loosely around their waists.

'Take this. . .this *thing* off at once! I can't breathe!' Lady Adeline ordered. Charlotte knew that her aunt was trying to sound firm, but panic spiralled her voice into a high, unimpressive squeak.

'Out 'ere, in this part o' the world, women ain't allowed to go about with their faces showing,' one of the sailors commented. 'You'd be in big trouble wivvout them veils. Doin' you a kindness, we was.'

He nodded his head tersely toward his companion, and the two men bent simultaneously to pick up Charlotte and her aunt, bundling them over their shoulders as if they were over-stuffed sacks of flour. Lady Adeline's moans quickly ceased, but whether it was because she lost her breath or because she had fainted Charlotte had no way of knowing. Poor Aunt Adeline, she thought with a flash of grim humour. Until these past few weeks the dear lady had never in her life had so many splendid reasons for fainting and so few people to pay attention to her when she did.

The journey down the gangplank to shore was not only undignified, it was also excessively uncomfortable. Charlotte was too relieved at finding herself upright again to complain when she was lifted into a palanquin and immediately carried off from the dockside.

By the time she had gathered her wits it was too late to ask questions, too late to find out what had happened to her aunt. She was alone in cushioned, perfumed, oppressively hot splendour. For a while fear threatened to overwhelm her. The unfamiliar veil increased her sensation of stifling, breath-taking heat, and her heart began to pound with a jumpy, erratic rhythm.

You are going to be imprisoned for life in a Turkish harem. Sir Clive has condemned you to serve as the Emir's concubine. Charlotte tried to visualise her fate, but in fact she wasn't at all sure what a concubine actually did, although she was sure it must be very unpleasant. She thought she might be less apprehensive if she knew what unspeakable degradations awaited her as the plaything of the Emir's old age. On the other hand, she reflected wryly, perhaps it was a blessing that she couldn't even imagine what lay in store. Perhaps there were advantages to being a virtuous, delicately reared English lady who had only the vaguest idea of what the duties of the marriage bed entailed.

For once her innate sense of the ridiculous could not vanquish the encroaching tentacles of fear, and for a few minutes she gave herself up to the luxury of full-scale panic. Then reason returned. This will never do, she told herself firmly. You should be spending your time becoming familiar with this strange new country. You don't have time to abandon yourself to useless palpitations. Drawing in several deep, calming breaths, she forced herself to take note of her surroundings.

Her palanquin was something like an old-fashioned English sedan chair, except that there was no separate bench to serve as a seat and she was obliged to sit cross-legged on the cushioned floor. The interior walls were completely lined in padded crimson silk, and the floor was stacked with tasselled cushions. If her bound arms hadn't made her feel so awkward and top-heavy, Charlotte thought she might have been quite comfortable.

There was no artificial light inside the palanquin, and thick beaded curtains blocked her view out of the window. With no way to mark the passage of time or distance she guessed that a quarter of an hour passed before she managed to nudge the window hangings aside with her chin and wedge them between the wall and her shoulder so that she could look out.

A street scene of incredible busyness and totally unfamiliar aspect met her gaze. Close by her palanquin an itinerant pedlar seemed to be selling some sort of drink, although the thick, pastel-pink liquid he was offering bore no resemblance to anything Charlotte had ever seen before. He attracted custom by clinking the metal cups suspended from his waist-belt in an endless, tuneful rhythm. Porters, the trays on their heads piled high with peaches and apricots, ran along the narrow strip of pavement, and an ox-cart full of vegetables jostled for position with three exotically garbed men on horseback.

At the far end of the street she could see a scribe seated cross-legged on the ground behind his tiny carved wooden desk. A line of heavily veiled women waited to buy his services, dark eyes gleaming from behind the enveloping folds of their muslin head-wraps.

Less appealing was the cowering group of bone-thin dogs that crouched beneath the shade of a gushing water fountain until a turbaned passer-by stopped for a drink and kicked them away with casual, brutal force.

Instinctively recoiling from the unpleasant sight, Charlotte accidentally allowed the curtain to fall back over the window. By the time she once again lifted it with her chin her bearers had carried the palanquin into a much quieter neighbourhood. Here she could see only high walls, occasionally overhung by fruit trees, and one large stone building, which she decided must be a mosque. A deep portico ran along the façade of the mosque, supported by elaborately carved columns and arches decorated with tiny pieces of coloured marble. The recessed door of the building was closed, affording her an excellent view of geometrically carved panels, inlaid with mother-of-pearl mosaics that glowed pink and creamy white in the sun. She saw a priest chanting in one of the towers at the corner of the building. The wailing notes of his call to prayer reminded her sharply of how different the religious beliefs of these people were from her own, and for a second or two she had to struggle to push away the renewed waves of fear.

The bearers scarcely slowed their pace as they carried her up a steep hill at the side of the mosque. They halted at the summit in front of an ornate iron-latticed entranceway. A single cry from one of the bearers secured the opening of the gate, and Charlotte was carried into a magnificent paved courtyard where flowering shrubs and cascading fountains seemed to occupy almost equal amounts of space.

Still at a run, the bearers carried the palanquin across the courtyard to another iron gate, this one built into a brick wall that was at least seven feet high. The gate swung open immediately to reveal a tall, clean-shaven black man, who wore a satin gown rather like an English dressing-robe, and a huge velvet turban decorated with iridescent peacock feathers and a badge of seed-pearls.

Charlotte felt the palanquin being placed on the ground, and then one of the bearers opened the door, averting his face as he assisted Charlotte out of the conveyance and on to her feet. As soon as she gained her balance the black door-keeper gestured to indicate that she should precede him into the inner courtyard.

The smell of flowers and crushed blossom was overwhelming after the stuffy confinement of the palanquin, but Charlotte refused to accept the support offered her by the turbaned doorman. She'd been brought here against her will, and she was going to make it on her own two feet, or else!

The rumble of wooden wheels on the cobbled paving-stones attracted her attention, and she sighed with heartfelt relief when she looked up and saw her aunt alighting from the rear of a velvet-draped ox-cart.

'Thank God they didn't separate us for long,' she said, leaning forward to kiss her aunt on the cheek—a difficult operation since both of them were still wearing muslin veils. 'Do you think this is the Emir Ibrahim's palace?'

Lady Adeline looked at the unimpressive building ahead of them and sniffed disparagingly. 'It's hardly what I'd call a palace, although I suppose the garden is quite nice.'

'Perhaps it's more luxurious inside. I don't think people here pay much attention to the outside appearance of their buildings.'

'That is certainly true. I've never seen such a ramshackle collection of houses as I saw on the way here. I don't know what the builders could have been thinking of. Each floor juts out further than the floor beneath, and half the floors don't seem to have any windows.'

The doorman clucked his tongue impatiently, indicating that they were to follow him along a narrow path that led between two cascading fountains. He chivvied them past the splashing water to where an open door offered access to a dark, high-ceilinged corridor.

Charlotte paused on the threshold, admitting to herself that she was terrified. The corridor looked as if it had been transported straight out of a nightmare. She half expected a covey of bats to come swooping down at any moment.

'Is it. . .is it a dungeon?' Lady Adeline whispered.

'I don't think so. Just a very dark corridor.'

'Maybe it's the corridor that leads to the dungeons.'

Charlotte gave a tiny gasp of laughter. 'No, I think it leads to the Emir's harem.'

Lady Adeline turned white. 'That's just as bad. In fact, it's probably worse. At least in a dungeon you would have some hope of preserving your reputation.' She leaned against the outside wall and stared defiantly at the towering figure of the doorman. 'I'm not going in there,' she said loudly. Despite weeks of stress and imprisonment Lady Adeline hadn't yet abandoned her belief that all foreigners could be brought to an understanding of plain English if you shouted loud enough. 'I'm the daughter of an English Earl and I *demand* to see the British Ambassador.'

The doorman smiled, revealing a row of perfect white teeth. He said something incomprehensible, then bent at the knees and tucked Lady Adeline under one arm and Charlotte under the other. He then marched calmly into the darkened building.

Coolness. The first thing Charlotte was aware of was how pleasantly cool the corridor felt after the heat of the palanquin and the burning sun of the garden. Then she heard a series of subdued rustlings and murmurings and realised that little trills of laughter were greeting their progress along the corridor.

As her eyes became accustomed to the gloom she saw that the hallway was nowhere near as narrow as she'd first thought. Bumping along against the doorman's hip, she grasped the fact that the corridor was lined on either side with latticed wooden screens, and behind those screens were scattered several groups of women and children—all of whom were giggling uncontrollably.

The gloom ended when they reached a shallow flight of stairs, illuminated by the coloured light streaming in through a series of stained-glass windows. At the top of the stairs the final traces of darkness vanished as they were carried into a tiled atrium whose walls and floor positively glowed with the brilliance of their mosaic designs.

A low dais was built at one end of the room, and seated on this dais was a wrinkled old woman with a painted face and extraordinary bright red hands. There were no chairs in the room, Charlotte realised. In fact furniture of any sort seemed to be in short supply. The old lady's body was supported by rows of embroidered silk cushions, and in front of her stood a crystal bowl containing bubbling water, surmounted by a clay pot from which extruded a long, flexible tube that she held clamped in her mouth. Occasional puffs of smoke billowed out from the tube, and a strange odour, faintly reminiscent of burning wood-smoke, became stronger as Charlotte approached the dais.

When they were about two yards away from the old lady and her crystal bowl the doorman finally allowed Charlotte and Lady Adeline to stand on their own feet. He then placed a large, firm hand on Charlotte's head and forced her to bow almost to the ground in front of the old lady. Her aunt, too surprised to protest, suffered a similar fate.

'I never thought the day would come when I'd bow down to a whore,' Lady Adeline muttered. At least, Charlotte thought that was what she heard, although she couldn't quite believe that the word 'whore' had actually crossed her aunt's chaste lips.

The old woman removed the tube from her mouth and issued some brief, incomprehensible instruction. The doorman immediately pulled off the muslin veils and a hushed murmur of astonishment rippled through the assembled crowd of women.

Charlotte had no idea what was so astonishing and at this moment she didn't really care. She drew in a deep breath and turned towards the old woman on the dais. After her experiences with 'Mr Alexander' she was no longer naïve enough to assume that the old crone didn't speak English because she chose to speak in Arabic, or Osmanlica, or whatever language she had just used.

'My aunt and I have been taken captive against our will,' she said, doing her best to sound both calm and dignified, although her insides had long since dissolved into a shivering mass of trepidation. 'We would appreciate it if you would first arrange for us to be untied and then arrange for us to have an interview with the British Ambassador.'

A gleam of amusement lightened the old woman's eyes, then she returned the tube to her mouth and sucked in silence for several agonisingly long minutes. Neither the doorman nor any of the assembled women uttered a sound. Finally she took the tube from her mouth just long enough to say two or three words. The doorman touched his hand to his breast, then raised it quickly to his lips and his forehead in a deferential salute. He then forced Charlotte and Lady Adeline to bow once again before hustling them across the atrium into a small chamber, whose bare marble floor and total absence of furniture gave no clue as to its function.

'They should have spent a little less money on decorating the walls and a little more on buying some chairs,' Lady Adeline remarked caustically. She stared up at the door-keeper, who loomed a good eighteen inches above her. 'Well, my good man, are you going to untie these ropes, or do I have to start screaming?'

The door-keeper's expression remained utterly impassive so that it was impossible to guess whether or not he had understood, but after fumbling briefly in the folds of his waist-sash he withdrew a small dagger and cut swiftly through the knots in the cord. As soon as she was free Charlotte flexed her hands gratefully, almost rejoicing as she felt the stinging pain of blood returning to her numbed fingers. She smiled at her aunt.

'With free hands and without those silly veils I feel almost normal again.'

'Humph! *Normal* is perhaps overstating the case. Have you looked towards the doorway?'

Charlotte turned and saw that the entrance to their chamber was circled by a crowd of exotic, silk-clad women who were all eyeing the two Englishwomen with as much unabashed curiosity as if they had been tigers caged at a circus. She smiled ruefully at her aunt. 'I suppose we should try to be friendly. They look harmless enough.' She started to walk towards the group of spectators clustered at the door, her hands outstretched in greeting. 'How do you do? My name is Miss Charlotte Rippon, and this is my aunt, the Lady——'

Her friendly words died away when she felt herself

grabbed by the waist and pulled back into the centre of the room. She whirled around, ready to protest, but the door-keeper grasped her chin and tilted it upwards at the same time as he reached for the top button on her travelling-gown. She stood stock-still, frozen into immobility for the few seconds it took him to unfasten the top three buttons of her tattered gown, then her power of movement returned in a surge of white-hot rage. She reacted instinctively, indifferent to her audience, slapping the door-keeper's face with a force that left her hand tingling.

She could literally feel the horrified silence that descended over the women, a silence so intense that it was palpable. Even Lady Adeline didn't speak. The door-keeper—too late it dawned on Charlotte that this man obviously had duties that extended well beyond opening and shutting the garden gate—looked at her without saying a word. Then he took a single step backwards and raised his hand. He clicked his fingers in a signal that was obviously recognised by all the women present except Charlotte and Lady Adeline. Their breath expelled in a collective sigh, and they all turned to watch the progress of a barefoot young girl who ran over to a concealed wall niche and returned carrying a short leather whip. She bowed low in front of the door-keeper, and he took the whip, continuing to stare wordlessly at Charlotte as he pulled the narrow leather thong through his fingers, testing its flexibility.

Charlotte was shaking from head to foot, but from anger almost as much as from fear. 'You had no right to touch me in such a fashion,' she said, re-fastening her buttons with a defiant flourish. 'In fact, you have no right to touch me at all. And if you beat me I shall see that the Prince Karim Alexander hears about what you have done. The Prince will not tolerate brutality towards me.'

The door-keeper spoke for the first time since they had left the presence of the old lady on the dais. Charlotte understood nothing except the words 'Emir Ibrahim' and 'Karim Alexander', but she saw, with profound relief, that the black man tucked the whip into his sash alongside the knife he had used to cut their bonds. He clapped his hands imperiously and issued what seemed to be a series of orders. The crowd of women disappeared almost instantaneously, melting away behind doorways, pillars and carved screens. Soon there was nobody left except two dark-eyed, long-haired girls, who advanced into the antechamber, smiling nervously. They introduced themselves as Miriam and Alia, daughters of the Emir Ibrahim.

'The Chief Eunuch says you will prepare for a bath,' Alia translated. 'We wish you much enjoyment of your washing,' she added courteously.

Some time later, her hair washed, her skin clean and perfumed, Charlotte was enveloped in a linen robe, and led to rejoin her aunt. She then discovered that there was another room to explore. This one was cool and high-ceilinged with attractive stained-glass windows admitting the sun to dance on the white marble floor in a dazzling rainbow of colour. Aunt Adeline was already ensconced on a pile of cushions, leaning back and sipping an aromatic, steaming liquid from a small porcelain cup. She had lost a considerable amount of weight during her battle with seasickness, and her previously chubby face was now revealed as an unexpectedly perfect oval. Her hair, fresh from its encounter with egg yolk and bowls of hot, scented water, hung around her shoulders in a rich cloud of golden-brown curls. With a start of astonishment Charlotte realised that her aunt could be considered an attractive woman. It was not necessarily a comforting thought. She suspected that her aunt might literally prefer death to the dishonour of being taken into the Emir Ibrahim's bed.

'Come and sit beside me,' Lady Adeline said. 'This tea I am drinking is flavoured with mint, of all the extraordinary things, but it is surprisingly refreshing.'

Charlotte sank down next to her aunt, accepting a cup of tea from one of the serving-girls. 'How did you like your bath?' she enquired teasingly.

Lady Adeline refused to fall into the trap. 'It was nowhere near as refreshing as a decent English tub, of course, but I dare say it was better than we could have expected from these heathens.'

The servants returned at that moment, bearing a selection of clothing—including what were obviously two pairs of brightly coloured silk trousers. Lady Adeline put down her empty cup and raised herself ominously against the cushions.

'Take those unmentionable garments away,' she said to the servant holding the trousers. 'I am a lady, an *English lady*, and I shall *never* wear anything so unbelievably vulgar.'

The serving-girl smiled, understanding that the trousers were being discussed but obviously having no idea what was being said about them. She shook the offending garments out in front of Lady Adeline, displaying their baggy folds and glittering embroidery to what she hoped was their best advantage. Lady Adeline shuddered. 'I am going to faint,' she murmured.

'Of course you're not,' Charlotte responded crisply. 'You didn't faint all the time we were aboard ship when you had much better reasons for fainting, so you certainly aren't going to do anything so useless now.'

Lady Adeline glared at her niece. 'Fainting is *never* useless. It is one of the most valuable weapons in a lady's arsenal.'

Charlotte was amused. 'That may be true, Aunt Adeline, but I think we should save our weapons to use in battles we can win. If you don't put on those trousers. . .' Lady Adeline shuddered again, and Charlotte hastily corrected herself. 'If you don't put on those unmentionable garments we shall have to go naked, because I'm quite certain the Chief Eunuch has no intention of returning our own clothes to us. On balance, don't you think that trou—I mean, unmentionable garments would be better than nothing?'

'You know, Charlotte, even in the painfully reduced circumstances in which we find ourselves you really should strive to be a little less logical. Logic is never becoming in a lady, and I've tried repeatedly to bring you to an understanding of that fact.'

'When we are back in England I promise that I will practise behaving illogically at least three times a day.

But while we are here would you mind very much if we used just a little bit of common sense?'

Lady Adeline sniffed disparagingly, then rose to her feet with as much hauteur as the soft pillows allowed. 'For your sake, Charlotte, I will put on those obscene garments, provided the servants supply some outer robe that totally conceals what I am wearing.' She swept into a dressing-alcove and turned to speak. 'You may tell the girls what I have said.'

The two women emerged from the baths some twenty minutes later, clad in the baggy trousers and thin gauze smocks, all of which were covered by brocaded silk caftans. In Charlotte's secret opinion the caftans were two of the most exquisite pieces of clothing she had ever seen, and they were certainly comfortable to wear.

The Chief Eunuch waited for them in exactly the place where they had left him. He eyed them in critical silence, then turned to address Alia, who stood patiently at his side.

The Emir's younger daughter smiled happily as she translated the Chief Eunuch's words. 'He says that now you are properly cleaned and dressed he is no longer ashamed to have you in his harem. With hard work, Charlotte, he thinks you may succeed in pleasing the Emir greatly. It is a most generous compliment. The Chief Eunuch does not offer such praise lightly.'

Charlotte knew that she either wanted to laugh or to cry, she just wasn't sure which. Her head had suddenly started spinning in the oddest fashion, and her legs displayed the most alarming tendency to buckle. 'Aunt Adeline,' she said, her voice seeming to echo from the end of a very long tunnel, 'I do believe I'm going to faint.'

CHAPTER FIVE

WHEN Charlotte next became aware of her surroundings she found herself back in the main reception hall, stretched out full length on a pile of cushions. Lady Adeline's pale, worried face was the first to swim into complete focus.

'I'm sorry,' Charlotte murmured, struggling to sit up. 'I've no idea why I did that.'

Her aunt slipped a cushion behind her back and held out a cup of mint tea. 'You're probably hungry. You went up on deck at dawn this morning, and so have eaten nothing all day.'

Charlotte managed a tiny laugh. 'What a horribly prosaic explanation of my first successful attack of the vapours.'

'Not the vapours, my dear, merely a common-or-garden faint. If you are feeling up to it I think it would be a good idea to eat. The servants have been waiting for some time to serve us dinner.'

'Actually I'm very hungry. And, now that you mention it, something smells wonderful. Where is the dining-room, do you think?'

'Here,' Lady Adeline said wryly. 'Have you ever heard of such a ridiculous plan for a palace? Special rooms for bathing, but nowhere to eat except the main hall. Really, I can't imagine why some of their architects don't take a trip to England and see what a proper house is supposed to look like.'

'Perhaps they think this is a proper style of house.'

Lady Adeline dismissed the absurd suggestion with an impatient snort. Meanwhile a little girl with riotously curly hair and huge brown eyes crept on to Charlotte's lap and stretched out a chubby hand to touch her hair. A murmur of approval went through the assembled women when Charlotte smiled back at the child and gently ruffled her dark curls.

'Congratulations. You have found a sure way to win the heart of every woman in the harem,' a mocking voice said in French. 'In the Ottoman Empire all women love children. It is the rule.'

Startled by the undisguised note of bitterness she heard in the voice, Charlotte looked up just in time to see a thin, elderly woman glide gracefully on to the cushion next to her.

'The Chief Eunuch has commanded me to keep you company while you eat,' the woman said, avoiding Charlotte's eyes. She clapped her hands in a quick staccato rhythm, and a group of serving-girls appeared, two of them sharing the burden of carrying a short-legged table and the remainder bearing various bowls and jugs. Within seconds the gleaming brass-topped table was set between the three women and the dishes of food dispersed over it. When several flat pieces of what looked like under-cooked pancakes had been added to the table setting a maid carrying a spouted copper pot and a small bowl positioned herself behind the elderly Turkish woman.

The woman glanced up at the servant and then across the table at Lady Adeline and Charlotte. 'It is necessary that you wash before eating,' she said, holding out her hands. The servant poured steaming water out of her copper pot, catching it skilfully in the small bowl as it trickled through the woman's fingers.

'Now it is your turn,' the elderly woman said, still in the same faintly mocking tone of voice. 'Remember that you must use only your right hand to eat. Leave your left hand lying neatly in your lap.'

'Her advice would be more to the point if there were any knives and forks on the table,' Lady Adeline said tartly. 'We can't use our right or our left hand when there are no implements anywhere in sight.'

Charlotte explained their predicament to the older woman.

'Here we find no need for knives and forks,' the woman said. There was no mistaking the laughter lurking in her eyes when she glanced across the table at Charlotte and Lady Adeline. 'In this country fingers are considered the most efficient utensils for eating,' she added. 'Please, *mesdames*, I beg you to join me in tasting some of the dishes that have been prepared for your pleasure.'

Charlotte decided that the hollow ache in her stomach was infinitely more important than the rules of etiquette existing in England.

'It is good that you do not resist the customs of the country,' the woman commented. 'You will save yourselves much grief. For me, I was not so wise. For eight days, when I was first brought here, I refused to eat. The Chief Eunuch of those days thought I would die and forced food down my throat.'

'When you were first brought here?' Charlotte queried. 'You mean, *madame*, that you are not Turkish?'

The elderly woman wiped her fingers delicately on her napkin. 'No,' she said at last. 'I was born in France.' Again the sardonic smile flickered briefly. 'Allow me to introduce myself, *mademoiselle*. I am Marie-Claire de Saint Michel, daughter of the Marquis de Saint Michel of Grenoble.'

Charlotte choked on her mouthful of rice, and Marie-Claire leaned back against her pillows, seeming to derive considerable amusement from the shock she had given her audience. When she could speak Charlotte translated Marie-Claire's information for her aunt. Not surprisingly Lady Adeline babbled for several seconds before reducing her tumble of words to one cogent question. 'How in the world did the daughter of a French Marquis find herself in the harem of an Ottoman Emir?'

Marie-Claire stared down at her lap as if seeing far back into a dimly remembered past. 'I was captured by pirates,' she said at last. 'The Emir Ibrahim tells me that the Barbary pirates have now been disbanded by the naval forces of Europe. But in 1789 they still threatened a significant part of the Mediterranean.'

'In 1789?' Charlotte breathed. 'But that is almost forty years ago! You cannot mean that you have been in this harem for forty years!'

This time Marie-Claire's smile contained more genuine humour. 'Can I not?'

'But you must have left France even before the Revolution! It's almost impossible to imagine.'

'It is ironic, is it not? My father was nervous about the course of events in France, and so he wanted to send me to safety. I was en route to the home of my cousins in Martinique when the pirate ship overtook us. In recent years the Emir Ibrahim has made enquiries in Paris on my behalf, and he discovered that my father, my mother and all my brothers died at the hands of Robespierre's Committee of Public Safety. I suppose you could say that in some ways the pirates rescued me from certain death.'

'Do you mean that you and the Emir. . .that you have been the Emir's. . .?'

'Concubine?' Marie-Claire supplied drily.

'Yes.' Charlotte swallowed hard against a rising sensation of nausea. 'Have you been his concubine for *forty years*?'

'No, I have never been the Emir Ibrahim's concubine. I was sold by the pirates to the Emir's father, Ali Mustafa, who at that time was already an old man approaching seventy. He died five years later, but, thank God, I was able to capture his attention long enough to become pregnant with his child. Unfortunately I gave birth only to a daughter, but you will find that having a child—even a girl—earns you a position of considerable respect within the harem. Start praying today that God grants you the gift of motherhood before the Emir Ibrahim loses interest.'

'What is she saying?' Lady Adeline demanded. 'I thought she mentioned something about having a daughter.'

Charlotte gave her aunt a severely edited translation of Marie-Claire's story. Lady Adeline gazed pityingly at the elderly Frenchwoman. 'Is your daughter still living with you in the harem?' she enquired kindly.

Marie-Claire laughed, displaying genuine amusement for the first time. 'Ah, no, indeed not. She was married many years ago on her fourteenth birthday. I have two grandsons who are themselves married and the fathers of children.'

'But why are you still here in the harem?' Charlotte asked, too surprised to be tactful. 'The Emir's father has been dead for so long, so why haven't you gone back to France after all this time?'

The laughter faded from Marie-Claire's face. 'You do not think before you speak, *mademoiselle*. I was *sold* to Mustafa, the Emir's father. A slave does not demand to be returned to her native land when her master dies. Besides, for what reason would I return to France? My daughter is here, and I am allowed to visit her often. From time to time I see the wives of my grandsons, and their children. In France I have nobody. My immediate family are all dead, but perhaps it is better so. Do you think they would wish to acknowledge me, the enslaved mother of a bastard daughter?'

'You must not think of yourself so. . .' Charlotte began.

'How else would people in France think of me? Be advised, *mademoiselle*. If you do not kill yourself before the Emir takes you to his bed, then resign yourself to the destiny that has been written for you. You will never be able to return to England; your life there is over. Forget the past, and save yourself much grief.'

Charlotte's stomach closed in a tight knot around the food she had just eaten. She and her aunt were prisoners—slaves—who might end up spending the rest of their lives enclosed behind the elegant scrollwork bars of the Emir's harem.

'Dear God, Charlotte, you have gone as white as a ghost!' Lady Adeline exclaimed. 'What did Marie-Claire say to you? What is wrong?'

With a supreme effort Charlotte forced her panicky emotions back under control. 'Don't worry, Aunt,' she soothed. 'Marie-Claire said nothing we haven't heard before. She merely commented upon the fact that she has no family left in France.'

'Revolutions always cause a lot of unnecessary trouble,' Lady Adeline agreed.

The servants cleared away the table and the empty dishes, returning with the copper pot full of hot water so that the ladies could once again wash their hands. Marie-

Claire spoke sharply to the serving-girl who appeared at her side. 'We shall drink tea and eat sweetmeats while I tell you about the Emir and his son,' she explained, speaking slowly for Lady Adeline's benefit. 'The ladies of the harem always like to talk about Prince Karim. They think he is very handsome.'

'But how do they know what he looks like if they are never allowed out?' Lady Adeline asked in her mangled French.

'Prince Karim lived here with his father until he left to go overseas three years ago. We are always permitted to view important ceremonies from behind special screens, so that we have plenty of occasions to see the men of the household, although they can never see us. Also, the women of the Prince's harem visit the baths at the same time as we do, so we have many occasions to gossip. They are all desolate that he has been away so long.'

Charlotte succumbed to the longing to learn something more about the Prince's background. She turned to Marie-Claire. 'Why did Prince Karim spend so much time travelling in Europe? Was he sent overseas by his father?'

'Not exactly.' Marie-Claire settled back against her cushions, pleased with her role as story-teller. 'Penelope, the Prince's mother, was the love of Emir Ibrahim's life. Their marriage, you understand, was arranged in the usual way. Penelope was a member of the Greek Phanariot family who ruled Wallachia on behalf of the Sultan, and she was a princess in her own right. The match began prosaically, but it turned out to be a passionate love-affair. Within seven years Penelope gave her husband three daughters, as well as twin sons who died in a measles epidemic and—her last child—the Prince Karim Alexander. His birth was difficult, and after that she could have no more babies.'

Remembering the information she had been given by Sir Clive on board ship, Charlotte said, 'I thought that titles in the Ottoman Empire couldn't be inherited.'

'That is true, and Prince Karim's title comes from his mother's family. Many people have claimed that it is evidence of the Emir's infatuation that he allowed Penelope to give her son a foreign title, and also the Greek name of Alexander. Others say that it is further proof of the Emir's blind devotion to Penelope that Karim was sent overseas to complete his education when he was only sixteen years old. However, I am certain that the decision to send Prince Karim overseas was taken by his father, not by his mother. The Emir Ibrahim would like the Sultan to have more advisers who are trained in the European ways. He believes that the Ottoman Empire will die if it does not change its political systems in the very near future.'

'Are there many in the Government who share his point of view?'

'Not many at all. The mullahs, the teachers of Islam, do not approve of European ways, and the Grand Vizier struggles to retain all the decision-making power in his own hands.'

'Does Prince Karim hold an office in the Ottoman Government?'

'He was considered an official counsellor to the Sultan, but I am not sure if he still holds that office after such a long absence. The Emir Ibrahim is powerful in the councils of the Sultan, but the Grand Vizier would like to see his power diminished.'

'Perhaps Karim left Istanbul on a mission for the Sultan?'

'No, I think not. It is well known that he left because of arguments with his father. He married a girl chosen by his father and set up his household here in the palace according to the traditions of Islam. But when his wife died in childbirth Karim refused to take a new wife, and the blazing arguments with the Emir began—arguments so angry that we could hear them even in the depths of the harem. Instead of consoling himself by enjoying the pleasures to be offered by his concubines, the Prince announced that he intended to return to his mother's estates in the Greek peninsula. He informed his father that the lands had been criminally mismanaged by their Turkish overseers and that he would make them profitable again. He said that the owners of property had an obligation to see that their dependants did not starve. He left Istanbul totally against his father's wishes and has not returned until today. Perhaps, at last, he is ready to oblige his father by taking a wife. The Emir grieves that his only son is not willing to give him the gift of a grandchild.'

Marie-Claire halted her story-telling as a visible tremor of excitement rippled through the women of the harem. Everybody watched in tense silence as the Chief Eunuch strode through the hall and, ignoring the agitated whispers, walked over to the group of women clustered around Charlotte and Lady Adeline. The women all rose to their feet as he approached, and he spoke to them softly before addressing the elderly Frenchwoman.

When he finished speaking Marie-Claire inclined her head in respectful acknowledgement, then turned to look at Charlotte and Lady Adeline. Her dark eyes gleamed with a curious mixture of sympathy and suppressed envy.

'The Emir Ibrahim has summoned you both to his private rooms,' she said finally. 'Go now with the Chief Eunuch, and he will see that you are properly prepared for the great honour in store for you.'

Charlotte stared up at the impassive features of the Chief Eunuch and willed herself to faint. Unfortunately her success outside the bath-house was not to be repeated, and she remained obstinately, vividly, *terrifyingly* conscious.

'Hurry,' she heard Marie-Claire murmur. 'Do not think, Charlotte, just go. You must not keep the Emir waiting.'

Lady Adeline soothed down her caftan. 'Well, Charlotte, my dear, what are they saying this time? Goodness, I do wish Marie-Claire spoke French a little more clearly.'

Charlotte's mouth was so dry that her tongue felt too thick to shape a complete sentence. 'The Emir wants to see us,' she managed at last.

'Thank goodness for that and about time, too,' Lady Adeline said briskly. 'Now perhaps we'll see somebody who can extricate us from the dreadful mess Sir Clive has plunged us into. Dreadful little man, Sir Clive. I never did like him.'

Before her astonished niece could gather her wits to protest this outrageous mis-statement Lady Adeline drew in a deep breath, threw out her bosom and tapped the Chief Eunuch on the arm. 'Very well, my man, what are you waiting for? Take us to see your master.'

It was a measure of how far they had both travelled in the preceding few hours that neither Lady Adeline nor Charlotte protested when the Chief Eunuch inspected them with what should have seemed insulting minuteness. Satisfied that the newcomers to his harem wouldn't disgrace him, the Chief Eunuch summoned two of the ubiquitous maidservants, who draped the women from head to toe in silk veils, using jewelled hair-pins to secure the fragile fabric.

With a little grunt of approval the Chief Eunuch ordered the women to follow him down a narrow hallway. The maidservants fell into step, trailing along at the rear. To prevent any attempt of escape? Charlotte wondered. If so, the precaution was unnecessary. The labyrinthine layout of the palace defied understanding, and since all the gates to the outside world were locked and guarded escape didn't seem a very realistic possibility. Quite apart from the fact that neither she nor Aunt Adeline had a brass farthing to their names, nor any idea where to run to.

Their little procession came to a halt at the foot of a dais similar to the one in the main hall of the *haremlik*. The Chief Eunuch moved to one side, unblocking her view, and Charlotte looked up, almost glad of the veil she wore. At least it served to hide the ignominious quaking of her body.

There were three men on the dais and her gaze flew to the only one she recognised. Sir Clive Bottomley was seated on a carved wooden chair, looking none too comfortable with his situation. Next to Sir Clive an elderly man—presumably the Emir—reclined upon a cushioned piece of furniture that reminded Charlotte of an oversized *chaise-longue*. A young boy sat at the Emir's feet, holding a silver goblet, and at least a dozen lavishly dressed servants, all male, lined the walls on either side of the dais.

However, neither the Emir nor Sir Clive could hold Charlotte's attention. Her eye was caught by the forbiddingly tall and grim-looking Turk who stood behind the Emir, dominating the room by his very stillness. Clad in a crimson, jewel-encrusted gown and wearing a turban decorated with a crest of peacock feathers, his arrogant gaze rested on Charlotte and her aunt for no more than a second before he lifted his head slightly and stared into the middle distance with every appearance of utter indifference.

Charlotte's heart lurched in her breast, then turned a series of bounding somersaults. Dear heaven, she thought dizzily. That man standing behind the Emir is Prince Karim Alexander!

The pounding of her heart slowed into a heavy, aching rhythm and the blood racing through her veins slowly froze into the coldness of despair. Until this moment she hadn't realised how much she was counting on the Prince to save her and Aunt Adeline from their fate. She had never quite believed that 'Mr Alexander' would be prepared to abandon the women who had saved his life to whatever fate Sir Clive chose to assign them.

Now, at last, she saw how mistaken she had been. Sir Clive seemed to be an honoured guest, which must mean that Sir Clive and the Prince were working together. Which meant, in turn, that she and her aunt had been sadly betrayed.

Against her better judgement Charlotte stole a second glance at the remote, aristocratic profile of the man standing motionless and unblinking behind his father's cushioned couch. His features might have been carved out of best quality Scottish granite. They certainly bore no trace of the laughing man whom she had known as Mr Alexander. How impossible it was to believe that this harsh, glittering stranger was a man whom she had held in her arms as he shivered with fever. Even more impossible to remember that they had spent a sunlit afternoon driving around the English countryside, sharing the triumph of finding his precious secret papers, and laughing together as they hid their discovery from the peevish eyes of Archdeacon Jeffries.

'Courage,' Lady Adeline whispered. 'Those knives the servants are holding probably don't even cut.'

'I wouldn't count on it,' Charlotte whispered in return.

The Chief Eunuch stepped forward angrily, silencing them with a violent downward sweep of his staff. He then knelt in front of the Emir, obviously begging pardon for the temerity of the two women who had dared to speak before they had been spoken to.

The Emir accepted the eunuch's apology with a languid wave of his hand. He certainly didn't seem to be overwhelmed with lust at the sight of the latest additions to his harem, Charlotte thought. In fact he seemed to pay no attention at all to either woman. The Chief Eunuch, head almost touching his knees, retreated towards one of the rows of servants, then Sir Clive sprang to his feet and walked down from the dais to position himself close to the two women. He, too, bowed low before launching into speech.

'Your Excellency, I beg your indulgence for speaking in my own language.' Sir Clive nodded towards Alexander. 'I rely upon you to act as interpreter, Prince.' His mouth tightened into a hard smile. 'But please remember that I do speak a certain amount of your language.'

Prince Karim moved for the first time. He placed his hand on his heart and bent his head deferentially. 'Your wish must always be my command, Sir Clive.'

Charlotte decided that she must have imagined the hint of irony in the Prince's voice. His expression didn't alter even slightly as he turned to his father and began to speak rapidly, presumably translating Sir Clive's opening words.

The Emir did not seem to be a man much given to wild displays of emotion. When the Prince finished speaking he swivelled his head in Sir Clive's direction and murmured a very brief response.

'His Excellency, my father, wishes me to convey the information that he hears what you say, Sir Clive.'

Sir Clive beamed ingratiatingly. 'Your Excellency has been more than generous in offering me your superb hospitality,' he said, tugging at his waistcoat. 'However, I wish to point out to Your Excellency that I have other obligations to fulfil in the city of Istanbul, and I request your permission to leave the palace early tomorrow morning. Your gate-master this afternoon refused to allow me to leave.'

Charlotte's head jerked up as she and her aunt exchanged surprised glances. Sir Clive surely had no reason to lie at this moment. If so, it seemed that he was as much a prisoner as they were. She listened intently to the murmur of the Prince's translation, wishing passionately that she understood Osmanlica.

Alexander's voice was devoid of all expression as he intoned his father's reply. 'His Excellency urges you to rest after the rigours of your long sea voyage, Sir Clive. He asks me to warn you that he cannot allow you to leave before you are recuperated from the stresses and strains of the past few weeks. He begs you not to trouble yourself with trivial details of commerce or politics so soon after your arrival in this beautiful city. He humbly suggests that you should tell him what urgent business requires your attention so that he may assist you in completing it.'

Only the presence of a dozen armed servants restrained Sir Clive from doing physical violence to the sleepy-eyed Emir. 'His Excellency, your father, is too kind,' he said through gritted teeth. 'But my business unfortunately requires immediate *personal* attention. Much as I regret relinquishing the exquisite pleasures of your father's hospitality, I really must leave first thing tomorrow morning.'

Charlotte thought she detected the faintest gleam of amusement in Prince Karim's eyes as he translated the Emir's reply. 'His Excellency, my father, bids you to learn the virtue of patience, Sir Clive. He also points out that the Grand Vizier is temporarily indisposed and not receiving visitors.'

Sir Clive stretched his lips into a smile. 'Your Excellency was good enough to command me to find your son, the Prince Karim Alexander, and to persuade him to return to Istanbul. I have not only fulfilled your command, but in addition I bring you an extra gift of two English women to add to the treasures of your harem. They are both comely, but I am sure you will find the younger one to be of surpassing beauty. Her complexion and hair alone make her worthy of note even by so great a connoisseur of feminine charms as Your Excellency. Her skin carries the bloom of a fresh peach, and her hair is the colour of spun gold.'

He stepped forward, planning to raise Charlotte's veil so that the Emir could admire her attributes, but Prince Karim moved swiftly to prevent him.

'Do not unveil these women if you value your life,' he said, his voice quiet but deadly.

Taken aback, Sir Clive allowed his hand to fall to his side. Then he realised that he was delighted by the Prince's unexpected intervention. His eyes took on a malicious gleam as he looked up at the tense figure. 'My dear sir!' he murmured, rather pleased with his convincing portrayal of shocked outrage. 'I cannot believe that you honour His Excellency the Emir so little that you would deprive him of a gift freely offered by one of his friends. That, surely, is not the act of a loving son. He will not be pleased when he discovers what you have done. Despite my inadequate command of your language I really feel constrained to inform the Emir that I bring him a gift.'

Well pleased with himself, Sir Clive turned to the Emir and did his best to convey in fractured Turkish that the two luscious women standing in front of him were intended as additions to his harem.

The Emir's gaze flicked appraisingly over Charlotte and Lady Adeline then switched to his son. 'Is there something you wish to say on the subject of this gift, Prince Karim Alexander?'

The haze of fury melted from in front of Alexander's eyes. Schooling his features into impassivity, he forced himself to betray no hint of unseemly emotion in front of his father's household. Charlotte and Lady Adeline could only be saved now by his personal intervention, and he owed them his protection. It was too late for regrets, too late to bemoan the fact that he was on such bad terms with his father, too late to think that he should have found some way to prevent Sir Clive exploiting this situation.

Alexander knelt swiftly in front of the Emir's divan, feeling a tremor of excitement unfurl deep inside his heart. He tried to ignore the sensation. This was not the moment to analyse what such a tremor might mean. Certainly it could not mean that he secretly rejoiced at the need to throw the mantle of his safekeeping over Charlotte. Why would he rejoice at such an obvious inconvenience?

'Your Excellency, and most honoured father,' he said, rising again to his feet. 'I beg your forgiveness for failing to translate the words of Sir Clive Bottomley, your guest, but there has been a grievous misunderstanding. My life was saved by the efforts of the two English women who have been brought before you, and, in truth, I owe them more than we can repay. Moreover their family in England is an important one, high in the councils of the English King. It would not be wise to offend them. Sir Clive wishes to offer these women to you as a gift for your harem, but in truth they cannot be so offered.'

The Emir clicked his fingers and the serving-boy immediately sprang to his feet, handing him the silver goblet. 'Why not?' he asked.

Alexander wished that he could simply explain what a violation of English honour and custom would be involved in such a transaction but he suspected that his father, although an exceptionally intelligent man, would not be able to grasp concepts so foreign to his tradition. A gift, once offered, could not be rejected honourably, and Alexander knew that only one course of action would save Charlotte and Lady Adeline from lifelong incarceration in the Emir's harem. He had to show, beyond any shadow of doubt, that the women were not free to be given away. He drew in a deep breath.

'First you should know, Excellency, that Sir Clive Bottomley is no friend of mine, or even of yours. He offers you these women, knowing he thereby does me great wrong. I promised to wed Charlotte Rippon, the younger of the two English women. The older lady, who is Charlotte Rippon's aunt, accompanied her niece to this country according to the customs of the English tradition. My promise to protect Charlotte Rippon and her aunt has been given to her brothers. The betrothal papers are signed. In all ways, save for the wedding ceremony, Charlotte Rippon is already my bride. Therefore, obviously, she cannot be given into your keeping.'

The Emir raised himself slightly against his cushions, the faintest flicker of interest lightening his dark eyes. 'In all ways save for the ceremony? Are you telling me, my son, that your marriage to this English woman has already been consummated?'

Alexander swiftly debated the merits of lying. One more untruth added to the pile he had just presented to his father scarcely seemed worth bothering about. However, he could see no advantage to lying so he told the truth.

'No, Excellency. Our betrothal has been formalised according to the traditions of her people, but the wedding ceremony has not yet taken place. Charlotte Rippon is still a virgin, but she is contracted to me by honour, by my word and by the traditions of her country.'

The Emir looked at his son's studiously impassive features and felt a surge of emotion that hovered somewhere between deep joy and faint amusement. Allah be praised, but it seemed that Alexander the Invulnerable had allowed a woman to creep into his heart at last. The emotion pulsing as a deep undertone to Alexander's words had not been put there by duty or honour. It sprang, the Emir did not doubt, from desire. A burning desire to possess the Englishwoman Charlotte.

The Emir studied the two women in front of him, wondering what qualities of enticement lay hidden beneath the clinging folds of Charlotte Rippon's veil. He had been reading widely these past three years and he knew that in England, as in other European countries, women were allowed to move freely among the men. He didn't doubt that Alexander had seen Charlotte Rippon's face many times, and even spent hours talking to her in private. It was intriguing to think that after all these years—and all those concubines!—his son had finally found the woman who could penetrate the camel-hide thickness of his indifference. He suspected that her mind, as much as her body, must have lit the spark that set his son's desires to burning.

With all the advantages of hindsight the Emir realised that he should have found a foreign bride for his son as soon as little Fatima died. The Emir's household might think that Alexander had remained unwed because he mourned his dead wife but the Emir knew better. Alexander had felt stifled by the prospect of another marriage contracted according to the customs of the Ottoman Empire. He had wed his first wife out of duty and nothing more. He had grieved for her death in childbirth, but his grief had been impersonal—sorrow for a young life cut off too soon and sorrow for an infant son too weak to fight off the jinns who had stolen away his breath. Perhaps it was the threat of another similar marriage that had sent him running into the battlefields of Greece.

He would talk to his son, the Emir decided suddenly. Not tomorrow, perhaps, but some time very soon. Perhaps there were reasons why he had chosen to betray his country and fight alongside the Greek rebels. In the meantime he knew that his son was honourable at heart, even if his actions seemed inexplicable. Whereas that skulking dog, Sir Clive, had probably never experienced an honest emotion in his entire life. If Sir Clive wanted to give him the English women for his harem and Alexander wanted one of them to wed, it wasn't difficult for the Emir to decide that his son should be allowed to do as he wished. He sipped honey-sweetened pomegranate juice from his silver goblet then rose to his feet, rather pleased by the drama inherent in his exit.

Ah, you're becoming a showman in your old age, he chided himself, and frowned ferociously to hide the pleased smile that threatened to form itself on his lips. Perhaps, after all, he would live long enough to see the sons of his son.

The silence in the great hall beat pleasurably against his ears. 'Prince Karim Alexander, you have my blessing upon your forthcoming marriage. I expect the wedding to be celebrated within three days. Begin the necessary celebrations first thing tomorrow morning.'

Alexander salaamed courteously. 'It shall be as you wish, Excellency. I am honoured by your blessing.'

'You will come to my room at noon tomorrow so that we may talk of your marriage and of other things.'

Alexander raised his head, meeting his father's eyes with a hint of challenge. 'It is my deepest wish, Excellency, to explain to you what I have been doing during the three years of my absence.'

The Emir swung abruptly on his heel, scarcely noticing the serving-boy and half a dozen male guards who fell into a step behind him. As the damask curtain into his private rooms closed behind him he heard Sir Clive's high-pitched voice demand to know what had been said. The Emir smiled. He wondered what the pompous ass of an Englishman would say if he knew the Emir spoke quite passable English.

'Oh, dear heaven, he's gone and I never even asked to see the British Ambassador,' Lady Adeline wailed. 'One minute the wretched man's lying there half asleep, and the next minute he's disappeared!'

'Don't worry, Aunt,' Charlotte said wearily. 'I don't think we would be seeing the Ambassador any time soon, even if you'd been allowed to speak.'

'Prince Karim, I *demand* to know what your father said.' Sir Clive's fair complexion was rapidly turning to purple. 'Are the women to be taken into his harem? And has he arranged for me to leave the palace? It is imperative that I go now—tonight!'

'You must be patient, Sir Clive. Is that not a lesson you urged Miss Rippon to learn? His Excellency the Emir wishes you to relax and enjoy his hospitality.'

'But I don't *wish* to enjoy his hospitality, dammit!'

The irony in Alexander's voice became more pronounced. 'When contemplating treachery, Sir Clive, a wise man remembers that it is much easier to walk into a den of lions than it is to walk out.'

'For heaven's sake, you don't suppose I entered this palace voluntarily, do you?' Sir Clive screeched. 'I was supposed to go straight to the Grand Vizier's cabinet in the Sultan's palace, but your father *abducted* me. Sent his damned servants to the boat and forced me to come here. It's an outrage, I tell you, an absolute outrage, and the Grand Vizier will hear about it, I warn you!'

'Dear me, it certainly seems that he should. Because you, Sir Clive, would never dream of abducting anybody, would you?'

The spluttering Sir Clive showed every sign of succumbing to apoplexy, and Charlotte was astonished to hear herself giggle. A dozen pairs of accusing eyes immediately turned in her direction. Laughing, it seemed, was yet another breach of the rules governing female behaviour. The Chief Eunuch took a menacing step towards her, but he retreated at the merest hint of a restraining gesture from the Prince.

Encouraged by the thought that perhaps some trace of 'Mr Alexander' still lingered beneath the crimson robes and haughty exterior of Prince Karim, Charlotte plucked up the courage to address him directly. 'Sir. . .Your Excellency. . .would you please explain to us what has happened? Has your father given orders for my aunt and me to be set free?'

Alexander turned slowly, not sure if he was ready to look at her. She was trying so hard not to sound scared—just as he was trying not to respond to her vulnerability. Her eyes shone bright with hope beneath the veil. She looked so damn trusting. . .and altogether too desirable for his peace of mind. Not to mention his peace of body, he reflected ruefully, allowing his gaze to run hungrily over her silk-misted form.

Deliberately he cut off the dangerous surge of tenderness. His harem was full of desirable female bodies and Charlotte was merely one more. A body, moreover, that he had no intention of touching. This marriage would be a legal fiction lasting long enough to get her and Lady Adeline safely out of Istanbul. The sooner it was contracted, the sooner he would be able to set her free, and then they would both return to the original course of their lives. Charlotte would sail back to England and he would sail to Brindisi to see if he could meet up with Hank Barrett.

But in the meantime how was he to explain to her that she really had no choice other than to marry him? However much he racked his brains, Alexander couldn't think of any tactful way to inform Charlotte that the pair of them would be married within three days. He looked at Lady Adeline, wondering if she would faint when she heard the news. On balance, he thought wryly, it might be rather convenient if she did. In any event there was no point in delaying the inevitable, so he drew in a deep breath and plunged into speech.

'You ask what arrangements have been made for your future, Miss Rippon,' he began cautiously. 'I explained to His Excellency the Emir that you and your aunt were not free to be given into his keeping.'

'Oh, well done, dear sir!' Lady Adeline exclaimed. 'I knew we could count on you! Will the British Ambassador be sending somebody to escort us home soon?'

'Er—not exactly.' Alexander tried to explain the Byzantine intricacies of their current situation. Failing hopelessly, he took refuge in a curt summation of his father's instructions.

'His Excellency the Emir has agreed to release you both from his harem on condition that Miss Rippon and I are married within the next three days. I have informed him that we are both looking forward to the ceremony.'

'Married!' Charlotte exclaimed, her voice shaking. 'But how can we be married? We're not even betr——'

He intervened swiftly, cutting off her denials. 'Celebrations for a Turkish wedding can often last more than a week. However, my father has ordered that in our case the preparations should be completed three days from tonight. He himself has graciously consented to officiate at the ceremonies on Friday—a most auspicious day.'

'On Friday!' Lady Adeline exclaimed in unison with her niece. Sir Clive simultaneously recovered his voice and burst into protest. 'This is absolutely preposterous! I have never heard such a farrago of nonsense in all my days. Married! You and Charlotte Rippon married—the very idea of it is absurd!'

Alexander decided that he'd had about all he could take of Sir Clive. Eventually the wretched man would be allowed to 'escape' so that he could carry his false information to the Grand Vizier, but it was still several days too early for such an escape to appear convincing. In the meantime the Prince couldn't resist administering the pompous, scheming baronet a small dose of his own medicine.

'Sir Clive, you overstep the bounds of courtesy,' he said coldly. He clicked his fingers and two of his father's guards appeared, curved scimitars raised with deadly intent. Alexander ran his finger meditatively along the glittering flat of the blade, meanwhile murmuring a couple of low-voiced instructions.

In a split second Sir Clive's face turned from livid puce to deathly pallor. 'Wh-what are y-you telling them, Prince Karim? I meant no discourtesy. I'm sure your marriage is a wonderful idea and M-Miss Rippon the image of perfection.'

'Do not speak her name again,' Alexander ordered with sweeping arrogance, concealing a grin with difficulty. 'Sir Clive, I believe your presence is no longer required.' He nodded curtly to the waiting guards.

Sheathing their weapons, the two men each seized one of Sir Clive's quivering arms. They salaamed deeply, forcing Sir Clive to bow with them, then marched rapidly out of the hall.

White-lipped, Charlotte watched the trio depart. 'Dear God, what will happen to him?' she asked.

'What do you think will happen to him, Miss Rippon?'

She gulped. 'You have. . .you have ordered him beheaded?'

He smiled tightly. 'Not quite. He is to spend the evening in his room, eating the best food we have to offer and watching some of my father's dancing girls. You need not fear for him, Miss Rippon. I save my rat-infested dungeons for prisoners who will not dishonour the rats.'

Once again Charlotte was glad of the veil which hid her fiery cheeks. 'Sir. . .Prince Karim. . .do you not think that for once Sir Clive has some measure of right on his side? The idea of our marrying on Friday is absurd. I think the Emir cannot have understood the situation——'

'Miss Rippon, believe me, there has been no misunderstanding.' He spoke as quietly as he could, praying his father would not be able to hear. 'You have a clear-cut choice to make, a choice that affects your aunt as much as it does you. We can be married on Friday, and you will then join my household with your aunt. Or you may both remain permanently as concubines in the Emir's harem. As my wife, Miss Rippon, your chances of a return to England will be infinitely greater than as my father's concubine. In the circumstances, do you find the decision so difficult?'

Only because she loved him, Charlotte realised with a sudden, blinding flash of self-awareness. Only because at the advanced age of five-and-twenty she still harboured the secret girlish fantasy of marrying a man who loved her as passionately and as deeply as she loved him. Marrying Prince Karim would be a torment if it meant that she was compelled to compete for his attentions with ten or fifteen other women. Dear heaven, what was she supposed to say? Captivity in the Emir's harem might mean boredom and physical degradation. Captivity in Karim Alexander's harem would mean a lifetime of searing, seething jealousy and unfulfilled dreams. She gazed down at the curling toes of her shoes, tongue-tied by the enormity of her own feelings.

Lady Adeline, however, was not afflicted with any such excess of emotion. Despite all she had recently endured she clearly understood the difference between being a wife and being a concubine. Prince Karim had offered her niece his hand in marriage. And marriage was the goal of every sensible woman, whereas concubinage was a mortal sin. Even worse, it was death to any claim to respectability. If Charlotte became the concubine of the Emir Ibrahim her life in England would be over. If she married the Prince she could return to Rippon Manor on a cloud of glory.

Lady Adeline's bosom puffed up in proud anticipation. She could on occasion be amazingly practical and this was one of those occasions. Lord knew, Charlotte was sometimes given to the oddest starts, no doubt brought on by her excessive quantity of education, but this time Lady Adeline had every intention of saving her niece from the consequences of her own folly.

'Charlotte,' she said firmly, 'you will thank the Prince for his kind proposal and tell him you are most happy to accept.'

'But Aunt Adeline,' Charlotte murmured desperately, 'you don't understand. This will not be a marriage as you and I understand the term——'

'Charlotte, my dear, marriage is marriage and you are not in a position to quibble about details.' Lady Adeline turned graciously towards the Prince. 'Charlotte is delighted to accept your offer of marriage,' she said. 'We shall look forward to meeting you in Church on Friday.'

Alexander, who had ridden many times into the thick of battle without flinching, discovered all at once that he was a coward. At the prospect of explaining to Lady Adeline just how a Muslim wedding was solemnised he became an abject, cringing coward.

'We shall meet on Friday,' he agreed. 'Meanwhile, the women of my father's harem will help you to prepare for the wedding ceremony.'

He beckoned the Chief Eunuch. 'Please escort my bride and her guardian to the harem of the Emir,' he said in Turkish. 'You will see to it, I know, that they are adequately prepared for the ceremony to come.'

The Chief Eunuch permitted himself the luxury of a very small smile. 'Yes, master. I shall see to it that your bride is adequately prepared.'

After two endless days and nights the preliminary ceremonies had all been completed, and the culminating moment approached. The wedding procession had formed in readiness to conduct Charlotte out of the Emir's harem and into the specially decorated bridal-room where she would meet Prince Karim. The bride and groom would be alone together for no more than a few minutes before separating once again to participate in the two final, lavish wedding feasts: one in the *haremlik* for the women, and the other in the *selamlik* banqueting hall for the men.

Charlotte stared straight ahead, her gaze fixed on the imposing rear view of the Chief Eunuch, who was leading her out of the Emir's harem into the garden which connected with Prince Karim's private quarters. Aunt Adeline walked on her left. Nassarah, the Emir Ibrahim's mother, supported by two serving-girls, walked on her right, and all the women of the harem, ordered by rank, tailed along behind. The late afternoon sun was hot, and Charlotte could feel her skin starting to itch beneath the sequins that had been stuck on to her forehead, cheeks and chin. She wondered if it was considered a bad omen if they fell off.

Their walk, fortunately, was brief. The Chief Eunuch led them across the garden to another door set into the same section of the palace they had just left. Charlotte swallowed over the sudden lump in her throat. The bridal party had arrived at the entrance to the harem of Prince Karim Alexander.

The door stood open in anticipation of their arrival, and Nassarah swept forward to pass a swift exchange of bows and courtesies with the women lined up in the hallway. Charlotte was conducted upstairs and seated on a wooden chair in the corner of a room decked almost from floor to ceiling with coloured silk flowers.

'Now this looks a bit more like a wedding,' Aunt Adeline remarked. 'Those flowers are very pretty. Garish, of course, but that's only to be expected.'

Marie-Claire came over to speak to Charlotte. 'Soon I and the other women of the Emir Ibrahim's household will return to our own section of the harem. The women left here will all be members of Prince Karim Alexander's household.' She paused. 'I think I do not have to warn you, Charlotte, that most of them will not be your friends.'

Charlotte, whose stomach had begun to perform a vigorous Irish jig, did not relish the reminder that she had more problems to contend with than the imminent arrival of her groom. 'I suppose they feel the Prince should have married one of them,' she said.

'They *wish* he had married one of them. That is not quite the same thing.' Marie-Claire's eyes looked suspiciously bright, although she would have been the last person in the world to admit to feeling sentimental in the presence of a bride.

'The Prince and his friends have already left the mosque. On his return he will be urged by his friends to come into this room and lift your veil. Do not be offended if he appears unwilling to enter. It is the tradition, you understand, that he should appear reluctant to meet his bride. He is supposed to be overwhelmed at the prospect of seeing the beauty of your face unveiled.'

'When he lifts your veil he will kiss you,' Miriam explained. 'It is very romantic, is it not? The first kiss of a man for his bride?'

Charlotte thought of the kiss she and the Prince had already exchanged. 'Yes,' she agreed breathlessly. 'It is very romantic.'

'He will give you a Face-See gift,' Alia interjected. 'But he will only kiss you for a little while because his friends will be waiting outside for him to start the feast.'

'After all these feasts surely nobody is hungry!'

'This will be the last one. It will finish early and then Prince Karim will come to take you to his bedchamber.'

'How exciting,' Charlotte said hollowly.

Her sarcasm was entirely lost on the Emir's daughters. 'It is of all things the most exciting,' they agreed in unison. 'We shall look forward to hearing everything that happens when we meet at the bathing-rooms.'

'Of course,' Charlotte said. 'All the details.'

A flurry of anticipation rippled through the women. 'The Prince and his friends are coming! We must go,' Marie-Claire explained. '*Au revoir*, Charlotte. May you and the Prince find many years of joy in each other's company.'

Lady Adeline bent to kiss her niece, tears streaming unashamedly down her cheeks. 'Dearest Charlotte, you look nothing like the bride I once dreamed of seeing in our little village church, and yet I truly think the Prince may be able to make you happy.'

A Highland fling was added to the Scottish reel and the Irish jig already being danced by Charlotte's stomach. She tried to smile, but all she could produce was a hiccup. 'I think, dear Aunt, that you are becoming a relentless optimist.'

Aunt Adeline had time only for a final kiss as Marie-Claire and Miriam virtually tugged her from the room.

In the distance, approaching from an entirely different angle, Charlotte heard the rumble of laughter and deep, male voices. Miriam paused in the doorway, glancing back over her shoulder. 'They are calling out, "The Groom is Coming,"' she explained and ran from the room in the wake of her sister.

A door opened quite close to the bridal chamber and for a moment the sound of laughter and encouraging shouts became almost deafening. Then the door closed again and the sounds of revelry were dimmed. Within the space of a few heartbeats Prince Karim Alexander entered the room.

She had thought him compelling when she saw him two nights previously. Now, clad in a crested turban and a royal blue caftan that was clasped at the waist with a jewel-encrusted gold belt, he was simply magnificent. He strode across the room, no hint of the shy or reluctant groom lingering in his manner now that his friends were not present to observe the performance.

Charlotte's entire body froze into a block of solid ice. The Prince stopped only inches away from her, stretching out his hand to touch the edge of her veil. For an instant her heart stopped beating before it raced forward again at twice its previous speed. It was ridiculous, because Mr Alexander had seen her unveiled face on a hundred different occasions, but this man was Prince Karim, son of the Emir Ibrahim, and she felt as shy as if this were truly the first time he had ever seen her.

Slowly, taking care not to catch the filmy fabric on any of her jewels, he lifted the spangled gauze over her head-dress and allowed it to settle in a soft cloud around her shoulders. Then he crooked his finger beneath her chin, gently forcing her head upwards until her eyes met his.

'I am dazzled by the beauty of my bride,' he said huskily, taking her hands into his clasp. 'You do honour to my gifts of jewels and clothes by deigning to wear them.'

'Th-thank you,' she whispered. 'You look—er—you look nice, too.'

She thought she saw the faintest trace of a smile on his lips before he raised her hands and kissed the tips of her fingers. Her hands began to burn with a tingling, icy fire. It must be the henna, she thought. That's why they dye a bride's hands scarlet—so that she will feel this incredible tingling sensation.

The Prince reached inside his caftan to extract a small, linen-wrapped package tied with coloured ribbons. 'Please accept this small gift as a token of my delight in the start of our marriage,' he said, placing the embroidered handkerchief in her lap. Without giving her any chance to react he bent towards her. Before Charlotte realised what he planned to do he had pressed his lips to her forehead, cheeks and chin in the precise spots decorated by the sequins. Goodness me! she thought wildly. The sequins have just the same peculiar effect as the henna.

He stepped back, the formality of his manner unexpectedly dropping from him, like a cloak shed at the outer door. 'Charlotte, I must go. It is considered an insult to the bride as well as to my guests if I stay alone with you too long. Tonight, when we have more time, I will explain everything. Take heart, Charlotte. You need not fear the hours ahead. This marriage will be in name only; you have my word.'

He turned on his heel in a whirl of royal-blue satin and she strained to hear the muted sounds of his footsteps retreating along the hallway. The door into the *selamlik*, the men's quarters, opened on to a burst of cheering and music-filled festivity, then quiet descended once again.

Charlotte sat, staring blindly at the Prince's gift of a handkerchief. A tuft of white hem poked through her grotesque bright red fingers, startling in the contrast of colours. For no explicable reason she burst into tears.

The bridal chamber was immediately filled with a bevvy of women, all proffering cambric squares for her to dry her eyes. A mixture of envy, sympathy and longing appeared plainly on their faces as they removed Charlotte's floor-length veil and began to brush her hair. Nobody in the Prince's harem spoke English or French, but by gestures they indicated that Charlotte should open her present.

Only too willing to have something to contemplate other than the battered state of her emotions, Charlotte untied the little package. Inside, instead of the comfits or hard sugar plums she had expected, lay a pair of sapphire earrings, the stones mounted in an exquisite setting of filigree gold.

The gasps of awe from the women were accompanied by gestures obviously designed to indicate that she should put on her new jewels. She did as she was asked, feeling the delicate gold quiver coldly against her skin. A round of applause greeted her action and servants began to carry in platters and trays of food, including a huge steaming bowl of orange-coloured saffron rice. Charlotte's stomach rebelled at the prospect of absorbing any more food. She ate a spoonful of the traditional bridal rice, then pushed aside her plate of unleavened bread. For once the women didn't urge her to eat against her will.

They themselves made short work of the meal, although they lingered with obvious enjoyment over the thick coffee and the sticky, honey-drenched array of sweetmeats. Once hands had been washed and the trays cleared away the women whispered to each other with knowing nods and smiles until, at yet another of the signals that always remained invisible to Charlotte, they all sprang to their feet, waited while the serving-girls re-draped her in the spangled wedding veil, then bowed deeply and retreated from the room.

The bridal chamber filled with silence, a silence so profound that Charlotte was sure that she could hear each individual beat of her heart. She heard no warning sounds, but she still knew the precise moment when the Prince crossed the threshold of the door.

'I'm sorry I was so long,' he said quietly. 'Will you come with me to my bedchamber? I think it's probably the only place in the entire palace where we can be alone to talk.'

She stood up, stiff from too many hours of sitting on the hard wooden chair. He extended his arm in the English fashion and, after a moment's hesitation, she accepted his offer of support.

'Good,' he said, smiling a little. 'Shall we scandalise the ladies of the harem by walking along the corridor to my room arm-in-arm?'

'Why would they be scandalised and, anyway, how will they ever know?'

'How will they know?' He laughed. 'Charlotte, my dear, you have spent three days in my father's palace already, so you must have discovered that it's impossible for a mere male to keep anything secret from the ladies of the harem. Look around you as we walk down the hallway. Every closet and every wall niche will have a pair of eyes peeking out through some crack in the decoration.'

'But why will they be scandalised?'

'We are in Istanbul, not London. Here men and women never walk arm-in-arm. In fact, as you must have observed, men and women are very rarely together at all.'

They had, by this time, progressed along some twenty feet of hallway. Charlotte swallowed a giggle as she glanced towards one of the decorative wall cupboards, designed to hold bedrolls during the daytime, and discovered herself being observed by a pair of very wide, very shocked brown eyes.

The Prince stopped outside an arched door. 'This is the entrance to my private suite of rooms,' he said. 'When I returned to Istanbul after completing my studies I had them decorated in a style somewhere between the European and the Oriental. I hope you will find them attractive.'

Her nervousness returned with overwhelming force as the Prince opened the door and ushered her into a spacious, white-ceilinged room with windows set Turkish-style between decorative arches. She looked hurriedly away from the bed, fixing her gaze instead upon the two comfortable armchairs, each flanked by a small boulle table. The wall behind the chairs was lined with shelves crammed full of books. The first books she had seen since boarding Sir Clive's ship, she realised.

'Why don't we sit down?' the Prince suggested. 'Nobody will disturb us here.'

Charlotte didn't find that thought particularly comforting. He must have felt the sudden stiffness of her hand against his arm. 'Charlotte,' he said, turning her gently towards him, 'I have told you there is nothing for you to fear from me tonight. We are only going to talk together, which is surely something we have done with pleasure many times before.'

Her breath caught on a subdued gasp of laughter. 'Then you were Mr Alexander. Now you are the Prince Karim.'

'No,' he said softly. 'Then and now I was Alexander, just as then you were Charlotte Rippon, and now—now you are still Charlotte.'

She turned abruptly, twisting away from him. 'I don't feel like the same person,' she said in a small voice. 'I feel as if I no longer know myself. I look in the mirror and there is nobody there I recognise.'

'Charlotte, let me take off your veil.'

His deep-voiced request brought a flare of heat rushing into her cheeks. You're English, Charlotte, she reminded herself. You don't care if every man in the world sees your face.

She forced a casual smile. 'Well, yes, of course, we must take it off. In fact, I'd almost forgotten it was still on.'

'First we will need to remove your head-dress.' He unpinned the silk-padded diadem that held her veil in position and placed it on one of the boulle tables. Then, as he had done before in the bridal chamber, he slowly lifted her veil until her face was completely uncovered. The words they had both meant to speak died away, unremembered and unspoken.

She appeared more beautiful every time he saw her,

Alexander thought helplessly. The blush on her cheeks tinted her complexion with the pink of an English rose, and her eyes were brilliant with unshed tears. He could only guess at the incredible courage it required for a woman from her background not to give way to panic at the situation in which she found herself.

He touched her lips with the tip of his finger and felt them tremble beneath the fleeting caress. He was swept by a wave of tenderness so intense that he took her into his arms without any thought for the consequences. His hands wove into the golden softness of her hair, drawing her against him. She looked up, startled and a little scared—but totally, *damnably* trusting.

He wouldn't betray that trust, Alexander promised himself. He had given his word that his marriage would remain unconsummated, and he had never yet broken his word.

'It's very odd to think we're married,' Charlotte said, her words muffled against his shoulder. 'I don't really feel married. We never exchanged vows and there was no minister——'

'Marriage isn't a religious celebration for Muslims,' Alexander explained distractedly.

'Then how do people know when they're legally wed?'

'The two families exchange written contracts.'

'But my family is in England.'

'In the circumstances, I acted on your behalf,' he said quickly, not wanting to raise the issue of the Rippon family signatures he had forged. Dear God, her mouth was so incredibly desirable! Phrases like 'petal-soft' and 'rosebud-fresh' danced around in his mind. Surely there would be no harm in kissing her? Nobody in England was ever going to know what had transpired in Istanbul, and as long as she was still a virgin her hopes of a respectable marriage would be as good as ever.

He would only kiss her for a moment, Alexander swore to himself. A brief, reassuring kiss just like the ones he used to give his younger sisters. There couldn't possibly be any harm in a friendly, affectionate kiss.

Even while he debated the wisdom of what he was about to do his head was descending slowly, inexorably towards her lips. When their mouths were no more than a breath apart he held himself back for a split second. Then their mouths touched—and he was lost.

Her lips were warm and soft with surprise, and they tasted of honey. His hands framed her face, holding her captive as he drank in the delicious taste of her. He felt her stiffen as their kiss deepened and once again he tried to draw away, but somehow his body was no longer working in harmony with his mind. His conscience reminded him that he had sworn to preserve Charlotte's innocence. His tongue, meanwhile, caressed the outline of her mouth, arrogantly demanding admission.

She parted her lips on a tiny sigh of bewildered acquiescence, and Alexander chose to ignore the rapid increase in his state of arousal. He explored the hot sweetness of her mouth as his hands caressed the length of her spine then curved around her hips, urging her close to his body. The warm pressure of her belly against his erection was torment of the most enchanting kind but, even through the stiff satin of their wedding clothes, he could feel the fear beginning to tremble through her.

The claims of his conscience slowly reasserted their control over the demands of his body and, with great reluctance, he broke off their kiss.

It was a long time—a very long time—since he had last experienced such difficulty in curbing his own desire. He didn't doubt there was something distinctly comical about his situation: a man blessed with a brand new wife and a harem full of concubines who nevertheless seemed destined to spend the night in a state of sexual abstinence. Perhaps in a few years' time he'd be able to laugh at the absurdity of it all. At this precise moment he found it difficult to appreciate the joke.

His breathing was still shallow and uneven when he finally drew away from Charlotte. He ran his hands down her back one last time, then walked determinedly to the other side of the room.

'The servants have left us *serbet* for our refreshment. Shall we sit down in the chairs and drink some while we talk?'

'Sherbet?' she questioned, looking a little dazed—and adorably aroused.

Overcoming her resistance would be so easy, Alexander thought. Her body was ready for him, even if her innocence caused her to deny the attraction. He could so easily carry her over to the bed, where he would slowly unfasten the traditional one hundred buttons of her caftan, kissing her each time one of the satin fastenings surrendered to his touch. Her breasts would be full and firm and he would take her nipples into his mouth——

'*Serbet* is our traditional drink of sweetened and thickened fruit juice,' he explained hurriedly, turning away in an affort to control his rising passion. 'I'm sure you have tasted it several times already.'

'Oh, yes, it's very good. And on my way here to the palace I saw men selling it in the street. But thank you, I'm not thirsty.'

'As you wish.' Alexander poured himself a drink, chiefly because it gave him something to do other than seize Charlotte and start ripping off her clothes. God knew, they had plenty to talk about. Surely he ought to be able to think of something other than how desirable she would look lying naked against the silken cushions of his bed. . .

Alexander poured himself another drink. This ridiculous daydreaming had to stop. Perhaps if he told Charlotte his plans for her future they would both be able to relax and get some sleep.

He walked over to the window where she was standing, staring out into the darkness. 'The scent of the flowers becomes even stronger at night,' she said as he came up behind her. 'It doesn't smell at all like an English garden even though some of the flowers are the same.'

It had been a mistake to come so close to her. When she was near he didn't want to waste time telling her how simple it was for a Muslim to get divorced. He didn't want to tell her that before he left for Greece he would book passage for her and her aunt on some respectable ship returning to England. When she was near all he wanted to do was hold her.

His arms slipped around her waist, pulling her back against his body. 'Do you miss England very much?' he asked softly.

'Usually only at night, when I'm alone. In the day too much has been happening recently and there has been no time for regrets. And in some ways, when I'm not feeling scared, seeing so many strange new things is very interesting.'

He smiled down at her. When he was with Charlotte he found that he often wanted to smile. 'Tonight you will not be alone,' he said huskily. 'And I will try to leave you no time for regrets.'

She looked up, her eyes betraying uncertainty about his meaning. Whatever she saw in his face caused her breath to come more quickly and brought a hectic flush of colour to her cheeks.

Alexander knew in that instant that he didn't have the will-power to send her away from his bed untouched. He wanted to see her naked beneath him. He wanted to be inside her, watching her body convulse with pleasure as he thrust deep into her. He wanted to hear her cry of joy in their final moments of ecstasy. He wanted to possess her, and claim her innocence for his own.

You have no right to take her virginity, an aggravating inner voice reminded him. Your life will probably be forfeit in Greece, even if you manage to escape the machinations of the Grand Vizier. And suppose, by some miracle, you do survive the battlefronts of Greece; what do you have to offer a gently reared English girl?

Alexander forced the unpleasant truths from his mind. Even if he made love to Charlotte he knew how to protect her from the calamity of bearing his child. After poor little Fatima died in childbirth he had made sure that none of his concubines ever became pregnant. Charlotte would still be able to marry her respectable Englishman, he assured himself. Nothing would change because of one short night spent in each other's arms. And he would bring her pleasure such as she had never imagined possible, he vowed. A gratification of the senses that would transport her into a realm of enchantment.

'Alexander?' Her hesitant question interrupted his

attempts at self-justification. 'Can you tell me what is going to happen to my aunt and me?'

'Don't worry, I will take care of everything,' he said grandly. 'Trust me, sweet Charlotte.'

A tiny smile tugged at her lips. 'You would look a great deal more trustworthy, you know, if you took off your hat.'

He pretended indignity. 'You don't find this exquisite creation to your taste?'

She shook her head and he laughed, tossing his turban carelessly towards one of the chairs. 'Better?'

'Yes, thank you. Much better.' She smiled diffidently. 'Now you look a little bit more like Mr Alexander.'

'And that is pleasing to you?'

Shyly she snuggled her face against his chest. 'It is pleasing to me,' she whispered.

'Well, I would never have believed that such a boring fellow could find favour with you. But, since he did, from now on I shall make sure only to seek you out when I am feverish, muddy, blood-spattered and generally incoherent. How depressing to think that when I am in full possession of my faculties you no longer care for my company.'

She laughed, the silvery laugh he treasured in his memory. 'With enough time I dare say I could learn to tolerate your company even when your wits aren't wandering.'

'I shall live in hope.'

She smiled, obviously completely unaware of what the little wriggles of her body were doing to him. Thank God, or maybe Praise Allah, that Turkish wedding clothes were so concealing, otherwise his state of arousal would be obvious even to one of her innocence. Patience, he reminded himself. Charlotte was probably more naïve than the youngest and least sophisticated of brides in this part of the world. Given the English prudery in sexual matters, he might find himself explaining step by step what he was doing before the night was over. A somewhat intimidating prospect, he reflected ruefully, even for a man of his experience.

'You are so silent,' she said quietly. 'What are you thinking, Alexander?'

He looked down at her, no longer making any attempt to conceal his desire. 'I am thinking that I want to kiss you.'

'How odd,' she whispered. 'We were both thinking the same thing.'

'A truly amazing coincidence,' Alexander breathed. Then his lips covered hers in an endless, passionate kiss.

She was drowning, Charlotte thought dreamily, drowning slowly in the waves of delicious sensation swamping her body. The only way to stay afloat was to cling to Alexander and let him support her. Oddly enough, the closer she got to him, the more waves rolled over her body and the more she needed his support. She clasped her hands behind his neck, running her fingers frantically through his thick, dark hair. Her body was slowly dissolving into liquid fire. She hoped it would be a long time before she finally disintegrated.

Somewhat belatedly Charlotte remembered that virtuous ladies were not supposed to enjoy their wifely duties. Horrified, because Alexander must already have guessed how much she liked being kissed, she screwed her eyes tightly shut and tried her best to think about England. But, instead of serene summer sunsets, all she could think about was how wonderful it felt when Alexander's tongue slowly, caressingly explored her mouth. Her breasts were heavy and aching and she suddenly thought how wonderful it would feel if he caressed her breasts with his tongue, the way he was caressing her mouth. The image was so clear, and so appallingly wicked, that she gave a little gasp and momentarily froze in his arms.

Immediately, Alexander drew back. 'I'm sorry, Charlotte. Did I hurt you?'

'No, you didn't hurt me. It's just that we shouldn't. . . I think that I should not. . .'

Alexander smiled. 'Sweet Charlotte, do not think, just allow yourself to feel.' His voice was a velvet caress, seducing her back into blissful lethargy. His thumbs traced the outline of her lips then trailed reverently down the whiteness of her throat. 'Does it not feel good when I touch you so?' he murmured.

It felt far more than good, it felt positively wonderful, and Charlotte gave up her attempts to remain limp and unresponsive in his arms. She made a final half-hearted protest when he swung her up into his arms and carried her across to the bed.

'Alexander, please listen to me. We must not do this. It isn't. . .it can't be right for us. . .'

'Why not?' he asked simply. 'We are married, Charlotte, and we have every right to share this night together. Trust me, sweetheart, you have nothing to fear. I will take care of you; you have my promise.'

Those words again. 'Trust me'. Her brain sent out one last faint warning signal, a feeble reminder that so far Alexander had provided very few logical reasons for her to trust him. But he kissed her again before she could form a coherent protest, the touch of his mouth burning away logic as his mouth left a trail of fire from her lips to her throat. He insinuated skilled, knowing fingers into the flow of golden hair that tumbled over her shoulders, spreading it out over the pillows, and her body arched instinctively towards him.

Unhurriedly his mouth sought hers as he began to unfasten the buttons on her wedding gown, kissing her each time he opened the caftan a little further, so that she soon lost all awareness of how masterfully she was being seduced. Drugged by desire, she watched his face, mesmerised by the passion tautening his features even though, until this moment, she had never understood the meaning of the word.

His eyes were slumberous, dark and heavy with desire as he finally eased the gown from her shoulders, revealing the thin white muslin of her chemise. 'Dear God, you are even lovelier than I imagined you would be,' he murmured, his fingers lightly grazing her breasts. Lowering his head, he slowly drew one of her nipples into his mouth, kissing her through the thin muslin.

Charlotte gasped. Her fantasy had not prepared her for the intensity of her pleasure. No longer in control of her own body, she trembled at the wild sensations his touch aroused, her breath rasping harshly in her throat as he removed her chemise and kissed her naked breasts. Her hands clutched randomly at the silken coverings of the bed as his fingers stroked along her thighs, turning her core to flame. Reality at that moment was bounded by the curtains of the bed and the magic that Alexander was working on her body. She felt no shame, only frustration, when he stood up to strip off his clothes, tossing aside the jewel-laden belt and heavy silk caftan with quick, impatient movements.

She met his lips with fierce abandon when they descended to claim hers once again. Intuitively she sensed that Alexander's kisses were hungrier, less controlled than they had been earlier and she experienced an unfamiliar thrill of satisfaction when she felt his hands tremble as he caressed her breasts.

But Alexander didn't allow his own passion to outrun Charlotte's arousal. A master in the art of seduction, he brought her to a state of mindless, white-hot readiness. His kisses left her aching, craving for something more, and the touch of his hair-roughened chest against her naked breasts set her body on fire. Their thighs rubbed together, his muscles hard against her softness, burning hot against her heat. With a little moan of pleasure she pressed against him, trying to ease the odd pain seething deep inside her, a pain that wasn't really a pain but an ache of pleasure, coiling itself tighter and tighter until she wanted to cry out for release.

Sensing her readiness, Alexander slowly moved his hand between her thighs. Her body stiffened immediately, and yet he detected almost as much desire as panic in the instinctive tensing of her muscles.

'Sweet Charlotte, you must not close yourself against me now,' he said thickly. 'Let me bring you to the ultimate pleasure. Let me touch you here.'

She could not admit the terrible truth that she wanted him to touch her. Surely no other woman, even in Turkey, had ever willingly allowed her husband to take such incredible liberties with her body? She twisted her head away, burying it in the pillow so that she would not have to look at Alexander. At the same time, with a shudder of shamed surrender, she opened her thighs.

The probing touch of his fingers was the sweetest of torments, and Charlotte felt reason spin away from her as sensation radiated out from the gentle, persistent caress of his hand. Tension gathered within her, convulsing her body, but the hunger for release seemed only to grow and, of their own accord, her hips began to move, rising rhythmically to the touch of his hand.

He had always sensed the core of passion hidden beneath Charlotte's cool English reserve, Alexander thought, and now he was sharing in the joy of its release. He kissed her passion-swollen lips, experiencing a surge of masculine triumph as he felt her body quiver at every slight stroke of his finger. The temptation to enter her now was enormous, the strain of fighting back the demands of his own body almost more than he could bear but, for the first time in his life, the satisfaction of the woman in bed with him seemed more important than the clamorous needs of his own body.

'We are nearly there, sweetheart,' he murmured against her mouth, trembling from the effort of holding himself back. He heard the tiny gasp of astonishment as pleasure finally exploded inside her. Her body arched into his, curving into his hand, waves of satisfaction pulsing through her and washing him with their warmth.

Dazed by what had happened, Charlotte turned slowly to look at her husband. Alexander's eyes were dark with hunger, his skin drawn tight with the strain of control. Then he smiled, and her heart seemed to turn a giant somersault. 'That was only the beginning,' he said softly. 'Now let me show you the rest.'

There couldn't possibly be anything more. Charlotte knew that it was going to take at least a hundred years before her body recovered from the amazing things that had happened to it during the past half-hour. She lay limp and passive in Alexander's arms, only vaguely aware of what he was doing until she felt his hands slide under her hips, lifting her to receive him and pressing inexorably against the resistance of her virginity.

Passivity vanished in a burst of pain. She twisted away

from his kiss, her eyes flying open. She cried out once, biting her lip to control the sounds.

'I'm sorry,' Alexander said gravely, stroking the hair away from her sweat-dampened brow. 'The first time there is no way to avoid a little pain. I think it is all over now.'

She closed her eyes, not believing him, and he murmured, 'I'm sorry,' again before bending his head to claim her mouth in a long, passionate kiss.

He wished with all his heart that he had not hurt her. He wanted to see the incredulous joy return to her face when she reached the ultimate pinnacle. He lay still within her, contained and disciplined, kissing her and caressing her breasts until the hardening of her nipples and the little shudders of her body told him what he wanted to know. Then he began to move slowly, carefully. His body ached with the need to thrust hard into her, but he would not do it. He would be gentle for her. He would do nothing to increase the pain he had already inflicted.

At first Charlotte didn't recognise what was happening to her body. But then another need began to grow inside her, the same yearning she had experienced before, and yet somehow even more intense because the sensation was more diffuse. Lying beneath him, her skin suddenly seemed unbearably sensitive to every slight movement of his body and, with a feeling of utter disbelief, she heard the renewed murmurs of pleasure escape from her lips.

Her body quickened to the pace he set, actively seeking his kisses, and when he sensed that her passion had finally returned he abandoned patience and possessed her with a thrusting, climactic urgency.

The surging force within Charlotte exploded a second time. For a moment she felt suspended in darkness, flung into a realm of pleasure so intense that it was almost impossible to comprehend. Then gradually the tumultuous ecstasy receded, leaving her exhausted and shivering, survivor of a savage storm, cast up on a deserted shore.

Alexander slowly withdrew from her body, turning her gently towards him so that he could offer his shoulder as a pillow. Remorsefully he saw that her lips were faintly bruised, although her eyes were drowsy with satisfaction. Tired out by the conflicting clamour of too many new experiences, Charlotte slept.

Looking down at the exhausted woman in his arms, Alexander's passion fled, leaving his brain icy cold and his conscience once again in active command. He had made Charlotte his wife and perhaps she had enjoyed the experience. But when she woke up what apology could he offer? His life was still forfeit to the cause of Greek freedom. He still had no right whatsoever to tear her out of the country in which she had grown up. Their marriage could never become a reality.

And what if she is carrying your child? he asked himself coldly. Even in that, you failed her. In the pleasures of the moment of climax you forgot the consequences of the future.

Cursing silently, Alexander forced himself to face the unpalatable truth. In seducing Charlotte he had betrayed every tenet of his personal code of honour. And, to compound his utter foolishness, he'd fallen in love somewhere during the process.

CHAPTER SIX

DARKNESS still veiled the bedchamber when Charlotte awoke—to find herself nestled in Alexander's arms. Horrified, she crept to the side of the bed, leaving a good two feet of space between herself and her new husband. Dear God! What if he had woken up and assumed she wanted a reprise of their sinfully enjoyable union?

Scarcely daring to breathe, she peeped at him through half-closed eyelids. Thank heaven, he seemed to be deeply asleep, so the ordeal of speaking to him face to face was temporarily postponed. She would get some clothes on, Charlotte decided agitatedly. Please God, if she was wearing clothes, he might forget some of the incredibly unladylike actions she had performed the previous night. Oh, Lord, how was she ever going to make him love her if she couldn't learn to behave with suitable wifely decorum? Why, oh, why hadn't she managed to lie stiff and unresponsive like any other virtuous woman? Why was she so abnormal? Even the pain of losing her virginity hadn't been sufficient to temper her response. Surely, in the cool light of morning, Alexander would be unable to conceal his disgust for a wife who had moaned with ecstasy as he possessed her body.

That excruciating memory embarrassed Charlotte enough to propel her out of bed with the speed of lightning. Clothes! She had to find clothes. Her chemise was nowhere in sight, but her caftan lay on the floor in a disordered heap and she picked it up with the eagerness of a beggar discovering the remains of a banquet.

Lying motionless in bed, Alexander watched as she thrust her arms into the loose-sleeved, silken wedding gown. A familiar ache of tenderness lodged itself in his heart. This time he didn't attempt to deny its meaning. Having waited nearly thirty years to experience love, he finally allowed himself to recognise what he had been feeling for the past few weeks.

Even in the grey light of dawn he could see that Charlotte's fingers shook as she fumbled with the tiny satin buttons. His stomach plummeted at this evidence of her distress. Fool! Idiot! he castigated himself. Did you think that one night of pleasure would be sufficient to have her cast aside all the traditions of her people? Did you hope that after one night in your bed she would join you on the battlefields of Greece and count the world well lost for love?

He would have liked to drag her back into bed and silence all his doubts in the glory of their lovemaking, but he could no longer ignore the strictures of his conscience. They would talk coolly and rationally, he decided, as they should have done last night. He would ask her if she had any idea what had happened to Mr Canning's vital documents, then he would explain how he planned to send her and Lady Adeline back to England on the first suitable ship——

Except that, because of his carelessness, she might already be carrying his child. And if she was her chances of finding a husband in England were almost nil.

Alexander tried to ignore the spark of joy that leaped through his veins. If Charlotte was pregnant with his baby, would he not be justified in asking her to remain with him as his wife?

And where do you plan to have her live? he mocked himself bitterly. Along with your concubines here in Istanbul, locked up in a golden cage? Or perhaps she would be more comfortable on your estates in Greece, surrounded by brigands-turned-freedom-fighters, and peasants starving after years of civil war?

He didn't have time to answer his own angry questions. Some inadvertent movement must have alerted Charlotte to his wakefulness, and she turned swiftly, her cheeks flooding with colour the moment their eyes met.

'G-good morning. I hope I didn't disturb you. I didn't realise you were awake.'

She edged away from him as she spoke. Almost as if she expected him to jump out of bed and throw her to the floor, he thought grimly. Her nervousness was understandable, of course. Their lovemaking, which for him had been so wonderful, for her had probably brought nothing but pain. Scowling at the unpleasant thought, he raised himself in the bed, dragging the coverlet with him in deference to Charlotte's obvious embarrassment.

Seeing his frown, Charlotte winced. Dear God, he was furious with her! 'W-would you like me to leave?' she asked, staring at her bare toes and wondering what rules of etiquette applied in this sort of situation. At least in an English house she'd have been able to retreat to the sanctuary of her own room. Here she wouldn't know how to find the women's quarters even if she were allowed to go there unescorted.

'No, I don't want you to leave.' If anything, Alexander sounded angrier than before. She saw him draw in a deep breath. Obviously he was having a hard time forcing himself not to shout, she reflected miserably.

'Charlotte, we need to talk,' he said abruptly. 'There is much that I should have explained to you last night.'

'About. . .what we did together?'

'No, I'm afraid there is little to be said about what happened between us, except that I cannot in all honesty pretend to be sorry. I should apologise, Charlotte, but I cannot.'

Her head shot up in amazement. *He* couldn't apologise? Apologise for what? she wondered. For the first time the breath-taking possibility occurred to her that Alexander might not have objected to her terrible behaviour. Charlotte was so lost in wonder at this delightful possibility that it was several seconds before she realised that Alexander was speaking to her again.

'It is past time for me to explain to you what I was doing in England. Many lives still depend upon the success of my mission, and I cannot speak to you with the frankness I would wish. However, I can tell you that my actions have the full support of Mr Canning, the English Foreign Secretary, and I believe they would even receive the grudging support of the Sultan himself.'

'You *believe* the Sultan would approve? Don't you know how he feels?' Charlotte asked.

'Unfortunately in this country it isn't easy to discover the opinion of our ruler.' Alexander's smile lacked any trace of humour. 'He is hemmed in by so many court officials that even to obtain an audience with him can sometimes take weeks of careful manoeuvring. And, thanks to the machinations of Sir Clive Bottomley, my father assures me that it's unsafe for me to leave the protection of his palace at the moment.'

'Unsafe? How can that be?'

'The Grand Vizier has bitterly opposed my actions over the past few years and Sir Clive Bottomley is working hand-in-glove with the Vizier. Only my father's quick thinking saved me from being taken straight from the ship to one of his prisons. My father intercepted Sir Clive's messenger and immediately sent his own men to the harbour. However, the Vizier knows we are in Istanbul, and I shall be captured if I attempt to leave the sanctuary of my father's house.'

'Surely you cannot be forced to stay within these walls forever?'

'No, but I must wait on my father's skills to negotiate an audience for me with the Sultan. Even the Vizier would hesitate to abduct me if I am en route to an audience with his master.'

Charlotte sighed with relief. 'Your father is a very important man in the Government, isn't he? He should experience no difficulty in arranging an audience.'

'If only it were that simple!' Alexander hesitated before continuing. 'There are two problems,' he admitted finally. 'First, you are still assuming that the Government of the Sublime Porte operates much like the British Government——'

'The Sublime Porte?' Charlotte queried.

'That is the English translation of the name we give to the Sultan's Government,' Alexander explained, turning away so that he wouldn't have to see how the rising sun outlined the shape of Charlotte's breasts against the satin of her caftan, positively inviting him to take their weight into his hands, or to bend his head and seek out her nipples. The mere thought of holding Charlotte was enough to arouse him, and he hastily returned to the safer subject of the Sultan's foreign policy. Reluctantly he reached for his caftan.

'Even my father, who is the chief financial adviser for the entire Ottoman Empire, cannot just walk into the Sultan's presence. But there is another problem, a more personal one. . .'

'Between you and your father?' Charlotte asked quietly.

He was surprised by her perception. 'Yes,' he admitted, closing his caftan and walking to the window. He stared out into gardens, now dappled with the sparkling light of early morning sun. 'My father isn't at all sure he wants to plead my cause with the Sultan. I have yet to convince him that the course of action I am pursuing in Greece will ultimately benefit the Ottoman Empire. He has always thought that instead of galloping around the battlefields of the Morea I would be more usefully occupied employing my skill in foreign languages to keep the Sultan informed of foreign opinion.'

'Have you been given a chance to talk with the Emir. . .with your father. . .at length? I would have thought you amazingly persuasive.'

He smiled at the dryness of her tone. When she spoke so, he was reminded of the Charlotte he had known in England—surely it had been half a lifetime ago?

'Alas, my father has good reason to consider me hot-headed. When I left Istanbul I breathed fire—or at least hot air—and spouted romantic illusions, heavily influenced by some of Lord Byron's more inane poetry. In consequence I must now convince the Emir that I'm a wiser man today than I was three years ago.'

'And are you?'

His smile became sombre. 'Let us hope so. There are few things more effective in cooling hot-heads than campaigning in freezing mud for a few months. Battlefields are amazingly efficient at stripping away illusions.'

'And yet you still support the cause of Greek independence?'

'That cause is just,' he said quietly. 'For nearly four hundred years the people of Greece have seen their lands raped to support the corrupt Government of an alien empire. It is time that Greece was ruled by Greeks.'

'And your father doesn't agree?'

'He is uncertain. He points out that wherever five Greeks are gathered together you have five different opinions as to how their country should be ruled. Indeed, on a bad day, five Greeks may well give you six or seven different opinions.'

Charlotte laughed. 'Then could you not compromise with your father and work for some halfway measure? Not quite an independent Greece, but a more independent province, perhaps?'

'Unfortunately such a solution won't work, Charlotte. The Pasha of Egypt is only waiting for Greece to be subdued and he will launch his armies into an attack against Istanbul itself. For his own safety the Sultan has to negotiate with the European powers to establish an independent Greece.'

'I'm surprised your father won't accept your vision.'

'Other, more personal problems cloud my relationship with the Emir,' Alexander admitted. 'Like many other fathers viewing their sons, he has seen too much of my youthful folly to accept that I might finally have reached a stage of reasonable wisdom.' He paused, then said softly, 'I'm sure the women of the harem have told you that my wife, Fatima, died in childbirth. My father made no secret of the fact that he wished me to marry again and provide him with the grandson that Allah had chosen to deny him previously. I found myself unable to fulfil his wishes and left Istanbul in part to avoid our constant arguments on the subject.'

He couldn't marry again because he loved Fatima so much, Charlotte thought painfully. She turned away, hiding the ridiculous tears that sprang, unbidden, into her eyes. She wouldn't torment him by asking questions about Fatima, she reflected wearily. Better to return their conversation to the safe subject of politics. The battles of Greeks and Egyptians were much less dangerous to discuss than beautiful dead wives.

'I still don't understand what you were doing in England,' she said flatly, her words clipped from the effort of hiding her tears.

Obviously she had no wish to learn anything about his personal life, Alexander concluded with a hint of bitterness. He had hoped to explain his complex feelings towards the religion and traditions of his father. And yet, logically, he realised that there was no reason for her to trouble herself with details of the endless struggle he waged between loyalty towards his father and the promise he had given his mother to abide by the laws of the Christian religion. Naturally she had no interest in hearing about his guilt over the death of sweet-natured, boring little Fatima.

Alexander ran his hands through his hair, then shoved them into the pockets of his caftan. What the hell? he thought grimly. If she wanted to talk politics he could certainly oblige.

'Only the great powers can bring the blood-bath in Greece to an end,' he replied curtly. 'If I ever manage to obtain an interview with the Sultan I can tell him that Mr Canning is his last great hope for settling the revolution with some measure of honour and justice for all concerned. The Sultan, like Mr Canning, fears the Russian Emperor. He would like to find some solution to the Greek rebellion that ensures no Russian interference in the affairs of the Greek people. Mr Canning is willing to use British diplomatic power and the British Navy to guarantee a Greek nation independent of Russian imperial control.'

'Why in the world would the Russians bother to interfere with events in Greece?'

'Partly because they would like access to the seaports of the Greek peninsula and partly because the Greeks and the Russians share the same religion. You may remember they are all members of the Orthodox Church and the Russian Emperor truly believes he has a divine mission to liberate Greece from the horrors of Muslim domination. But mostly the Russian Emperor interferes because he will never be satisfied until he has gobbled up all the European countries that currently belong to the Ottoman Empire. Many Russians, not just the Emperor, dream of an empire that will one day encompass the whole of eastern Europe.'

Charlotte found her interest caught and, scarcely noticing what she was doing, she walked over to the window-seat, settling down close to Alexander as they admired the brilliant colours of the flowers. 'I suppose it isn't surprising that the Sultan doesn't want such a huge new empire sitting on his doorstep, especially since it would have been carved out of his territory. So why doesn't he negotiate?'

Alexander smiled tightly. 'The Grand Vizier and most of the other government counsellors are violently opposed to any negotiations with foreign countries. They live in the past and they refuse to accept the fact that the Ottoman Empire no longer has the strength to impose its will upon nations such as France and England. They cannot tolerate the thought that we are so weak that we *must* negotiate with the great powers, whether we wish to or not.'

'But if the Sultan is the supreme ruler, why doesn't he order the Grand Vizier to negotiate?'

'The Sultan, in theory, wields absolute power. In practice, he is often a puppet, dancing to the whim of his damned eunuchs.'

Charlotte sat bolt upright on the window seat. 'Eunuchs!' she exclaimed. 'You mean even the Sultan has them? Alexander, what in the world *is* a eunuch?'

He was half amused, half pained by her question. Dear God, but she had led a sheltered existence! 'A eunuch is a disgrace to the so-called civilisation of my native land,' he said with quiet conviction. 'A eunuch is a slave, a man deprived of all possibility of marriage or fatherhood by a surgical operation performed upon him while he is still a young boy. Eunuchs are very valuable pieces of property because they cannot found dynasties, nor can they threaten the virtue of their masters' womenfolk. That is no excuse, in my opinion, for depriving thousands of young boys of their chance to live a normal life, and killing many hundreds more during the course of the barbarous surgery. I myself will never allow a eunuch to hold any place in my household.'

'Is that why I didn't see any of them in your harem?'

'That is why,' he agreed.

'But you have slaves,' she said, avoiding his eyes. 'The women of your household. . .the concubines. . .'

'Charlotte, they were all gifts to me, presented by my father in an effort to tempt me into marriage.'

'You could have set them free.'

'They have been freed,' he told her quietly. 'All of them. But where are they to go, what are they to do with their gift of freedom? In England, perhaps, I could find them some form of respectable employment. In this country women are either slaves or they are kept in some man's harem.'

'You could find them husbands,' Charlotte suggested.

He looked up quickly, something in her voice alerting him to the turmoil of emotions bubbling beneath her calm exterior. 'Is it possible,' he asked, his voice soft with interest, 'that you are jealous of my concubines?'

'Of course not,' she denied hastily. Too hastily. 'It is

of no consequence to me if you keep a *million* concubines. Why in the world would I be jealous?'

'There is only one reason I can think of.'

'Well, I'm not jealous in the slightest,' she repeated firmly. At least, she hoped she sounded firm. 'I simply don't like to think of all those poor women locked up in your harem with nothing to do.'

'Perhaps I should find time to alleviate their boredom,' he suggested innocently.

Her breath threatened to burst her lungs. 'That is entirely your own affair, Prince Karim.'

'You are suddenly amazingly formal, dear wife. Last night I seem to remember that you called me many names, but Prince Karim was definitely not one of them.'

'Last night. . .last night was a terrible mistake,' she blurted out. 'And anyway, you still haven't explained why Sir Clive Bottomley is so anxious to hand you over to the Grand Vizier.'

Alexander sighed, sorely tempted to ignore her all-too-obvious attempt to change the subject. And yet he really had no right to overcome her resistance to his love-making. True, he had already taken her virginity. That deed was done and there was no going back. But if his seed was not growing within her he could divorce her in a couple of weeks and she would be able to return honourably enough to her own country. Lord knew, she would not be the first woman in the world to go to her husband already experienced. If she married Archdeacon Jeffries. . . But no, he would not torment himself with images of his own sweet Charlotte lying in the arms of that dried-up excuse for a man. Whoever she married would be English and suitable, and able to give her the sort of life to which she was accustomed.

Alexander could no longer deceive himself as he had done last night. He knew now that he would never be able to make love to her and yet avoid the risk of giving her his child. With Charlotte captive beneath him, her legs wrapped around his hips, and her lips parted to receive the thrust of his tongue, he would never be in sufficient control to withdraw at the crucial moment.

There was no doubt some obscure form of divine

justice in his current situation, Alexander reflected. For years he had denied his father the joy of grandchildren. Now he himself was praying for a child that he really had no right to wish for. God, or perhaps it was Allah, undoubtedly had a perverse sense of humour.

'Alexander, are you angry?'

Charlotte's hesitant question interrupted his restless thoughts. What had she asked originally? he wondered tiredly. Oh, yes, something about Sir Clive Bottomley.

'Sir Clive wants to hand me over to the Grand Vizier because he believes he has successfully stolen the secret papers Mr Canning gave me. He thinks he has in his possession an outline of England's plans for dealing with the Greek rebellion. He knows the Grand Vizier will never accept those papers as genuine until he has tortured somebody into validating their worth. Sir Clive intends me to be the torture victim. No doubt he anticipates collecting a large reward for his treachery.'

'Sir Clive intends to hand you over, knowing you will be tortured. . .?' Charlotte turned around, pleasure slowly replacing the revulsion in her face. 'But Sir Clive doesn't have the right papers, does he? You hid Mr Canning's secret plans in Archdeacon Jefferies's wall and the men who attacked you made off with a set of false papers. Sir Clive has come racing back to Istanbul with a set of forgeries!'

She really was incredibly quick-witted, Alexander reflected with an odd little surge of pride. 'Yes, you're right. But the situation isn't as happy as it sounds. Quite apart from the minor problem of keeping myself out of the hands of the Grand Vizier's master torturer, I have another, far greater difficulty. As you must know, Charlotte, I have no idea where the genuine papers are.'

'But I do,' she said smugly. 'And what's more, I think they are probably quite safe.'

'They are?' He forgot his stern resolution to keep relations between the two of them strictly impersonal. He seized her hands, grinning exuberantly. 'Are they somewhere we might hope to recover them? I have been waiting for another opportunity to ask you about them ever since you gave me that crushing set-down on board Sir Clive's ship.'

She tried to frown. 'I think you will agree you deserved a set-down.'

'I would certainly never admit any such thing.' He brushed his thumb lightly across her lips and his teasing smile faded. 'Tell me, Charlotte. Where did you hide Mr Canning's papers?'

She had sworn that she would never reveal what she had done with the package of documents, but that seemed like a decision taken by another woman for reasons which she could no longer begin to comprehend.

'I gave the documents to Tom, our coachman, and asked him to take them to Henry Barrett,' she said, laughing out loud as she saw the wonder and relief spreading across Alexander's face. 'I even asked Tom to give Mr Barrett a message saying that we were being brought to Istanbul. From my brief acquaintance with the enterprising Mr Barrett, I wouldn't be surprised if he comes pounding on your father's door any day now.'

Completely forgetting that he wasn't supposed to touch her, Alexander pulled Charlotte into his arms, hugging her tightly. 'You are positively a jewel among women, Charlotte, my sweet! A gem among wives! How am I ever going to repay you, most intelligent of women?' He kissed her teasingly on the tip of her nose.

She forced herself to remain stiff and rigid in his embrace. Whatever happened, she warned herself, she mustn't destroy his delight in her achievements by melting into his arms and turning her face up to receive his kisses. She bit her lip, determined not to display any unseemly emotion. Dear God, but she wanted to kiss him!

She closed her eyes, screwing them tightly shut against temptation. What in the world would Aunt Adeline say if she ever discovered that Charlotte craved the touch of her husband's mouth upon her breasts, that her stomach was already knotting tight in anticipation of the caress of his hand between her thighs?

Her thoughts alone were more than enough to make her cheeks flame scarlet. Mindful of her aunt's instructions, Charlotte ignored the melting sensations of her body and willed herself to think of England. She would learn how to behave like a proper wife whatever it cost her in terms of will-power!

Alexander felt the unyielding tension of his wife's body and his moment of carefree passion died, stillborn. Dear God, but she must loathe his touch! He moved away from her, schooling his features into blankness. He had planned to suggest that they spend the day together, but now he wasn't sure that he would be able to tolerate the frustration of so many hours spent celibate in her company. It would no doubt be better, he decided bleakly, if he didn't see her again except in the company of other women.

He strode to the door and flung it open. As he had expected, two little serving-girls waited outside. 'Conduct your mistress back to the *haremlik*,' he ordered curtly in Turkish. 'See that she is given every attention needed for her comfort and pleasure.'

Turning to Charlotte, he deliberately avoided looking into her eyes. 'You will be relieved to hear that your duties as my wife are now complete,' he said coolly. 'You and Lady Adeline are at liberty to entertain yourselves in my harem until I can arrange for your passage back to England. My servants have been instructed to provide for your comfort.'

Unfortunately his servants could not provide the comfort she needed most, Charlotte reflected miserably. Obviously she had offended him again, although she couldn't think how. She had held her body so still that she would have sworn not a single tremor escaped to betray what she was actually feeling. Pride came to her rescue, preventing her from revealing the extent of her despair.

'My aunt and I will look forward to hearing the date and time of our departure,' she replied with a coolness that she hoped exceeded his. With a final dignified nod she swept her wedding veil off the arm of the chair and walked blindly from the room.

* * *

Machmet, one of the Emir's most trusted servants, waited until the sound of the foreigner's footsteps faded into silence then sprang nimbly to his feet. He made his way swiftly into the palace, where the carefully orchestrated fire had long since been extinguished and the serving-girls were now working busily to clear away any lingering trace of smoke. At the entrance to his master's sleeping chamber he performed a graceful *temena*, touching the floor, his knees, his heart, lips and forehead in the customary ritual.

The Emir returned the salute. 'Enter, old friend,' he ordered gently.

'I come to tell you that the foreigner has escaped, Most Excellent One.'

The Emir contemplated his fingernails. 'Has he indeed?'

Machmet permitted himself a small smile as he traversed the bedchamber. 'Everything took place exactly as you wished, Excellency. The foreigner thought himself amazingly clever when he discovered the flower-pots we had placed in the corner of the garden. I confess that for a moment I feared he would not succeed in climbing over the wall, so feeble is his body. But in the end he triumphed. From the sound of his footsteps, I know that he ran south, towards the mosque.'

'No doubt to hire transportation.' The Emir smiled. 'Thank you for your careful observations, Old One. Now let us be sure that our informer inside the Grand Vizier's office knows to expect a visit from this despicable Sir Clive.'

'It shall be as you command, Excellency. I run to obey.'

'When you return, old friend, I hope you will find time to join me in some coffee and a pipe.'

Machmet bowed low. 'For such pleasure, Excellency, there is always time.'

The Emir Ibrahim's palace was located in the luxurious Eyub district of Istanbul, and Sir Clive hurried towards the local mosque, where he hoped to find some form of transportation. On discovering that nothing was available save a malodorous ox-cart, he decided that it would be more sensible to return to the ship, where he could change his clothes, hire a suitably prestigious conveyance, and travel to the Grand Vizier's office with appropriate dignity, taking several of his sailors as an armed escort. Sir Clive had no intention of executing a brilliant escape from the Emir only to find himself a prisoner of the Grand Vizier.

The journey by ox-cart was both demeaning and uncomfortable but his schooner, thank God, was still in the harbour. Sir Clive had no doubt that this apparent display of loyalty was due to the fact that his crew lacked money to provision themselves for the return voyage to England. As he paid off his driver he noticed the smart new brig resting at anchor only a few feet away from his own ship. Its name, the *American Beauty*, was emblazoned in jet-black paint against the gleaming stern and an American flag flew from its mast, flapping noisily in the brisk breeze. American shipping was not common in this part of the world, and Sir Clive made a mental note to find out as soon as possible who owned the brig. Just like his brilliant observation of the flower-pots and the missing bricks in the wall, he reflected complacently, it was this meticulous attention to detail that brought him such stunning success.

Lieutenant Haye greeted his employer's return with unconcealed relief. 'Sir Clive, we've been so worried! I was on the point of notifying the British Ambassador of your disappearance.'

The man was a total fool, Sir Clive thought angrily. 'I was detained on business with the Emir Ibrahim,' he said coldly. 'And I've told you, Haye, that my business here requires absolute secrecy. Government orders, direct from the Foreign Secretary himself. Do not discuss my presence here with anybody.' Sir Clive tossed down a couple of gold coins. 'Here, buy yourself a woman for the night, with my compliments, and stop trying to think.'

'Yes, Sir Clive. Thank you, sir. Do you have any idea when we might be leaving for home, Sir Clive? As you know, my wife is sick——'

'Probably by the end of the week.' Sir Clive flung himself into his chair and reached for the bottle of port.

God, a drink was going to taste good after five days of that eternal pomegranate juice! 'Send Sam to me with some hot water, Haye. I need to change before I go out again.'

'Yes, sir.' Lieutenant Haye hesitated on the threshold. 'Do you have any word as to Miss Rippon and Lady Adeline, sir?'

'Miss Rippon is married to Prince Karim,' Sir Clive replied shortly. 'What do you know about that American ship berthed next to ours, Haye? Looks like a brand new vessel.'

'It's a merchantman, sir, carrying cargo between here and Boston. Docked first thing this morning and the captain is an American, name of Henry Barrett. As far as I can tell the whole crew's still on board. They certainly haven't started unloading their merchandise, whatever it is.'

'Henry Barrett, eh?' Sir Clive downed his port in a single swallow. He had a good memory for names, and remembered that a Mr Barrett had gone calling at Rippon Manor when the Prince was lying there wounded. He stared, unseeingly, at his lieutenant. 'Get Sam here,' he ordered. 'On the double.'

He hardly noticed when the lieutenant left the cabin and Sam came in with the requisite supply of boiling water and fresh body linen. Sir Clive allowed himself to be washed and dressed in silence, his thoughts racing. He had made some discreet enquiries after his original trip to Rippon Manor and had learned that a Bostonian by the name of Captain Henry Barrett had once operated a merchant shipping line with many ties to the Greek Peninsula. Now it seemed that the same Captain Henry Barrett who had rushed to the village of St Leonard's in pursuit of Prince Karim was bobbing at anchor in the port of Istanbul. Very interesting.

Sir Clive's good humour returned in full flood. He decided to pay a visit to Captain Barrett en route to the Grand Vizier's office. He would almost certainly pick up some useful information and he had learned that it was always wise to keep one or two tricks up his sleeve when negotiating with slippery Orientals like the Grand Vizier.

Besides, he hadn't forgiven Prince Karim for causing so much disruption to his clever plans, and he didn't want to miss any opportunity to do the Prince harm.

If it had not been such an incredibly vulgar habit, Sir Clive might have been whistling as he made his way up the gangplank on to the freshly swabbed deck of the *American Beauty*. He was stopped by an impertinent sailor. 'Sorry, matey, no visitors. The captain's too busy.'

The guard spoke with the offensive, grating accent of a backwoods American colonial. Sir Clive winced. Reluctantly, however, he conceded that this was not the moment to treat the upstart fellow with the disdain he deserved. He produced his most ingratiating smile.

'I think you'll find that Captain Barrett is willing to make an exception in my case.' He leaned forward, lowering his voice conspiratorially. 'Tell the captain that I bring an urgent message for him from Prince Karim Alexander.'

The sailor regarded him through narrowed eyes, then summoned one of his colleagues with a piercing whistle. 'Tell the captain he has a visitor,' he ordered the young boy who came running to his side. 'Somebody who bears a message from the Prince Karim Alexander.'

As Sir Clive had hoped, the Prince's name proved a most efficient passport and within less than five minutes he found himself being escorted into the presence of Mr Henry Barrett, captain and owner of the *American Beauty*.

Captain Barrett was not, at this moment, a figure to inspire awe in any observer. His old-fashioned wig rested askew over his left ear. His uniform was unbuttoned and his stockings bagged untidily over his ankles. His desk overflowed with charts and papers, several of which had been pinned haphazardly into piles by empty brandy bottles. Sir Clive surveyed the scene, his lip curling in contempt.

'Captain Barrett?' he murmured. 'My name is Sir Clive Bottomley, and I'm obliged to you for sparing me some of your valuable time.'

'My pleashur,' the captain hiccuped. 'Never too busy

for friendsh of my friendsh.' He held up a bottle. 'Join me in a spot of brandy, Shir. . . Sir Clive?'

'No, thank you.'

'You won't mind if I do.' The captain's colonial accent was as thick as the sailor's up on deck. 'It'sh bin a long and frush. . .long and frushtr. . . It'sh bin a damned hard voyage.'

'I'm sorry to hear that.'

'Yesh. One frush. . .one frushtra. . .one damned problem after another.'

Captain Barrett slumped into his chair and Sir Clive began to wonder if his visit was worth the time involved. This drunken sot wouldn't have any information worth passing on to the Grand Vizier or to anybody else. Still, since he was here, he might as well make sure that the captain didn't make contact with Prince Karim, or even the Emir Ibrahim. The Emir didn't seem like much of a threat, but one never knew.

Sir Clive leaned forward. 'I have a message for you,' he whispered hoarsely. 'From Prince Karim Alexander.'

The captain sprang to his feet. 'Shhh. . .' he sputtered, sending a copious spray of brandy fumes in Sir Clive's direction. He pressed his finger to his lips and, in a grotesque parody of caution, blundered around the cabin, knocking into furniture on his way to the door. He pulled this open with a force that sent him reeling backwards, then grinned sheepishly at Sir Clive.

'Nobody there,' he said. 'Ye can give me the mesh. . .give me the message now. There's nary a soul to hear us.'

Sir Clive almost laughed aloud. Good lord, Prince Karim ought to have had more sense than to hire such a bumbling drunkard. If all the men fighting for Greek freedom were as foolish as this one the war would be over before the summer ended.

'What dosh the Prinsh say?'

'He wants you to know there is great danger waiting here in Istanbul,' Sir Clive whispered dramatically. The information Captain Barrett possessed might not be very useful, but it was better if Prince Karim didn't share it, and Sir Clive was determined to prevent any contact between the two men. He leaned forward.

'The Prince told me to warn you. Whatever you do, don't go to the Emir Ibrahim's house, or try to get any messages to the Prince himself. The Grand Vizier has spies everywhere, even inside the Emir's household. You will be seized if you go anywhere near the Emir's palace.'

Captain Barrett tugged at his cravat, his face turning pale. 'Mebbe we'd better turn the ship around,' he said. 'I never wanted to come to Istanbul in the first place.' With trembling fingers he attempted to pour yet another serving of brandy into his glass. When it was clear that his hands lacked the co-ordination to achieve his purpose he shrugged resignedly and up-ended the bottle straight into his mouth.

'Knew we shouldn't've come here,' he muttered, sidling up to Sir Clive. 'Last thing we want is for some damned Mussh. . .Musshel. . .some damned Turk to come poking his nose into the holds of our ship.'

Sir Clive stiffened, then forced himself to relax again. 'I'm sure you're right, Captain Barrett. Although I don't quite understand why we can't have any Turks inspecting the holds. . .?'

Winking broadly, Henry Barrett attempted to give Sir Clive a playful dig in the ribs. 'No reason for heathen Ottomans to get their hands on ammunition intended for honesht Greek Christians, no siree, bob.'

'Indeed there is not,' Sir Clive murmured, barely able to conceal his excitement at this drunken revelation. So the holds of the *American Beauty* contained weapons for the Greek revolutionaries, did they? That was certainly information which the Grand Vizier would pay generously to receive. Now, however, he had to find some way to prevent the idiot of a captain from turning tail and sailing out of port. He rose to his feet, counting the minutes until he could get to the Grand Vizier.

'Now, Captain Barrett, remember that Prince Karim is relying on you. Whatever happens, don't leave Istanbul until the Prince sends you another message.'

Henry Barrett lurched drunkenly toward his desk. 'Find the sextant,' he mumbled. 'Think I'll give orders to set sail for Corfu. The British are there. The Navy, they'll look after me.'

'No!' Sir Clive fought back his dismay and managed to produce another persuasive smile. 'You must not go to Corfu, Captain Barrett. The Prince needs you here. You mustn't leave Istanbul. Remember, Prince Karim is relying on the *American Beauty* to provide his escape route from the city.'

'Oh, ah, I remember now.' The captain scratched under his wig, sending it even further askew. 'Eshcape route. Can't leave.' He muddled his charts around on the desk, narrowly avoiding yet another accident with the brandy bottle. 'Well, I guess I oughta stay here for the Prince since he needs me.'

'Indeed you should.' Sir Clive's smile mingled relief and scorn in almost equal parts. 'Good man,' he said, clapping the captain on the arm. 'I am certain Prince Karim will reward you as you deserve for all your loyal service.'

'Oh, ah,' agreed Captain Barrett. 'I reckon he might at that.'

'Don't trouble to ring for an escort. I can find my own way back up on deck.'

'Your escort is already here,' Captain Barrett said with a clarity which Sir Clive might have found amazing if he hadn't been so busy congratulating himself.

The captain nodded almost imperceptibly to the sailor, who inclined his head in acknowledgement, then turned politely towards the baronet. 'If ye'll follow me, please, sir, I'll show you the quickest way off the ship.'

3ank Barrett scarcely waited for Sir Clive to leave his cabin before he tossed his rarely used wig into a corner and began to re-button his uniform. Straightening his hose, he poked his head out into the corridor and yelled for his cabin boy.

After two long voyages Edwin was used to his captain's informality, and he ran up, grinning cheerfully. 'Dougal's following the English toff just like you told him to, sir.'

The captain was busy tying his garter and his only reply was a satisfied grunt. Returned to his usual state of immaculate neatness, he beckoned Edwin to his desk, and the two of them worked swiftly to restore order to the scattered charts and papers.

'Shall I throw these all away, sir?' Edwin spoke over an armload of empty bottles.

'Yes, and don't let the cook know we raided his supply store, or he won't speak to me for a week.'

'The men'll appreciate the brandy, sir, and they sure won't mind if it comes out of a stewpot instead of a bottle. Fancy Sir Clive never stopping to think how strange it was that you were so drunk and the ship was so clean and tidy. He ought to know that you can't run a ship with a drunken captain.'

'Sir Clive was too busy congratulating himself on his own cleverness to find time to think.' Hank Barrett gave the cabin boy an affectionate cuff on the arm. 'Don't cut yourself on those bottles, you young rascal, and tell Dougal to report back to me as soon as he returns from following Sir Clive. Once I know what our pompous little baronet is up to I shall be leaving for the Emir Ibrahim's palace.'

Alexander was definitely not enjoying himself. Not only was he confined to his father's palace when he ought to have been sailing away in search of Hank Barrett, but married life was not proving at all easy. For thirty-six long, weary hours he had remained resolute in his noble decision not to spend time alone with Charlotte. So far the only practical result of his nobility seemed to be an acute case of sexual frustration on his part, and a determination on his wife's part to avoid all contact with him whenever he entered the harem—which he only entered, of course, in order to see her. It did not help his state of mind in the slightest to know that everybody in the palace, from the Emir down to the youngest and newest kitchen boy, watched the progress of his and Charlotte's relationship with unconcealed curiosity.

To compound his problems, the Emir was being as uncooperative as only he knew how. A dozen times Alexander had tried to ask his father to arrange an audience with the Sultan Mahmud II. The Emir, for all practical purposes, became deaf whenever his son raised the subject.

This afternoon's interview had so far proceeded no differently from many that had gone before. Alexander introduced the subject of international politics. The Emir ignored him and returned to his own favourite topic.

Alexander gritted his teeth and answered the Emir with the courtesy that tradition demanded. 'I thank you, Father, for your kind enquiries as to the state of my bride's health. Allah be praised, she fares well.'

'Long may her good health continue. Soon I hope to hear that she awaits the child who will ease the sorrow of my declining years by making me a grandfather.'

'Most honoured father, I beg leave to suggest that you have many years still to complete before you enter your decline. I would also respectfully remind you that you are already a grandfather many times over.'

The Emir waved a dismissive hand. 'The children of my daughters, though much beloved, cannot mean the same to me as the son of my only son.'

Alexander decided to break the news to his father that Charlotte was unlikely ever to produce the longed-for grandson since he planned to arrange passage home to England for her and for Lady Adeline as soon as he could leave the palace. Even as he started speaking one of the gatehouse slaves ran into the hall. Alexander welcomed his arrival with a slightly guilty sigh of relief.

The slave touched his head to the marble floor in a swift genuflexion. 'Most Excellent Emir, there are foreigners outside your gates, requesting admission.'

The Emir fanned himself. 'Do they have names, these foreigners?'

'Most Excellent Emir, their names are too difficult to be remembered by this feeble brain of mine. They carry weapons, but they do not look intent upon doing battle.'

'Are they wearing any sort of uniform?'

'I regret, Excellency, that the ridiculous clothes worn by foreigners all look alike to me. And of course they wear no turbans to show their rank or office. But the leader gave me this piece of paper. Perhaps Your

Excellency's great wisdom will enable you to understand its meaning.'

The Emir took the small white card, glanced at it briefly, then handed it to his son. 'Do you know this man, Karim Alexander?'

'Captain Henry Barrett'. Alexander read the three simple words and his heart began to pound with excitement. 'Yes, Father, I know him well. He is an old and trusted friend. I would be honoured to make him known to you.'

The Emir turned back to the slave. 'Show in the foreigners. Leave them in possession of their weapons, but have an armed guard escort them.'

The slave bowed to the ground. 'It shall be as you say, Excellency.'

Alexander hadn't realised how much he missed the company of his friend until Hank Barrett strode into the reception hall, flanked by a neatly uniformed contingent of ship's officers and his father's personal guards. He watched with satisfaction as Hank, experienced in the ways of the Orient, bowed low to the Emir before acknowledging Alexander's presence with a smile and a brief inclination of his head.

'Karim Alexander, you may introduce your military friend to me,' the Emir said in Turkish.

Alexander moved from behind his father's divan, clasping Hank's hands in a warm, enthusiastic grip. 'So you made it out here, you old reprobate. Trust you to follow your nose and land in the thick of trouble.'

Hank grinned. 'Seems to me, I was just following you. I suppose you wouldn't like to tell these friendly fellows here to sheathe their scimitars? All those curved blades make me nervous.'

'The command is not mine to give, but you needn't worry. My father knows that you are my friend and the scimitars are merely for show.'

'I wonder why that doesn't seem quite the reassurance that it ought to be?' Hank's smile was faintly quizzical as he clapped Alexander's arm. 'Never seen you all decked out in fancy dress before. The hat suits you, old chap. It must be something about that arrogant profile of yours. Looks just right under a spray of peacock feathers.'

'Your compliments, my friend, carry the unique American flavour that makes them all sound suspiciously like insults. But we cannot continue this conversation, delightful as it is. My father wishes me to make you known to him.'

Alexander swung around to face the Emir and performed a graceful *temena*. 'Honoured sire, I wish you to meet my closest friend, Captain Henry Barrett of Boston, Massachusetts.'

The Emir's eyebrow raised in mild interest. 'He is an American?'

'Yes, sire. But he has sailed for many years as a merchant in this part of the world. He has traded especially with the merchants of the Greek ports.'

His face expressionless, the Emir turned towards Henry Barrett, examining him closely. 'You and your servants are welcome in my humble home,' he said finally.

Alexander translated his father's remarks, then asked for permission to speak with his friend in private. The Emir once again stared at the captain in silence for several seconds before clapping his hands to summon a slave.

'You will see to it that the American friends of the Prince Karim are entertained and given refreshment,' he ordered, rising from his divan. He nodded to his son. 'Bring your captain to my private chamber. I believe we have much to talk about.'

Once in his room, the Emir wasted little time in preliminaries. 'You and your friend will please be seated, Karim Alexander. Then, perhaps, you will ask your friend why he has come here.'

Alexander sat down and indicated that the captain should do the same. 'I'm certainly pleased to see you, Hank, but how did you know I was in Istanbul? Did Tom find you and give you the message?'

'Yes. He caught a bad chill, but his wounds were superficial and he managed to make his way to my lodgings in Portman Square only two days after your abduction. He brought me some papers that Miss Rippon had entrusted to him, and begged me to follow you to Istanbul. The *American Beauty* was already docked at Tilbury, so I figure we set sail only three or four days after you and Sir Clive. We ran into a spot of bad weather off the coast of Portugal, but aside from that our journey was uneventful. So here we are.'

'And a most welcome sight,' Alexander replied, translating the gist of Hank's remarks for his father's benefit. 'You have the papers safe?' he added eagerly.

'Aye, they're safe. And obviously you yourself came to no harm, but what of the women, Miss Rippon and Lady Adeline? Tom was worried sick about what had happened to his mistress. Said she fought like a tiger when Sir Clive Bottomley tried to abduct you. He was afraid she might put up so much resistance that Sir Clive would do her a mischief.'

To his utter dismay Alexander felt his cheeks grow warm. He cleared his throat to cover his confusion, causing both his father and Hank Barrett to look at him with renewed interest. 'I am happy to report that Charlotte and her aunt are both well,' he said swiftly, avoiding his friend's all-too-penetrating gaze. 'As a matter of fact Charlotte and I were married two days ago and her aunt remains with her in the *haremlik* as a companion and chaperon. In the circumstances, you understand, it seemed advisable that we should wed.'

'Well, my sincere congratulations, Alexander.' Hank spoke heartily, barely able to conceal his astonishment as he recognised all the signs of acute embarrassment in a man whom he had known for years as an inveterate and carefree womaniser. 'I would like to pay my respects to Lady Adeline and to your new bride,' Hank said. 'If your father wouldn't be offended by the breach of his customs.'

Alexander had to fight back an immediate impulse to refuse. He found himself victim to a rush of conflicting emotions and didn't immediately translate Hank's comments for the Emir's benefit. On the one hand he wanted very much to give Charlotte and her aunt the pleasure of seeing somebody familiar and English-speaking. On the other hand he felt a primitive, irrational rush of jealousy at the thought of bringing his wife out of the protection of his harem and exposing her to his friend's interested gaze. Neither the fact that Hank Barrett had already seen Charlotte's face, nor the fact that he himself had protested a thousand times at the absurd separation of the sexes insisted upon by Muslim tradition made any dent in the reflex surge of male possessiveness that swept through him.

'They will have to be veiled,' he heard himself say. He excused himself by adding, 'You understand it is the custom of my father's household.'

The Emir looked up at his son, sympathy and humour gleaming in the depths of his very dark eyes. 'Do not ascribe your personal jealousies to the traditions of my household,' he said softly in Turkish. 'I think your feelings for your wife are more intense than any you have experienced for a woman before, and you are finally beginning to understand why so many men take comfort in the seclusion of their women.'

Alexander turned to face his father, astonishment driving out embarrassment. 'You have understood my conversation with Hank Barrett!' he exclaimed in Turkish.

The Emir leaned back against his cushions. 'On rare occasions a father may learn wisdom from his son. You urged me to open my mind to the ways of the Europeans by learning to speak one of their languages. I have studied both French and English during the years you have been away.'

'And yet you did not tell me what you had done.'

The Emir regarded his son with a hint of sadness. 'Have you chosen to tell me all that you did during the past three years, Karim Alexander? Sometimes those who love each other best find it most difficult to say what is in their hearts.' He clapped his hands sharply before Alexander could reply and a slave appeared almost instantly in the doorway.

'The wife of my son and her aunt are to be brought to my son's private quarters,' he told the servant. 'See that they are ready to come immediately after the evening meal has been served.'

For Hank's benefit Alexander condensed the Emir's words into the brief comment that Charlotte and Lady Adeline would join the men after dinner. 'I shall be pleased to see them,' Hank said. 'And in the meantime I think you and your father will be interested to hear that I had a visitor on board my ship this morning. None other than a certain Sir Clive Bottomley, who warned me that on no account was I to come to the Emir Ibrahim's palace. Naturally I came here as soon as possible.'

Alexander smiled. 'Sir Clive "escaped" from this palace only this morning. He seems to be having a busy day of it. My father and I expected him to go straight to the Grand Vizier's office.'

'He went there directly from my ship with a contingent of his own crew. One of my men followed him.' Hank's eyes took on a decided twinkle. 'I expect Sir Clive thought he had hot news to deliver to the Grand Vizier. For some reason—I guess it must have been something I said—he seems to think that the Turkish Customs officials will find supplies and ammunition for the Greek rebels when they search the holds of my ship.'

Alexander looked up swiftly. 'But of course they will find no such thing?'

Hank looked offended. 'How can you ask such a question, Alex? You know me better than that. My holds contain nothing more exciting than a consignment of American deerskins, intended for the Turkish leather-working guild.'

'Sir Clive is more easily deceived than the eunuchs of the Grand Vizier's office,' the Emir said softly. 'If Captain Barrett's ship has false holds the eunuchs will find them.'

'There are no false holds, Father.'

'Point out to your friend that because his storage holds are now empty of treasonous weapons, it does not mean that they will always be so. And I cannot condone treason.'

Alexander made the appropriate translation, and Hank bowed politely to the Emir. 'What Your Excellency says is true. However, we live in difficult times and it is sometimes difficult for a man to judge which acts are treasonous and which are necessary for the achievement of justice. To supply food to people who are starving could be considered a simple act of human kindness.'

'Karim Alexander, you should tell your friend that he is old enough to have attained wisdom. In war many people must suffer, not only the soldiers,' the Emir responded.

Alexander felt his fists clutch into tight balls of frustration, and he hid them within the sleeves of his caftan. 'I cannot allow the people on my estates to starve, Father. They are my responsibility.'

'And your loyalty to the Sultan? Is that not also your responsibility?'

Hank saw the pain flash briefly in Alexander's eyes, and he intervened swiftly. 'Because all foreign news is censored here, you may not know that the Greek Provisional Government has just sent a letter to the British Government, officially requesting British help in negotiating an end to their war with the Ottoman Empire. They have suggested creating a new kingdom of Greece and they wish to offer the throne to Prince Leopold.'

Alexander flashed a look of gratitude towards his friend. Angry words would never convince his father of the imperative need for the Sultan to negotiate. Rational argument, however, might succeed where emotion failed. He quietly translated Hank's words, adding an explanation that Prince Leopold was a very wise and good man, the widowed son-in-law of King George IV.

The Emir frowned. 'The fact that the Greek rebels are cunning enough to win the British over to their side does not make their war any less treacherous, just as the fact that this Prince Leopold possesses a kindly nature does not make him a lawful king.'

Hank waited for a translation and then bowed again. 'With all due respect, Your Excellency, the Greek struggle for independence has progressed so far, and now involves the interests of so many foreign powers, that your Sultan will risk the entire future of the

Ottoman Empire if he attempts to continue governing the Greek peninsula under the old system.'

The Emir listened to Alexander's translation, then spoke sadly. 'The fact that our Sultan may be required to surrender part of the lands that are justly his does not mean that my son should fight to hasten his loss.'

'Father, I did nothing to aid the rebellion in its early stages. Indeed, it was only when I left here three years ago and saw what was happening in the Morea with my own eyes that I knew the Ottoman cause was already lost. Everything that I have done in these past few years has been designed simply to hasten the end of a brutal war and to alleviate the suffering of the innocent victims of battle. Father, the people on my estates are starving. Whole towns have been wiped out by the ravages of disease and starvation. I seek only the chance to deliver food to the people of my estates in Greece. For my mother's sake I wish to ensure that the next generation of Greek children will not be forced to live in a world of permanent hunger and official corruption.'

'The study of history shows that such high-flown and noble wishes inevitably require the reinforcement of guns and ammunition,' the Emir said drily.

'It is true I shall have to provide ammunition to my people. If you had seen the rape and pillage perpetrated by the Egyptian Army, father, you would understand why weapons are necessary. Without ammunition to defend their smallholdings my estates will be laid waste in an orgy of plunder and destruction.'

Silence settled thick and heavy over the room. The Emir finally spoke. 'So, it is as I feared. In effect, my son, you ask me to give you permission to leave my palace in order to fight against the Sultan.'

'No,' Alexander replied. 'I ask only your permission to seek an audience with the Sultan so that I might convey to him the secret plans of the British Foreign Secretary. I found in the past that Mahmud II is far-seeing in his actions and in his understanding of world events. I believe I can convince him that the best interests of his Empire and his subjects will be served if he agrees to negotiate a peaceful settlement to the Greek revolution.'

'A peaceful settlement? It seems to me that you speak not of a settlement, but of an abject submission.'

'Father, I seek freedom for the millions of Greeks who have suffered under a corrupt and oppressive regime. If you saw the situation in Greece you would acknowledge that our Sultan has not been well served by many of his deputies. Most of all I seek an end to the rebellion that will keep the Russian Emperor out of Greece—and out of Turkey's back yard. I beg you, Father, do not waste your time fearing the Greek phoenix when the Russian bear prowls at our door.'

The Emir placed the tips of his fingers together and stared at them sombrely. 'I will give consideration to your words, Karim Alexander. Now I am tired and wish to rest for a while alone. Tell your friend Captain Barrett that he and his officers are invited to eat with us at sundown.'

Alexander bowed, trying to control the faint leap of hope that at last his father understood what he, Alexander, had been working to achieve during the last three years. 'May Allah grant you easeful repose, Father.'

The Emir's eyes gleamed with a flash of sardonic humour. 'I scarcely need Allah's help in such a simple matter, my son. I do not have a new and beautiful wife, so for me, unfortunately, repose is all too easy to find. Enjoy the torment that your bride causes you. One day, when you are old, you will wish you could again feel such a fever of the blood.'

'My bride causes me no torment,' Alexander replied instantly.

The Emir smiled and closed his eyes.

Quite apart from the fact that Charlotte's emotions were torn and bleeding, life in Alexander's harem had not proved easy. None of his concubines spoke anything except Osmanlica, which meant that only the most basic forms of communication were possible. Moreover, Aunt Adeline—although she would have died rather than admit it—missed the cosy bustle of the Emir Ibrahim's much larger household.

Charlotte, on the other hand, was quite glad of her isolation, and her aunt, fortunately, was a much less penetrating observer than the other women of the harem. Best of all, she was even less anxious than her niece to discuss precisely what had happened during the course of Charlotte's initiation into the mysteries of married life.

Reunited with Charlotte, she soon convinced herself that her niece remained a virgin, and her only questions about the Prince concerned his willingness to help them both return to England. Charlotte replied—with perfect truth—that he had promised to book them passages on the first available ship out of Istanbul. Lady Adeline's rapture at this news was so heartfelt and so prolonged that she quite failed to notice her niece's conspicuous lack of enthusiasm.

It was therefore with decidedly conflicting feelings that Charlotte and her aunt finally grasped the information being mimed to them by the most senior of Alexander's concubines.

'They want to take both of us to see the Prince!' Lady Adeline concluded triumphantly. 'What splendid news! No doubt he's already found us berths on a ship sailing for England. It's scarcely forty-eight hours since your wedding, so he's really been very prompt in his attentions. You see, Charlotte dearest, I told you he wouldn't fail us.'

'And you were right,' Charlotte agreed miserably, handing her empty coffee-cup to a servant. This summons presumably meant that she would be sent back to England without ever being ordered into Alexander's bed again. She tried hard to feel deliriously happy. How wonderful to think that she would never again be forced to submit to Alexander's brutal masculine desires. How gratifying to know that she would never again be caressed and held by a man who was not even her husband except by the laws of a heathen religion.

Charlotte swallowed over a large lump in her throat,

wondering why the emotion she felt seemed so much more like frantic despair than delirious happiness.

She blinked her eyes, then stared numbly at the arm-waving concubine. 'I think she wants us to wear our veils,' she said.

Lady Adeline snatched up the length of white muslin held out by a serving-girl, and tossed it impatiently over her head. 'Such an incredible piece of nonsense when the Prince has seen us both a hundred times. But I suppose, if it keeps them happy, it's easier not to complain.'

Charlotte adjusted her veil more slowly, admitting to herself that she wished her final interview with Alexander were going to be private. Why? she mocked herself. Because you hoped against hope that when next you were alone with him he would take you into his arms and carry you to his bed? Do you have no more sense of self-preservation than to actively seek the shattering storm of sensations that Alexander arouses in you?

'Charlotte, dear, could you please hurry a little? The servant is really becoming quite agitated. Dear me, you've been so scatter-brained these past couple of days, I can't think what's come over you.'

'Sorry, Aunt.' Not scatter-brained, Charlotte thought, pinning her veil. Merely incapable of concentrating on anything except Alexander. She shook out the folds of her silk gauze trousers, wishing she could shake the fuzziness out of her brain with equal ease.

'Charlotte, dear, we're all waiting.'

'Coming, Aunt,' she said dutifully. Dear God, if only he would kiss me just one more time, she added silently.

For a moment Hank Barrett didn't recognise the exquisitely beautiful and exotic young girl who drifted into Alexander's room in the wake of Lady Adeline and a retinue of servants. Beneath the subtle concealment of her veil he saw a gently rounded female figure, clad in glittering harem clothes, and an oval face framed by a cloud of golden hair that hung loose almost to her waist. He swallowed a most ungentlemanlike exclamation when the girl lifted her eyes and he realised that he was looking at none other than the former Miss Charlotte Rippon.

He watched, torn between amusement and a faint feeling of envy, as Alexander and Charlotte exchanged glances, loaded on each side with almost equal amounts of uncertainty, longing and sexual tension. He and his dear wife Sukey had once felt that way, he thought tenderly, in those long-ago days when they'd been courting. But Sukey had been dead for many years, and that sort of intensity surely wasn't something that a middle-aged man could recapture with any of the women he bought and paid for.

Hank had very little time to reflect on the startling transformation of Miss Rippon, unawakened English lady, into this tantalising creature who breathed passion and sensuality. Lady Adeline, overcome by the pleasure of seeing the familiar face of a Christian gentleman—even if he was, regrettably, American—flung herself into his arms and burst into a flood of heartfelt, noisy tears.

'Oh, Mr Barrett,' she gasped between sobs, 'it's so *wonderful* to see you.'

Hank's cheeks grew scarlet with embarrassment. He could command a crew of two hundred men without blinking an eye. A crying woman, however, was considerably more than he could handle, particularly one who seemed to regard him in the light of her personal saviour.

'There, there,' he mumbled awkwardly, patting Lady Adeline's back and simultaneously flashing a look of urgent appeal towards Alexander. He fumbled in his pocket for a clean handkerchief and held it out with a hint of desperation. 'No need for tears, my lady,' he suggested hopefully. 'Everything's going to be all right, you'll see.'

Lady Adeline's only comment was a distraught snuffle and Hank managed a feeble grin as he caught Alexander's ironic glance of male camaraderie. Oddly enough, he was beginning to enjoy the warm feeling of Lady Adeline's plump body pressed against his chest. Her very softness made him feel strong and protective, sensations which he had rarely experienced in the arid years since Sukey's death.

Charlotte felt Alexander's gaze turn towards her and

she lifted her head proudly, blinking back almost as violent an attack of tears as Aunt Adeline, although the cause was quite different.

She saw at once that Alexander's expression was at its most sardonic and his voice was laced with the mockery she dreaded. 'In view of your aunt's copious tears you will no doubt be delighted to learn that Captain Barrett has come expressly to rescue you both from the horrors of your imprisonment.'

Charlotte was so preoccupied with controlling her own emotions that she entirely failed to recognise the hurt underpinning Alexander's sarcasm. Inevitably she responded to the sarcasm while completely ignoring the hurt.

'If he is come to rescue us, then of course he is doubly welcome. But it's a pity, is it not, that he didn't manage to arrive here before you were compelled to marry me? However quickly you ship me away, our marriage will remain a legal fact.'

Alexander's mouth tightened and he spoke far more harshly than he'd intended. 'On the contrary, our marriage is a trivial detail that need trouble neither of us. In a Muslim country like this one our union can be ended a great deal more swiftly than it began. If I speak the words "I divorce thee" three times in front of witnesses our marriage is legally at an end.'

Lady Adeline perked up. She threw back her veil, mopped her eyes and thanked Captain Barrett prettily for the loan of his handkerchief. By now she had genuinely forgotten her original fear that 'something dreadful' might have happened to Charlotte on her wedding night. She smiled radiantly at her niece. 'Well, this is certainly a night for happy news,' she said. 'I am sorry for all the poor Muslim women who must get abandoned by their husbands, but from our point of view such an easy divorce is certainly a blessing.'

Charlotte found her aunt's cheerfulness hard to bear. 'But Aunt Adeline, when the Earl of Leinster applied to Parliament for a Bill of Divorcement from his Countess, you said that marriage was indestructible except by death.'

'That was an *English* marriage,' Aunt Adeline retorted. 'Not at all the same thing, as I'm sure you'll agree. The Earl and Countess were married in church, but your marriage was celebrated in a bath-house. Need I say more? Dear Charlotte, what a relief! You will be able to return to England and resume your life just as if this horrid episode had never happened.'

Charlotte looked down at her henna-red hands and so failed to notice Alexander's wince at the words 'horrid episode'. 'Yes, Aunt,' she said dully. 'We'll go back to England just as if nothing had ever happened.' Despite her best efforts her sentence ended in an odd sort of hiccup.

Lady Adeline finally became aware of the fact that she still stood clasped within the somewhat clumsy protection of Captain Barrett's arms. She blushed rosily and quickly removed herself to a more decorous distance.

'I hope I haven't ruined your uniform,' she said. 'But it was such a pleasant shock to see you. I don't usually cry quite so *copiously*.'

'Don't give it another thought,' Hank said gruffly.

Their conference was interrupted at this point by the arrival of the Chief Eunuch, who conveyed a low-voiced message to Alexander, waited while Alexander replied, and then went swiftly from the room.

'My father, the Emir, wishes to join us,' Alexander explained to the others. 'He has something urgent to tell us.'

The Emir entered the room just as his son finished speaking. Waving his hand in dismissal of his trail of servants, he acknowledged the presence of the captain and the women with a brief inclination of his head.

'I will speak in English,' he said, to the astonishment of everybody in the room. 'Perhaps the time is come for me to set aside tradition and also pride. It humbles me that I speak your language with so many errors.'

'I have heard none so far, Excellency,' Hank remarked politely.

'You are kind, Captain Barrett. I know that I pronounce your words in ways that are not correct. I do not sound as my son, Karim Alexander, sounds when he uses your language. But the message I bear is of some urgency. I come to tell you that Sir Clive Bottomley is at this moment with the Grand Vizier. He has passed on secret papers from Mr Canning, the British Foreign Secretary, and he has told the Grand Vizier that Karim Alexander is actively working for the cause of the Greek Rebellion.'

'But how can you possibly know all this?' Charlotte cried, her curiosity causing her to forget that women in the Ottoman Empire were only allowed to speak when spoken to.

Alexander held his breath, but the Emir didn't rebuke Charlotte for daring to question him. 'It is necessary for me to know what happens in the Grand Vizier's office, therefore I have made arrangements to ensure that I am informed. Even in the Vizier's most secret councils there are men who are loyal to me.'

The Emir spoke without a trace of boastfulness, but Charlotte realised for the first time just how powerful a figure he was in the Government of the Ottoman Empire. She watched Alexander, her heart beating faster than she wanted to admit, as he crossed the room to the Emir's side.

'Father, I beg your forgiveness for the trouble my presence here in this city has caused you, but the papers Sir Clive gives to the Grand Vizier are forgeries. The real documents have been brought to Istanbul by Captain Barrett. It is these documents I wish to present to His Highness the Sultan.'

'You believe the documents Captain Barrett brings are likely to be helpful to the Sultan and our Empire?'

'Yes, I do. They convey personal messages from Mr Canning to our Sultan. England and Russia have recently signed a secret agreement which guarantees that the British Navy will prevent Russian interference in the affairs of the Greek peninsula while the Sultan and the leaders of the Greek Provisional Government work out a settlement to end the war.'

'The laws of our empire are based on the profound wisdom of the Prophet of Islam. It is hard to surrender Ottoman territory to the Christian infidel.'

'But inevitable, Father,' Alexander said softly. 'Let me help to make the inevitable as painless as possible. I swear to you that in all my dealings with the British Government I have striven always to preserve and protect the interests of our Sultan. As for my activities in Greece, I have explained to you already that I wish only to protect the people of my estates from plunder and starvation. In calling upon the aid of the Egyptian armies to defeat the Greek rebels, the Sultan has set free a monster which fattens itself upon the blood of innocent peasants.'

'I myself do not trust Ali Pasha, the Egyptian ruler,' the Emir admitted. 'I have thought much about what you said this afternoon, my son, and, in view of Sir Clive's activities, I have decided to use my influence to obtain you an immediate audience with His Highness the Sultan.'

Alexander knelt swiftly in front of his father. With consummate grace he touched his forehead to the back of the Emir's hand. 'I kneel at your feet in gratitude,' he murmured, the words sounding oddly formal in the coldness of the English language.

'Your gratitude may be premature,' the Emir replied drily. 'Even if the Sultan accepts your advice it will be essential for you to have your escape route planned. The Grand Vizier is not alone in his opinion that you have brought untold harm to our Empire by encouraging the Sultan in his liberalising tendencies. Your life, my son, will be measured in hours once your interview with the Sultan is over—and the danger will be all the greater if your interview is successful.'

'Hank Barrett will be ready to take me from Istanbul.' Alexander paused. 'Will you come with me, Father?'

The silence lasted no more than a second, but in that instant Charlotte realised that not only was Alexander's life hanging in the balance, but the Emir's also.

The Emir smiled. 'Your offer is kindly meant, but do not worry, my son. I have taken the necessary precautions. Believe me, I plan to spend many more years cultivating my garden, and enjoying my grandchildren.'

Alexander's eyes darkened in challenge, but his smile

was warm. 'May your *daughters' children* provide you with unending joy, most honoured father.'

The Emir chuckled. 'They will. And, I think, my son's children also.' He turned abruptly, his smile fading, and faced Hank Barrett. 'I will arrange an escape route for my son from the Sultan's palace to your ship. I will rely upon you to arrange a safe passage out of the harbour.'

'You can count on me and my men, Excellency. We'll be ready.'

'It is good, and best, perhaps, if I have no precise knowledge of your destination. That way I cannot reveal it.' The Emir turned back to his son. 'I have one further request of you, Karim Alexander. I would speak with your wife, Charlotte Rippon. Alone.'

Charlotte had already learned enough of Turkish customs to understand how extraordinary such a request was. She glanced quickly at Alexander and saw that his face had become totally impassive, a sign which she had learned to recognise as indicative of intense inner turmoil. The silence in the room thickened until Alexander finally inclined his head in acquiesence.

'Your wish, Father, is my command.' He clapped his hands and summoned a servant to escort Lady Adeline back to the harem. 'With your permission, Father, I shall take Hank to rejoin his men in the main hall.'

'I shall be with you both shortly. I know we still have much to discuss before your interview with the Sultan tomorrow morning.'

Hank Barrett and Alexander bowed as they left the room. The Emir smiled faintly as he watched his son's departure. 'Poor Karim Alexander,' he said, gesturing to indicate that Charlotte should sit down. 'He loves you a great deal more than he finds comfortable.'

Charlotte wished very much that she could believe the Emir, but she saw no grounds for thinking that he was right. 'He can't possibly love me,' she burst out. 'We've been married only three days, and he's already talking about our divorce! He plans to send me back to England the minute he can find a boat to take me.'

The Emir actually chuckled. 'How very noble of him,

and how very misguided. Do you not see, Charlotte Rippon, that he loves you enough to set you free of the bonds that fate has tied around you?'

Charlotte was astonished to find herself admitting to the Emir a truth she had scarcely admitted to herself. 'I am not sure, Excellency, that I wish to be set free.'

'Then my son is blessed. To love and be loved is a great joy. I have felt affection for many women in my life, but only once have I truly felt love. That was for Penelope, the mother of Karim Alexander. When she died I wondered at the cruelty of Allah who ordained that I should not die with her.'

'I am sorry for your loss, Excellency.'

'I thank you for your sympathy, but I no longer mourn her death. Instead I offer thanks for our years of happiness together. Not only do I have the memory of untold hours of joy, but Allah, in his great wisdom, has allowed me to live long enough to see Karim Alexander grow to full manhood. So bountiful is Allah's mercy that he has even sent you to me, the one woman my son needed to complete his happiness.'

'I don't think I could have been chosen by Allah,' Charlotte protested. 'I'm afraid I would make a terrible Muslim wife.'

'Fortunately Allah's vision is not limited as mortal vision is limited. He sees far enough and deep enough to dismiss the divisions we humans impose.' The Emir walked over to his son's book collection and ran his fingers along the leather bindings. 'My son is a mixture of two cultures that do not easily reconcile with each other. Duty, tradition and personal feelings are constantly at war within Karim Alexander. When he came back from school in Europe he tried to please me by marrying Fatima, the bride I chose for him. He fulfilled every obligation imposed by courtesy, honour and tradition, but his life with her was no more than an endless round of obligation, unleavened by any spark of passion or admiration. Poor little Fatima! She was so lost and unhappy, and Karim Alexander felt so guilty when he saw her misery.'

'The women in the harem thought your son was so

much in love with Fatima that he couldn't bear to marry another woman!'

'The story is kinder so, and the telling prettier. But, in truth, my son refused to marry again because he dreaded the heavy weight of another loveless marriage. It was only during the long years of our separation that I acknowledged in my heart that the woman to inspire his love would not be Turkish. And it is only since I saw you, Charlotte Rippon, that I knew the right bride for my son had been found at last.'

'But how can you know such things, Excellency? You have never seen my face clearly. You have never heard me speak with Alexander, never seen me——'

'I have no need to see *you*,' the Emir replied gently. 'I need only observe my son. Knowing him as I do, it was not hard to guess that obligations to your family played only the smallest part in his decision to marry you. Beneath the careful coolness of his expression I saw that he burned with the desire to possess you.'

'You are wrong, Excellency.' Charlotte's denial was all the more vehement because she wished so much that the Emir might be right. 'Alexander offered to marry me because he felt obliged to rescue my aunt and me from a lifetime of captivity in your harem.'

'He might have used such an excuse, even to himself. A moment's calm reflection would have shown him that he needed to make no such gesture. However little my son may understand me, he knows me well enough to be certain that I would have released you both into his care without any need for the formality of a wedding.'

'But it was you, Excellency, who insisted the wedding should take place at once!'

'That is so,' the Emir agreed, smiling complacently. 'Your marriage to my son was destined by Allah. When I insisted upon an immediate marriage I merely ensured that neither pride nor the evil machinations of others would stand in the way of your joyful destiny.'

Charlotte knelt beside the old Emir. 'But your son plans to send me away. How can I bring him joy if he divorces me?'

'Fight for him, Charlotte Rippon. If you fear to

confess your love, show him passion until you gain courage. You are a beautiful woman and have powerful weapons at your disposal. Use them.'

'I don't think English women are very well trained in the use of weapons of passion,' she said in a small voice.

The Emir smiled. 'I suspect that my son is an excellent teacher, Charlotte Rippon. Perhaps you need do no more than relax and learn to enjoy his instruction.'

She gulped. 'In England a lady is not supposed to enjoy passion.'

'How very odd,' he said softly. 'Here in the Orient there are many things we can learn from your country. This one thing, perhaps, you can learn from us.'

Charlotte drew in a deep breath, almost unable to assimilate the wealth of new information and ideas. 'You have been very kind to me, Excellency.'

'Because I am a selfish old man, and I want to know that my son is happy.'

'I will try to make him happy, Excellency.'

'And I am sure you will succeed. While my son is away, fighting the world's battles, I shall tend to my garden. Then one day, a few years from now, you will bring my grandsons home for me to admire and spoil. That will be my reward.'

CHAPTER SEVEN

CHARLOTTE and Lady Adeline were smuggled out of the palace in the early hours of the morning. Escorted by a phalanx of the Emir's sturdiest fighting men, they arrived at the docks before sunrise and were carried on board almost unnoticed.

Hank Barrett showed them to their cabin: a small but comfortably appointed room with a mirrored chest of drawers set between the two bunk beds, and a tiny desk and chair standing in the corner opposite the porthole.

'Real beds! And furniture!' Lady Adeline sighed in

ecstasy, tossing aside her veil with joyful abandon. 'Oh, Captain! I cannot tell you how magnificent this cabin looks to my homesick eyes!'

He beamed, gratified by her excitement. 'I'm glad you like it, my lady. This is normally Lieutenant Fitzroy's cabin, but he's bunking with the other officers. Now, if you'll excuse me, I have to get back on deck.'

'Of course, we quite understand how busy you are.'

'So busy, I almost forgot to tell you of my surprise.' Hank paused in the doorway, his eyes twinkling. 'If you two ladies would care to open the chest I think you might find something to please you stored within.'

'Oh, Captain Barrett, can it be. . .could it be that you have somehow procured us decent clothing?' Lady Adeline ran to the chest with the eagerness of a child and tugged open the top drawer. 'Oh, Charlotte, just look! We can wear *skirts* again!'

Hank chuckled benevolently. 'Now, now, you're spoiling my surprise, Lady Adeline.'

Charlotte slowly unhooked her veil, allowing it to fall across her shoulders. 'How long will it be before Alexander arrives on board, Captain Barrett?'

'Not too long, I don't expect.' Hank sounded reassuring enough, but his vagueness irritated Charlotte. She wasn't a child, and even if the news was bad she wanted to hear it.

'I would prefer to know the truth, Captain. In your opinion, is he going to make it here safely?'

'I'm sure he is. That man has more lives than our ship's cat.' Hank's cheerful expression sobered somewhat. 'However, until we're safely out to sea, I must ask you two ladies to remain in the cabin. We don't want any last-minute accidents to spoil our get-away.'

'Indeed not.' Lady Adeline shuddered. 'Dear heavens, I couldn't bear to think of spending another night in this dreadful town.'

'Don't worry, my lady. I guarantee we'll be at sea before sundown.'

Lady Adeline blossomed under his reassurances, her complexion becoming rosier by the minute and her eyes sparkling with unexpected liveliness. Charlotte turned away and stared out of the porthole, not wishing to dampen her aunt's cheerful mood. The captain had promised that they would be at sea by nightfall and she didn't doubt his word. But would Alexander be with them?

Lady Adeline dragged her niece over to the chest of drawers the moment Hank Barrett left the cabin. 'Charlotte, dearest, just see what that nice man has found for us! Petticoats and spencers, and knitted stockings! Two gowns and even a pair of mittens! Dear child, we can dress respectably again.'

Charlotte tried to feel cheered by the prospect of changing her highly improper harem garments for linen drawers, three layers of patticoats, a stiff white under-blouse and a grey polished cotton gown in the style of a pelisse. She failed.

Lady Adeline suffered from no such inexplicable fit of melancholy. She abandoned her caftan and the unmentionable trousers with a speed and an expertise that would have astonished the maids back home in England. Within fifteen minutes, only slightly out of breath, she stood before her niece, transformed once again into the familiar Lady Adeline of Rippon Manor. Charlotte burst into tears.

Lady Adeline, who found Charlotte's usual common sense almost impossible to deal with, experienced no difficulty whatever in handling a minor bout of female hysteria. She recalled that, during the past few days, her niece had given way to a fainting fit, had indulged in odd moods of introspection, and now had broken down into this positive storm of weeping. Thank the Lord, but it seemed as if Charlotte was beginning to behave like any other woman at last. It was almost worth being abducted to find out that her niece *could* behave like a lady when she set her mind to the task.

'There, there,' Lady Adeline said soothingly, stroking her niece's back. 'All this has been too much for you, Charlotte, dearest, but we shall soon be home and this dreadful nightmare can be forgotten. In a month or so Prince Karim and the Emir will be no more than a distant memory.'

Her words reduced Charlotte to a further paroxysm of tears, but Aunt Adeline merely availed herself of one of the clean handkerchiefs, thoughtfully provided by Captain Barrett, and waited for the sobs to cease.

Charlotte debated telling Aunt Adeline that she was crying precisely because she feared that her marriage to Alexander would be declared finished almost before it began. Deciding that such a revelation was calculated to send her aunt into strong hysterics, she resolutely quelled her tears.

'You are assuming we shall sail away from here without incident,' she said, trying to make some sort of explanation which her aunt might understand. 'But we have no way of knowing if Alexander. . .if Prince Karim is safe. First he must present his case convincingly to the Sultan, and then, even if he is not charged with high treason, he still has to make good his escape from the Grand Vizier and Sir Clive.'

'Well, that is no cause for tears,' Aunt Adeline replied comfortably. 'Captain Barrett is one of Prince Karim's oldest friends, and, if he has no concerns, I don't see any reason for us to trouble our heads about the Prince's safety.'

'There are dozens of reasons! Sir Clive, for one, cannot *afford* to allow Alexander to escape. He must realise Alexander will inform the British Government of his treachery.'

'I'm sure Emir Ibrahim is perfectly capable of taking care of an annoying little man like Sir Clive. The Emir struck me as a crafty gentleman. Not at all what one would wish for in an Englishman, of course, but the sort of character that must be very useful in a country like this. Don't fall back into bad habits, Charlotte, dearest, just when you were behaving so well. There is no reason in the world to burden your poor little brain with unnecessary worries when we have Captain Barrett to do our worrying for us. We shall be out of here before tea-time, you'll see. Now, why don't you sit down for a minute and I'll pop my head into the corridor and try to find somebody who will bring us a nice cup of morning coffee?'

Lady Adeline's sublime optimism was proved justified when Prince Karim arrived on board late in the afternoon. He wore full court ceremonial costume, having ridden straight to the harbour from his audience with the Sultan. To the vast entertainment of the watching crowds, the Emir's entire personal bodyguard escorted him to the quayside, harness jingling and scimitars flashing in the dazzling June sun.

Prince Karim dismounted, spoke briefly to his father's Captain of the Guard, then strode up the gangplank on to the *American Beauty*. Captain Barrett barely allowed his friend time to step on board before he called out the commands to draw up the gangplank and weigh anchor.

Charlotte had only felt the first tentative sighs and creaks of the ship preparing to set sail when Prince Karim Alexander arrived at the entrance to her cabin.

'Come in, Prince, do come in!' Lady Adeline bubbled with good humour. 'What a pity, we just sent the teapot back to the galley.' She laughed. 'You see, dear sir, how I have become a sailor already? I know I mustn't say kitchen. Will you come in, Prince, and sit for a while?'

Alexander remained in the entrance, his gaze fixed rigidly on Lady Adeline. 'Thank you, my lady, but I will not come in. I stopped only to assure myself that you and your niece were safe and. . .comfortable.'

'Captain Barrett has been very kind,' Charlotte said, willing her husband to look at her. Her entire body ached with the need for his touch. Her mouth trembled as she imagined the caress of his kiss. What would happen, she wondered, if she ran across the cabin and threw herself into his arms? Aunt Adeline, of course, would undoubtedly faint. But what would Alexander do?

She hovered on the verge of casting caution to the winds and flying into his embrace, then he turned slowly in her direction and her feet froze to the ground.

He surveyed her swiftly, taking in all the details of her changed appearance in a single arrogant glance. For a fleeting instant she thought she saw disappointment in the depths of his eyes, then his feelings were once again hidden behind a blank mask of courtesy.

'I'm pleased that the European clothes have met with your approval,' he said coolly.

'It's such a blessing to be respectably clad again.' Aunt Adeline smiled, supremely oblivious to the lightning shafts of electric tension swirling all around her. 'I hope your meeting with the Sultan went well, Prince Karim?'

'I think so. I am optimistic that he may sign the Anglo-Russian Protocol as Mr Canning urged him to do.'

'So now all our problems are solved. How very nice!'

'Some of our problems are solved,' Alexander corrected gently. 'But if you and your niece would care to join Captain Barrett and me for a late dinner tonight I shall be able to explain our situation to you more fully.'

'We shall look forward to it,' Aunt Adeline assured him.

Hank Barrett greeted their arrival at the dinner table with a bluff heartiness that contrasted strongly with Alexander's restrained courtesy. 'We're still in the Sea of Marmara, heading for the Aegean,' Hank said as his cabin boy served a simple but well-cooked meal of chicken stew and rice. 'We hope to run the Dardanelles before first light tomorrow. No point in drawing attention to ourselves if we can avoid it, even though we're flying the American flag. We should reach our destination some time on the morning after next. The wind is in our favour.'

'Where exactly is our destination?' Charlotte asked.

Captain Barrett exchanged a quick glance with Alexander before replying. 'The island of Pakos,' he said at last. 'We have supplies to take on board there.'

'And then we'll be sailing for England?' Lady Adeline enquired.

This time it was Alexander who replied. 'No,' he said. 'I'm sorry, my lady, but an immediate return to England simply isn't feasible. We have supplies to ferry into Greece and it's essential to get them there without any further delay. A voyage to England would add several weeks to our delivery schedule, and we cannot afford those weeks. The people of my estates will be dead of starvation if I don't bring them food soon.'

'Don't worry, my lady.' Captain Barrett was at his most encouraging. 'Alexander here has special navigation charts showing all the favoured routes of the Turkish Navy. They were provided by the British Foreign Secretary himself. We're going to be able to slip in and out of Greek harbour without so much as sighting a Turkish fighting vessel.'

Lady Adeline seemed comforted by the captain's suave reassurances. Charlotte, too, cheered up slightly—although for vastly different reasons. If they weren't sailing straight back to England her chances of coming to some sort of an understanding with Alexander surely must be improved, she reasoned.

Alexander's next words betrayed the shaky foundations of her optimism. 'You will be pleased to know, Miss Rippon, that the Sultan has entrusted me with personal messages for Mr Canning, so it is imperative that I should return to England the moment we have delivered these supplies. You will not long be burdened with my company.'

She lifted her eyes until their gazes locked. 'Why do you call me Miss Rippon?'

He didn't answer her immediately, and Lady Adeline broke into the silence. 'Well, dearest, what else should he call you? The Prince realises as well as any of us that the ceremony you went through in his father's house has no legal standing.'

'On the contrary,' Alexander remarked swiftly. 'Our marriage has every possible legal standing until I pronounce the decree of divorce.'

Aunt Adeline looked shocked, and Charlotte asked swiftly, 'Then why did you call me Miss Rippon?'

His eyes darkened. 'Perhaps because I did not wish to cause offence by reminding you of the true relationship existing between us. What else would you have me call you, *Miss Rippon*?'

The vision of his bed, and her body twined intimately with his, sprang into her mind. She recalled all too vividly the murmured words of passion, the names of endearment that had passed between them, and her cheeks flamed with heat. Hank Barrett looked at the pair of them and covered a grin by swallowing some wine. Young lovers, he thought with a combination of irritation and envy, before taking pity on them both.

'Alex, we should tell the ladies what happened to our old friend Sir Clive Bottomley,' he said with a tactful change of subject. 'They don't know as yet that his interview with the Grand Vizier didn't go exactly as planned.' Hank chortled. 'The Grand Vizier handed him into the custody of the British Ambassador, together with all the Government papers he was trying to sell.'

Lady Adeline clapped her hands, and Charlotte smiled. 'I'm delighted to hear he met his just reward, Captain, but why in the world did the Grand Vizier do something so convenient for us?'

'Not because it suited us, I can assure you,' Alexander said. 'The Grand Vizier saw that the Sultan was not prepared to accept the truth of Sir Clive's information, so he simply decided the man had outlived his usefulness. Thirty years ago he would have been tossed into a dungeon. Nowadays even the Vizier is a little more cautious in his treatment of powerful foreigners.'

As far as Lady Adeline was concerned it was enough to know that Sir Clive had been taken into custody—British custody. She had no wish for a long dissertation on the foreign-policy recommendations that Prince Karim had made to the Sultan, and she quickly changed the subject. 'How long will it take to load the provisions once we reach this island of yours?' she asked.

'Not more than five or six hours,' Hank said. 'We plan to load the minute we arrive, whatever hour it is, day or night. The islanders are only too glad of the work, so we have no shortage of willing hands. Besides, they are Greek, even though their island lies so close to the Turkish mainland, and they know these supplies will keep their fellow countrymen in the Morea alive through the winter.'

'Could we send word to our family, Captain Barrett, to let them know that Charlotte and I are on our way home?'

'I wish it were possible, my lady, but there's no mail service from Pakos. We might manage to find somebody to carry a letter from one of the larger islands, but the *American Beauty* is so fast, I expect we'll be sailing into English harbour long before any of your messages could arrive.'

'I suppose, in a way, that is good news.' Lady Adeline seemed determined to be cheerful. She rose graciously to her feet. 'Well, gentlemen, my niece and I will leave you to the enjoyment of your port. Let us hope that the winds remain favourable and we arrive in Pakos on schedule the day after tomorrow.'

In the event the winds proved less than co-operative, and it was well past noon on Thursday by the time Hank navigated his brig into the deep natural harbour on the western side of the Isle of Pakos.

Alexander and three other crew members were first off the ship, rowing themselves ashore almost before the anchor was secured. By the time Lady Adeline and Charlotte were ferried ashore, some two hours later, at least twenty islanders were already hard at work, dragging huge barrels and crates across the beach, while another dozen men rowed boats loaded with supplies out to the *American Beauty*. Alexander, clad only in breeches and a cotton shirt, stood knee-deep in the sea-water, directing the loading operations, while Hank Barrett took charge of the placement aboard ship.

Lieutenant Fitzroy and Edwin, the cabin boy, erected a makeshift canvas awning on the beach to protect the ladies from the blazing late afternoon sun, then spread another sheet of canvas to protect their clothing from contact with the sand. All the crew had been too busy to prepare anything at breakfast time, so Charlotte was delighted when the lieutenant handed over a small basket of bread, cold chicken, and bunches of delicious black grapes brought down to the beach by the children of the island.

'How thoughtful of you, Lieutenant,' she said, smiling up at him.

'It was Prince Karim who remembered you hadn't eaten,' the lieutenant replied.

'Well, you must thank him from both of us,' Lady

Adeline told him, sitting down on the canvas mat and settling her back against a convenient boulder.

Their late luncheon over, Lady Adeline announced that she planned to fill the remaining hours of the afternoon by taking a nap. 'You should do the same, Charlotte. You're looking positively peaky. The heat obviously doesn't agree with you.' She arranged her skirts decorously about her ankles, lay down under the shadiest corner of the awning and promptly fell asleep.

Charlotte was too restless to follow her aunt's sensible example and fall asleep. She watched Alexander heave one of the massive crates into a row-boat, the muscles of his neck cording with the effort. Her stomach coiled itself into an aching, yearning knot, and this time she recognised the sensation for what it was. Desire. The desire to hold Alexander and to be held by him. The desire to feel the hardness of his body covering her softness. The desire to have him caress her breasts and trail his hands across her hips.

She closed her eyes, shutting out images that were too painfully vivid. When she opened them again Alexander was walking up the line of sweating, straining workers, offering encouragement. His shirt clung damply to his back, soaked with a mixture of sweat and sea-spray. His black hair had grown since they left England, and now it brushed the collar of his shirt. He passed only a few feet away from Charlotte, but he seemed totally oblivious to her presence. A lock of hair fell forward into his eyes, and he pushed it away with a careless, impatient gesture.

Her heart contracted with a little squeeze of love. She wished passionately that she had the courage to kick off her shoes and stockings and run into the water to join him at his back-breaking chores. She could wipe the sweat from his brow before it dripped down into his eyes. She could offer him grape juice to drink. She could *touch* him. . .

Out here? In full view of about fifty interested observers? She was more likely to be swept off her feet by an incoming wave than to offer Alexander any practical help. Regretfully she turned back towards the canvas awning, almost stumbling over two beautiful and incredibly dirty young children who had positioned themselves right behind her.

The older of the two youngsters might have been four years old. Solemn-eyed, unblinking, he surveyed Charlotte in nerve-racking silence. The other child, scarcely old enough to toddle, was busily engaged in sucking his thumb. Tugging at her skirt, the older boy indicated that she was to follow him inland.

The heat of the mid-afternoon sun was greater than anything she had ever experienced before, and the rough, pebble-strewn path literally burned beneath the soles of her shoes. Close to fainting from the heat, Charlotte was immeasurably relieved when the barefooted youngsters finally drew to a halt outside a hovel that would not have been considered fit habitation for pigs on the Rippon Manor estate. The older of the two boys drew aside a tattered leather curtain and encouraged Charlotte to enter. The fetid air of the interior rushed out to meet her, but, drawing in several gulps of fresh air, she did as he requested.

Seated on the dirt floor, her back resting against the rough plaster wall, was a weary-eyed, bone-thin woman, probably somewhat older than Charlotte's own five-and-twenty. In her arms she nursed an infant who could not have been born more than a day or two previously.

Charlotte knelt beside the mother and her infant, making international cooing noises of approval. The mother smiled proudly, pulling aside the baby's rags so that her visitor could admire the full perfection of his body.

'Another boy,' Charlotte commented, smiling. 'Your husband will be pleased to have so many fine sons.'

The mother seemed to understand the gist of what had been said, and she smiled tiredly, but the boys continued to tug at Charlotte's skirts, and she soon realised that it was not their new brother that she had been brought to see. On the contrary, the boys' interest was entirely centred upon a large goat tethered to the hovel's only piece of furniture—a giant bed.

The goat, like the children's mother, had obviously given birth in the past few days, and her snow-white kids—the cleanest objects in the room—wobbled around her on shaky legs. Charlotte's young host removed his thumb from his mouth just long enough to sweep up the runt of the litter and thrust it directly into Charlotte's arms.

She accepted her temporary gift with a smile. The older boy meanwhile reached on to a low shelf for a pottery bowl and proceeded to milk the nanny-goat with amazing efficiency, considering the small size of his fists. Watched by his approving mother, he proudly presented the bowl of foamy blue milk to his visitor.

Her stomach turned threateningly, informing Charlotte in no uncertain terms that warm goat's milk was not its idea of an appropriate summer afternoon drink. But there was obviously going to be no reprieve from consuming this offering. She closed her eyes and drank.

Goat's milk, she decided as she drained the bowl, was never likely to become one of her favourite beverages. With a sickly smile and a firm gesture she refused her young host's offer of a second helping.

Upon reflection she realised that the goats probably represented a major part of this family's livelihood, and she wondered how she could repay the children's hospitality without causing offence. The stifling heat reminded her that she was wearing three lace-trimmed linen petticoats. Not allowing herself time to reflect on Aunt Adeline's probable reaction, she turned her back on the two little boys and quickly stepped out of one of her petticoats.

Folding it into a makeshift shawl, she handed it to the mother. 'For your new son,' she said, laying the petticoat in the wooden crate that obviously served as the baby's bed.

The mother touched the snow-white linen with hesitant fingers. Her face, when she looked up at Charlotte, reflected her awe. Her sons cut short what was obviously a profuse expression of thanks by the simple expedient of running out of the hut and tugging on Charlotte's skirts until she went with them.

The fierce heat was fading into the milder warmth of evening as they started their walk back to the beach. A sea breeze sprang up, ruffling her hair, and Charlotte realised suddenly how much she was enjoying herself.

The boys pranced ahead of her, agile as the goats they raised. They pointed with pride to a spring of water that spurted out of the rocky hillside and provided a narrow oasis of tough, spiky grass and brilliantly coloured flowers. Charlotte knelt down on the grass, taking off her sun-bonnet and unfastening the top few buttons of her bodice so that she could bathe her face and neck in the luxurious spray of cool water. The two little boys, she noticed wryly, watched her ablutions with interest but showed absolutely no inclination to follow suit.

'What the *hell* do you think you're doing?' Alexander's voice, quiet but deadly with anger, interrupted the chirrup of the boys' voices. 'Where have you been for the past hour? Do you realise your aunt is sick with worry? Do you realise that half my crew is wasting valuable time looking for you?'

Charlotte scrambled to her feet, humiliatingly conscious of the water still dripping from her face and hands. She wiped her forehead on the sleeve of her gown, her instinctive apologies dying away unspoken as she registered the full impact of Alexander's furious expression.

'*Your* crew?' she replied pointedly, fanning her anger to match his. 'I'm sure Captain Barrett would be interested to hear his men described in such terms.'

'The *Beauty* may be Hank's ship, but every penny of the money to support her operation over the past three years has come from me. It is *my* crew wasting time looking for you, Charlotte.'

'Do you call me Miss Rippon only when my aunt is around to hear you, Prince Karim? Are we supposed to have one relationship in private and another in public?'

The two little boys, not liking the sound of angry voices, crept closer to Charlotte's skirts. In their efforts to make themselves invisible they pulled at her gown, popping open two more of the buttons on her bodice. Too late she realised that her dress must by now be unbuttoned well beyond the point of decency. Lowering her gaze, she tried to repair the damage with fingers that suddenly felt like a collection of ten artificial thumbs. Dear God, but she could *feel* the heat of Alexander's gaze burning against the swell of her breasts.

Alexander took a few quick steps towards her, his pretence of anger draining away in a rush of uncontrollable desire. 'No,' he muttered hoarsely, covering her hand with his. 'Leave your dress as it is, Charlotte. Let me enjoy the torture of remembering.'

'We must get back to the beach,' she said disjointedly. 'Your men. . .the little boys. . .'

Alexander spoke softly in Greek, and the two children emerged from behind Charlotte's skirts, scampering off towards the distant shore.

'My men are nowhere in sight, Charlotte, and the little boys have run off to receive a sweetmeat.' His head lowered slowly to her mouth. 'Give me your lips,' he whispered. 'Let me taste you just once more.'

Hesitantly, she raised her face to his, still innocent enough to be shocked by the naked passion that she saw etched on to his dark features. All too aware of the pleasure mixed in with her shyness, she let Alexander capture her shoulders, dragging her effortlessly against the rock-hard strength of his body. Beneath the dampness of his cotton shirt she could feel the hurried, uneven pounding of his heart. Then desire flooded her, hot and remorseless, as his mouth seized hers in a hungry kiss.

She was soon helpless and shuddering beneath his expert caresses, her naïve desire brought from a tentative spark to a leaping flame by the sophisticated ministrations of his mouth and hands. His fingers probed the unbuttoned neckline of her gown and found the ribbons of her chemise. Slowly, tantalisingly, he untied them. She heard herself give a tiny groan of pleasure as he insinuated his hand beneath the chemise, seeking out her nipple. Her arms fastened urgently around his neck, heedless of anything save the demands of her own body. Dear God, but she wanted to be closer to him, to feel his skin naked against hers, to feel his hands caressing her body——

'*Charlotte*!' The anguished screech was unmistakably

Aunt Adeline. 'Dear Lord in Heaven, what are you *doing*, child?'

Alexander froze as if shot. At first Charlotte continued to cling to him, aroused beyond the point of pride, or even understanding. Then the clouds of passion cleared just sufficiently for her to realise that Aunt Adeline was speaking to her, and her entire body blushed dark red with humiliation. She jerked guiltily, trying to pull herself out of Alexander's arms, but he restrained her.

'Don't move for a minute,' he murmured into her ear, his fingers skilfully refastening the buttons of her gown. 'I fear your aunt would succumb to instant hysterics if she got a good look at either of us in our current state.'

Hank Barrett's voice, an undercurrent of amusement easily audible, interrupted the babble of Lady Adeline's frantic exclamations. 'When you're ready, Alex, the men are preparing to load the last few barrels of oil. I'll escort Lady Adeline back to the ship, if you'll take care of Miss Rippon?'

'Thank you, Hank, for your thoughtfulness.' The merest hint of rueful irony tinged Alexander's reply.

'No trouble at all, Alex. By the way, it's going to be another three and a half hours before the tide will be right for leaving harbour.'

'Don't worry. We're not likely to miss the boat.' Alexander spoke over his shoulder, his body still shielding Charlotte from Aunt Adeline's apoplectic view.

'Miss the boat! Now you listen to me, Prince Karim! I shall expect you both back at the beach within five minutes.' Aunt Adeline's command left no room for argument or denial.

'We shall be there,' Alexander replied quietly.

Rooted to the spot with shame, Charlotte listened to the sound of two sets of footsteps steadily retreating. Finally Alexander loosened the clasp of his arms around her waist and stepped away.

He regarded her gravely. 'I'm sorry, Charlotte. But perhaps it is fortunate Hank and your aunt arrived in time to prevent us both from committing some folly we would afterwards regret. Will you allow me to escort you back to the shore? I believe Lieutenant Fitzroy is ready to return you and Lady Adeline to the *Beauty*.'

Charlotte stared at a fragile pink flower, crushed beneath her foot. 'I am quite ready,' she said.

They walked back to the beach, a yard of empty space separating their bodies and a lifetime of cultural differences separating their souls.

Once they arrived back on board the *Beauty* Charlotte knew that there was no point in trying to delay the inevitable confrontation with her aunt. Lady Adeline closed the door to their cabin with a firmness that boded ill, her bosom heaving under the stress of her righteous indignation. Hands folded tightly across her stomach, she pursed her normally gentle mouth into a prim, reproving line.

'This is a *most* distressing moment for me, Charlotte.'

'I'm sorry, Aunt.'

'Apologies are scarcely sufficient to rectify the dreadful damage you've done. I stand here in place of your dear departed mother, and it is my *duty* to demand an explanation of your appalling behaviour. Although what possible explanation you can offer for. . .for——'

'For kissing Alexander?' Charlotte supplied helpfully.

Lady Adeline shuddered. 'Charlotte, how *could* you? And when we are on our way home to safety, too. It's not as if we were still in that dreadful harem, and subject to the whim of all those horrid people. What would Archdeacon Jeffries say if he knew that the lady he wishes to marry has *willingly* indulged in. . .indulged in physical embraces with another man? And with a man who is a *foreigner*, of all things?'

'Would our kisses have been easier to watch if Alexander happened to be English?' Charlotte demanded. She untied the strings of her cotton bonnet and tossed it angrily on to the bed. 'Do you know something, Aunt? I don't give a *damn* what the archdeacon thinks. Not about my embraces with a foreigner or about anything else for that matter. The man is a pompous hypocrite and I am never going to marry him. Besides, you seem to forget that I'm already married to Alexander, and he hasn't divorced me yet. With any luck maybe he never will.'

Lady Adeline took several deep, rapid breaths. 'I shall not faint,' she announced. 'Even though I heard you use the most unladylike profanity, I shall not faint, nor shall I have hysterics.' Her attempt at sternness collapsed, and two tears trickled slowly down her pink cheeks. 'Oh, Charlotte, I don't understand anything that's happening to us any more! What is to become of us both?'

Full of remorse, Charlotte swept her aunt into a warm hug. 'Don't cry, dearest Aunt,' she said, herself torn halfway between tears and laughter. 'I'm not surprised if you feel a little bewildered. The life we led at Rippon Manor doesn't seem to have much connection with Turkish Sultans and revolutionary wars, not to mention ferrying rebel supplies into occupied Greek territory.'

Lady Adeline's tears stopped and she looked much struck. 'If we ever do get back to the manor, only think of the stories I shall have to tell the Ladies' Sewing Circle! So much for the squire's wife and her visits to her daughter in Paris.'

Charlotte laughed. 'They will never believe you, Aunt.'

'Probably not.' Lady Adeline sighed. 'And, of course, a great many of our experiences simply can't be mentioned in polite company.'

'Like wearing transparent trousers in the harem, you mean?'

Lady Adeline gave a horrified shriek. 'Charlotte, promise me you will never mention those. . .those *garments* again!'

'I promise, Aunt.' Charlotte's eyes gleamed with mischief. 'At least not in company.'

Lady Adeline gave another shriek, but her heart wasn't in it. She sat on the edge of the bed and pulled disconsolately at a loose thread in the sleeve of her gown. Finally she drew in a deep breath, clearly nerving herself to speak.

'Charlotte, we have lived together nearly all your life, and you know how very fond of you I am, so you must not think I am a nosy old woman asking questions I have no right to ask. Would you tell me what you meant, dearest child, when you said that with any luck the Prince might never divorce you?'

Charlotte became much occupied with arranging her hair-pins in a neat row on top of the chest of drawers. 'I love him, Aunt,' she admitted finally. 'I cannot think of anything in this world I want more than to remain with him always.'

'He is nothing at all like any of the nice young men in our neighbourhood,' Lady Adeline commented in a small voice.

Charlotte knelt beside her aunt. 'Perhaps that is why I like him so well,' she said earnestly. 'Think about it, Aunt Adeline. If I fitted so perfectly into English country society, why did I reach twenty-five years of age without ever falling in love? Most of my friends were married long before their twentieth birthday.'

'Probably because they didn't confuse falling in love with getting married,' Lady Adeline pointed out sadly. 'Matrimony is a practical institution, my dear, designed to protect property and provide stable homes in which to raise children. Love is a very nice feeling while it lasts, but it is rarely of long duration. A sensible young lady first finds a suitable marriage partner, then persuades herself that she loves him. You have always wanted to do it the other way around. The wrong way around.'

'But perhaps Alexander *is* a suitable marriage partner for me.'

'He certainly seems to have sufficient funds——'

'No, I don't mean money. I mean that our characters are well suited, despite the difference in our backgrounds. He makes me laugh. He makes me think. He makes me feel alive.' Her voice fell to no more than a whisper. 'When he touches me I am on fire.'

'How. . .how monstrous uncomfortable that must be.'

'No,' Charlotte said softly. 'Not uncomfortable, dear Aunt. Bewildering. Agonising. Terrifying. And wonderful.'

Lady Adeline jumped off the bed and patted her hair briskly. 'Well, dearest, I suppose there is no more to be said on the subject at the moment. In some ways your brothers may feel there are advantages in acknowledging the marriage. After all, when you get right down to it, he *is* a Prince.'

'But only a Greek one, Aunt.'

Lady Adeline was sublimely unaware of being teased. 'Charlotte, a Prince is a Prince, and in London society I dare say people would not care so much about the fact that he is foreign.'

'How true. In fact, fashion is so fickle in London that next season Greek princes may be all the rage.'

'That would never happen in St Leonard's, of course.'

Charlotte's eyes twinkled. 'No, not in St Leonard's. But think of it this way, Aunt. As a Princess I would take precedence over Lady Thimbleby, and you know how much you have always longed for somebody to move into the district who would outrank her.'

'Good heavens, you're quite right. Even a foreign Prince and Princess must take precedence over an ordinary Earl and Countess.' Lady Adeline's normally jolly features took on a pugnacious glow. 'We shall give a ball as soon as we get back to Rippon Manor. All your brothers will have to come, and we shall introduce the Prince to the neighbourhood. My, my, how splendid it will be!'

Charlotte felt constrained to offer a word of caution. 'First we have to make sure that Alexander doesn't divorce me.'

Lady Adeline's glance was unexpectedly shrewd. 'I think, my dear, that you will be able to find some way to persuade him that he would prefer to stay married.'

The *American Beauty* sailed swiftly through the sparkling blue waters of the Aegean, seemingly alone in the miles of tranquil ocean. On board tension increased hourly as they sailed ever closer to the Gulf of Argolis, where Alexander's estates lay and where the Greek Provisional Government stood besieged.

'We plan to slip in and out of the bay under cover of darkness,' Hank Barrett explained to Charlotte and Lady Adeline over a hasty breakfast of coffee and dry biscuits. 'With so many Egyptian soldiers roaming the peninsula we cannot afford to be spotted while we are unloading the provisions.'

'Which bay have you chosen for the landing?' Charlotte asked.

'Alexander will navigate the last few miles,' Hank said. 'The decision is his. The Greek coastline has so many inlets that even a brig as large as the *Beauty* can find the occasional natural harbour deep enough to accommodate her. And fortunately the Prince knows this stretch of coast like the back of his hand.'

'Where is the Prince these days?' Lady Adeline asked. 'We've scarcely seen him since we loaded supplies from that little island three days ago.'

'He is very busy, my lady. He is the only person who knows the precise location of our landing-spot, and he feels a heavy burden of responsibility for our safety. He doesn't want to lead us into a bunch of Turkish fireships if he can avoid it.'

'Fireships? Dear God, what are they?'

'Don't worry about them,' Hank said hurriedly. 'I assure you, Lady Adeline, there's no real chance of our encountering any Turkish ships at all, especially a fire-ship. And if we do happen to meet up with a straggler we fly the American flag. They would never risk attacking us.'

Lady Adeline appeared relieved. 'That's good to know,' she said. 'Make sure our flag is kept flying high on the mast.'

Charlotte looked at Captain Barrett, wishing he was a better liar. His protestations had lacked conviction, leaving her with the horrid certainty that, when Greeks and Turks started fighting, American flags—however high-flying—provided little in the way of protection.

The *Beauty* was ten miles from shore when the Turkish naval frigate sailed out from its place of concealment behind a tiny offshore island. Charlotte happened to be on deck with her aunt as the look-out called the warning.

'All hands! All hands shorten sail!' Captain Barrett commanded.

The watch ran to their posts and the small crew of officers went to their stations. Courses and topgallants were got in. Alexander came running down from the bridge, taking the stairs two at a time.

He spoke quickly, curtly. 'Go to your cabins, please. It will be safer.'

'Are they going to attack us?' Lady Adeline asked fearfully.

'Possibly. My lady, please, we must clear the decks to position the carronades.'

A sailor ran up to Alexander. 'Sir, the cap'n says to get up to the wheel, sir. They're closing within range, sir, and signalling to board us.'

'Coming.' Alexander looked over his shoulder as he strode away. 'Get below and stay there,' he ordered harshly. '*Now*!'

Once they were in their cabin Charlotte found that the enforced inactivity was torment. Overhead she could hear the noise of pounding feet, the sounds of heavy equipment being dragged into position, the creak of the rigging. She could even hear Captain Barrett bellowing commands, although not clearly enough to distinguish his words. Unable to stand her isolation, she ignored Aunt Adeline's protests and opened the cabin door. The faintest echo of a voice drifted down to her. 'Ship cleared for action, sir.'

'Battle-stations secured, sir.'

'Thank you, Lieutenant. Prepare to attack!'

'Ready, sir.'

'Fire first gun!'

She grabbed the door-jamb for support and thirty seconds later a dull boom echoed across the water, expanding gradually into a louder explosion. The *Beauty* rocked violently, the hull shuddering with after-shocks.

Lady Adeline collapsed on to her bed. 'God help us, we're sinking!'

Charlotte slammed the cabin door shut and ran to the porthole. 'No, I don't think we were hit. Botheration, I can only see a little bit of the frigate! There's smoke everywhere.'

Another round of cannon-shot slammed over the calm water as she spoke, exploding against the hull of the Turkish ship. Smoke, this time interspersed with licking tongues of orange flame, temporarily blacked out her view.

She dashed back to the door, aware of the futility of her actions but unable to quell the frantic need for movement. Her hand was already on the doorknob when she was thrown headlong against the end of Aunt Adeline's bed by a tempestuous, convulsive heave of the *Beauty*. Dazedly, even as she flew through the air, she registered the boom of a massive explosion.

'Oh, God, Charlotte, are you dead?'

'It feels like it.' Wincing, she pulled herself slowly to her feet, the breath returning to her lungs in painful gasps. Prodding herself gingerly, she realised that by some miracle she had escaped all injury except a blow to her shoulder.

Lady Adeline, plump cheeks grey with fear, peeked out from behind the pillow that she had pulled over her head. 'Now we really have been hit,' she moaned. 'Charlotte, I can't swim!'

'One hit doesn't cause a brigantine of this size to sink, Aunt Adeline.' Charlotte tried her best to keep the quiver of panic from her voice.

'Dear Lord, there go the guns again! We can't even tell if they're ours!'

Down the gangway Charlotte heard the echoing call of an officer's voice.

'Report damage below!'

Almost simultaneously another voice bellowed, 'Three men wounded on the aft cannons. Stretcher party on deck! Lord in heaven! Where's the goddamned surgeon? Where's Doc Grimes?'

'The captain's been hit!'

A moan from her aunt indicated that Lady Adeline had heard the bad news. Charlotte ran into the corridor without any consideration for her own safety. 'Wait here,' she said to her aunt. 'Keep the door closed, and I'll be back in a moment. Everything's going to be all right.'

Acrid, foul-smelling smoke covered the deck in a thick haze, and at first she found it impossible to see. The smoke caught at her lungs, squeezing out air, so that she choked almost to the point of retching. Towards the horizon the smoke finally cleared and she could see the Turkish frigate listing badly to starboard. With a rush of triumph she realised that it was retreating.

A gust of wind blew away some of the smoke on deck, and she saw the surgeon huddled over a wounded sailor. Eyes smarting and arms outstretched, she clawed her way across the slippery deck.

'I've come to help,' she told the doctor when she finally reached him. 'The captain's been hit, and they need you at the helm. Can I take over here?'

The surgeon ran his fingers over his patient's face, closing the man's eyes, then dragging the body into the shelter of an overhanging spar. 'No,' he said, turning briskly from the dead body. 'There's nothing for you to do, miss. You'd better be going back to your cabin. These sights aren't for the likes of you.'

As if to reinforce his words a barrage of shot exploded on the deck, tearing great gouges into the planking. 'Get below, miss,' the surgeon shouted, then forged ahead, returning the instruments he had been using to a leather bag, and slinging a blood-stained towel over his shoulder. Charlotte ran after him.

'I can help,' she insisted. 'I'm experienced as a nurse.'

'Miss, get below. You'll be helping nobody if you get a lump of lead shot in your chest.'

'But the Turkish ship is retreating.'

He didn't even pause in his relentless march towards the bridge. 'No, miss. It's swinging around to leeward. It's going to attack from the other side.'

As he spoke they arrived at the helm. Pieces of jib and sail hung at drunken angles to the mast, and torn canvas snapped in the breeze. Debris of every kind littered the deck, making each step hazardous. Only two men remained standing: Alexander and Mr Wardle, the ship's most junior officer, both of them black with powder burns.

The surgeon, with an unerring nose for scenting out the location of the wounded, walked briskly to the masthead, where Captain Barrett, Lieutenant Fitzroy and Edwin, the cabin boy, lay stretched out on the deck.

All three of them were covered in blood and dirt. All three of them seemed to be unconscious.

With a non-committal growl the doctor knelt beside the lieutenant and felt for a heartbeat.

'You still here?' he asked Charlotte, when he could make himself heard above the boom of cannon. 'Since you are, make yourself useful and find me some sailors to help carry these men below.'

She refused to confirm the doctor's low opinion of her by asking how she was supposed to find either sailors or stretchers when the smoke was so thick that it was virtually impossible to see anything two feet from your nose. Doggedly she scrambled to her feet, realising, as she made her way back to the ladder, that Alexander had taken over command of the ship and now stood on the quarterdeck, a spyglass trained on the Turkish ship.

'Fire cannon four to port!' he shouted, his voice powerful enough to be heard over the roar of a dozen different voices. Swinging around to watch the gunners, his gaze fell upon Charlotte, and for a moment his entire body froze into utter stillness. The boom of exploding shot and a roar of triumph from his men brought him back to life.

'Get below stairs this instant, and that's an order, Miss Rippon.' His voice was icy with fury.

'I can't, Alexander. I'm sorry. The surgeon needs my help, and people will die needlessly if I obey you.'

She scrambled helter-skelter down the ladder, giving him no chance to say anything more. She ran in pursuit of a group of sailors, cursing her cumbersome skirts and her lack of speed. She finally caught up with an elderly sailor whom she recognised as a cook from the galley. She seized his arm thankfully.

'The doctor needs you at the helm. Three officers have been injured and we need stretchers to carry them below. We need some more sailors to help with the carrying, just for a few minutes.'

'I'll see to it,' he said. 'Wait here, miss.'

The smoke from another exchange of shots was already beginning to clear by the time she returned to the bridge with the three sailors. 'Took your time, didn't you?' the surgeon demanded grumpily.

'The men were all somewhat busy, Doctor.'

He grunted. Pointing to Lieutenant Fitzroy, he spoke to the cook in a low voice. 'Help me get him to the galley, will you? I'll have to amputate his leg. Thigh bone's smashed right through.'

'What about Captain Barrett and the cabin boy?' Charlotte asked. She had to ask something to avoid throwing up as two of the sailors lifted Lieutenant Fitzroy's mangled body on to a piece of canvas. She was sure she had seen a piece of bone sticking through the lacerated flesh of the lieutenant's leg. She swallowed hard. If she hadn't sensed Alexander's gaze once again fixed coldly upon her, she was quite sure she would have fainted. As it was she gritted her teeth and forced herself to speak with the appearance of calm. 'They're both unconscious, Doctor, and they're covered in blood.'

'They're not going to die, either of them. At least, not in the next half-hour or so. And the little lad's come round a couple of times already. Get them taken below and try to keep them comfortable. Don't let them move if you can avoid it. I've already taken the shot out the captain's wounds, and I'll stitch him up when I've operated on the lieutenant. The lad needs his wrist splinted.'

The Turkish frigate had finally retreated, its main mast in flames, but the sailors she approached all seemed as busy as ever when Charlotte requested their help as stretcher-bearers. 'Unless the captain's dying, miss, we can't come. We have to get the *Beauty* out of sight before the Turks signal for reinforcements,' one of the men explained to her hurriedly. 'The Prince is taking us into his secret harbour.'

In the end Charlotte and the cook carried the wounded men below decks by themselves. They made two trips up to the bridge, carrying first the cabin boy and then the captain on canvas sheets slung between them. Charlotte had never realised how heavy a slender thirteen-year-old boy could feel and, as for the captain, there were several moments when she was sure that her arms would fall out of their sockets before they arrived at her cabin.

To the accompaniment of alarmed squeaks and exclamations from Aunt Adeline Charlotte and the cook bestowed the captain on Charlotte's bed and the cabin boy on Lady Adeline's. Charlotte slumped against the wall, almost too exhausted to move.

Edwin stirred as his head touched the coolness of the pillow, and his eyes flickered open for a second or two. The cook ran a knowledgeable hand over the cabin boy's head. 'He's got a lump the size of a pigeon's egg on the back of his head, miss, and he's broken his wrist. But he's not badly wounded, for all he's so bloody. I think a fair bit of that blood must be from the lieutenant's wounds. They were lying real close.'

Charlotte rinsed a cloth with water from the carafe standing by her bedside. She wiped it over Edwin's filthy, blood-caked face. To her surprise most of the blood washed off on the cloth.

'I think you're right,' she said to the cook, much cheered by the thought that the little cabin boy wasn't at death's door. 'If you could just bring me some hot water, then I think my aunt and I could take care of these two patients quite well by ourselves.'

'I'll be right back, miss.' The cook's expression held a new respect. 'It'll be a real help to everybody if you ladies could get these two ready for Doc Grimes.'

Lady Adeline watched the cook leave the room, fanning herself with her handkerchief. 'Charlotte, I warn you that I am *not* at all able to take care of these men. In fact I am about to faint. This very minute.'

'Please don't, Aunt, because I simply haven't the time to attend to you. Why don't you see about removing Captain Barrett's shoes and perhaps his jacket? The surgeon has already cut half of it away to remove the gunshot, but I expect the captain would rest more comfortably in his shirt.'

Lady Adeline rose ominously to her feet. 'Charlotte, you are trying to turn me into one of those dreadful, *managing* women, and I'm simply not going to let it happen. In the face of death and disaster a lady's role is to have hysterics. It helps a gentleman to feel suitably manly.'

'But, Aunt Adeline, there are no gentlemen here to appreciate your contribution to their feelings of manliness. There is only me, and I need your help so that we can have Captain Barrett ready for the surgeon when he arrives—— Oh, thank you, Cook.' She broke off to address the sailor who stood in the doorway with a pail of steaming water. 'And you've brought some soap, too. How wonderful.'

'And clean rags, so you can bind up the captain till Doc Grimes gets here. If it's all right with you, miss, I'll be on my way. There's two or three other wounded sailors who could use a sip of water while they're waiting for Doc Grimes.'

'Then cut along to them and don't waste time dallying here.' The crusty voice of Captain Barrett spoke from the bed. 'The Turkish ship? We repelled her all right and tight?'

'Aye, we did that, sir. Sent her running for shore with her tail between her legs.'

'Damage to the *Beauty*?'

'Nothing serious, sir. The Prince is taking us into harbour now.'

'Casualties?'

'Two, sir. And Doc Grimes is operating on Lieutenant Fitzroy now.'

'He caught a ball right in the thigh. Saw it coming and yelled, but he didn't hear me. Is he going to lose his leg?'

'We don't know,' Charlotte intervened swiftly. 'But we do know Dr Grimes will clap me in irons if he comes in and finds you sitting up like that.' She nodded to the cook, who slipped out of the room. 'Well, Captain Barrett, are you going to lie down, or are you going to let the surgeon unleash his wrath upon me?'

'The captain is going to lie down,' Lady Adeline said, surprising herself almost as much as Charlotte. She moved forward, purposefully carrying a small bowl of hot water and a soapy wash-rag. She almost dropped everything when she got close enough to the captain to see the blood-soaked mess of his leg and arm, but somehow she managed to keep control of herself.

'You're turning into a managing female,' Hank told her, collapsing against the pillows with a great deal more relief than he was prepared to show. 'Did anybody tell you that?'

'I was commenting upon it myself only moments ago,' Lady Adeline remarked calmly. She sat down on the edge of the bed and began to bathe the captain's face. 'Dear me, whoever would believe that beneath all this grease and gunpowder lies a most handsome set of features?'

Hank scowled ferociously, but didn't quite succeed in concealing his blush of pleasure.

Edwin regained consciousness when Charlotte attempted to clean away some of the blood from his injured hand. He sat up, his newly washed face stark white, and immediately attempted to get out of bed. 'Lie down, you young whipper-snapper,' Hank Barrett ordered softly. 'If I can put up with two ladies playing nursemaid, you can certainly do the same.'

'I'm thirsty,' Edwin croaked. 'Could you please pour me a mug of water, Miss Rippon?'

'I'll see to that,' the doctor said from the doorway. 'Miss Rippon, if it wouldn't be too much of an imposition, the cook asks if you would go to the galley and help him serve some soup to the men who've been injured.'

'Yes, of course, if you and my aunt don't need me here.'

'All I have to do is check the splint on young Edwin's arm and sew a few dainty stitches into the captain's tough hide. There's no reason for you to stay and listen to them bellow.'

'We wouldn't have to bellow if you weren't so cow-handed,' Hank said gruffly.

'He's starting earlier than usual, Miss Rippon. I'd make my escape, if I were you.'

Charlotte entered the galley, keeping her eyes averted from the freshly scrubbed table where she knew Lieutenant Fitzroy had had his leg amputated. The whole kitchen reeked of the rum that had been poured into him in an effort to deaden the pain.

'How is the lieutenant?' she asked the cook.

'Sleeping. The rum's not worn off yet. He's tied to the doc's bed so's he can't move and bleed himself to death. Doc Grimes is an excellent surgeon, but it's touch and go whether he'll make it. It's the blood-poisoning that'll be the problem. That and the fever.'

'I can nurse him tonight, if that would help.'

'Best if Doc Grimes handles it, miss. He'll know what to do in an emergency.'

'The doctor said you wanted me to take some soup to the other injured men?'

'Yes, there's only four of them. They're up aft.'

She carried thick pea soup to the injured men, who were resting in hammocks under a specially rigged awning. The *Beauty* had cabin space for its small complement of officers but the men, as on most other ships, had to sleep wherever they could find room. The sailors, fortunately, didn't seem to be badly wounded and they were excessively grateful for the bowls of soup. All of them appeared embarrassed that such minor injuries should warrant special attention from a lady who was sailing as Prince Karim's guest.

When she returned to the galley the cook had prepared her a cup of soup. She drank eagerly, aware of tiredness seeping into every one of her muscles.

'I will take a tray to Captain Barrett and Edwin and my aunt,' she offered when her soup was finished. 'I know you still have supper to prepare for the rest of the crew.'

'Aye. I'd be grateful if you would, miss. My galley mate was one of the two who died and there's nobody spare to give me a hand.'

'I'm sorry about your mate.'

'Aye, he was a good man. Here you are, miss. This is the tray for Captain Barrett and the boy. Although I'm not sure they'll want to be eating by the time Doc Grimes has finished with them.'

The surgeon was just returning the last of his evil-looking instruments to his bag when Charlotte returned to her cabin with the tray of food. Both patients were propped up on pillows, looking pale and weary, but reasonably healthy.

The surgeon snapped his bag shut and made for the exit. 'If either of them tries to get out of bed, Lady Adeline, you send for me and I'll dose both of them with laudanum—and probably a purgative for good measure.'

'Damn it, man, I'm suppose to be the captain on this ship!'

'Tomorrow you will be again,' the doctor said calmly. 'For tonight, I understand Prince Karim Alexander is doing an excellent job. Miss Rippon, a word with you, please, once you've handed that tray over to your aunt.'

Outside in the corridor the surgeon spoke to her bluntly. 'You are dead on your feet, Miss Rippon. If I could see the colour of your skin under all that gunpowder and smoke decorating your face, I'm sure it would be grey with exhaustion. Get some rest, young lady, before you collapse on me.'

'The idea is appealing,' Charlotte admitted ruefully. 'But there's a slight problem, Dr Grimes. My bed is occupied by Captain Barrett.'

'Use his cabin,' the surgeon said promptly. 'He won't be moving from where he is tonight, so his bed will be free. You will be quiet and private there.'

'I cannot leave my aunt to shoulder all the nursing——'

'I'll see she is relieved as soon as one of the men can be spared. And I will be looking in on them all whenever I can spare time from Fitzroy.'

'How is the lieutenant?'

'Not good. But there is nothing you can do for him, Miss Rippon, so take yourself off to bed before you are added to my overlong list of patients. Here is the key to the captain's cabin. I took it from his jacket pocket.'

'Thank you, Dr Grimes.' Charlotte made no effort to protest any further. The prospect of a few hours' undisturbed sleep was too appealing.

'Thank *you*,' he replied with quiet emphasis. 'Without your help today a lot of people would have had to suffer a lot longer and Lieutenant Fitzroy wouldn't have had a chance.'

There was a cheval-glass directly opposite the door in Captain Barrett's cabin. When Charlotte first saw her reflection she didn't recognise herself and automatically jumped back in alarm from the filthy, grimy-visaged woman who confronted her. When she realised that it was only her reflection she would have laughed except that she was too tired to expend the energy.

Thank heaven the pitcher standing on the captain's dresser was full of clean water. It was cold, of course, but there was a bar of scented soap in a porcelain dish alongside the washbowl, and, with the aid of one of her discarded petticoats, she was able to do a fair job of wiping the sweat and grime from her body. Her hair probably reeked of gunsmoke, but she decided regretfully that she was too tired to attempt to wash it. In any case her supply of clean water was already exhausted.

She contemplated her pile of filthy, discarded clothing with disgust. She supposed she would have to put the chemise back on before she got into bed. Then her eye fell on a shirt of the captain's, obviously freshly laundered, and lying on his bed. The temptation to put on something clean was too great to be overcome. Charlotte reached for the captain's shirt.

She had rolled up the long sleeves, and was tying the last of the string closures, when she heard the sound of a key turning in the lock. Rooted to the spot, she watched the door open. Alexander, stripped to the waist and dripping water, entered the cabin.

He took two steps into the room, then stopped dead when he realised that he was not alone.

For several agonising moments neither of them moved or spoke. Then Alexander walked in and shut the door.

CHAPTER EIGHT

ALEXANDER'S exhaustion was leavened only by the simmering fury he felt at the day's events. It was not so much that the renegade Turkish frigate had violated international law by firing on the *Beauty*. The naval vessels defending the Greek mainland were crewed by mercenaries trained in the old Ottoman art of piracy, so both he and Hank had anticipated an attack. That was why the *Beauty* carried twenty hidden cannon and a crew composed mainly of veterans from the Napoleonic wars.

No, what disturbed Alexander wasn't the attack, but his fear: the blinding, paralysing fear he had felt when the Turkish frigate first appeared on the horizon. Thank God Hank Barrett had been commanding the helm during those crucial first minutes of battle! With a sick sense of shame Alexander acknowledged the unbearable truth. When battle was engaged, for several vital seconds he had been incapable of issuing a rational command. His mind had been filled with the single compelling thought that Charlotte was on board—and that he personally had led her into this appalling danger.

He had seen on other battlefields how love destroyed the efficiency of men fighting for a just cause. He had sworn many times that until the people of Greece were free he would never allow himself to fall victim to the weakness of loving a woman. Now he accepted the bitter truth that he was hopelessly forsworn. He loved Charlotte beyond any chance of change or redemption.

The maelstrom of Alexander's emotions left no room for logic. He didn't stop to thank God that Charlotte had survived her reckless bravery. He didn't stop to ask himself why she was standing, half naked, in Hank's cabin. His brain registered only that she was there, and that, despite his exhaustion, he desired her more than he had ever desired any other woman. In the next instant he was swamped with rage. He stared at Charlotte with something close to hatred as he acknowledged that this woman had the power to distort the entire direction of his life—and shred his heart in the process.

He closed the door, throwing the bolt as a barrier against intruders. A rush of emotion gripped Alexander as he turned to look again at the slender, graceful figure of the woman who was his wife. *His wife.* In other circumstances he might have laughed at the irony of those words, but tonight he found no humour in his situation. He loved Charlotte, but his love gave him no right to take her to his bed. As an honourable man he had no choice other than to return her to the safety and tranquillity of her family life in England. The conflict between honour and desire rubbed his self-control raw.

Not surprisingly Charlotte must have read the anger in his face, for she stepped backwards, crossing her arms over her breasts in an instinctive gesture of self-protection. The frustration still boiled hot and hard within Alexander, and her fear inspired him with a gratifying sense of male domination. He had no power to make Charlotte love him, but at least he had the power to make her fear him.

Through the red haze of his anger he finally realised how odd it was for Charlotte to be standing in the middle of the cabin which he shared with Hank, clad only in a man's shirt. Why in the world was she wearing such an odd garment? he wondered.

'What are you doing here?' he asked, his voice chilled with the ice of sudden jealousy. 'How did you get in?'

With a despairing attempt at modesty Charlotte attempted to conceal her bare legs beneath the flapping tails of the captain's shirt. 'Dr Grimes gave me the key. He said I needed some rest and th-the captain was sleeping in my bed.'

'No wonder you need rest,' Alexander commented furiously, succumbing to another surge of guilt as he realised that even the ship's surgeon had done more today for his wife's comfort than he had. 'You have been running all over the ship in absolute defiance of my orders, putting yourself and members of my crew at risk.

How dare you disobey me by leaving your cabin when I had expressly commanded you to stay there?'

'You had commanded me!' Charlotte breathed. 'You seem to be a little confused as to who I am, Prince Karim. I am not one of your harem women, to be ordered around at your whim. I am an Englishwoman, not a Turkish slave, and I'm perfectly capable of making my own decisions. If I choose to leave my cabin, no command of yours will keep me there.'

'You are my wife,' he ground out.

'In the Ottoman Empire that may be little better than being a slave, but in England a husband does not give his wife foolish orders and expect her to obey them. I was needed on deck, Prince Karim. Your men were wounded and dying. The surgeon needed help to save lives and relieve suffering. In a small way I was able to assist him. What's more, I would go up on deck again right this minute if I decided it was the proper thing to do. You have no power to make me obey you.'

Her hostility, and her painful reminders of the unbridgeable gulf between them, sparked a primitive reaction deep in Alexander's soul. He laughed, hearing the savagery behind the sound but not even trying to control it.

'Are you quite sure that I have no power to make you obey?' he said. Eyes glittering, he advanced steadily towards her, obscurely pleased when he saw her step back yet again. 'On the contrary, dear wife, I believe I have all the power I need to enforce my will.'

'Alexander. . .no. . . You are angry. You don't really want to frighten me——'

'Do I not?' He clenched his fists, deliberately fanning his rage. God, he needed to have her in his bed tonight! And if he allowed his anger to cool he would remember all the reasons why she was forbidden to him. 'Do not waste time by trying to retreat from me,' he said brutally. 'It will avail you nothing. It is past time for you to be shown precisely how much power I possess, and how little control you have over your own destiny.' His voice lowered to something between a threat and a husky promise. 'Believe me, it is a lesson which will give me much pleasure to impart.'

'Alexander, please! We both said things we did not mean——'

'Ah! You did not mean to defy me? That is good. Defiance sits ill on the shoulders of a Turkish wife.' As he spoke he dragged her into his arms, winding his fingers into the golden curls at the nape of her neck so that her head was jerked back. His gaze dropped to the fragile column of her throat and rested there with the harshness of a blow. 'Since you intended no defiance you will wish to give me the solace I seek from your body. When I order you to open your lips to receive my kiss, you will obey.'

For a moment Charlotte rebelled against his deliberate cruelty, but some primitive instinct alerted her to the fact that his ruthless behaviour was caused more by suffering than by arrogance. Somewhere beneath the caustic veneer she sensed that he was feeling the same curious mixture of pain, longing and desire that she felt. An odd feeling of tenderness swept over her as she looked up at him. How strange it was to think that, for all the women he had taken to his bed, at this instant he apparently felt as uncertain about their relationship as she did. Guided by nothing more than intuition, she stood on tiptoe and pressed a fleeting kiss against the corner of his mouth.

For several seconds he didn't move, then he groaned deep in his throat, gazing down at her, his eyes obsidian-black with the pain of indecision. Deliberately provocative, she lowered her gaze to the floor. 'Is it your wish that I kiss you again, Prince Karim?' she murmured.

With a muttered exclamation he bent her over his arm, looming over her, his mouth hot and seeking against her throat. An arrow of agonisingly sweet sensation flew through her body, headed straight for the pit of her stomach. His lips trailed up her neck until they covered hers, and his tongue invaded her mouth, demanding total surrender. Her body slowly went limp in his arms.

'Dear God, Charlotte,' he murmured against her

mouth. 'Tell me that I must not do this. Look at me with those defiant blue eyes and tell me that you will not obey my commands. Do not permit me to carry you to my bed. Tonight, when I need you so much, I shall not be able to save you from the possibility of bearing my child.'

Her soft curves moulded themselves even more closely to the hardness of his body. 'Alexander,' she said huskily, 'I forbid you to take me to your bed.'

It was easy for a man of his experience to know that she didn't mean what she said, that she was, in fact, deliberately encouraging him. Every quiver of her body told him that she was more than willing to surrender to his touch. Guilt tore at his heart. On their wedding night he had set out to destroy her virginal innocence, using every skill he had ever been taught to bring her to physical fulfilment. And now her body quickened with the remembrance of the ecstasy they had shared. He had awakened her to the sensual demands of her body. Was it not his responsibility to help her control the urges which he alone had aroused?

Alexander closed his eyes, forcing himself to remember the debt he owed to Charlotte, the obligation he had to protect her. But all he could think of was how incredibly perfect she felt in his arms and how passionately he longed to possess her. His fingers explored the contours of her breast, and he felt her nipples stiffen at his touch. He watched her eyes grow heavy, their azure brilliance dimming to take on the mystery of the sea at night. Her cheeks bloomed with delicate pink colour.

'Alex,' she whispered. 'I want you to kiss me properly, with your. . .with your tongue.'

'Dear God, Charlotte, don't tempt me!' Even as he spoke his mouth sought hers again, savage, ravenous, starving for the taste of her lips. His hand reached down to stroke her thighs and her whole body jerked in an exquisite agony of pleasure. Her slender hands clutched at his shoulders, then roamed freely over his body until he groaned with the forbidden delight of her touch.

Charlotte's hesitant caresses grew bolder. She fumbled with the heavy silver buckle of his belt, tossing it aside as soon as she succeeded in unfastening it. Her hands slid down his stomach until her fingers tangled in the matt of hair at his groin.

Alexander sucked in his breath, feeling the sweat break out on his brow. With an impatient movement he ripped off the shirt she wore, pulling her naked body back against him with a low growl of satisfaction.

The touch of her mouth was like flame on his skin, urging him onward to the point where they could quench the fire. She signed, a gentle sound in the world of deep, harsh breathing they had created for each other, and, all resistance at an end, he swung her up into his arms.

'Where are you taking me?' she asked softly.

'To my bed.'

'I. . .forbade. . .you. . .to take. . .me. . .to your bed,' she panted between kisses.

'So you did.' He paused by the side of the bunk and reached out to grab a woollen blanket and a pillow. He tossed the blanket into a heap at his feet and allowed the pillow to fall somewhere on top of it. He knelt down and laid her gently on the floor, pushing her back against the pillow and straddling her with an urgency he could no longer conceal. 'You see, sweet Charlotte, with what swiftness I obey your commands.'

Her face tilted up to him, dreamy with passion, but her mouth twisted into the teasing smile he had learned to love so well. 'In that case, Prince Karim, I order you to make me feel again the way I did on the night of our wedding.'

She arched her hips upwards as she spoke, and he buried himself within the silken prison of her body. 'Sweet Charlotte,' he said softly. 'I can imagine no command that would give me greater pleasure.'

Alexander had left the cabin and the ship was riding at anchor when Charlotte woke the next morning. Sun streamed in through the porthole, casting its bright light on the dark oaken beams of the cabin. For several languid minutes she lay on the bunk, staring up at the low beams of the ceiling, reliving the ecstasy she had experienced in Alexander's arms.

But one night's pleasure, however intense, did not

necessarily mean that a lifetime of married happiness lay ahead of her. Charlotte sat up in bed, hugging the sheets around her bare body. It was a measure of her preoccupation that she didn't once pause to reflect on the wanton state of her nakedness. The question was, how could she convince Alexander to remain married? After last night, after listening to the heated endearments he had whispered as he cradled her in his arms, she no longer doubted that he loved her. But love, unfortunately, did not necessarily conquer all. Alexander had decided that she would be better off living with her family in England, and he was stubborn enough to make them both utterly miserable by living up to his decision.

A child was the obvious answer, Charlotte thought. If she became pregnant with Alexander's child even he would see the impossibility of returning her to her family. If she carried his baby she could not pretend to be unwed, and, although divorce might be an acceptable facet of Ottoman society, in England it was anathema.

Her problem, therefore, had quite an easy solution, Charlotte decided. She simply needed to make sure that Alexander came to her bed often enough to get her with child before the *Beauty* arrived back in England. She gnawed thoughtfully on her thumb-nail, making and discarding schemes for luring her husband into her bed. Since she shared a cabin with Aunt Adeline, and Alexander shared a cabin with Captain Barrett, lurid seduction scenes would be difficult to stage.

Thinking of Captain Barrett reminded her that she had much more to do today than curl up in bed, daydreaming about her husband. Someone—presumably Alexander—had thoughtfully provided fresh water and clean towels so that she was able to wash, but her clothes had all been tidied away and were nowhere in sight.

Draping herself from neck-to-toes in a sheet from the bunk, she poked her head out into the corridor. After about fifteen minutes of waiting a sailor walked by, and she was able to send a message to her aunt.

Lady Adeline arrived promptly, bearing a bundle of fresh clothing and looking surprisingly rested. 'Dr Grimes had a truckle bed brought into our cabin for me, and really neither patient was a bit of trouble during the night. Captain Barrett will be getting up tomorrow morning, and Edwin is already back on duty, impressing everybody with the size of his bandages.'

'And the lieutenant?'

Lady Adeline's expression sobered. 'Not too good, I'm afraid. I understand he's in such pain, he begged the doctor to shoot him and put him out of his misery. Only time will tell if he survives the ordeal.'

'And if he dies?'

'The surgeon told me Captain Barrett is known for his generosity to widows and children. You may be sure they will not starve.' Lady Adeline spread out her bundle of clothes on the spare bed. 'Anyway, here is a clean chemise and petticoat for you, and I brought your caftan so you would have something to wear while your dress is being washed. The laundry boy assured me that with all this sunshine it's only a matter of hours before it will be dry.'

Charlotte dressed quickly. 'What can we do this morning to help, do you think?'

'Carrying food to the invalids is about all we are useful for. Prince Karim left in the middle of the night, taking half a dozen of the crew with him. From what the captain tells me, I understand he has met up with some of the Greek freedom-fighters, and they are helping him carry the grain and the oil to his estates. Tonight, when it's dark again, a band of soldiers fighting on behalf of the Provisional Government will unload the cases of ammunition and the special guns that the British have provided. The guns have a new type of bore—although what that means I have no idea.'

'I imagine it means they can kill more of the enemy faster than before,' Charlotte said, her voice dry.

'Probably. In any event, the Greeks are thrilled these guns have arrived and consider everyone on board the *Beauty* a positive hero.'

'When is Alexander due to return, do you know?' From the shrewd gaze Lady Adeline cast in her direction, Charlotte deduced that she had not managed to sound as casual as she'd hoped.

'He should be back within three days,' Lady Adeline said. 'His estates lie less than fifteen miles inland, according to the captain.'

'You and Captain Barrett seem to have had time for a great deal of conversation.'

Lady Adeline turned pink. 'Well, some light-hearted chatter helped to take his mind off the pain of his injuries, you know. We spoke a great deal about the city of Boston. I should like to visit there one day.'

'Visit America!' If her aunt had declared that she wished to visit the dark side of the moon, Charlotte could not have been more astonished.

'Well, I would not admit this to anybody else, but I dare say St Leonard's may seem just a teensy bit tame after our adventures of the last few weeks. We certainly have had an interesting time.'

'Please remember that thought, dearest aunt, when we wake up tomorrow morning and see a fleet of Turkish ships waiting to attack us.'

But their hiding place in the bay remained undiscovered, and only the death of Lieutenant Fitzroy marred the *Beauty's* return to a pre-battle state of pristine order and comfort. Captain Barrett conducted funeral services for his lieutenant and for the two sailors killed in the skirmish. Charlotte kept thinking about the lieutenant's widow and three young children. She wondered how they would feel when they learned that their husband and father had sacrificed his life in the cause of Greek freedom. The crew seemed troubled by no such worries. In fact they appeared almost relieved that Lieutenant Fitzroy's endless moans of anguish had finally ceased.

The *Beauty* sailed to the mouth of the bay and the bodies were dropped off into the dark depths of the ocean. Charlotte tried to imagine how she would feel if Alexander died in his effort to smuggle food through to his estates. At first the thought was too painful even to consider coherently. Then she decided that she would feel nothing but rage. Gradually it dawned on her that she loved Alexander precisely because he was the sort of man to tilt at windmills. He had chosen to put his life at risk to support people he cared about and a cause he considered just. That, in part, was why she loved him.

Captain Barrett, supported by a stout cane, had resumed active command of the ship when Alexander and his small landing party returned three days later. All of the men appeared dazed by the brutal pace they had maintained on their return march, and Alexander not only appeared grey with fatigue, he had lost weight to the point where his features were positively haggard. Charlotte waited for him on deck as he boarded the ship, and when he greeted her she saw the joy flare in his eyes for one unguarded moment before he clamped down on all trace of emotion.

'Go and sleep, Alex,' the captain ordered. 'Your men, too. I can sail this ship out of here tonight without any difficulty.'

'The peasants we met on land told me that the bulk of the Turkish fleet is gathering in the Bay of Argolis, which is what British Naval Intelligence also reports. Steer clear of them if you can, Hank.'

'Go to bed,' Hank said, cuffing his friend affectionately on the arm. 'Try to remember I was avoiding enemy ships when you were still cutting your milk-teeth.'

'Alexander saw some terrible sights in the countryside,' Captain Barrett told the ladies later that night as they sat down for dinner with his small complement of officers. 'He feels it all the more because it is his people who are suffering. Without this shipment of food we brought in he doesn't think a child or an old person on his estate would have survived the winter.'

'One shipment of food and ammunition is not going to solve the problem for more than a few months,' Charlotte said sadly.

'True; that is why we have to pray that the Sultan isn't persuaded to go back on his word. The sooner Alex can get to Mr Canning and pass on Mahmud's messages, the better for everybody. With Britain and France adding their weight to the demand for an end to the useless slaughter it is possible that the Greeks may yet win their way through to victory.'

'But I don't see what any of this has to do with England,' Lady Adeline said plaintively. 'Why can't all these foreigners be left alone to fight their own wars?'

'Because it isn't in England's best interests to allow the Greek peninsula to be overrun by Egyptian mercenaries bent on plunder or, worse still, Russian troops conquering new territory in the name of religious liberty and Christian solidarity. Nor can she allow France to become the dominating influence in the region.'

'Well, I dare say international politics is a subject I am never going to understand,' Lady Adeline said. She smiled encouragingly. 'Why don't you tell us some more stories about Boston, Captain Barrett? I am sure Charlotte would like to hear them as much as I would.'

Captain Barrett did indeed have a fund of witty and amusing tales to tell about life in America, but Charlotte found her attention wandering, and eventually, pleading fatigue, she excused herself from the table. Lady Adeline, curiously pink around the cheekbones, declared that she would keep the captain company for just a little longer.

Charlotte walked briskly enough down the narrow companionway that led to her cabin but her footsteps slowed to a halt outside the tiny cabin left spare by the death of Lieutenant Fitzroy. According to the captain, this was where Alexander would be sleeping. Here, she and Alexander could be alone. Not allowing herself time for reflection, Charlotte reached for the door-handle.

'Were you looking for me?' Alexander asked quietly from behind her, his hand descending to close over hers.

'Yes, I was.' Charlotte stared at her toes, overcome by a sudden shyness. 'I wanted to. . . I thought I would check to see if you were resting comfortably.'

'I slept deeply for five hours,' he said, his voice carefully uninflected. 'It was enough to revive me.'

'Have you had something to eat?'

'I am not hungry.' He paused, then said levelly, 'It seems that we both felt a similar need to see one another. I came to seek you out, Charlotte, hoping that we might be able to speak alone for a few minutes. There are. . .apologies. . .which I must make to you.'

'Apologies?'

He opened the door of the cabin. 'If you would step inside, we could leave the door ajar and yet we should still be ensured of a measure of privacy.'

She hated his formality, the guarded blankness of his expression. But if they could be alone—really alone—she thought that she might be able to break down the protective barrier of his indifference. He was tired still, and his face betrayed more emotion than he usually permitted himself to show. If he loved her, and she was almost sure that he did, surely she ought to be able to find some way to penetrate behind the guard of his ridiculous masculine sense of honour? Charlotte walked into the empty cabin, keeping her gaze fixed firmly ahead as he followed her into the tiny room.

Alexander gestured to the narrow bed and a small wooden chair. 'I'm afraid there is not much choice of furniture. Where would you prefer to sit?'

She perched on the edge of the bed, hoping that he would join her, but he chose not to sit down at all. 'Charlotte,' he said, selecting his words with obvious care, 'there are many things I must say, many apologies I should make, but I wish, first of all, to apologise for my brutal behaviour towards you on the night of the *Beauty*'s encounter with the renegade Turkish ship.'

'Your "brutal" behaviour, Prince Karim?'

He reddened. 'There are many aspects of our relationship which I regret, Charlotte, but, believe me, the manner in which I used you that night has haunted me more than all the rest. There is no excuse for the way I lashed out at you, except that I was angered by my inability to protect you from the dangers of battle. Instead of admitting the truth, I simply transferred my anger to you.'

'You did at first,' she agreed. 'Later. . .when we made love. . . I think it was not anger that you felt.'

Alexander drew in a deep, shaky breath. 'Well, and that is another thing we must discuss. I wish you to know that I deeply regret breaking my word to you in the matter of. . .in the matter of——'

'Keeping our marriage unconsummated?' she queried softly.

'Yes. Charlotte, I have betrayed your trust in the worst possible way, but I will make it up to you, I promise. Fortunately it is not only Lady Adeline who thinks of the Ottoman Empire as part of another universe. The events and happenings of Istanbul lack any semblance of reality for the leaders of London society. I swear no breath of scandal shall attach to your name once you return to England and to your family.'

She looked at him with pretended coolness. 'Are you sure you can make such a promise, Prince Karim?'

He was so caught up in his attempt at atonement that he didn't hear the hint of laughter in her voice.

'I am sure,' he said earnestly. 'Who is there to tell tales, after all? Sir Clive will never be in any position to circulate malicious rumours and I certainly will never reveal to anybody that we are married. You have my oath upon it.' He looked away. 'You told me once, long ago, that you wished to marry Archdeacon Jeffries. If you still feel that such a marriage would be right for you, from the bottom of my heart I wish you every possible happiness.'

'You know, it is the oddest thing, Prince Karim, but I was under the impression that, even in the Ottoman Empire, ladies were only permitted to marry one man at a time. And it might have escaped your memory, but I am already wed. To you.'

'It is of no consequence——'

'Is it not? Do you know, I have this lowering suspicion that Archdeacon Jeffries is one of those stuffy, over-conventional people who would consider it rather bad form to marry a woman who is already married to somebody else.'

'Don't worry about it,' he said quickly. 'I will pronounce a decree of divorce from you as soon as I can find the necessary Muslim witnesses.'

Charlotte rose to her feet and quietly closed the cabin door. With an appearance of tragedy that was rather hard to maintain in view of the laughter bubbling inside of her she remarked that she did not think a divorce would solve her problems.

'Why not? You would be legally and morally free——'

'Yes, but I have been corrupted,' she pointed out mournfully.

Alexander strode across the tiny room and seized her hands, dropping them as if they had been burning coals when he realised what he was doing. 'Charlotte, you must not think of yourself so! You are not corrupted, my darl—— That is to say, you are not corrupted at all, and Lady Adeline and I will concoct some story that is so perfect in all its details that no breath of scandal will ever attach itself to your name.'

Emboldened by the endearment which he had almost spoken, Charlotte curled herself against the unyielding rigidity of Alexander's body. Not by so much as the quiver of a muscle did he betray any reaction, but she was beginning to understand this complex man at long last, and she realised that the very absence of visible emotion hinted at a storm of feeling seething within.

'The trouble is,' she whispered, 'that I'm afraid I may cause the scandal myself. There will be no need of Sir Clive to spread rumours, or Aunt Adeline to slip up in her story. What do you think the archdeacon would say if I put my hands behind his head like this, and pulled his mouth down until it touched mine—like this?'

She brushed her lips very gently against his. Alexander's body might have been carved out of stone, but the agony of longing in his eyes betrayed him. She touched the tip of her tongue to the corner of his mouth and his iron self-discipline finally snapped. He dragged her into his arms, ravishing her mouth with the aching hunger of his kiss. When at last he drew back Charlotte looked up at him, her eyes dancing with silent amusement.

'Oh, dear, Alexander, I'm sure I don't know what will become of me.' She slipped her hands inside his jacket and slid them provocatively down the length of his body until she felt the hard thrust of his erection against her palm. She caressed him lightly with her fingers and felt his immediate tremor of response. She sighed with mock regret.

'I'm awfully afraid the archdeacon would die of shock if I did this to him,' she said, her caresses becoming considerably more daring. 'But the trouble is, you've taught me to enjoy doing it, and I fear it has already become an incurable habit.' She pretended not to hear Alexander's strangled gasp of ecstasy. 'If I caused the death of the archdeacon, what would happen to all his worthy parishioners? Surely you would not wish to leave his flock without a pastor just because you cannot bear to keep me as your wife?'

'It is not because I do not want you,' Alexander managed to gasp out. 'It is for your sake—only for yours—that I wish to repudiate our marriage.'

'But I don't wish to be repudiated,' Charlotte whispered, cradling her body against his. 'You have already corrupted me, Alexander, and now there is no hope of returning me to my old, boring existence.'

'But you were *safe*, Charlotte.'

She took his hand and carried it to her breast. 'I don't want to be safe if it means life without you. Feel how I burn, Alexander. It is you whom I crave.'

'Charlotte, dearest heart, there are a thousand reasons why I must not listen to you. As long as the Grand Vizier resents my influence on the Sultan my life will be at risk. Then there is my commitment to the cause of freedom for the Greek people—that is not a commitment to be made by a married man.'

'But with your help the struggle may soon be at an end.'

'Please God that it should be so. But even when Greece is technically independent her problems will not vanish. The peasants will still be unhealthy and ill-prepared to wrest a living from land that has been devastated by half a generation of war. My responsibilities lie in Greece, Charlotte, and to a lesser extent in Istanbul. If you remained married to me you would not be able to visit your family in England more than once every five or six years. Our children would be born in a country that is foreign to you. Their religion could not be yours, because there are no priests of the Church of England in the Morea.'

She pressed her fingers gently against his lips. 'You have left out the most important factor in the balance sheet,' she murmured. 'You have not given the most important reason why I should remain with you as your wife. I love you.'

He crushed her to him, kissing her with an aching intensity, and telling her endlessly of his love as he removed her clothes. When they lay naked together in the narrow bed he caressed her with hands that trembled with emotion. 'Dear God, Charlotte, I love you so much, but I have no right to take you as my wife when I have so little to offer you.'

'So much to offer me,' she corrected fiercely, pressing her slim body next to his. 'Everything I could ever want or need.'

'I will make you happy,' he vowed as he claimed possession of her body. 'Charlotte, I promise you will not live to regret this day.'

She gave a tiny sigh of contentment that died on a choked gasp of desire. 'Alexander, please, no more words! Love me *now*!'

Charlotte didn't return to the cabin she shared with Lady Adeline until the middle of the next morning. Her aunt, with a highly uncharacteristic display of tact, spared them both the embarrassment of asking where she had spent the night. There was probably no need for anybody to ask, Charlotte reflected wryly as she stared into the little mirror above the chest of drawers. Her sparkling eyes, glowing complexion and self-satisfied smiles surely ought to indicate to anybody just how she had been occupying her time.

Even so, she felt a little uncertain as she told her aunt that Alexander was arranging for Captain Barrett to marry them again as soon as possible.

Lady Adeline merely nodded. 'It is probably for the best,' she said. 'Once the captain has married you in a lawful Christian ceremony there can be no doubts raised by anybody.'

Charlotte hugged her aunt tightly. 'I shall miss you so much, Aunt Adeline. But we will visit you often in England, and you can stay with us in Greece whenever you want. Do you mind very much that I am going so far away?'

Lady Adeline looked surprisingly vague. 'Why, no, why should I mind, dear? After all, as you pointed out yourself, if you'd been suited for marriage to an ordinary Englishman you'd have married one years ago. I should have thought of that for myself since I had never contemplated matrimony until . . .'

Several small clues came together and an incredible suspicion began to form itself in Charlotte's mind. 'Aunt? Why won't you look at me? Are you suggesting. . .is it possible that you yourself might be contemplating matrimony?'

Lady Adeline seemed to find it necessary to bend her head deep into the recesses of the chest of drawers. She emerged after a few seconds, flushed and even more vague-looking than usual. She waved a handkerchief abstractedly and murmured, 'I knew there was a clean one in there somewhere.'

'Aunt Adeline. . .'

'Yes, you are quite right, dearest, we must think about your wedding, not about my hankies. When is the ceremony with Prince Karim to take place, my dear?'

Charlotte decided to be kind and followed her aunt's change of subject. 'Alexander estimates that we should be in reach of the Italian coast by late tomorrow afternoon. He thought we should have the ceremony on deck, just before sundown. He would like to invite the crew to attend, since they deserve some relaxation after all the trials and tribulations they have endured recently.'

'It sounds as if it will be very nice, dearest. Not quite as nice as a Church, perhaps, but certainly a vast improvement over a bath-house. It is quite impossible to take a ceremony seriously when one's hair is being rubbed with raw eggs.'

Charlotte wisely decided not to involve herself in a discussion of the relative merits of Christian and Muslim wedding customs. 'I wondered if you had any suggestions as to what I might wear, Aunt Adeline? This grey cotton is the only dress I have, and it's hardly festive enough for a wedding.'

As Charlotte had hoped, at the mention of clothing Lady Adeline's attention snapped into immediate focus. 'We only have today and tomorrow,' she murmured, the light of battle gleaming in her eyes. 'But with the material from your caftan and mine we might be able to produce some sort of a gown that won't disgrace us. Your caftan is sky-blue, mine is silver. Hmm. . . I dare say we could work something out, although it will be nothing conventionally white and bridal.'

'But then, our marriage is hardly conventional.'

'That is most certainly true.' Lady Adeline pulled out her caftan from the bottom drawer of the chest and shook it experimentally. 'Hmm. . . I don't think we shall want for fabric. Quick, Charlotte, get undressed so I can take your measure! There's no time to delay; we must start work immediately.'

The Italian Adriatic coastline was no more than a blur on the far horizon when Mr Wardle, the *Beauty*'s most junior officer, escorted Charlotte up the narrow wooden stairs to the deck. Captain Barrett had discarded his stick and stood at the helm, looking plump and imposing in his best uniform. Edwin, his right arm still splinted, balanced the open *Prayer Book* on his left arm, ready for the captain to read the marriage service. Alexander, Lady Adeline, and a small group of ship's officers stood alongside the captain.

A piper and fiddler provided a jaunty wedding march for Charlotte's progress across the deck between the rows of waiting sailors. The silk ruffles of her new gown rustled pleasurably around her ankles as she slowly approached Alexander's side. Her heart was beating so fast that she felt sure it would burst with happiness beneath the tight bodice which Aunt Adeline had sewn so carefully.

Mr Wardle tightened his clasp on Charlotte's hand and successfully navigated several sets of block and tackle before drawing to a halt in front of Captain

Barrett. The musicians gave a final cheerful flourish, then fell silent.

'This is a very happy occasion,' Hank beamed, hooking a pair of spectacles into position. He reached into his pocket for a handkerchief and blew his nose. 'Can't tell you how much pleasure it gives me to see my old friend Alex getting married at last. You are just what he needed, my dear. Just what he needed.' He cleared his throat noisily, and began to read.

'Dearly beloved, we are gathered together here in the sight of God. . .'

Charlotte looked at Alexander, who stared straight ahead, his expression sober to the point of grimness. Love swept through her as he turned to look down at her, the secrets of his heart betrayed by his eyes. She smiled, hugging to herself the glorious secret of her power as a woman. How wonderful it was to know that she could break through that austere mask to the warm, caring, passionate, *loving* man beneath. The rest of the congregation might not be able to read Alexander's thoughts, but she could feel his love and desire reaching out to envelop her in a blaze of fierce, protective adoration.

'Repeat after me,' Hank Barrett instructed Alexander. 'With this ring, I thee wed.'

Alexander took off his heavy signet-ring and slipped it on to Charlotte's finger, and this time the love in his eyes was naked and unashamed, plainly there for all to see. He repeated his vows quietly, as if they were just for her, and Charlotte trembled with the impact of so much emotion. She ached for the opportunity to show him how deeply his love was returned.

The service was soon over. Captain Barrett solemnly pronounced them man and wife, then glanced at Alexander mischievously. 'You may kiss the bride,' he said with a chuckle. 'It's the tradition among us heathen infidels, you know.'

'Even infidels occasionally come up with a good idea,' Alexander murmured. He raised Charlotte's hands to his lips, drawing her slowly towards him. 'Sweet Charlotte, welcome into my heart and into my life.'

She lifted her face to receive his kiss, completely indifferent to their interested audience. The kiss went on until a lusty cheer from the assembled sailors brought her tumbling back to earth. 'The captain has lent us his cabin,' Alexander whispered into her ear as they broke apart. 'I hope you aren't intending to linger over dinner?'

'May I not? Actually, I'm rather hungry.'

'I will take care of your hunger,' he told her softly. 'As you will take care of mine.'

The sailors approached at that moment to begin setting up trestle-tables. Aunt Adeline shook hands with Alexander and informed him that he was a lucky man, then hugged her niece with every appearance of warm affection. Charlotte wondered why she derived the oddest impression that her aunt's attention was really not on the wedding.

Hank Barrett solved the mystery when he rose to declare a toast to the health, long life and wedded bliss of the bride and groom. The sailors responded with a hearty cheer and several generous swigs of rum. The officers and Lady Adeline joined in the cheer and raised their more refined glasses of wine. Charlotte smiled modestly, as became a bride, and Alexander rose gracefully to his feet to acknowledge the good wishes with an elegant bow.

Captain Barrett, however, did not sit down. Before Charlotte's incredulous gaze he placed his arm around Aunt Adeline's waist and gently raised her to her feet.

'I have another toast for you all to make,' Hank Barrett said, his voice gruffer than ever. 'I ask you all to wish good health and happiness to Lady Adeline Spencer, who has honoured me by agreeing to become my wife.'

The sailors cheered even louder than before, although whether this was approval or the extra serving of rum was hard to decide. Charlotte simply stared at her aunt with her glass unmoving in her hand and her mouth inelegantly hanging open.

Alexander bent down and whispered in her ear. 'Dearest Charlotte, you will have to close your mouth or I shall be unable to resist the invitation.'

Lady Adeline, rosy-cheeked and laughing within the circle of Captain Barrett's arms, looked nervously at her niece. 'I hope you are not very shocked, Charlotte?'

'I am not shocked, I'm stunned,' Charlotte replied. 'But I think it's the most marvellous piece of news I've heard in ages. Dearest Aunt, will you tell me how it all came about?'

Lady Adeline toyed modestly with her wine glass. 'Well, Henry tells me he was most impressed by my bravery, first in the Emir's harem and then when the *Beauty* was under attack from those nasty Turks. And then, you know, his wounds were causing him considerable pain, although he wouldn't admit it. We started talking during the long hours of the night when he couldn't sleep and I suppose one thing just led to another.'

Lady Adeline's rosy cheeks became even rosier. 'The captain is a very masculine sort of man and he—er—assures me that I am a very feminine sort of woman. He's been lonely since his wife died, and I dare say he hasn't taken proper care of himself at all. You know how gentlemen are.' Lady Adeline gave her niece a woman-to-woman smile. 'Henry tells me his house is just crying out for a new mistress. He promises me I will be very happy living with him in America, and I'm sure he's right. Gentlemen are always right about these things.'

'Captain Barrett is taking you back to *America*? Aunt Adeline, you cannot mean that you're actually going to live in *Boston*?'

'Whyever shouldn't I live in Boston? You know, Charlotte, dear, I'm sorry to say that some of your remarks betray a very narrow, nationalistic sort of outlook. England is not the centre of the universe, you know. Hank tells me Boston is a very superior sort of city, and it cannot possibly be a more dangerous place to live than St Leonard's. After all, in America I shall have nothing worse to cope with than blizzards and bears and Red Indians, which I dare say will seem mere nothings to me when you remember that I've already survived an abduction, imprisonment in a harem, and battle with

Turkish pirates. Hank tells me his house is very cosy and I will like it a lot.'

Alexander smiled engagingly. 'And when you get tired of the bears and the blizzards you must persuade Hank to set sail and bring you to visit us in Greece.'

'We'll do our best to keep you entertained,' Charlotte said teasingly. 'Turkish pirates may be more than we can offer, but I dare say Alexander will be able to conjure up a brigand or two.'

'Some great-nieces and nephews will provide all the excitement I need,' Aunt Adeline replied briskly.

'Speaking of which,' Alexander said, without the slightest regard for Charlotte's blushes, 'I think it is time for my wife and me to bid you all goodnight.'

'Feeling sleepy, are you?' Hank chuckled.

'Something of the sort,' Alexander replied, unruffled. He offered his arm to Charlotte, and they walked together to the far side of the deck. Out of sight of the wedding party, they leaned against the deck-rail, Alexander's arm resting about her waist. The setting sun cast a red glow over the Italian coast, and overhead the sky gradually became dark.

'Are you pleased to be nearing home?' Alexander asked.

'I'm looking forward to seeing my brothers again, and reassuring them that I'm safe.' She smiled. 'I'm also looking forward to buying some new clothes in London.'

'I think you are not telling me the whole truth, Charlotte. You have lived all your life in England. You must long for your friends, and your first glimpse of the white cliffs of Dover and the grey skies made soft with summer rain.'

Charlotte reached up and stroked her fingers over the hard plane of his cheek. 'Yes, I look forward to seeing England again, but I am not homesick—at least not in the way you fear. I love you, Alexander. If I am with you I am content. England without you at my side would seem a very lonely place.'

Alexander took her hand and pressed a burning kiss into her palm. His eyes suddenly twinkled with laughter.

'Do you think Mrs Stubbs will ever forgive me for dragging you away to foreign parts?'

Charlotte laughed. 'She may forgive *you*. Since you're a foreigner, you can't be expected to have a real sense of what's right and proper. It's me she'll be so cross with. Unless. . .'

'Unless what? Don't stop now.'

'She was my nurse once, before she became the housekeeper, and she loves babies. If we offered her the job of nanny to our children I think you might be surprised at how willingly she abandoned Rippon Manor for the shores of Greece.'

'It must be a conspiracy,' Alexander muttered. 'First my father, then your aunt. Now even the housekeeper, it seems, is clamouring for babies.' He tilted her chin and kissed her lightly, teasingly on the tip of her nose. 'Well, what do you say, my dearest wife? Shall we go down to the captain's cabin and start procreating all these little Princes and Princesses who have been so urgently requested?'

Charlotte raised herself on tiptoe so that she could kiss her husband full on the mouth. 'Thank goodness,' she murmured. 'I was beginning to think you would never ask.'

Look out for the two intriguing

MASQUERADE *Historical*

Romances coming next month

TEN GUINEAS ON LOVE

Alice Thornton

To Charity Mayfield's shock, she discovered a year after her father's death that his debts could mean losing her home. Only by marriage could she touch her inheritance and save Hazelhurst. The only sensible candidate would be Edward, newly come into the Earldom, and the Mayfields' neighbour, so impetuously Charity wrote to propose!

But she'd made a mistake, the new Earl was *Jack* Riversleigh, and he wasn't at all disposed to help out – which led Charity rashly to bet him that she *could* find a husband within a month...

THE GOLDEN PHOENIX

Hazel Smith

San Francisco in 1906 was not a safe place to be, either from rogues or earthquakes. So Charisse Linton was relieved that her father knew the owner of The Gateway Hotel, and that George Davis would help her search for her brother Ralph. John Linton, estranged from his only son for eight years, wanted to make amends before he died, so Charisse's mission was urgent.

Dace LaVelle, having won The Gateway Hotel from George, was equally determined to win Charisse, but this dangerous gambler had met his match...

Available in July